SEED SOWER

A Novel by

Leonard J Rampello, MD

ISBN: 978-0-9997641-0-7

First printing edition 2018

Copyright 2017 by Leonard J Rampello

Library of Congress catalogue number 2018900500

Wachusett Mountain Press

755 West Street

Leominster, Massachusetts 01453

PROLOGUE

First, came the blinding flash, then the sensation of being hit by a powerful blast of hot air. Deaf from the blast, Captain Jeff Blake struggled to see through the dust and smoke. His eyes were burning, and the salty taste of blood from his nose had already reached his lips.

All he could see were the gray spots caused by blunt trauma to the head that dislodges the gel like substance in the eye producing floaters. Everywhere he looked, only floaters. It wasn't until the floaters settled that he could see many of his medical team laying dead or dying on the floor. Time was standing still. The disorientation was paralyzing.

The air was dense with the unmistakable smell of exploded munitions. The grittiness of desert sand choked his breath. Unable to call out, all he could do was struggle on all fours with a sinking feeling of helplessness. Finally, he came to the realization that Field hospital Ranger Three, twenty miles outside of Mosel, had been hit by an RPG attack.

Struggling to get control of himself, and gasping for air, his mind began to race. Where are my guys? Is anybody left? How could any of this had happen?

The doctors and nurses of Ranger Three Field hospital were protected by a secured perimeter almost a mile away. Motion sensors scanning the desert horizon failed to sound the alarm. Even Shadow, their German Sheppard mascot never stirred or made a sound.

Jeff's sight was beginning to return, and for the first time, he saw the extent of the carnage. Even as a doctor, he wasn't prepared for what he saw. Blood and body parts were still smoking from the heat of the blast. Shadow was dead on the floor with a smoking piece of shrapnel protruding from his left hindquarter. The exam tables were charred black and medical supplies strewn about everywhere. His heart began to fill with rage.

The deafness finally gave way to a loud ringing in his ears over which he began to hear the sounds of vehicles approaching and sporadic machine gun bursts. Almost reflexively, he realized that the savages were coming in closer to finish the job.

Corporal Manny Alvarez, medic first class, appeared through the haze. He was bruised and bleeding from a gash over his left ear. Manny had served three tours of duty in Iraq. He was a seasoned combat veteran who had been in more than a few firefights before becoming a medic.

Alvarez managed to get over to where Captain Blake was struggling on the floor trying to regain his bearings. He could see that the Captain was stunned with multiple superficial cuts from small shrapnel, but was otherwise ok.

"Sir, we're messed up pretty bad! Rogers, Flores, Peterson, and Sergeant Collins are grabbing the M4s, grenades and as many clips as they can carry."

His voice was quivering with emotion as he wiped the blood and sand out of his eyes.

"The rest are all dead, Captain. Those motherfuckers killed everybody, even Shadow."

Jeff somehow found the strength and presence of mind to begin shouting out orders.

"Get everyone out of this fucking tent. The Humvee out back with the 50cal is the only cover we've got. Wait for them to come in close. That's when we make our stand!"

There was no time for fear, only the adrenaline rush and the primordial urge to survive. The only good news that day was the fact that all the wounded had been moved out the day before.

The enemy came up close and personal, concentrating their firepower on what was left of the hospital tent. Incredibly, the tent was still mostly standing. Jeff and his men, sweaty and bloodied, with hearts pounding, took up positions atop and around the Humvee.

The invaders continued to empty their ammo clips into the tent, making sure no one could get out alive.

The snapping sounds of rounds hitting everywhere reminded everyone that they could be dead in an instant. The entire tent came down under the withering barrage of automatic weapons fire exposing the attackers with no cover.

They looked up, only to be starring down the barrel of the 50cal ant almost point blank range. Jeff and his men opened up with a barrage of blistering and concentrated fire on the thirty or forty invaders who had dismounted their vehicles. They were decimated where they stood. They had never expected serious resistance, let alone, a counter attack. Some began to flee toward their vehicles, most of which were bullet riddled by the destructive force of the 50cal.

There would be no mercy shown that day. They were cut down with a vengeance. Filled with rage, Jeff continued running after the few fleeing attackers firing his M4 and yelling, "Nobody kills my dog!" over and over until dropping face down in the sand from sheer exhaustion.

By the time it was over, fourteen medical personal lay dead under the tent and thirty-six al Qaida met the virgins. For their action, Jeff and each of his men were awarded a Bronze Star.

Chapter 1

Jeff Blake was no ordinary ER physician. In a former life, he was a rising star in the world of molecular genetics and cancer research. The son of a factory worker and a seamstress, Jeff had come up the hard way. There was no pedigree in his background, no connections, and no money. Despite a humble beginning he enjoyed success in the world of academics and medicine, a world of fierce competition and privilege He was the only American ever invited to study at Moscow's famed Academy of Sciences. Though it all he never lost site of the kid who swept floors at Star Markets, pumped gas at Joes Roadside, and drove a school bus during college to make ends meet.

His father was an Irish immigrant who broke the rules and married an Italian girl. Something you didn't do back in the day. They lived in the North End and didn't give a shit about what anybody thought. They were happy and in love. Jeff was an only child. His father was killed in an accident while unloading a freighter in the Boston shipyards. Jeff was only nine years old when it happened. He never forgot the vivid memory of his mother crying uncontrollably the day she got the news. His mother never remarried. She died when Jeff was seventeen from breast cancer. Maybe that's why Jeff decided to go into medicine.

The young Jeff, the one who worked menial jobs growing up, never really went away. He was always there, just under the professional and polished veneer of the grown Jeff, always ready to call up when needed. His war experience had taught him special skills and tested him as a man. At thirty-seven he had never married, but not because he was incapable of love and commitment. Everyone he grew up with were already out of school, married, pursuing a job or career, while Jeff's medical studies seemed to go on forever.

He was brought up Catholic, but like so many of his generation, had fallen away from the Church. It wasn't that he didn't believe in God. It was more that he began to question the Church's wisdom which he believed suffered from the same pressures, frailty, and human failings that all of us share. Beliefs, values, and spirituality don't die easily. Jeff case was no exception.

A light snow was falling in Boston's North End. Hanover Street shimmered with streetlights reflecting off the wet pavement. The neighborhood was alive with shoppers coming and going. Italian restaurants, pastry shops, and bakeries dotted both sides of the street. The unmistakable aroma of espresso coffee lingered in the air. This was the lively and famous "Little Italy" of Boston.

The North End had a cool yet old world vibe. Leftovers from the old immigration days mixed with new young millennials moving into the old world apartments. It's a place where shopkeepers know their customers on a first name basis, and the feeling of belonging to a community still survived. Even the sketchy homeboys respected the neighborhood and kept things safe.

Jeff rushed up the slippery steps at Saint Bart's to begin his shift. It didn't matter that a moment of melancholia had briefly entered his mind for the academic life he had left behind. His life was in a kind of limbo. Everything seemed to be on hold. He knew it better than anyone else. He had learned to leave those feelings at the door. He was there to give one hundred percent to anyone who needed him.

The waiting room at Saint Bartholomew Hospital in the North End of Boston was timeless. It was typical of an urban hospital that was built back in the days of the first Italian immigrants. The only difference was Spanish had replaced Italian. It didn't matter what time of day it was. The ER waiting room was always full with the mostly poor and uninsured, languishing under dim fluorescent lighting for hours on end.

Babies crying in the arms of their exhausted mothers, senior citizens clutching their shopping bags and derelicts sleeping in the corners seemed to be permanent fixtures. The place was painted "institution beige "color. Whoever chose the color really wanted to complement the overall feeling of hopeless waiting.

Jeff was always a few minutes late. Even as a boy, no matter how early he got up for school, he would make it into the classroom just as the bell sounded. He tried desperately to sneak in unobserved, but as luck would have it, he was greeted by the ever present, commanding and decidedly Irish voice of Maggie Burns, nursing supervisor.

Tufts of red hair visible through the gray gave hints of the fiery Irish matron who reigned and commanded over the nightly drama of life in an urban ER. As a mother, about to scold her little boy for being late, Jeff could see her looking at him with a put on scowling face, holding up her wrist, and checking the time on her old worn Timex.

Maggie was one tougher than nails battle- scarred nurse. She was feared and respected by all. She'd seen and done it all. Jeff knew that when the shit hit the fan you'd better hope that Maggie was around. Under the hard veneer lived a heart of gold with enough compassion to go around.

"Well, if it isn't the illustrious Doctor Blake! So nice of you to join the party tonight. We have a delightful array of guests in attendance," she exclaimed in her still decernable Irish brogue.

Jeff smiled at her as if to say, "Ok I get the message." He made his way through the atmosphere of ordered chaos of hallways cluttered with stretchers, carts, and EMT's, moving ahead with Maggie in tow, finally reaching Jeff's workstation.

"Maggie, where are my charts?"

"Where they always are," Maggie shot back with her signature smile and hands folded across her ample bosom.

"Their right where you left them. Mixed in with all your personal crap and clutter!"

He smiled again, ignored her, and pressed on.

"Where's the P.A? Is Chris on tonight? Need to get report."

As he started down toward the exam rooms, Chris appeared through the chaos and began the report.

"Room 5....31-year-old female with gross hematuria, right flank pain, temp 101, elevated white count, CT pending, question kidney stone. Blood and urine cultures already submitted, antibiotics started, urology called for possible stent placement."

One by one, Jeff reviewed patient evaluations, performed examinations, checked labs and x-rays, wrote orders and directed care.

As they moved along he noticed the patient in room 13, a rather odd appearing middle-aged man. He seemed different than the typical Saint Bart's client. He was sitting on the exam table with his legs dangling over the side, wearing a hospital Johnnie, wing tip shoes, and white socks. He was bent over starring down, seemingly engrossed in his ipad. He looked very much out of place.

"Chris, who's that guy in room 13?"

14

"Oh him. He came in with hives after eating calamari at Vincenzo's. Got assigned to Dr. Rivers but said he wanted you. He said he looked you up online on one of those doctor review sites."

"His blood work, and EKG are ok. Chest film and KUB still pending. Benadryl seems to have done the trick. His name is Mr. Spikes, Leonard Spikes. Oh, a weird thing is that his temp was crazy low. He feels cold to the touch but tells us it's normal for him. We're looking for an old mercury thermometer to double check it."

As Jeff and Chris entered room 13, Mr. Spikes put down his iPad and looked up with an annoying grin on his face.

"You must be Dr. Blake. I looked you up on the internet. They say you're pretty smart. Too smart for this place."

Jeff had to control the feeling having been stripped naked by a stranger using the internet. It was one of his pet peeves. The good the bad and the ugly, all available to whoever wanted to peer into your privacy. What else had he learned? Maybe something about the incident at Harvard?

"Well, Mr. Spikes, Chris tells me you're feeling much better after the medication we gave you. Did you know you were allergic to seafood?"

Still looking down at his iPad and ignoring the question, he answered.

"It says here you were doing some pretty impressive work unlocking the biological secrets of human cancer cells. It's a subject that fascinates me immensely. I'd love to talk to you about that sometime. I have some ideas of my own."

"Well, Mr. Spikes, do you work in the field or have experience in the academic world?"

"Well, actually I don't. Let's just say I have considerable knowledge in that arena."

Always maintaining his professional demeanor, Jeff tried not to look annoyed at this armchair scientist wannabe and got right back on point.

"Mr. Spikes, Chris, our PA, will go over your discharge instructions. Get some rest tonight and be sure to come back if you experience any shortness of breath."

Just then, Maggie came over.

"Dr. Blake, Dr. Stieger from x-ray is on line three. Wants to talk to you."

"Hey, Stieger, Blake here."

"Jeff, you gotta get down here. I have something to show you on your patient Leonard Spikes, I'll bet even YOUR smart ass has never seen before."

"I'm discharging him as we speak." Jeff said.

He looked over to Chris signaling him to hold Spikes a bit longer.

X-ray departments are always in the dark basements and bowels of most hospitals. You can always spot the radiologists. They're the pale ones with dark circles under their eyes. They work in darkened rooms bathed in the glow of computer screens.

They never see the patient or deal with medical drama. No patient interaction or bedside manner needed, just a deep knowledge of complex disease processes and the identifiable changes they manifest in the body, not to mention

16

understanding the physics of the incredibly high tech machines that make the specialty possible.

Blake spotted Charlie Steiger, smiling from ear to ear like a first-year medical student jubilant over having made a first correct diagnosis. Steiger was a brilliant radiologist with specialties in interventional MRI and CT scanning, so it didn't really matter that crumbs from his lunch were all over his shirt and keyboard.

Stieger clicked a few times on his keyboard and brought up the first image of a routine chest film on the monitor. He then, turned and looked at Jeff.

"Well, what do you see"? "

"Except for normal lung fields and cardiac silhouette, only the fact that the film is mislabeled. The left and right markers are reversed."

"That's what I thought until I checked," Stieger shot back. "I did a chest and abdominal CT, off the grid of course, and wa la! What do you see now?"

"Wow, I knew Spikes was weird," exclaimed Jeff, "but this is incredible!"

Together, almost in chorus, they exclaimed "SITUS INVERSUS!"

It's a rare condition every doctor has studied but will never actually see during his or her entire medical careers. Spikes' case was complete. Positional reversal of all his internal organs. It doesn't usually lead to any problems but confounds the hell out of any doctor, or worse yet, any operating surgeon unfortunate enough to come across a case without prior knowledge. Jeff couldn't wait to run upstairs and tell everyone they had a rare medical anomaly sitting right in front of them.

Back on the ER floor, Jeff quickly rushed into Spike's room.

"Mr. Spikes, you are indeed, a unique fellow".

Before Jeff could finish, Spikes looked up again with a mischievous grin on his face.

"I was wondering how long it would take you to find out that I was put together all wrong. I know all about it, dear doctor. By the way I always run a low body temperature. It's normal for me. We'll talk about it another time. I'm feeling well and have so much to do tomorrow."

Spikes scooped up his paperwork,signed an discharge against advice form, got dressed quickly, and abruptly left before anyone could say a word.

Chapter 2

Almost two years had passed since Jeff and Amanda met. It occurred at a boring reception for the new department head at Harvard University's Fermi physics lab.

Jeff was there reluctantly. The reception was a mandatory social event for science faculty. A lot of rich donors and deep pocket corporate types would be in attendance. It would be great chance to talk up his research on the genetics of cancer hoping to attract research donors.

The room had a quiet elegance about it with fine drapery and solid oak upholstered furniture. Large floral bouquets had been placed around the room. The open bar was stocked with only the upper shelf brands. Drink orders were being taken by a small army of white jacketed staff. It was truly a fitting venue for a crowd of upscale wealthy donors and academic types.

Amanda, a Ph.D. candidate in the physics department, was given the job of greeting the attendees and handing out nametags.

There she was in her little black dress and uncomfortable high heels. She stood there, a perfect beauty, smiling away and thinking to herself.

"I graduated from Rensselaer Polytechnic summa cum laude in physics with a second major in Applied Mathematics. I got into Fermi at Harvard, and here I am in these shoes that are killing me, smiling at rich people and handing out nametags. Well it could be worst. I could be dressed in the silly waiters outfit bringing cocktails around like my male student colleagues. Anyways, I guess I should be grateful that I'm here at all. I beat out a ton of candidates from all over the world to get this position. Ok, I'm lucky to be here, but these shoes are still killing me."

Jeff saw her at the reception line and for a moment forgot why he was there. He had that wow moment when a man sees a woman that makes him pause... that makes him think that possibly the primordial search for a mate might be over. It's something that can't be explained. It's an impulse that was buried deep in a man's genetic code a millions of years ago.

Her silky long black hair glistened under the chandelier lighting. She possessed a perfect waist to hip ratio which anthropologist researchers have proven attracts a man without him even being aware of it. It has something to do with a caveman instinct indicating a woman's fertility status, her ability to bear children and pass along the male's genetic code.

Her little black dress revealed a line every man craves. Her soft and demure smile completed the picture. Jeff was smitten in an instant.

What about the age difference? A quick computation, ten years max. Amazing, he thought, the crap that runs through your mind when you only have a few seconds to say something cool. The line moved forward. When their eyes met, Blake came up with a lame,

"So how'd you get this job?" "She shot back with a put on sexy smile and voice,

"I graduated top of my class in physics with a double major in applied mathematics."

"Wow, that was it!" Jeff thought to himself, "she's smart, sarcastic, accomplished, and beautiful. He noticed she was not wearing a wedding ring. He knew he couldn't let this one get away. Maybe I'm out of my league, he thought. She probably has a million horny guys chasing after her. What the hell, what's one more?

Amanda, for her part, knew that Blake was no rich donor. She could tell by what he was wearing that he had never seen the inside of Louis of Boston clothiers. However, his tall and athletic physic, boyish good looks and engaging smile did not escape her attention.

Earlier she had looked over the attendee list that gave a brief description of the faculty attendant's background and remembered that Blake's was quite impressive.

She couldn't help but think of his dumb opening line. Was he coming on to me, she thought, or maybe he's just socially awkward, or both?

Little did they both realize that this moment was the beginning of a special union.

Love for a man who made her feel whole, protected, and cherished. Love for a woman, an intellectual equal, whose nurturing warmth and supportive spirit made everything right. He would become her rock. She would become his perspective, and the love of his life.

Chapter 3

Sunlight peeked through the bedroom window creating a comforting silent glow. Amanda could hear the sound of the front door unlocking. The room was a little chilly. It's the way she liked it. Toby, their black lab, barely stirred, instinctively knowing it was Jeff, home from his shift at Saint Bart's. He quietly entered the bedroom and slipped into the bed beside Amanda. Her body was soft, smooth, warm, and so comforting to his gentle touch. She began to purr, a sound that women make when they feel comforted and loved. Gently kissing her ear, he whispered.

"Honey, it's time to get up."

Referring to her passion for the charities that she supported, he quietly chided her in a whisper voice.

"The starving people in Chad are counting on you to get to the fundraiser and figure out a way to get them supper tonight."

Barely awake, she stirred and slowly opened her eyes. She was able to muster a comeback.

"Are you making fun of my noble endeavors? You, the dispenser of toxic medications, radiation and painful remedies!"

Jeff continued to gently kiss and caress her under the covers. As she awakened enough to respond to his advances, she realized that he had fallen asleep.

She thought to herself. "Must have been a rough night in the ER."

Amanda returned from her morning schedule just as Jeff was awakening. Her cheeks were still red from the cold Boston winter wind. She was wearing the hand knitted blue scarf that Jeff had got for her on their last weekend away in Vermont. They both loved their weekends in Vermont. Bicycling the Champlain bike path and breakfast at Luenig's. Memories they both cherished.

She put on a pot of Jeff's favorite Star Bucks French Roast, grabbed a cup for herself, and began to head out the door to start her day.

This day would be special. She would be presenting her proposed Ph.D. research project that had to do with the theory of time as it relates to space, and the possibility that time could be used to create a more efficient model for space travel. Her faculty adversary panel would have already reviewed her presentation and would weigh in on whether or not they would support her project. She was very excited and anxious at the same time.

"Oh Jeff, a big envelope came for you. I think it must be from that sweet old nutty professor you studied under in Russia. It's on your desk."

"Professor Romilov is not nutty! He's a brilliant man!"

"Ok, he's a brilliant man who happens to be a bit of an eccentric! Don't take offense, Jeffery. I actually think he's very sweet and smart, but even you have to admit he's been known to express some, shall we say, odd notions."

"How do you know it's from him?"

"Who else would address an envelope like that?"

Jeff made sure to jump up and run to the door before she left. He didn't want her to leave before wishing her good luck on her presentation, and to tell her how much she meant to him. He grabbed her hand, as she was moving toward the door causing her to swing around in his embrace.

"Sweetie, those old stuffed shirts are going to be blown away by how smart you are. And if there not, they'll have to deal with me."

A hug and kiss on her now warm cheek, produced a beautiful smile shining through the obvious apprehension of the review she would be facing.

Opening the door, she turned one last time before leaving, smiled and glanced back at Jeff, before disappearing into the cold morning air.

After coffee and a shower, Jeff readied himself for his day job, overseeing and directing graduate students in their research projects. It helped pay the bills and kept him engaged in academics. Everyone knew his career and potential were running on idle.

Gone were the days when he directed his genetics research lab that turned out new discoveries and advancements at an envious rate. Insiders affectionately called it Harvard's version of Motown's "Hitsville USA."

Almost forgetting, he found the large envelope that had come for him. Amanda was right. No one else would address the envelope to "The illustrious Professor Jeffery Blake, M.D." It had to be from Professor Romilov. The professor had a penchant for the dramatic and humor. Opening the envelope, he made himself comfortable noticing that it was postmarked from Paris.

Dear Jeffery,

I am not sure that you will receive this letter. I gave it to a French colleague in the hopes that he could mail it from Paris. As usual, they watch my every move, even when I am taking a piss! If they find out about this, I could spend the few years I have left in some cold dark place. They do not trust me but need me for their bullshit ideas. Detente!

Please tell me that you are not still working in that dreadful emergency ward. Such a waste of talent! I hope Amanda is well. You know that I have the greatest affection for you. However, I must tell you that I have no idea what she sees in you other than the fact that you are brilliant and good looking. You lucky bugger!

I am excited to tell you that I have made an incredible discovery in my work that was right under my nose. I had failed to see it before. I made the acquaintance of a very interesting fellow who gave me a different perspective on my work and who sent me in the right direction. I want so much to share what I have found with you. The authorities must not know. I am not ready yet.

I suspect that something big is happening in the global scientific community. There has been a lot of gossip and unusual emails. That sort of thing. The authorities have been monitoring my daily activities more closely. I don't know how much longer I can stay here. For the first time they have barred me from traveling abroad for scientific meetings. I am concerned that I am marked for forced retirement.

Soon, I expect you will be invited to attend a conference to be held in Geneva at the site of the new linear accelerator complex. My impression is that many in the global scientific community have been invited, but nobody here at the Academy is talking about it. There is something odd about the invitation. I received it on my office fax. The sponsor is not entirely clear. The title reads "Modern Day Revelations in Science and Global Applications.

More unusual is the fact that there is no formal speakers list. It states that never before concepts of biology, physics, and information technology will be presented. The event is not posted in the usual journals. It sounds like there will be some crazy theories thrown about.

Should be very interesting and an excuse for me to get the hell out of here. I am going to beg them to let me go. I have a few persuasive tricks up my sleeve. We will see what happens. I will get word to you. Whatever you do, I am counting on you to be there, and do not forget to bring the lovely Amanda. I am truly excited to see you both. Try not to disappoint me.

It has been to long since we enjoyed each other's company and lively discourse. If you contact me through the usual channels, please be sure not to mention this communication.
Your friend,
Yuri

Jeff put the letter down and for a moment wondered if the effects of all that vodka had finally gotten to the old man. That notion was quickly dispelled.

Eccentric? Yes. Crazy? No.

He wondered why he hadn't heard about the conference. Maybe he had strayed too far professionally and was no longer in the loop of scientific announcements.

He poured a second cup of coffee. He was still a little groggy from the night before. He knew his circadian rhythm could never get used to night shift work. Just then his cell rang. It was Maggie from the ER.

"Jeffrey, thought you should know. There are some suits and ties snooping around Saint Bart's asking questions about you and of all people, that weird patient from last night, Leonard Spikes."

"What kind of questions?" Blake asked.

"Stuff like if you know him from before or if he hangs out around the hospital. Don't know what they're looking for, but they sure seemed persistent."

"Did they say who they were or show an ID?"

"They flashed a badge but I was too frazzled to look at. Said they were from the FBI. They weren't the cops."

"Thanks Maggie.I owe you one."

Jeff logged on to the Hospital's electronic medical record program and located Leonard Spike's chart listing his address and phone number. Forty-seven Prince Street Apt 2A. He knew where that was. It was in the heart of the North End just across from Bove's Bakery. A call to the number listed reached only a voice mailbox with a quirky message.

"I am not at my phone at the moment as I generally prefer to be doing something else. If you are so inclined, you may leave a message. If your message sparks my interest I may or I may not respond. May the rest of your day be fruitful and filled with purpose."

Jeff left a message identifying himself and asking Spikes if they could meet to discuss his unusual anatomic findings and maybe get some history about his family, that sort of thing. Who knows, there might just be a publishable article somewhere in his story. Jeff left his personal contact information at the University.

He finished his part time day job early that day. Only two projects to review and make recommendations this day. He had the night off from Saint Bart's and was looking forward to dinner with Amanda. There was so much to tell her.

He planned to make this night special. It was their two-year anniversary of the night they met. He was, after all, a romantic at heart, albeit an awkward one. Besides, he knew that women love that kind of stuff. Flowers and dinner at the trendy Jean Paul's Bistro in Cambridge. That should make her happy, and him a Prince. There was more. A surprise she wouldn't be expecting. This night would be a lot more than an anniversary dinner.

Jean Paul's had an authentic Paris feel. Gentle lighting accented the gold textured faux painted walls found in many of Paris's most intimate restaurants. White tablecloths, fine crystal, and a small arrangement of colorful flowers adorned each table. The upholstered furniture was made of dark wood matching the elegant wainscoted walls. Parisian music in the background and an impeccably dressed wait staff complemented the jacket and tie dress code.

Jeff got to the restaurant a little earlier and was seated at the table. Amanda arrived looking radiant in the glow and reflection of the gold colored walls. Her eyes searched for a moment and then connected to Jeff's, producing an instant smile.

"This place is so nice. I'm feeling very special. Did you pick it out yourself?"

"You ARE very special, about as special as you can get and still be real. Not only did I pick it out myself, but also I wanted to pick a place neither one of us has ever been to before. I want this night to be a new and lasting memory."

Then Jeff put on his silly voice and face, and whispered.

"Someday, when we are really old, living in a nursing home, sitting next to each other sipping our laxative protein packed drink, we'll share this special memory. That is, of course, if we still HAVE a memory."

Amanda laughed then leaned over, gave Jeff a kiss on the cheek and whispered, "Don't drink too much wine. I need you awake tonight."

When they both settled down, Jeff took Amanda's hand.

"Are you going to tell me how your presentation went today?"

"Let's just say they were all very impressed with my presentation and gave me full approval. Their letting me work independently. I'm so excited to get started!"

"Wow, that's so great! Another reason to celebrate tonight."

Dinner exceeded expectations, starting with fois gras and hot French onion soup followed by a perfectly cooked chateaubriand with pommes frites. Everything went well and as planned. Amanda's lovely and demure face was visibly pleased. They held hands and reminisced about the ups and downs in their lives, reaffirming the love, loyalty, and partnership they both felt for one another.

The waiter came over and put one serving of the traditional French pastry, Clafoutis on the table. It was adorned with one lit candle.

Jeff took Amanda's hand again and looked directly into her eyes at the same time reaching into his left jacket pocket.

Leaning in to her, he spoke slowly and deliberately in a whisper.

"Sweetheart, you're the best thing that has ever come into my life. I thank God every day for having brought you to me. You're a gift that I don't deserve. If you marry me, I promise to love you and be deserving of your love for as long as I live."

Jeff placed the gray velvet ring box on the table and opened it. The ring had a one carat round center diamond with two half carat round diamonds on each side sparkling in a platinum setting. He placed it on her finger. A perfect fit. He had borrowed a ring from her jewelry box and brought it to the jeweler for sizing. He wanted everything to be perfect.

Amanda's eyes welled up as a smile spread across her face. Her answer?

"YES"

Some of the dinners had taken notice of the proposal. They raised their glasses, and broke out with applause.

After a wonderful dinner the couple left the restaurant and decided to take a long arm in arm walk along the well-lit Charles River Walkway. They wanted to enjoy the fresh air and come down from the high they both were feeling. The conversation was excitedly fast. Amanda began to rattle off a million things racing through her head. Jeff stopped, turned, held her, and said jokingly.

"Slow down before you give yourself a heart attack. We've got plenty of time to figure it all out."

She nodded yes and gave out a sigh of approval.

Jeff recounted the events of the day, Professor Romilovs letter and the bizarre encounter with Leonard Spikes. Amanda was all ears and especially excited about the possible conference trip to Switzerland. The chilly winds of a Boston winter night cut their evening stroll short.

They hailed a cab home to their apartment in the South End. As the cab crossed the Charles River onto Storrow Drive, Jeff felt an impulse and instructed the cabby to go by Prince Street, where Spikes address was listed. After all, it was not much out of the way and he was determined at some point to interview Spikes about his strange anatomical condition. Amanda joked that maybe Spikes might be outside on this cold night smoking a cigarette and waiting for someone to offer him conversation and a drink.

"He's probable dying to hear about our engagement."

"Don't make fun of me, Miss Bride to be, I just want to see where he lives."

They turned onto Prince Street and stopped in front of forty-seven. There were three windows in the front and no lights on. Everyone noticed the black SUV across the street that had government surveillance written all over it.

"Only the Feds or the Mob brings a ride like that into the North End," said the cabby.

"You're right let's get out of here," Amanda replied.

Reaching Boston's South End, they turned right from Tremont onto the narrow Dwight Street, where they lived. Blake and Amanda felt an unsettling sensation when they saw another black SUV blocking the street in front of their building. The cabby flashed his lights signaling the SUV to allow them to pass. Two men dressed in top coats exited the SUV and started walking slowly toward the cab. Blake stuffed a large bill into the cabby's hand, thanked him, and suggested he back up the street and leave. They both got out.

Pointing toward Blake, one of the men shouted.

"Dr Blake...Dr Jeffery Blake?"

Yes, I'm Dr Blake. Who are you and what do you want?"

"Nothing to worry about". Said one of the men, flashing an ID badge high above his head.

"I'm special agent Rossi and this is my partner, special agent Barnes. We're from the FBI. We have a few questions to ask you."

Amanda's protective instincts kicked in. She clutched Jeff's arm and forcefully directing them both toward the entranceway of their apartment.

"Its ten o'clock at night. Can't this wait until tomorrow?" she called out.

"I'm afraid it can't. Now please get in to the car!'

"We're not getting in the car." said Jeff.

"Oh, but you are, commanded Agent Rossi."

And with that, Jeff and Amanda found themselves in the back seat of the SUV with the dome light on. Agent Rossi shoved a photo in front of them.

"Do you know this guy?"

"Yes, Jeff replied, its Leonard Spikes, he was in my emergency room last night"

"What is your relationship to him?"

"Doctor, Patient .I have no other relationship."

What about this guy, pushing another photo into Blake's hand. Shocked and astonished Blake replied, "That's my friend and mentor, Professor Romilov! But, what's he doing with Spikes in the background?"

"That's what we were hoping you could tell us."

Jeff, with an agitated voice began, "Romilov is a good man! He stays out of politics! He wouldn't hurt anyone! His only love is science! As for Spikes, I don't know him! What has he done? Is he wanted for something?"

"He hasn't done anything that we know of, at least not yet. Russian intelligence sent this to us and told us they thought Spikes might be in Boston. It seems they want to talk to Spikes about this Romilov guy."

"Somehow this guy Spikes got into the US without a paper trail. He doesn't exist in our system. No passport, no family, no social, no credit cards or employment history…nada".

"Nobody walks around this country without us knowing about it. Even the wetbacks coming across the southern border are processed. We got his address from the hospital. We've been watching his place all day and so far he's a no show."

"Look… Doc… We're really sorry about bothering you and your girlfriend this late at night. We know this night was special for the two of you, but on this one, we're on a tight schedule. Here's my card. If Spikes contacts you give us a call."

"How did you know this was a special night for us?" Jeff asked.

"Like I said Doc, there's not much we don't know about."

Agent Rossi jumped back into the SUV, and out of Amanda's line of site, flashed Jeff a double thumbs up sign before speeding off into the night.

Chapter 4

The road of life is a strange and wondrous journey. The road gets wider or narrower, speeds up or slows down, turns right or left. Sometimes it even goes around in circles. There are STOP and CAUTION signs everywhere along the road. Everyone travels the same road arriving at different destinations.

At times, in a person's life, there are seminal events that define that life, an event that causes change, or sets a new course. Something happens that gives a mission, purpose, or new direction. For Jeff Blake that moment happened just out of medical school. Jeff's first assignment was a rotation in pediatric oncology at Boston's famed Children's Hospital. It was on his first day that he met Ronnie Maguire. Ronnie's parents, Joe and Linda, were fresh out of high school when they learned that Linda was pregnant.

They were high school sweethearts who had grown up too soon in the tough streets of Boston's Southey neighborhood. Three decker housing, Irish gangs and bad schools were a way of life.

Strong family values and loyalties kept the whole thing from falling apart. Joe worked as a roofer when he could and Linda tended bar part time.

When little Ronnie was born Joe and Linda dedicated themselves to Ronnie and each other. It didn't seem to matter that they were poor with few resources for a bright future. Ronnie brought them closer together and gave them hope that everything would be all right.

Life was good for the Maguire's until Ronnie turned three. Mom noticed some bruising on Ronnie's body and thought it was probably from the rough horseplay Ronnie loved. Joe and Ronnie liked to play a game called Suma where the goal was to force your opponent out of an imaginary circle. Ronnie won every time and Joe would pretend that Ronnie was just too powerful.

It wasn't until the daycare service, that Ronnie had just been enrolled in, noticed the bruising and alerted DCF to investigate suspected child abuse. That's when things turned bad. Ronnie had seen his pediatrician only three months prior and been given a clean bill of health.

Another physical brought the devastating diagnosis of acute lymphocytic leukemia.

Over the next two years little Ronnie would win the hearts of all who knew him. He united distant family members, and inspired grownups to never give up in the face of adversity. Ronnie redefined the meaning of the word "courage" and set an example of love and goodness.

There was something about Ronnie that captivated Jeff more than just doctor –patient relationship. Jeff seemed drawn to Ronnie. Maybe, Ronnie stirred up Jeff's deep feelings of having a family of his own. Whatever it was, Jeff had developed a special bond with Ronnie and loved him like a little brother. During his nights on call at the hospital, he would sit with Ronnie at night giving Joe and Linda a break to get some sleep.

It was 12.30AM, and Jeff had finished making night rounds. Rather than go back to the on call room and wait for his beeper to go off, he decided to join Joe and Linda in Ronnie's room.

The room was darkened and quiet. The only light or sound came from the monitors screens and the occasional beeping alerts. Joe and Linda were sound asleep on the recliners provided for parents by the hospital. Ronnie looked peaceful but gaunt. The chemo had robbed him of his hair and turned his skin a salo white from the anemia it causes.

Suddenly, the cardiac monitor emitted a flat line high pitch alert. Jeff jumped up from the chair to start resuscitation. Instead, Ronnie sat up with eyes wide opened and said in a clear adult male voice,

"Why can't you do something? I'm losing my battle. I don't want to die."

Jeff felt a chill run through his body. He was frozen from what had just happened. Then, in an instant, he awoke, only to realize that the entire incident was only a dream. Or was it? He realized that he had dozed off. Joe and Linda were still sleeping and Ronnie was resting comfortably.

Ronnie died on an overcast Boston day, surrounded by Joe and Linda, family and friends, nurses who cared for him, father Murphy from Saint Bernard's Parish and Jeff Blake who had come to show his support for the McGuire's.

Close family and friends had gathered for the deathwatch at Ronnie's bedside. When it looked like Ronnie had stopped breathing, Joe, with his eyes full of tears, handed the lifeless boy to Blake and asked, "Is he gone?"

At Ronnie's wake, Jeff watched as the long line of people who had come to pay their respects to Joe and Linda pass by. The line included many caregivers from Children's Hospital.

Feeling a sinking sense of guilt, Jeff kept thinking. "Did we do too much? Did we put Ronnie and his family through too many painful tests and experimental treatments trying to save his life? Did we lose site of the humanity in our quest to

40

triumph over this dreadful disease. Ronnie taught us a lot about what worked and what did not. But at what price?"

One thing was for sure. Jeff had been so affected by this tragedy and the bizarre dream, that he made the decision, on that day, to make his life's work defeating the scourge of cancer. Whatever this thing is that wakes up inside a person and destroys the precious gift of life had to be stopped. There had to be an answer and he had to do everything he could to find it.

Joe and Linda went on to have two more healthy children. The legacy of love that little Ronnie left behind would forever be present in their lives.

As for Jeff, he found success. The small part-time lab he started in his last year of residency attracted enormous talent. At first, they were mostly volunteers eager to work and try out new ideas unfettered by corporate money and direction. The founders of this new enterprise rejected the notion of being forced to look for a new drug that no one could afford. Funding began as a trickle, then grew substantially when word spread that this small group of cancer warriors were on to something.

The lab grew in both size and prestige, attracting government as well as private equity capital. It was monetized under the name of "GenOnc Corp". The whole team working there was driven to make progress.

Culture dishes of cancer cell lines filling the large incubators had goofy handwritten signs that read "doomed to die" and "little bastards."

Over the months that followed, his team would discover that cancer cells making up a primary tumor evolve into cells with a different genetic code from the original parent cells. Their offspring would have their own personalities with different strengths and weaknesses. This explained why specific chemotherapy medications, taking years to develop, might be effective against the original tumor only to fail against its metastatic offspring.

They learned that the same cancer was genetically different in different patients. This explained, why one size fits all treatment chemotherapy protocols, had different outcomes.

These discoveries spawned a whole new approach to the war on cancer developing the field of "targeted therapies" and "vaccines."

Groundbreaking, was the discovery of "ligands." These tiny strands of protein acted as ferries, attaching themselves to cancer cells and carrying them across cell membrane barriers. This, for the first time, explained how cancer spreads. Jeff and his team were being considered for the Noble Prize in Medicine when the whole thing came crashing down.

Over time, the Universities money and resources partnered with GenOnc. Their job became providing the expertise for the creation of protocols, legal issues, and quality control services, leaving Jeff and his staff able to concentrate and have complete autonomy over the scientific work.

Chapter 5

Six months later

Barry Stone was a thirty eight year old dairy farmer from Mission Creek Idaho who was losing the battle against a malignant melanoma that began as a small mole between the toes of his left foot. He had undergone surgery and multiple rounds of chemotherapy only to be told that the cancer had spread.

The tumors growing in his lungs were getting larger. His oncologist had heard about an investigational clinical trial being conducted in Boston at GenOnc. They were looking for patients like Barry. Not yet very sick or debilitated but facing a grim prognosis. His application was accepted after a rigorous review by the universities' investigational candidate review committee. All guidelines and criteria were scrupulously adhered to.

When Barry and his wife Janice arrived, the staff explained to them that they had developed a tumor vaccine specific for melanoma, and had genetically engineered it to work against different patterns of known melanoma cancer cell lines. It had proved highly effective in different animal models, but had never before been used in humans.

Jeff and his team explained to Barry in a video recorded session the risks and possibility of unknown reactions that could potentially result in death. He would be supervised closely by a handpicked medical team led by Dr Michael Gibbons, chief of intensive care at MGH.

The vaccine would be administered in small ever-increasing doses until a maximum calculated dosage was achieved. There would be continuous monitoring of any changes or side effects. An antidote of protein antibodies specifically designed to attach to the vaccine components and neutralize their effects had been developed as a backup safety measure. Barry had passed a complete reevaluation of his medical status and given the green light.

On the morning of the study Barry entered the mini one patient lab, smiling, full of hope, and confident in the team. He signed all the consent forms and exclaimed to everyone,

"Ok, let's get this show on the road!"

The nurse attached an IV to Barry's arm and so began the infusion of the vaccine. That little bottle hanging on a pole represented more than just the years of hard work and

44

dedication of twenty-six men and women. It represented more than the millions of research dollars raised by ordinary people in walk a thons, bake sales, and fundraisers all across the nation. It represented HOPE!

During the infusion which stretched out over eight hours, Barry delighted and entertained everyone with his stories of life on his family's Idaho farm. He researched the Boston restaurant scene and let everyone know that he expected the famous porterhouse steak at Abe & Louis. He proved to be the quintessential "salt of the earth" type of guy.

At the end of eight hours the maximum dosage of vaccine had been infused without a hitch. Barry reported feeling fine. His only complaint jokingly was about the quality of the clinic food, even though he managed to eat every morsel.

When the nurse declared "infusion complete" Barry smiled and gave a thumbs up sign. A round of applause resounded, reminiscent of NASA space launch tradition. It had been a long day full of tension, exhaustion, and anticipation.

After three days in the lab under a medical microscope, the only changes in Barry detected were a slight fever and an acceptable spike in the white cell blood count. Both indicated an immune system response. Barry was developing cabin fever and after clearance by Dr Gibbons was allowed to leave the lab.

He and his wife,Janice, were put up in the Harvard University dorm suites and given free meal passes at all campus food concessions. Other than avoidance of alcohol, there were no dietary restrictions. He would report to the lab for a physical and blood work twice a day. They would stay in town for three weeks then set up the appointment for a chest CT to access the tumor response, if any.

The agonizing three weeks had passed and for Barry the day for his follow up chest CT scan had finally arrived. Other than some mild fatigue, Barry had been feeling well and was eager to get back home. He had grown tired of life under the microscope and longed for the comfort of familiar surroundings. Regardless of his outcome, he was resolved to accept his fate, and rejoice in having been given a chance to be healed.

Jeff and a few of his closest team had gathered together with Barry's wife Janice in the CT viewing console pod. Lips could be seen quietly mouthing private prayers. The computer generated voice command "breathe…don't breathe" and the whirling of the generators was the only sound heard as Barry was transported through the scanner. Thirty seconds later, it was over.

As the first images arrived, Jeff resisted the temptations to scroll through them until the entire complement of images was delivered. In two and a half minutes the completion icon green LED began flashing. The moment of truth had arrived. No one expected what happened next.

The large tumors in Barry's lungs had not just decreased in size as hoped, but could no longer be identified. Complete resolution! Total response! It was NASA control room all over again. Cheers and thumbs up through the glass partition to Barry. There were tears of joy everywhere. They had done it!

It took a few days for the enormity of these findings to sink in.

Had they discovered a way to cure cancer? Had one of man's greatest achievements been realized? The team, following scientific protocol, deciding that they would remain silent about the experiment until a complete review of the methods; data, outcome, and follow up could be prepared for scientific publication. They knew they would be in for rigorous scrutiny from the global scientific and academic community.

Barry and Janice were ready to head back home to Idaho with a new lease on life but not before experiencing Boston's Freedom Trail Tour, Duck Boat Tour and that legendary porterhouse steak at Abe and Louis on Boylston Street.

At Boston's Logan Airport, Barry and Janice were waiting at gate 15 for United flight 309 direct service to Boise Idaho with mixed emotions. Joy for the outcome of the experiment, and sadness, for leaving the people, with whom a deep emotional bond had formed filled their hearts. They were accompanied by Nurse Cheryl Amato from Dr Gibbon's team who was familiar with Barry's case. She had been on Barry's case from the beginning and was in charge of monitoring his follow up care.

Like everyone else involved, she had come to develop a kindred spirit with Barry and Janice. She was glad for them that they were going home but knew she would miss their homespun humor and genuine affection.

As their flight was called and they said their final goodbyes, Cheryl noticed some blotchy red spots on Barry's face.

"Barry. How are you feeling? I'm noticing some red spots on your face."

" I'm fine just a little itching, that's all".

"Barry, I want you to come here and sit for a minute."

"We're going to miss our flight."Barry exclaimed. Janice quickly took control.

"Barry,do what Cheryl says! We can get another flight if we have to."

As Janice consoled Barry, Cheryl called Jeff's cell.

"Dr Blake, this is Cheryl Amato. I'm with Barry and Janice at Logan. He's developing some blotching and itching. I don't think it's safe for him to leave. Might be some sort of allergic reaction."

"Right, Jeff replied, don't let him leave. We've got to get him back to the lab ASAP. I'll get Gibbons down here. The traffic is murder at this hour. Get security. Explain to them the situation. Give them my number. He needs an ambulance. If he starts going downhill tell the EMT's to start full anaphylaxis protocol. Do it now! Call me on the way!"

Sirens blared and lights flashed as the ambulance sped through rush hour traffic. Janice's face had grown grim. Barry realized he was in trouble. What began as a sensation of flush was quickly becoming uncomfortable as evidenced by a grimace on Barry's face. Cold wet towels seemed to help. The EMT's could be heard shouting out Barry's vital signs over the radio to the team waiting at the lab.

"I feel like I'm burning up, how much farther?"

"Don't worry." Cheryl tried to reassure them both.

"You'll be ok once we get some meds on board. ETA, five minutes."

As Barry was being rushed on a gurney into the lab he cried out, "I'm burning up. Somebody help me" Oh my God I'm burning up!"

The EMT's were yelling, "BP 80/60! .5cc of epinephrine IM stat. Decadron 10 mg IV. Dilaudid 2 mg IV. Let's get an airway! Come on, intubation now! He's got shitty BP. We need to get those fluids in guys."

All of a sudden Barry woke up with a learch and began screaming in pain. He had a scary demonic look in his face. It caused a panic in the room. Seasoned professional hands began to tremble and fumble, dropping syringes on the floor. Uncontrollable agitation set in requiring restraints on Barry plus the addition of IV Ativan.

Everything seemed to be spiraling out of control. Barry fell back limp on the stretcher and went unconscious. With Barry unconscious, Jeff was able to intubate, establish an airway and start100% oxygen. Dilaudid helped calm the agitation and controlled the pain. Dr Gibbons noticed that Janice was shaking with her eyes fixed on Barry. She was going into shock.

"Get her out of here! Get her out of here!"

Dr Gibbons watched as Cheryl struggled with the IV's.

"Cheryl, why aren't the IV's working? We need fluids! We need them stat!"

"The veins keep dissolving. They won't hold the needle. I can't get the IV in! Jeff grabbed the IV needle from Cheryl's shaking hand. Barry's both arms were bleeding from failed IV attempts.

"Go for the subclavian or jugular! We need fluids!" Gibbons yelled out again.

Jeff tried to get an IV line but failed. Even the large peripheral veins dissolved at the touch of the needle. In desperation he ran to the lab fridge, grabbed the vial of antidote that had been prepared and injected it into Barry's shoulder.

Barry's skin had turned a frightening bright red color. The agitation returned with a vengeance testing the strength of the restraints. Something, not Barry, was shaking his body violently.

" Are we getting this? Is the video on?" Dr Gibbons gasped.

Then, as if on cue, Barry's skin began to undulate like a fluid wave. Small eruptions began to pop spewing blood and tissue. The process intensified. Dr Gibbons commanded in a loud and controlled voice,

"Evacuate the pod! Evacuate the pod! Everybody out now!

What followed was an explosive decomposition of a human body never before seen or described in the annals of science or history. In a few short seconds the glass walls of the pod were covered in splattered blood and tissue. The unbearable stench of decomposition permeated the air.

Jeff and the team huddled outside by the hundred-year-old oak tree shell-shocked and dazed. Janice was devastated, crying and shaking uncontrollably. Everyone's attention was on Janice but she was inconsolable. The only saving grace was the fact that she was not in the room and did not witness the actual moment of death.

It would take over forty-eight hours for the EPA and Harvard's own biological decontamination team to clear the area for safe entry. Barry's remains were gathered as best as they could. Tissue samples were set aside for examination and study.

In the days and months that followed there ensued an extensive and exhaustive investigation into every aspect of the research methodology and experiment protocols. The details of what happened were legally sealed and never released to the public. The press was told that equipment had malfunctioned resulting in an explosion and death. No names were released.

Janice went back to Idaho with Barry's remains. She had no animosity toward the staff or GenOncCorp. She accepted a large financial package to help her defray any personal expenses and buy her silence regarding the events surrounding Barry's death. There would be no tell all book or tabloid articles. She understood the importance of the research, the risks they took, and was satisfied by the review boards conclusions that all possible safety protocols had been followed.

Jeff was emotionally traumatized by these events. He took on an irrational personal responsibility for Barry's death. He blamed himself and agonizing over the possibility that he had missed something that led to this debacle.

Despite the urgings of his fellow research staff members, Jeff decided to take time off from research and head in another direction. The door, however, remained open. GenOnc Corp's scientific agenda was placed on hold as everyone regrouped.

Chapter 6

Several months had passed since the night encounter with the FBI agents. Blake had given up trying to contact Leonard Spikes. He seemed to have disappeared. Repeated calls went unanswered and finally a recording that the phone had been disconnected. The apartment on Prince Street had a "For Rent" sign in the window. Inquires to the landlord drew a blank. It seems that no one had ever heard of Leonard Spikes. No invitation had come for the international meeting that Romilov had promised and Jeff thought it time to give his old friend a call.

He checked his iphone world clock and calculated the nine-hour time difference. He knew Romilov lived alone and would most likely be home settling in for the night. The call connected with ease. An older woman's voice answered. Jeff had to quickly muster up whatever Russian he could remember.

"Professor Romilov please" The voice responded in a nasty tone "wrong number" and hung up. Jeff checked the number again. It was correct. He called again and the same nasty voice answered and hung up. Calls to the Academy of Science became worrisome. Employees reported that Romilov "doesn't work here anymore" and gave no further information. A quick check on the internet for Romilov's possible obituary drew a blank. What had happened to his old friend? Jeff called Amanda to tell her about Romilov being out of touch.

"Amanda, I'm really worried. They say he doesn't work there any more like he's some kind of janitor or something. For God's sake, he's the director of the molecular genetics program, not just any old employee!"

"Don't worry, I'm sure there's a reasonable explanation, and that he's fine. Maybe he moved or took another position? Anyways, I was just about to call you. I have quite the surprise for you. You'll never believe who I'm having tea with this very moment."

"Who?"

"Leonard Spikes!"

Jeff's heart sank. Had Amanda lost her mind? A man wanted for questioning by the FBI, a possible fugitive!

"Amanda, listen to me. Excuse yourself and get out of the house immediately. I'm on my way over. I'm calling the police."

"No you're not! Don't you dare!"

"He's a harmless soul and a delight to talk with. He knows a lot about everything and we're discussing the most interesting conundrums of quantum physics. Get over here and you might learn something. I've asked him to stay for dinner." She hung up the phone.

Jeff was in disbelief as he raced through the Boston traffic. Arriving home, he opened the door to see Spikes with that annoying signature grin on his face. A grin that Jeff remembered from the ER. Amanda was smiling and looking charmed out of her mind.

"What's going on here? What are you doing in my house?"

Before Jeff could say another word Amanda jumped to her feet.

"Jeffery! Mr. Spikes is a guest in our home and you WILL treat him with the courtesy and the respect he deserves!"

Just then Spikes calmly spoke.

"I'm sorry if I upset you Dr Blake, but I was told you were looking for me and wanted to discuss something. I know it's not customary, but I thought I would drop by and at least give you my contact information. I prefer the direct approach and given certain circumstances find it to be more advantageous. I can assure you I am no danger to you or your lovely Amanda. I think we have a lot in common and much to talk about. Amanda has invited me to stay for dinner but I'll decline if that makes you uncomfortable. Maybe I should be on my way."

"No one's going anywhere," said Amanda handing Jeff a comforting glass of Merlot. "Dinner was already ready before Mr. Spikes stopped by and I've kept it on the warmer."

By this time Jeff had begun to calm down. The shock of Spikes popping into his life was fading. He found himself being drawn in by a powerful yet unintimidating personality. It was almost as if this Leonard Spikes emitted some kind of reassuring presence that mitigated any feelings of suspicion or ulterior motives. As much as Jeff tried to resist and maintain his objective position, he felt an uncommon sense of goodness and calm around his new guest.

As the evening progressed the conversation was light. Shared experiences of travel destinations and the history surrounding them made for a lively exchange. It seemed as though there was no subject that Spikes could not demonstrate a depth of knowledge. Quite a remarkable persona indeed. The subject of his odd anatomy never came up. Suddenly it seemed like the wrong time and place to discuss such matters.

Amanda again reminded Jeff how lucky he was to have her in his life. That night she proved to be the perfect hostess.

"Was there anything she didn't excel in." he thought? Could any woman possibly be this perfect? Was he observing a one in a million or maybe just in love?"

After dinner Spikes complemented Amanda and said he had forgotten how good a cup of coffee could be. How it awakens the senses.

"You know Jeffery, I must confess that our meeting in the emergency department at Saint Bartholomew was no chance encounter. You probably know that already."

Spikes began to move closer, walking slowly in a circular pattern keeping his eyes always trained on Amanda and Jeff who began to feel, almost, as if they were being stalked.

"I've been following your career Jeffery, and have been very impressed by your work. No one came closer than you in unlocking the secrets of cellular life. What happened to Barry Stone was indeed unfortunate. There was nothing more you could have done. I hope you realize that the disease was fighting for "ITS" life. The the cancer has a life of its own and was fighting for own survival. Your brilliant treatment was about to kill it forever. It had to get out. I am in a position to help you move ahead more rapidly, that is, if you allow me to do so."

Spike's tone and demeanor began to change. Slowly, as he spoke, his persona seemed to transform into a stronger, darker, and more powerful presence, a presence commanding complete attention. Spikes took another sip of his second cup of coffee and fixed his gaze on both Amanda and Jeff.

"There is something that I need to share with you both. I have a purpose for coming into your lives and I hope you'll forgive me for the intrusion."

He turned his gaze directly toward Jeff.

"Dr Blake, we have identified you and Amanda as potential players in major events about to happen in the not so distant future. What I am about to tell you will sound preposterous. I don't expect you to believe or trust in me, but am hoping, that in time you will give me your confidence."

"You will be asked to help in bringing about changes already set in motion. There is a plan that must succeed. I want you both to remember that you will always have your free will to say yes or no."

Spikes motioned for them to sit down to listen to what he had to say. A powerful quite engulfed the room allowing only Spike's deliberate voice to be heard. Amanda and Blake felt helpless to interrupt or say anything before he was finished. It was as if they had entered into a hypnotic trance like state with a feeling of being controlled, and almost paralyzed.

"Truths will be revealed to you. I hope that you both will embrace and open yourself to them. They are precious gifts for you to nourish and protect."

Next he turned toward Amanda.

"Amanda, you will be a full partner in these endeavors. Your knowledge of particle physics and quantum mechanics, with my help, will enable my reveals to come into focus. My aim is to move the body of human scientific knowledge ahead. I do not do this for personal gain and neither should you. I am hoping that doing this will give you both the confidence in me to do what needs to be done."

"There will be many others privy to my reveals. No one outside our circle should know about our little conversation for now. When the time is right the whole world will know."

Amanda was speechless. Jeff was aware that something very unusual had just happened. It left him with a creepy and uneasy feeling. He was skeptical about everything that Spikes had said. He was shocked that Spikes seemed to know everything about the experiment gone wrong, even Barry's name. No one had that information. How could he possibly know? Blake gathered his wits and then demanded,

"Who are you Spikes?"

"I am you! I am your friend."

"Don't give me any mumbo jumbo. Maybe you're unbalanced. Maybe you're a spy of some sort. We know that the FBI is looking for you. How do you know professor Romilov? What happened to him? Maybe you need to leave us alone!"

Spikes went quiet for a moment as if he was taking some time gathering his thoughts. Then he looked up at Jeff with a stern look on his face.

"Get back to the lab where you belong, Dr Blake! There's work to be done!"

Spikes got up moved toward the door and opened it part way. Lingering for a moment, he turned back to Jeff.

"Oh and those ligands you discovered? Maybe you should think about "reversing the polarity."

As Spikes walked out and down the sidewalk Blake ran outside after him.

"What do you know about ligands? How are you getting home? You don't have a car." From a distance Spikes retorted,

"I enjoy walking."

Jeff ran out after him a little farther, "How do I contact you?

"You can't. I'll know when we need to talk."

Jeff reached the end of the street and the rounded the corner. Spikes was nowhere to be seened.He had disappeared.

Jeff dashed back into the house to find Amanda sitting on the sofa looking very disappointed and angry at his behavior.

"What's wrong with you? I can't believe how rude you are. "She said.

"What's wrong with me? How about you? He had you eating out of the palm of his hand. All that crap about "reveals "and stuff. I'm calling Agent Rossi."

"Like hell you are," she yelled back. "You're acting like an alpha male asshole! He's committed no crime!"

She stormed into the bedroom and slammed the door.

The sun made its way through the lace curtains illuminating the weathered oak wood floors, announcing the beginning of a new day. Amanda was already up. She made her way quietly by the couch where Jeff was still sleeping. He was in a most uncomfortable position with his neck at almost a right angle to the armrest. He began struggling to get into a more comfortable position, but couldn't seem to find it. He finally gave up and got up.

"How was your night on the couch?" Amanda sarcastically inquired.

"I don't know what got into me. That Spikes. He rattles my cage. What does he want from us? I don't feel comfortable with him coming around here. He never answers any of my questions. He creeps me out."

Amanda walked over to Jeff and sat beside him on the sofa. She sat quietly as Jeff vented his suspicions. Finally, in a calm voice she replied.

"Look, all I know is this. He's a well-mannered gentleman who behaved himself with grace. He's probably the smartest and most interesting person I've met in quite some time. I know you'll think I'm crazy, but I believe and sense that he has a genuine affection for both of us. I don't know why, but I can feel it. If you remember, asked that you keep your mind open. I can't believe the inquisitive scientist I know could make a snap judgment call without thinking things through. You need to start acting like the like the Dr Jeffery Blake I fell in love with."

She hesitated and then raised her voice up a notch.

"And by the way. He's right on another point. I don't know why I haven't pushed for this before. Not a day goes by that I don't say. Today's the day. Well, today IS the day."

"You have got to get over that accident that happened in the lab. Barry Stone was a dead man. We both know he had less than two months to live. The experiment was his only chance. You need to get back to where you really belong, and stop feeling guilty. You are guilty of nothing! You're losing your identity Jeff. It's like your life is walking around in circles with destination unknown. It's not you. Get back before you turn into someone nobody recognizes."

Jeff had a lot to think about. As usual, he knew that Amanda, and by extension Spikes, were right about getting back to the lab. He kept thinking about what Spikes said about the ligands on his way out the door. "Think about reversing polarity."

He began to think, "What if the way ligands bond themselves to cancer cells were not by chemical bonds as are found in all biological entities? What if they were instead by electrical or magnetic bonds?"

He knew that his colleagues were working very hard to create or identify chemical substances to block the bonding mechanism. Blocking the way ligands attach themselves to cancer cells, would block the way cancer cells are ferried from the original tumor to distant locations in the body. If it turned out that ligands bind instead by electrical potentials or magnetic fields then reversing polarity could disrupt the whole process! Cancer would have to find another way to spread.

"WOW," he thought to himself. Why didn't I think of this? This could be a breakthrough."

Chapter 7

That night Jeff couldn't sleep. The whole night would be spent at the kitchen table designing an experiment to prove or disprove the theory that Spikes had revealed.

The next morning, Jeff couldn't wait to tell Amanda about the experiment he had designed, and the idea that Spikes had given him. He explained the entire thought process to her. There was a quickness and excitement in his voice that she had not heard in a long time. She shared his excitement and had the feeling that maybe, just maybe, a cloud had been finally lifted. Amanda watched with a sense of relief, as Jeff scurried around that morning, prepping, for a foray back to the lab.

"Amanda, please do me a favor. Call the hospital. Tell them I'll be in tomorrow but that I can't make it tonight. Make up something."

Jeff didn't waste any time paying a visit to GenOnc Labs where David Misner had taken the reins. He realized he had been away too long when the security officer wouldn't let him in without an appointment. A call to David's office did the trick.

As he made his way down the long corridor to lab 101 he could see that the place hadn't changed much. Everything still in place gave him a sense of being home again and everyone seemed delighted to see him again.

"Hey Doc, good to see you. hope you're coming back" was the general comment of former coworkers, as they spotted Jeff in the hallway. After all the, so good to see you's were over, David motioned to Jeff to come into his private office. They shook hands.

"So Jeff, to what do we owe this honor?" David said, tongue- in- cheek. "Please tell me you're thinking about coming back."

"Thanks David, you've always been such a good friend. Yes, I'm giving it some consideration. How are things going with the work?"

David got up from his desk and walked over to the whiteboard. He began drawing a schematic of ligands, marking the locations of binding receptor sights.

"Look Jeff, you know, now that you no longer work here, I'm not supposed to talk to you about the work but I've got to tell you that things aren't going well. Fact is, we're making very slow progress inhibiting ligand binding."

He pointed to each receptor site and explained that the biological model for blocking the attachment of ligands to the cancer cells just wasn't working.

"We just can't seem to find the key. We've followed a lot of dead ends. It's proving to be a hard nut to crack."

"David, that's one of the reasons I came over today. I've got something I want to run by you and see if you think there might be a chance it could get to the next level."

Jeff explained, in great detail his theory of a possible blocking mechanism using reverse polarity. He could not reveal that it was not entirely his idea for fear that the story of where he got the idea would sound too preposterous.

After kicking it back and forth, they both agreed the idea was worth a shot. The experiment would be tried in mice and hamsters that had been implanted with cancerous tumors. The only problem would be finding the right energy source with reversal capacity. David's idea was to consult his friends in the physics department. They always seemed to come up with some brainy solution. They agreed but not before David urged Jeff to come back and join the team. Jeff knew it was time to get back in the fight.

On the way home, Jeff's brain was working overtime trying to come up with a solution when all of a sudden a light went on.

"Oh my God, how could I be so stupid."

He was disappointed in himself. Why hadn't he thought to run this problem by Amanda. After all, she WAS working toward her PhD in physics. How could he be so condescending? She deserved better than that.

When he got home Amanda was working on the physics project at the kitchen table. He made sure to tell her how beautiful and professorial she looked wearing her pair of new brown horned rimmed glasses.

"Amanda, I need your brainy help with something."

"Not before I get my, hello I'm home kiss."

She had a way of slowing him down in a hurry and reminding him of his manly relationship obligations. She got the kiss.

Jeff explained to her in great detail again the problem of polarity reversal and asked if she had any ideas on how to achieve it.

Without hesitation and very matter of factually, she said.

" Why didn't you ask me that earlier? Wait don't answer."

She put her finger over Jeff's lips to save him the embarrassment of having to come up with some lame excuse.

"As to your problem, that's easy enough. Just put your little cancer cell critters through the magnetometers."

"The what?" said Jeff.

"The magnetometer. It's a device we use to test the strength of attraction between two or more atoms. It reverses polarity in a step wise fashion to pull atoms apart. We can then insert new atoms in an attempt to create new elements. At low power it will scramble up the little critters a bit but they should be all right. I wouldn't try it on a human subject without a lot of tweaking."

66

Jeff grabbed Amanda and gave her a big hug.

"You're amazing! I love you!"

Looking surprised at Jeff's over the top reaction, Amanda said,

"Why all the fuss? It's no big deal."

"It is to me!" Jeff said.

Three weeks would pass before the phone call from David Misner. The magnetometer had detected positive electrical potentials on the membrane surfaces of the cancer cells and negative potentials on the ligands. The perfect attraction to bind them together. The magnetometer was able to reverse the positivity of the cancer cells making ligand binding impossible.

"Jeff, congratulations!

"We inoculated the critters little livers with melanoma and watched to tumor grow. The critters that got the treated melanoma cells had no metastasis to other areas after two weeks. The other group was loaded with metastasis everywhere. Amazing results!"

"Where do we go from here? We need new equipment and new protocols. Everything's changed."

Everything had changed. It was a whole new direction. A true breakthrough, and all because of a flippant suggestion by Leonard Spikes. Jeff knew he had to contact Spikes and tell him the news, apologize for his behavior, and thank him for his help.

More importantly, he had to find out who this man was and how he came to know these things. What is his background? Where does he come from? What else does he know?

Jeff had to admit to himself that these so-called "reveals" might have some merit after all. He remembered the instructions to" keep an open mind and embrace the precious gifts." Amanda was right again.

Chapter 8

Spring came early to Boston. The unseasonably warm weather brought out hoards of Bostonians suffering from the long winter blues and cabin fever. Pale bodies on bikes, and people jogging, rollerblading, and walking dogs were everywhere.

Amanda and Jeff were not immune to the effects of Spring. Dusting off their bikes from winter storage, they set off on one of their favorite pastimes, cruising along the Charles River bikeway.

The warm breeze and comfort of sunshine on skin seem to energize and restore what winter's gloomy cold and gray days had worn down. Sailboats, highlighting the sunny Charles River's white peaks, were everywhere. The Cambridge skyline on the other side of the Charles River sparkled with sunshine reflecting off of the buildings windows.

Jeff had the habit of cruising along, on his bike, a little ahead of Amanda, in a sort of semi single file style pattern, to help avoid pedestrians.

Without warning, Jeff slammed on his brakes causing Amanda to narrowly miss colliding with him. When they stopped Jeff turned to Amanda looking startled.

"That guy on the bench over there, sunning himself, is that Spikes?"

There he was, soaking up the sun. Spikes was quite the sight, slumped back on the park bench. He was wearing black loafers and long black pants rolled up above the knees. He had on an unbottened white dress shirt exposing his skinny white chest. His black fedora hat was pulled down low, as if he wanted to avoid getting any sun on his face.

Jeff and Amanda backed tracked and pulled their bikes up in front of him. Amanda spoke first

"Mr. Spikes, how are you? Where have you been? We wanted to contact you but didn't know how."   Then Jeff jumped in.

"I wanted to apologize for the way I behaved and thank you for the tip you gave me about the ligands. It turned out to be truly remarkable."

Spikes was sporting his annoying grin which by now had become his signature trademark.

"Well, Jeffery, I'm glad you took my advice."

"By the way, you both rode right by me. Never even noticing me! Ah, the story of my very existence!"

He was smiling and seemed to be enjoying a private joke. Then he added.

"I guess I tend to be invisible at times. Have you both had time to think about our last conversation?"

"Yes, that's almost all we talk about." said Jeff.

I need to apologize again for my rude behavior and thank you again for the insight you gave me which led to a most astounding discovery. I promise to give you full credit but how could I divulge the source when I had no way to explain who you are? We have so many questions to ask you about your background, scientific training." As Jeff was excitedly rattling off, Spikes motioned to him "that's enough."

"Well, it seems that you two are finally ready to have a serious conversation."

Jeff and Amanda got quiet and nodded.

"You must understand, first and foremost, that I am a benevolent being that means no harm to any living thing. There is evil in this world but I am not it. For us to go forward you must believe this. You must truly believe this. I know that you both do not completely believe in me at this point and that's ok. I have not shown or proven enough to you yet to merit your full confidence. Besides, humanity is skeptical by nature. Not your fault...a good thing...a trait that affords you protection. I cannot answer all the questions you put forth at this time. At this moment in our relationship, you are not ready to fully comprehend what I have come to accomplish."

"From now on, when referring to myself I will use the pronouns I and WE interchangeably. Don't try to understand it. Just accept it."

Jeff and Amanda stood there transfixed, trying to resist a wave of anxiety, and at the same time wonderment, that began to sweep slowly over their bodies. Their heart rates began to quicken. A strange goose bump chill formed on their skin like frost on a leaf. Neither one knew exactly what to say or do next. There was a quiet pause.

Spikes broke the awkward silence.

"I will communicate with you both in a novel way. There will be nothing to fear and no harm will come of it. In this new way of communication, "reveals" will flow in an environment better suited for a more complete understanding. You must both always remember. You will always have FREE WILL."

"Our relationship will end whenever you WILL it to end. If you choose to do so, you will have no recollection of me, our conversations, or of the reveals."

Amanda and Jeff stood there speechless.They needed a moment to gather their thoughts. There were so many questions that needed answering. In an instant, Spikes tipped his hat and said,

"Well, it was so nice to see you both again today. Please enjoy the rest of your day. I'll, be in touch."

They watched as he disappeared into the crowd of spring revelers.

Jeff turned to Amanda; "I need a drink" Amanda hesitated as if she had trouble focusing,

"Me too."

Boston Founders Pub was just across the street. A landmark watering hole dating back to the Revolutionary War. It wasn't their first choice but it was close, just a few steps away. Usually packed with tourists, they were surprised to be able to find two seats at the bar.

The smell of beer and spirits permeated the air. Revolutionary war era oak wood floors and paneled walls lined the room. Pillars made from old ship masts supported the beams. It was easy to imagine colonials in three pointed hats drinking British ale and complaining about the Crown.

A red faced and portly middle-aged bartender approached with a congenial smile. He took one look at Jeff and Amanda and exclaimed,

"You two look like you've just seen a ghost! Nothing a shot of Jameson Whiskey won't cure!"

Amanda looked up,

"Make it a double."

"Me too." Jeff chimed in.

The Irish whisky was true to form. Smooth in the beginning with the right sting at the finish. After a few sips a calm began to replace the strange unsettling emotions they both experienced.

"Amanda, I'm starting to ask myself questions that feel absurd. Questions that are way out of my comfort zone. I'm trying to rationalize everything that's happened since we met Spikes but I'm finding it very difficult to put it all together. There is no rational explanation. Sometimes I think that maybe Spikes is a hoax or some kind of twisted joke, but on the other hand his "reveals" have born amazing results .He's right about one thing. I'm still not a true believer in all this, but fascinated by the whole thing."

"I feel the same way but go one step farther," Amanda said. "I'm excited and scared at the same time."

"I'm not sure what to think except that we have been brought into something that is bigger than we can imagine. My gut tells me we've been given a unique privilege to participate in something extraordinary. Spikes is no ordinary man. I'm afraid and excited at the same time to find out what or who he really is. He said he would communicate to us in a novel way and that we shouldn't be afraid. I know that I have little reason to trust him, but I somehow I do."

They went home after an emotionally exhausting morning. Cuddling on the sofa they both fell asleep. Jeff woke up earlier than Amanda. His neck was sore again from the uncomfortable position sleeping on the sofa. He placed Amanda in a more comfortable position and kissed her soft cheek as he gently pulled the covers over her. He knew her first class wasn't till three in the afternoon and that she needed to sleep. She looked so peaceful and beautiful. For a moment he became almost envious of the total serenity she seemed to be enjoying.

Jeff had decided that this would be the day he would give his notice at Saint Bart's. He had mixed feelings. Excited to resume his research at GenOnc but knowing he would miss the great team of care giving professionals he admired so much, especially Maggie and Chris. He left Amanda a note before leaving.

"Good morning Sleeping Beauty. You looked like you were having the best dreams ever. Maybe you'll tell me about them tonight. Don't make supper tonight. I'm bringing home some take out. Love You, xo"

When Amanda awoke she had to compose herself. She had just had a most unusual experience. A dream like no other dream she had ever had before.

"Jeff where are you?" She said out loud.

She found the note. Something had happened to her while she slept. Something she needed help in understanding. It was very unsettling. Instinctively, she knew she had to go outside her usual daily sphere to find the answers.

She was glad that Jeff wasn't home. He would have noticed that something was wrong. She would be under pressure to come up with an explanation. She wasn't ready. She needed to figure it out for herself first. As chance would have it she got a text that class had been cancelled. A free day couldn't be better. She needed time to sort things out.

Chapter 9

Saint Anthony's Parish was one of Boston's oldest churches. The waves of Italian immigrants arriving in Boston at the turn of the nineteenth century were not welcomed in the already established Irish Parishes. The Italians were the new workers, the new fodder for the sweatshops.The Irish had moved up the hierarchy ladder becoming "bosses."

Mostly from Italy's poorest southern regions of Calabria and Sicily, the Italians had darker skin than their English and Irish predecessors. They didn't speak English, and were for the most part, uneducated.

What they did have, however, were skills in the construction trades handed down from father to son, an incredible work ethic, love of family, faith in God, and the will to succeed.

Saint Anthony's Parish was built by the sweat and pride of these early immigrants. Perched atop Margaret Street, the steeple looked out over the Atlantic Ocean. On any given Sunday morning a welcoming bell could be heard all over the North End.

As Amanda approached the large oak doors of Saint Anthony's she remembered the family pictures taken on this very spot. She recalled, with fond memories, Easter Sunday's, her cousin's wedding, and the old wedding picture of her parents standing in front of these very doors.

Being there brought back the childhood memories of all the Sundays, when for years, she and her parents, attended the traditional Latin mass. She remembered reading along from the missal in Latin during the Mass and not understanding what the words meant, but how special she felt reading, in this mysterious language, used by the ancients.

The feelings of looking forward to the after church Italian Sunday feast, and belonging to a community came rushing back. She missed her parents, who had been taken from her at an early age. She remembered her mother, a strong and beautiful woman, and the stories about the old country, her kind, and loving smile. She recalled her father, a loyal and good man, a good provider, and the day he taught her to ride a two-wheel bike.

Inside the church, not much had changed. The wooden pews were still as shiny as before from the many layers of varnish applied over the years. The white marble alter with high spires soaring toward the ornate dome reflected the adoration of the faithful workers who built this historic church. Dozens of special intention candles, flickering in low lighting, brought back memories of a time when closeness to God occupied a special place in her heart.

Other than two elderly women saying their Rosary, the church was empty. Amanda settled in to a pew near the back, and began to pray.

"Dear Lord, well here I am again. I know it's been a long time. I know I have no excuse. I remember Father Melucci telling us that God is our father, and like any father, he loves and forgives his children no matter what they have done."

"I still have faith. I am asking you for your guidance. As you know, I have met someone who has made me question so many things. I am being drawn into his spell. My heart tells me he is good, but I remember being taught not to follow false prophets. Please give me the wisdom to make the right choices."

Just then, with an echoing voice, a white haired older Father Melucci appeared.

"Is that you Amanda Fiore? Do you remember me? I gave you your first communion! It's so good to see you again. Your parents were such good people. I miss them so much. I heard you're quite the scientist at Harvard and all."

"Well, I'm not so sure about that, but it's good to see you too, father. I've kind of fallen away...

The good priest interrupted, Now, Now, Now
"No need to explain anything. Many in your generation have embraced the secular world and gotten caught up in its powerful distractions. Both I and the Lord know that you have been blessed with Baptism and a good foundation in the Faith. I'm just so glad to see you here today. Is there anything I can help you with?"

"Well father, I've just asked the Lord to give me direction on a matter of upmost importance. Do I have your fullest confidence?" The priest nodded in the affirmative.

"You see, as crazy as this may sound, I think I may have been visited by an entity not of this world and don't know where to turn."

Father Melucci's smile turned to an expression of concern.

"Child, I am very good at performing weddings and baptisms, hearing confessions and spreading the word of the gospel."

He nervously hesitated and then began again.

"For matters such as you have described, I would advise you to meet with a colleague of mine, Father Timothy Ryan of the Harvard Divinity School. He has studied and written extensively on such matters. In fact, he recently reached out to me, asking me to be on look out for requests like yours. I'll call him and give you a proper introduction."

They exchanged contact information. Father Melucci blessed Amanda with Holy Water. She left the church feeling refreshed, uplifted, and renewed.

That evening, as promised, Jeff came home with takeout Chinese food and a rented movie. Before Amanda could even greet him, he embraced her and began to gently kiss her neck and hold her tightly as if to say, "Tonight you're mine"

Still holding her he whispered in her ear.

"Tonight it's only me and you …no talk about anything else." That night, their lovemaking was more intense than ever. They became like one. The physical reflecting the ever-stronger emotional connection.

Checking her emails and texts the next morning, Amanda noticed a text from Father Ryan.

"Wow that was quick, she thought.

"Please meet me this afternoon at two pm, conf room 203b, at the Newman Center. Eager to meet with you. Yours truly, Father Ryan.

Amanda checked her schedule and quickly confirmed she would be free for the meeting. She felt a sense of guilt keeping all this from Jeff.

The Newman Center at Harvard began as a campus-meeting place for like-minded Catholics to enjoy mutual fellowship. Over time, the organization established chapters in major secular universities across the country. Today the Newman Centers welcome students of all faiths to participate in discussion of religious topics and reflect on societal issues.

After a short search, Amanda found the conference room. Father Ryan was waiting outside, almost as if he wanted to intercept her before she entered. He was tall and distinguished. He was wearing the standard black priest suit with white collar that glowed in contrast to his red Irish face.

"You must be Amanda Fiore," Father Ryan said, offering his handshake. "So glad you could come. Father Melucci told me all about you and your considerable accomplishments here at Harvard."

Amanda shook Ryan's hand.

"Thank you for taking the time to listen to my dilemma. Father Melucci recommended I talk to you almost immediately after I expressed to him my concerns. I had barely told him anything when he asked me to contact you. Obviously, you have an insight into the matter I wish to discuss.

The priest smiled and nodded.

"Let's just say I've been involved in some bizarre matters as of late."

"Amanda, before we go inside, there is something I need to ask you. Have you been visited by any unusual dreams?"

Almost reflexively, Amanda answered,

"Yes, but how could you know that?" It was the reason I went to church and ran into Father Melucci. I needed answers and asked God to help me figure it all out. It's the reason we were put in contact. I haven't told a soul! Not even the most important person in my life."

Father Ryan escorted Amanda a little way further from the door.

"Amanda, there are many people, across the globe, who have experienced this phenomenon. Before we go inside, I must warn you. The people inside have all shared the same experience. We have been meeting in secret trying to make sense of it all. You may recognize some of them. Many of them are, shall we say, high profile individuals. They share one commonality. They are all people of character, integrity, and faith. We have been brought together by a common experience, and are all sworn to secrecy for the time being."

He turned and looked over his shoulder to be sure they were alone then back at Amanda.

"Please Amanda, it is important that you understand that if the news media were to learn of our meetings, our members would be subject to ridicule and unwelcomed scrutiny. You can walk away now if you wish, but if you enter and join our little group, we must be guaranteed your strictest confidence."

Amanda was taken aback by the revelation that others had also had the "dreams." Then she remembered the words of Spikes, when he told her and Jeff, "others are privy to the reveals."

She was compelled to learn more. There was no going back.

Entering the conference room Amanda was startled by the number of people present around the conference table. She immediately recognized US Senator John Mitchell, Jessica Blumenthal CNX news anchor, Reverend Jeremiah Johnson, a prominent civil rights leader, and Rabbi Meacham Feingold, famous author, Boston University professor, and Nazi hunter.

"Please welcome Harvard doctorial candidate in Physics, Amanda Fiore."

The group seemed formal and in a somber mood, but managed to produce nodding smiles toward Armand's introduction.

Father Ryan began to lead the meeting. "This is what we know so far."

"The "Dreams "began approximately two months ago. They don't follow any timeline or pattern. They are so vivid and compelling that the recipient can recall every detail. During the dream the subject enters into a state of calm euphoria similar to that experienced by morphine. The dream contents are tailored to each recipient's life experience and area of expertise. A common theme of hope and preparation for a new world order permeates the dream's message. Then, there is the infamous Leonard Spikes, whom we have all met."

This last statement really threw Amanda off guard. Pride and presumption had gotten the better of her. How foolish it was of her to think that she and Jeff somehow, had a special and exclusive relationship with Spikes.

"We have reason to believe that this may be a worldwide phenomenon involving thousands if not millions of people. The Holy Father has secretly reported to me and others in our church's hierarchy that he has been besieged by Bishops from all parts of the world regarding this phenomenon. We believe that there are probably other groups like ours trying to come to grips with this situation. With your help, we are putting together a databank of our collective dreams in an attempt to form a picture from a mosaic. Maybe our new member, Amanda, can provide us with another piece of the puzzle."

Looking directly at Amanda, Father Ryan said,

"Would you care to share with us your dreams?"

The whole room focused on what she was about to reveal.

"First, let me thank you all for permitting me to be a part of your group. Frankly, I'm not ashamed to admit that I'm a bit shaken up by all this."

"My life partner, Dr Jeffery Blake and I met Leonard Spikes several months ago. He gained our confidence by helping Dr Blake make a significant breakthrough in understanding cancer."

"In my first, and thus far, only dream, I was invited to focus on my knowledge as a particle physicist. I was given a different point of view or perspective. In the dream, I felt as if I was in a trance like state, totally relaxed, profoundly peaceful, and open. The dream was vivid beyond anything I had ever experienced before. Unlike other dreams, it was not fragmented but seemed to flow in an instructional format. Oddly, I was aware that this was only a dream but I did not want to wake up. The background of the dream was the conception of a human life."

"Everything we see, touch and feel is composed of Matter. Matter is composed of molecules and molecules of atoms, and atoms, of course of sub-atomic particles. They are all whirling around each other held together by a force we call energy. The laws of thermodynamics tell us that energy cannot neither be created nor destroyed. When matter disintegrates its energy persists, explaining why the universe continues to expand."

"In the dream, I was shown, that for a new life to form, whether plant or animal, an infusion of energy or life force is required to run the process. Energy is essential for cell formation, division, and growth. That energy is the LIFE FORCE. It is the fuel of life, without which, the atoms that form the molecules that then compose living organisms, require to grow and function."

"That energy or life force does not die with the organism. It persists and becomes one with the universe."

" I think it was revealed to me that the SOUL, or what we call self consciousness, or that part of us that makes us unique and who we are, really does EXIST, and that it is UNIVERSAL and that it NEVER DIES."

There was dead silence in the room. All were visibly moved. There followed a lively debate with different points of view. It was clear that everyone was afraid by the notion that dreams could be communicated to them out of their control. It was a power that made them feel helpless, small, and venerable. They had to remind each other that they had been told about free will and the ability to opt out. At the end of the meeting they resolved to remain silent and stay in touch. Father Ryan told Amanda that he would like to meet with Jeff. The meeting ended.

Chapter 10

 While searching through her pocketbook for a return receipt, Amanda came across the business card that agent Rossi had given her that night on Dwight Street.

 "Maybe the agent had learned something about the fate of Professor Romilov." She thought.

 She knew this issue was wearing heavily on Jeff's mind. Jeff's father had died in a work accident just before Jeff had entered High School. The professor had filled the role of father figure that Jeff had missed out on during his formative years.

As for the professor, Jeff had filled the role of the son he always dreamed of having, but never would. They had a special bond that went far beyond their mentor / student relationship.

Amanda decided to take a chance. With considerable reservation she proceeded to enter the number on her cell phone. It began to ring.

"Agent Rossi, I don't know if you remember me, Amanda Fiore?"

"Oh sure, you're the Doc's girlfriend. Before you begin I'm really sorry for how things went down that night. Me and my partner Barnes could have been more professional. That case is pretty much closed now. So what's this call about?"

"Agent Rossi, Dr Blake has been trying to reach his friend Professor Romilov, the man you were inquiring about. He hasn't had any luck and is worried about his friend's whereabouts and well-being. I thought you might have some information in this regard that you could share with us."

"Well, here's how it works. Ordinarily we gather info but never share it outside the agency. I guess, after that night, I'm going to break the rules. Seeing how we kind of strong-armed you guys, I owe you one. What's your email address?"

Amanda provided Agent Rossi with her email address.

The very next day an email from agent Rossi arrived with a single attachment. Opening the attachment she learned the sad news.

It contained a Russian newspaper article with a short story of how professor Romilov had been killed in a tragic auto accident. A translation accompanied the article. The article contained two photos, one of the mangled vehicle, and the other of a closed casket service with a few dignitaries present.

That night after supper Amanda approached Blake as he was working on a scientific presentation.

Handing him the article she said, "Jeff I have some bad news. I'm so very sorry."

She sat next to him with her arm around him as he read the news article. Transfixed and silent, tears welled up in his eyes.

"I knew something had happened to him." He repeated this several times.

"He was such a good man. He was all alone. He had nobody to take care of him. There was this woman, Marlena who lived outside of town. I don't know. I don't know. Of all the things. Why wouldn't anyone tell me when I called?"

"Why?"

Amanda could feel his loss. She held him tight. She knew she needed to tell him about her dream and the meeting with Father Ryan. It would have to wait until the loss of his friend had settled in.

Over a week had passed since the news about the Professor. Jeff seemed to be going about his business with a brighter attitude and indicated that things at the lab were progressing well.

That night Amanda told Jeff about her dream, the meeting with Father Ryan and the group's efforts to make sense of it all. Jeff admitted to Amanda that he too had had a dream which he wanted to share with her but couldn't find the right time. His dream had revealed notions that were so far out he was afraid she would think he was losing it.

In his dream he learned that cancer is the result of a quasi-intelligent tiny strand of DNA code that evolved from a single mutation in the human genome. It occurred in humanoid X, the first carrier, several hundred thousand years ago when the first humanoids were migrating north from the African continent to Europe and the Middle East. It also found its way into the animal kingdom. It's like a parasite, with its own life, that lives in the human genome, struggling to survive in order to avoid extinction. It passes from one generation to the next.

The older humanoid host, with its ever-deteriorating aging immune system, provides the perfect vehicle for its reemergence. An aged weakened immune system can't hold the code in check, making the elderly more susceptible.

When the host's immune system is too weak to suppress its activity, it reprograms the cell's DNA to replicate and grow new cells at an ever increasing and dizzying rate, using the energy of metabolism as a life force. It continually changes and adapts its DNA footprint to evade whatever man invents to destroy it. It never goes away. It hides in the healthy cells. Killing the cancer cells only slows the process. It's transmitted to the host's offspring and waits in most cases many years for the favorable conditions to develop.

Poor health habits or environmental damage can cause these changes to occur earlier by weakening the power of the immune system. If life were extended another fifty years and the immune defense weakened with time, cancer would touch just about everyone.

Jeff learned that what happened to Barry Stone was just as Spikes had said. The deadly genetic code life form had to escape the host in a hurry. For the first time it sensed that it could actually be completely extinguished. It was fighting for IT'S own life.

Chapter 11

Maggie and Chris had organized a surprise going away party for Jeff at Vincenzo's in the North End. Vincenzo's was everyone favorite spot. Big smiles by the staff always made everyone feel welcomed. Neapolitan music playing softly the background, red and white checkered tablecloths, and the aroma of their signature red sauce everywhere, created a homey comfort that complimented the food. A flask of Ruffino Chianti adorned every table whether you wanted it or not. The food was good and the place was affordable. It was the working class family's neighborhood restaurant.

On the night of the party Jeff knew that something was up. When he walked in with Amanda, the place exploded with cheers. Like the gentleman that he was, he put on a very convincing surprised act. As the party progressed, he became truly moved, grateful, and a bit overwhelmed, by what seemed to be a genuine outpouring of good will and affection.

Maggie and Chris performed a roast, highlighting, and in true roast tradition, exaggerating all of Jeff's "personality quirks." It was fun for all. In the end, they presented him with a watch that had a special voice function reminding him to be on time… a personality trait he has struggled with since he was a kid. It was called the "never be late again watch."

The evening was winding down. Everyone was saying their goodbyes and well wishes. The staff was busy cleaning up and preparing for closing. As the last guest left, Jeff and Amanda were thanking the owner for helping put on a wonderful evening. Just then a voice rang out from a dimly lit corner of the restaurant.

"Congratulations."

It was Leonard Spikes with a large napkin tucked in his collar stained with red sauce. He was slurping up the spaghetti strands and drinking the Ruffino.

Amanda and Jeff now looked at him with different eyes. A quick chill came over their bodies. That fleeting chill you feel when startled by something that evokes anxiety like coming upon a snake in your garden.

"Now, now." Spikes said.

"No need to be frightened. Just a friendly hello."

"Nice party. Well deserved. These people think very highly of you Jeffery. Actually, a tribute to you, for fostering such feelings."

"How long have you been here?" Jeff managed to get out.

"If we had seen you we would have come over to say hello."

"Well," Spikes said chuckling, like I said, I have a tendency to be invisible at times."

Spikes put his wine glass down and pushed his chair away from the table.

"Would you two care to join me for a glass of wine?They're closing here, but we could go across the street to the espresso bar. It's quiet there."

Across the street, they found a quiet table and exchanged pleasantries until the waiter delivered three glasses of Cabernet.

"You two have been very patient with me and have shown strong character. Many others have found all of this to be more than they want to understand. They have used their FREE WILL and have no recollection. You both have many questions that need to be answered and rightfully so. As my plan unravels things will become much clearer."

Spike's face and entire demeanor seemed to be changing and morphing into a more serious and darkening persona. He commanded and produced an almost hypnotic state, capturing Jeff's and Amanda complete attention. The timber of his voice lowered and became more deliberate. He looked around as if to be sure no one could hear what he was about to say and then declared,

"I am not of this world."

Jeff and Amanda were visibility shaken by this statement. They clutched each other out of fear and a feeling of being helpless. They became completely absorbed in anticipation of what was to follow. No other sound or image could penetrate their consciousness.

"Once, you asked me who I was. My answer was "I am you. You see, it was my way of telling you that we are all ONE. We are all citizens of the same universe. We are all made of the same elements found everywhere in the universe"

He took another sip of wine.

"The Universe is eternally large and incomprehensible in scope. This planet is but a grain of sand in the vastness of the universe. It is a grain of sand hidden in the vast beach of time."

"When we discovered this planet many ions ago, it became abundantly clear the all the conditions necessary to evolve our type of life could be found right here. The size and distance of this planet from your sun or what we calculate as heat ratio, gravitational strength, speed of rotation, abundance of water, oxygen, and carbon were all ideal for us. It became our mission to plant the seeds of life here. We needed to insure the propagation and survival of our species."

"The seeds of life are what you call you call DNA. It is a code so complex and so perfect that even your greatest scientific minds like Einstein, Hawking and others have concluded, after a lifetime of study, that the complexity of it all, cannot be rationally explained by mere chance alone. In the case of DNA, trillions of circumstances would have been necessary in an exact order to construct such a complex entity and the laws by which it functions."

94

"Jeffery, you have learned through your brilliant research, that the complexity and vastness of DNA defies the laws of probability or natural selection. Every cell in your body is producing thousands of proteins every minute, each with a specific function to sustain and continue your life."

"This glorious, harmonious and enormously complex thing you call life did not, and could not, have occurred by mere chance like winning a lottery. You're most gifted mathematicians and statisticians have already concluded and published their findings, that winning every lottery in the world on the same day by the same player, every day, forever, is more probable than constructing an intelligent code with commands and functions such as those found in DNA."

"Amanda, as a physicist, you know that Albert Einstein with his proven theory of relativity demonstrated that the universe is expanding and that time is not linear but instead warped with peaks and troughs such that time travel and parallel universes could actually exist. Logic would dictate that for something to be expanding there would have to have been a point where it was smaller and therefore a beginning.

Your scientists are reluctantly coming to a conclusion. They are being dragged, kicking and screaming, to the table, forced by facts, to admit that there IS a GRAND DESIGN to the universe and that nothing in the universe happened by chance."

"For there to be a design there had to be a designer, a force that created the immutable laws that govern the existence of all things"

Spikes paused and looked at Jeff and Amanda as if to ask, "Are there any questions?" None followed.

"Your science tells you the Earth is six billion years old. That figure is not even close. This wonderful planet has been inhabited by many civilizations that have gone extinct thousands of years before your Egyptians and Romans. Time has erased almost all evidence of their existence.

"Modern man is a mere two million years old."

"We have been silent observers of your remarkable progress. Watching from afar and visiting occasionally to collect data and check on your progress"

"We have witnessed savagery and love, kindness and indifference. For the second time we have reluctantly decided that an intervention is necessary. We have come to warn mankind that you are about to go extinct".

Amanda found the courage to blurt out "How did these other civilizations go extinct? "

"They chose Evil over Good."

"Mankind is born with the intuitive capacity to distinguish Good from Evil. There is an Evil presence in this world. Evil always seeks to destroy. Evil's greatest trick is to convince man that Evil does not exist. Evil uses free will provided by Good to accomplish this end. The capacity to distinguish Good from Evil can be lost when the most powerful tool used by Evil is Pride. Pride is the great destroyer. I am not referring to the type of pride one has, for example, in a job well done. I am referring to a different type of pride."

"Pride enables those who fall under its spell to believe they are superior to others and that they have been given

96

certain rights and privileges over others. They begin to believe that they have dominion over all things when in reality they have dominion over nothing. They start to believe that others must do their bidding. Your story in the in the book you call the Bible, about the fallen angel, is the perfect example of Pride. Those who embrace Pride are capable of the most heinous crimes against humanity…all in the name of Pride.

"Are you an agent of the Creator or a messenger?" asked Jeff.

Spikes seemed to avoid the question, looking away as if to say, "not now."

"There exists an Energy that keeps the universe ordered. Everything in the Universe follows a certain order, defined and measurable. Man's Laws taken from the Universe follow a predictable order. Remember that the absence of ORDER is Chaos. The Good is Order. Evil, being the absence of good, is Chaos."

"Wait, you didn't answer the last question." Jeff said.

"Are we to believe that are you a messenger of the Creator? When was the first intervention? How long ago did it happen?"

"All in good time…all in good time my dear Dr Blake. I must go now."

"But wait!" Why didn't you tell me about my friend, Professor Romilov? Surly you must have known that he died in a car accident."

"You will see your friend again." Spikes said.

Then, to their fear and amazement, Spikes simply evaporated in front of them, leaving the check on the table.

Amanda and Blake paid the check and left the bar trembling and clutching each other. For the first time in many years they recited Hail Mary's all the way home. Both of them called in sick the next day and spent most of the day holding each other in the warmth, comfort, and safety of their bed. For the first time in their relationship they could not find the words to express their fears and apprehension. Why were they chosen? Why were they told that they would be major players in the forthcoming changes about to happen? They considered opting out. Maybe Father Ryan's group could offer them a safe refuge to vent their fears. There was no one else they could confide in without sounding like lunatics.

Amanda told Jeff all about her dream and Father Ryan's group. They both agreed that they had to contact the group and add their new experiences. Maybe they could gain a new insight into what was going on. Spikes disappearing act had really spooked them. Things seemed to be moving too fast.

The very next day an email arrived from Father Ryan. "Meeting 7'o clock same place …bring the doctor."

Jeff told Amanda that he would not be able to reveal all the specific details of his dream to the group. One specific reveal contained information about a medical breakthrough too sensitive to divulge to such a diverse group.

Chapter 12

When Amanda and Jeff arrived to the meeting Father Ryan was waiting outside the door as before. He welcomed Jeff and again asked for discretion and secrecy. Jeff affirmed and they all entered.

"Let me introduce to all of you Doctor Jeffery Blake, pioneering cancer researcher here at Harvard."

Jeff told the group his relationship with Spikes and the insights he was shown leading to the breakthrough with the ligands. He ended his report describing the most recent meeting with Spikes and the disappearance before their very eyes. This fact really got the groups attention stirring emotional remarks from Reverend Johnson.

"This guy Spikes, with the disappearing act and all scares me. Either he's a magician of some sort or he could be the Evil One himself leading us down the primrose path. At the

END OF TIME the bible warns of false prophets and seductive lies."

Father Ryan responded in, "His Holy Father has expressed the same concerns and when pressed would not discuss his dream worried that it could be a portal for malevolent sprit to enter. He is praying for guidance."

Jessica Blumenthal of CNX looked around the table making sure that no one else was about to speak.

"There has to be a logical explanation to all of this. My guys on the ground in the Middle East are reporting all kinds of weird rumors of mental issues and strange behavior breaking out amongst the ruling class. There have been a rash of unexplained suicides in those groups. We are also hearing stories about Mullahs and Imams absent for days at a time, sending out surrogates in their places. There issuing press releases that they are ill or indisposed. That sort of thing. As a news reporter it's very hard for me to keep from talking to my producer and keep this thing under wraps. It won't be long before this story will get out. If another network gets it first my career will be toast. I'll try to keep it quiet for a little while longer."

"Well," said Senator Mitchell, looking over at Jessica Blumenthal, "I guess after that statement, that just about wraps it up for me. Don't need to be a part of this type of publicity or accused of keeping secrets or being part of a conspiracy by the press."

Blumenthal rolled her eyes and thought to herself, "what an asshole." As the members filed out there was a sense that

100

there would be no more meetings. Only Rabbi Feingold lingered.

Looking at Amanda and Jeff the Rabbi said, "The Christians are waiting for the second coming and judgment day. My people are waiting for the Messiah. The Muslim world waits for the Mahdi to come. Maybe we all don't have very long to wait.

Father Ryan stood quietly at the door. When everyone had left he turned to Amanda and Blake.

"Well, aren't you two leaving also?"

"Not until we get answers to what we came for."

"You said you would present a compilation of the collective dreams from the group…..a kind of summary of what has been and learned so far."

"Right, that was my intent until all hell broke loose and the meeting dissolved. Let's go back inside and I'll show you. The others pretty much know most of this."

Father Ryan pulled a thick folder from his old weathered black leather bag and began.

"We believe that Spikes is not of this world. He never reveals his true nature but leaves the impression that his kind had something to do with the creation of the world we live in."

"In one dream he revealed that his species came to the realization that they needed to spread out beyond their world in order to survive. There were indications that their planet was getting old and resources were predicted to be inadequate in the distant future. They also came to realize that interstellar exploration was limited by their corporal bodies. They developed technology enabling them to deconstruct their molecular containers/bodies and preserve their unique energy or essence. That would explain how Spikes was able to evaporate before you, be in two places almost instantaneously, or appear out of nowhere. Our friends in the physics department call this phenomenon "teleportation." These "beings" seeded our nascent atmosphere in an experiment to see what would develop in a way that would always respect the laws of nature. They took a keen interested in chronicling what direction we would take. We became their mice in a lab. Over time they developed affection for the wonder of what they had nourished and fostered."

"The dreams message a notion of an opposing Force to what they have created. The dreams together seem to indicate that mankind has now acquired the ability for extinction which is being nourished by the opposing Force. They have been deliberating what to do for a long time and decided to intervene in our behalf."

"They have begun by giving us the tools to help us accept the next chapter in this story. These tools seem to be advances in science and technology designed to gain and give them credibility. They seem to want to push Mankind to the next level, creating a sort of partnership and trust, which may in time, become a new belief system. This would seem to enabling man to resist the powers of the force that wants to destroy us."

Amanda and Jeff thanked Father Ryan for his insight. They all agreed to stay in touch, but tacitly knew, this was probably the last time they would meet.

102

On the way home, Amanda and Blake decided to grab a bite to eat at Richard's Table on Tremont Street. Richards had joined the bursting South End restaurant scene. Somehow, the chef's at Richards were able to take a traditional tavern menu and infuse it with new cuisine flavors and twists. As usual, the place was hoping and tables were at a premium. Jeff spotted two seats at the bar which he quickly claimed. They both actually preferred the more lively and community feel of dining at the bar. After ordering two Sam Adams on tap and Atlantic haddock sandwiches, Amanda noticed that Jessica Blumenthal was on the TV that hung over the the bar reporting for CNX. The din of the bar patrons made it difficult to hear the audio. Luckily the closed caption was turned on.

"CNX is reporting that Iran is considering abandoning their nuclear ambitions…this following a mysterious rash of illness and suicides in the ranks of the ruling class. CNX reports that the leaders of numerous Middle Eastern nations are calling for an emergency meeting to discuss a consensus policy statement which may indicate a change in traditional political posture. Stay tuned for a special report at 10 Eastern Time."

They both remembered what Jessica Blumenthal had said at Father Ryan's last meeting…that the lid was ready to blow on this story.

Chapter 13

Three Months Earlier

Valstov was a small town forty-three miles east of Moscow. It was home to two thousand mostly poor Russian farmers. The town was famous for the fine goat cheese produced in that region for generations. The entire cheese making process is still done by hand with little or no changes from the way it was produced hundreds of years ago.

It was also the boyhood home of Yuri Romilov. Rumor had it that this was the town where Czar Nicholas kept his mistress and that she was murdered just before the revolution to preserve the honor of the royal family.

Valstov was also famous for the genocide that took place at the hands of the Nazi's during WW2. The citizen's crime for being murdered was hiding grain from the German troops.

Yuri Romilov was ten years old when, together with his schoolmate Marlena, he managed to escape the slaughter and destruction he witnessed of their school and village at the hands of the Nazi's.

There was no warning on that sunny cold winter day. It began with the distant clattering sound of the armored column approaching. Everyone ran to the schoolhouse window to see what the noise was all about. Through the tall trees that surrounded their schoolhouse they could see speckled sunlight and alternating shadows cast by the vehicles approaching. Plumes of dark smoke from the noisy diesel engines confirmed that the vehicles were tanks.

The first round of incoming munitions exploded with a force that devastated the classroom next door to where Yuri and Marlena were standing. The blast sent debris, and body parts flying in every direction. Yuri and Marlena were buried by debris but miraculously unhurt.

They managed to get outside running as fast as they could before falling face down in a snow bank. Marlena was wearing only a blue flannel dress. She lost her shoes in the explosion. Yuri had on a long sleeve white cotton shirt and brown homemade wool pants. He still had his boots on. The cold clean air outside seemed like a gift of life but the feeling wouldn't last long. They were shell-shocked and disorientated as to what direction to go. A young German soldier appeared, standing before them. He was albino with snow-white tufts of hair protruding from under his helmet. His eyes were pink and scary to the two young children. Marlena hugged Yuri. They were both trembling from the cold and the fear that they were about to be shot.

"Are we going to die?" Marlena said looking up at Yuri.

Before Yuri could respond the soldier commanded,

"Come with me now!"

He grabbed them both by the back of the neck, and in an instant, dragged them to the tree line and out of the sight of his comrades.

"I'm not going to hurt you." He reassured them.

"Stay here and hide yourselves…you are not going to die."

He quickly stripped off his uniform revealing a white muscular body. He threw his rifle into the woods.

"Take this coat and these clothes and cover yourselves. There are rations in the pockets."

Before he disappeared into the snowy surroundings he glanced back at Yuri and said,

"I will see you again someday."

Yuri was struck by the German soldier's ability to speak perfect Russian without a trace of German accent. Yuri quickly tore the soldier's shirt into strips and wrapped the pieces around Marlena's feet to prevent frostbite.

From their vantage point, the children watched as the German soldiers methodically burned the town and murdered all who were unable to flee. They hid out in the woods for two days enduring the cold nights, the smoky smell of the village burning, and soulful sounds of suffering. They survived the cold night by clutching each other under piles of leaves and the wool coat left behind by the strange young German soldier. He had saved their lives. They blocked out the horrors going on around them by reciting prayers, taught to them, by parents they would never see again.

It would be several years before the war ended. During that time they suffered the cold, hunger, death, and destruction that war brought. They were like the many other war orphans who lost their families that day. They were left to fend for themselves. They were lucky to be taken in by a childless couple and worked on the couple's farm until the war was over.

During those difficult times a love bloomed between them. Their love never had a chance to blossom. Their world had fallen apart. It was full of death, destruction, and poverty, the result of war. The war had put everyone's life on hold.

After the war, they went their separate ways never forgetting the closeness and shared experience of survival and the strange young soldier who saved them.

Marlena went on to marry a local farmer and had two boys. She was left widowed by a farm accident many years later.

Yuri went on with his studies at the university. He became a successful and noted scientist in the new and emerging science of genetics. Whatever oppression the Czars had been accused of had been replaced by the Communist party. Yuri never bought in to the communist philosophy. He worked hard to make the best life he could. The war had not changed his desire to leave the world a better place. He devoted himself to science. It became his passion and served to fill the void left in his heart from losing the love of his life.

Yuri had become quite the chess player. He won several local tournaments and was considered the man to beat at the informal chess games that took place every Sunday in Gorky Park. Rumor had begun to spread that a newcomer named Olav was making the table rounds and beating everyone he played. Yuri was eager to meet this Olav and try his hand defeating the newcomer. He didn't have to wait long.

"They tell me you're the best chess player in Gorky. Let me introduce myself. I am Olav. I have been looking forward to meeting you. Maybe you would consider a friendly game of chess as a way of introduction and the beginning of a new friendship?"

Yuri had expected him to be older. His facial features were chiseled with very smooth skin. Olav looked very familiar, like someone he had seen somewhere before. Yuri couldn't place him. He was tall and slim with an athletic build. He was wearing a military type green sweater with patches, and camo pants with big pockets. Heavy black leather boots with thick heels made him look taller.

Yuri stood up, smiled, and shook Olav's hand.

"Your prowess in the game of chess precedes you my new friend. I would be delighted to play you. Please have a seat."

Yuri reached into the inside pocket of his coat and produced a silver flask and two shot glasses which he placed on the board. He then proceeded to fill them with vodka.

Staring into each other's eyes, the two men clicked their glasses in a toast and down the hatch the vodka went.

They played for hours with no winner. It was a stalemate until Yuri could play no more. A small crowd had formed and onlookers were going out and bringing back hot coffee for the two.

"Olav, you are indeed a formidable opponent. I am too exhausted to continue and will concede the game to you, but only under the condition that we play again soon."

Olav raised his cup of coffee in a salute to his opponent.

"Professor, it is I who must concede! You are the formidable one. Not I. We will continue this game at another time to its conclusion, but only if you allow me the honor of dinner tonight."

The two men shook hands and proceeded to the restaurant as the small group of onlookers that had gathered applauded. During dinner, Olav asked lots of questions about the professors work to the point that the professor began to think that maybe Olav was a government operative prying into his work. Olav seemed to have a deep knowledge of genetics. As they prepared to leave, the professor was thanking Olav for the game and his generosity with dinner. Olav put his hand on the professor's shoulder and looked directly into his eyes producing a moment of transcendent connection.

"Do not worry professor. I am not from the government." He smiled eerily. "I am your new friend who will send you a gift of knowledge. Use it wisely."

Olav turned and walked away into the night. Yuri stood there wondering how he was able to read his thoughts and know his suspicions.

Yuri would become the recipient of dreams that would give him deep insights into his work and revelations that would take his research to another level. He would come to understand what Olav meant by his parting remarks. He had no way to explain what happened and no one with whom to share this bizarre experience. There would never be a rematch.

Yuri rented an old barn in Valstov under an assumed name. The barn's roof had caved in years before and it had the appearance of an old dilapidated abandoned structure. It was perfect for his purposes. No one would be snooping around or asking any questions. He had made a possible breakthrough in his research in the field of agriculture and had to put it to the test. The experiment would have to be conducted in secret.

Inside he would be planting a garden. The open roof provided plenty of natural sunlight and rainwater. The plants were genetically modified to resist destruction by insects. Extensive testing had proven that the genetic modification produced no toxins and passed the UN criteria for being classified as an organic product completely safe for human consumption.

There was another motive for choosing this site and her name was Marlena. He mustered up the courage and made the decision to contact Marlena who was still living there with her two grown sons. He admitted to himself that in his heart, even after all these years, he still had feelings for her.

He fantasized that maybe, just maybe, he might have a second chance. He wondered what her reaction would be getting a call from an old love interest. He prepared himself for rejection but knew it was worth taking a chance. When he got home for the day the first thing he did was pour himself a shot of courage.

He took a deep breath and picked up the phone. When the number began to ring he had to remind himself to calm down.

"Hello,Marlena?"

"Yes?"

"This is Yuri Romilov. I hope you don't mind that I am calling you. I know it's been a long time, but I'm going to be in Valstov and I thought it might be nice to see you again. I will understand if you don't agree."

To his relief, at least over the phone, she seemed very willing to meet with him. It took a lot of courage to make the call but he was quickly put at ease after listening to her sweet voice and welcoming comments. They agreed to meet the next night at the old tavern on the outskirts of town. After putting down the phone, he recalled the strong emotions he felt the last time he saw her at a WW2 commemorative town event and how crushed he was to learn that she was engaged to be married.

During the drive to their meeting Yuri's heart was filled with mixed emotions. He feared what she would think, seeing him as a much older man, grayed with a weathered face. Yet, the excitement to see the girl he once loved won over his fears. What would she be like? People change he thought. The anticipation of their meeting continued to build.

The tavern hadn't changed much except for one wall covered with WW2 news clippings and memorabilia all framed and neatly displayed. The wait staff seemed so young, giggling, and flirting with each other behind the bar. There were very few patrons in the tavern that night. Yuri positioned himself at a table giving him a clear line of vision to the entrance door. He was thinking how lucky he was that the lighting was so dim, self-conscious of the older man he had become. What would be her reaction?

It wasn't long before Marlena walked in. He recognized her instantly. She looked around and quickly produced a big smile when she spotted him. Walking quickly toward him Yuri quickly got up from his chair and put out his hand to greet her.

"Yuri Romilov," she exclaimed. "Look at you... Still so handsome!"

Ignoring his out stretched hand, she grabbed both his shoulders and kissed him on both cheeks in true European tradition. Feeling awkward and stupid, he returned the gesture.

He couldn't believe how beautiful she had become in her maturity. His heart felt a joy he had forgotten was possible.

"Marlena, you look beautiful... It's so wonderful to see you"

"So wonderful that you regret not coming back to see me before I was engaged?" she jokingly said.

He was visible taken aback by her statement but managed to regain his composure.

They caught up for the many years apart recounting the events in their lives. He learned that her boys had finished their education and moved to the Balkans where they both worked. There was an undertone in their conversation of lost opportunities, regrets, but also notes of happiness in being together. Yuri's spirits were lifted.

Marlena's body language and eyes revealed the good heart and the warm spirit that had originally attracted Yuri so very much. Seeing this brought him comfort that the girl he once knew had not changed. He knew he had made the right decision to call her. After only a few hours together, he felt as if the years had melted away, and that there was nothing he couldn't tell her.

It was getting late and although it now seemed almost secondary, Yuri knew that the time had come to tell Marlena about the other motive leading him to contact her. He knew he ran the risk of sounding selfish and did not want to break the magic of the evening.

"Marlena, there is something I must tell you."

Marlena listened intently.

"I confess that for whatever its worth now, the day I learned of your engagement to Ivan I was crushed. Until then I had not realized the true feelings I had for you. I knew I had lost something I could never replace. My pride had gotten in the way of making my feelings known. I remember thinking that I had nothing to offer you…that I was poor with an uncertain future and that Ivan was a good man, and a land owner, who would provide you with a better life than I could."

"Not a day has gone by that I haven't thought of you with great affection. Now that I see you again I realize what a fool I was in not contacting you sooner. When I learned of Ivan's tragic accident my heart and prayers were with you. I had become a stupid old man, lost in academia. I was trapped in my comfortable world."

"Oh Yuri, enough of that talk." she said.

"No one goes through life without regrets. The trick is to keep moving forward."

Relieved by her response, Yuri proceeded to tell her about the barn he rented under an assumed name and the experiment he would be conducting. He asked her if she might know a trustworthy individual to help with the tending and maintenance of the small plot he would be planting. He explained that the authorities could not know about the plot and that he would pay a handsome sum for their discretion.

To his delight, as he had secretly hoped for, Marlena stepped up and offered to help. She would make sure the plants were sufficiently watered and call him only if a problem arose. Yuri had set up a secured telephone line.

As time went on, Yuri would drive out to the old barn infrequently so as not to attract attention stopping a mile before the barn and parking is car in the rear of a small roadside tavern. He kept a bicycle hidden in the woods behind the tavern and would peddle the rest of the way. Marlena would meet him bringing some wine, the town's famous goat cheese and some crusty bread. They gathered plant and soil samples, check on the progress of plant growth all the while enjoying each other's company. The flames of love lost rekindled between them as time went on.

About six weeks into the experiment Marlena called and left a message on the secure phone line. Insects were eating the leaves. She was worried that if she waited for his next visit there may not be anything left to tend. She asked if she should spray insecticide.

When Yuri got home he called back immediately and left her a message.

"Marlena, whatever you do…do not spray the plants! I'm coming out tonight."

He drove out to the barn that night without stopping at the tavern. The barn was cold and dark. A musty humid scent filled the air. He had brought a battery-operated spotlight with him. As he turned it on over the garden bed, he was delighted with what he saw.

The garden bed was teeming with insects, covering and eating only the first low hanging leaves. They seemed to reach a certain point, eat their fill and turn back down the plant. The rest of the plant remained intact and thriving. SELECTIVE FEEDING.

It was just what he had hoped for. The insects were happy and so were the plants. Just as the insects were programmed to be eating machines with no stopping mechanisms the genetic modification in the plants influenced their behavior to simply stop eating at a certain level. The genetic modifications that Olav had revealed to him somehow traveled from plant to insect imparting a learned behavior allowing them both to live in symbiosis. If only humans could learn this behavior, he thought.

He began to think that the problem of feeding the masses with genetically engineered crops impervious to pests might be solved. No pesticides contaminating the soil and water! No foods or livestock containing cancer-causing chemicals! No harm to the ecological balance of insect life! Nevertheless, what about the problem of GMO foods evoking an immune response with allergic reactions? Isn't that the issue with peanut allergies? Plant testing had already proven that the plants contained no new allergens, not already found in nature.

All kinds of notions raced through his head. Had the genetic modification had actually worked? Would anyone, anywhere, with few skills, be able to grow food with only three ingredients; modified seeds, sunlight and water? Had the Holy Grail of agriculture finally arrived? Was the problem of world hunger solved? The possibilities seemed endless.

Yuri could hardly contain himself!

He frantically busied himself taking more plant, soil, and now insect samples.

The pain in his arthritic right knee that he has endured for the better part of a year was becoming more intense, but at that moment it didn't matter. Off he went, in a hobbling run to Marlena's modest farmhouse. He knew it was late but had to see her and share his exciting discovery. He also knew that she was alone. At least, that's what she said. He was about to find out.

Gently knocking on the door so as not to alarm he kept repeating in a low whisper like voice,

"Marlena...Marlena, its Yuri...don't be afraid...open up."

She came to the door wearing a white night shirt. The candle she held in her right hand cast a glow illuminating her soft cheek line and long graying hair.

"What are you doing here so late? Is something wrong? Are you all right?"

"I could not be better," he responded.

Grabbing her shoulders he held her tight and kissed her cheek. The candle fell from her hand extinguishing itself on the floor. A dog could be heard barking in the distance barely perceptible in the silence of the night.

"Marlena, I just came from the plot. I think I have made an important discovery! I am here to share my excitement with you and to thank you for all your help and taking the risk I have exposed you to."

"Marlena, I think this may be the reason that God spared us the fate suffered by so many of our family and friends at the hands of those Nazi bastards! The nights we spent freezing the woods, smelling the smoke from the fires, hearing the shots and screams…It may have been all for a reason! It may have been for this moment."

"Do you remember that albino boy, the young German soldier, who led us to safety? Well, I may have met him again. He may be the one who led me to this incredible discovery!"

"Now, I know why we survived. It was for this moment!"

Yuri was so excited and caught up in the moment that he could not contain himself.

"Marlena, there's something else I must tell you. My joy of this moment would not be complete if I did not tell you that I have loved you since we were little kids playing sticks in the schoolyard. I always let you win so that you would want to play again and we could be together.

117

"Ours was not to be. So many things got in the way...so many things."

Marlena had tears in her eyes. She held Yuri closer.

"It's ok...It's ok." She whispered. "The world was on fire …there was nothing else we could do."

He took her by the hand and this time kissed her on the lips. Yuri grabbed the coat hanging by the door and draped it over her shoulders. Together they rushed back to the barn. He wanted to show her everything.

"Look, "he said. The insects are only eating the bottom leaves leaving the rest for us!

"At the Academy my projects were mainly in developing biological weapons. Work that I despised. I would give them just enough to wet their appetites. It was becoming increasingly more difficult to hide my stalling and lack of interest in the projects. It had become clear to me that at some point, I may have to defect to the West or fake some sort of disability and go into retirement. My passion in molecular genetics has always been in agriculture. Farming is in my blood."

Marlena looked him straight in the eye.

"If there is one thing I know about Yuri Romilov, it is that he is driven to achieve and never gives up. Some day that brilliant brain in your head will cease to function. That day will be the day you die. Until then you will continue to achieve greatness as you have done today."

"Marlena, my life in Russia has come to an end. Soon, I will no longer be able stay here. My discovery must remain a secret. If my work, the gene sequences, and formulas were to become known, my life would be in danger. The consequences of this discovery would be far reaching. There are those who would pay a king's ransom to keep this information from coming out. There are also those who would do anything to possess the rights on this technology."

"It must be tested and released in the public domain so as to benefit all of mankind. No one person or entity can own or control it. It is a sacred promise I made to the person who gave me the key in unlocking this wondrous discovery .Without his opening my eyes to the research I had already done I would have missed a small alteration in the genetic code that led to all of this. It was literally right under my nose."

"I can't even thank him. I have no way to contact him. Just trying to explain how I came about this would make me sound preposterous. Only my friends in America would understand."

"Marlena, I must leave Russia as soon as possible. I have been working on a plan for two years. But now the plan has changed."

"Listen carefully. I love you, and I can't leave you behind. When they know I am gone they will start looking and you. You will be in danger. You must come with me. We can start a new life in America. I have a plan and friends who will help us. We can do it. I promise. We still have a few good years left. I will do everything in my power to make them happy years for both of us."

"My sweet Yuri, I love you also and want nothing more than to be with you in the last phase of my life, but my life is here. All I know is here. My two sons are here. I don't know any other way to live. If I leave, I can never come back. What will my boy's think when their mother is gone? I may never see them or the grandchildren I hope to have."

"Marlena, from what you have told me, I know that your sons are good boys who want their mother to be happy .They are well educated and working in the western Baltic States. They have little hope for a better future. This could be the spark that leads them also to America and a better life. I can arrange acceptance for all of us through my contacts in Boston. The Americans have been encouraging me for years to defect."

They went to Marlena's house and spent the night together. Their hearts were filled with emotion, joy, and uncertainty for the future.

That night Yuri told Marlena the details of his defection plan knowing he could trust her with anything. She promised to consider his offer, and without revealing the details of the plan, look for her family's approval. He asked her for her identity card with her photo. He would need it to forge documents.

Yuri always knew the day might come when he would have to leave his homeland. He devised a plan. A government exit permit would be impossible to obtain and a secret land trip through the Baltic States with all the border crossings and document checks would expose him to almost certain arrest. Leaving by air was even more risky and out of the question. KGB security was focused more on passengers leaving rather than on those entering. After considerable study he concluded that the safest way out of the country would be by sea.

Chapter 14

The port of Taganrog, a gloomy industrial container port on the Sea of Azov, became the center of Romilov's research for a suitable place to begin an escape route. A ship that made no stops traveling to the West would be ideal, minimizing the chances of detection to only three points; embarking, the voyage, and disembarking.

The Canadian Star was such a ship. At 126 feet wide, she was able to pass the width limit of 147 feet required to sail through the Strait of Dardena and on to the Mediterranean Sea without having to stop in Istanbul.

He knew from studying the ships logs online that she made the trip regularly, at least twice a month, sailing from Taganrog, and returning to Montreal Canada. Security at Montreal's container terminal was notoriously lax. His friends in the Ministry of Transportation had told him that sensitive shipments with phony documents were routinely sent through this channel. Blueprints of the ship obtained online revealed numerous storage rooms in which to hide. The ship was big enough for a stowaway to make the eight-day trip undetected.

Bribes are a way of life in Russia, and are an acceptable way of showing "gratitude" for a "favor."

Yuri made the acquaintance a Port Authority functionary named Victor. Victor was someone you could count on to look the other way for a fee. He was typical of low-level government lifers who trudged through their daily lives melting out favors for gifts or harsh bureaucratic obstacles for those who needed services the old fashion and slower way.

Victor had already been in Romilov's favor and assured him he could get him on the ship posing as one of the ship's dockside maintenance workers. Romilov had already paid for a forged employee ID badge. For the equivalent of five thousand American dollars, Victor would provide access to a locked storage room and supply it with bottled water, enough packaged food to last the eight-day journey and a sealable waste container.

Yuri contacted Victor and told him the plan was on. He asked to get things ready for the Canadian Stars next landing. It would be less than ten days away. Time passed quickly once the decision to defect was made.

The professor lived in a decidedly upscale apartment provided by his employer, the Moscow Academy of Science. Hilda Korsikof was the professor's dedicated housekeeper. Over the years, she had taken on a protective role of screening visitors and fielding inquires at the home. She was fiercely loyal to the professor who had treated her with kindness and generosity.

There was nothing unusual about this clear crisp morning on Bolshoy Street. The tree-lined street was quiet. Most of the well-healed neighbors had already left for work.

As Hilda went about her housekeeping chores, a loud and angry knock sounded at the door.

"Who thinks a knock so loud is necessary? What manner of person with such rudeness knocks like this?" Hilda exclaimed as she approached the door.

"Open the door!" a man's voice said.

Opening the door Hilda replied," And who might you be?"

"I am Regional Inspector Dardoff. Where is the professor?"

Dardoff had the look of a career bureaucrat with his ill-fitting pinstriped suit and spit shined shoes. The two thugs with him looked like KGB enforcers.

"I imagine he is at work at the Academy," Hilda replied, starting to worry that something serious was wrong. She remembered that she had not seen him that morning and that his bed was still made. There was no sign that he had actually slept there the night before.

"He's not been seen at the Academy for two days. Did he tell you where he was going? If you know what's good for you, you had better tell us! You and your daughter could be in great danger for holding back information!"

Hilda, visibly upset, stuck to her story and told the men the truth, she knew nothing.

They forced themselves into the apartment pushing Hilda aside. Hilda began to protest the intrusion only to be warned that any interference would be met with harsh action. She watched in fear as they trashed through all the professors belongings and books. In the end, they carried out the Professors laptop, private papers, and a box of computer memory sticks. They repeated the stern warning.

"Report any contact or face the consequence!"

Hilda resisted the impulse to pick up the phone and called the Professor, knowing the phone line was no doubt being monitored. Too upset to remain in the apartment she went home. A manila envelope addressed to her was stuffed in her mailbox. Opening it she found a note from the professor and a plastic bag full of cash…the equivalent of six months pay.

Dear Hilda,

It is with a heavy heart that I bid you goodbye. Circumstances have compelled me to leave Moscow. Please forgive me for not being able to say goodbye in a proper manner but I was left no alternative. I want to thank you for the service and friendship you have provided me all this time. I truly appreciate all you have done. May you remain happy and healthy in the coming years. I will remember you always in my prayers. Your Friend, Yuri Romilov.

The day of departure had arrived. Romilov had made his way to Taganrog the night before. He turned in his government car to the owner of a chop shop who gave him a cash deal. Victor had turned him on to these criminals knowing that he would be in line for a cash referral fee. Romilov knew that the chop shop would only sell the parts and never the intact vehicle. Intact, the car would be traceable and impossible to resell. The chop shop could strip the car down to a thousand different parts categorizing them by number to be sold one part at a time through a network of middlemen. After the usual haggling the owner handed Romilov two hundred and eighty thousand rubles in neatly packed larger bills. It the equivalent of roughly four thousand dollars. Next stop would be meeting Victor and setting the plan in motion.

The Professor reached the terminal gate and Victor was there waiting…wrinkled suit, tobacco stained fingers and all.

"Well, if it isn't my old friend," Victor said with a greedy smile on his face. "You have picked a dismal day to travel with the rain and all. Come into my office and we can go over the details of your voyage. Before Yuri could put his bag down, Victor turned and said,

"First there is the matter of a few incidental expenses I have incurred in your behalf. Have you come prepared?"

"What expenses? I have already paid you the agreed sum."

Yuri struggled not to betray his anxiety of something going wrong at the last minute.

The professor dug down deep and pulled out his authoritarian and professorial persona. He knew that under different circumstances this lowly government functionary would be tipping his hat and treating him with respect for the position he held in Russian society. This was the culture and class distinction was alive and well in Russia.

"My dear Victor. I have powerful friends in Moscow who are capable of making things very difficult for you. I think you know who I am. I can assure you that those powerful friends want to see my voyage go well."

Sporting his phony smile Victor moved toward the professor as if to greet him warmly.

"Comrade... Don't worry!" Victor is here to make sure that all goes as planned. I had to employ a friend and associate...one of the crew who has helped me in the past. He provided me with a key to the storage room where you will stay. It is amply stocked with food and water as agreed. He will keep prying eyes away and allow you to get out for some fresh air at night. He will coach you on how to disembark without being noticed. A service well worth the mere one hundred dollars a day. He can be trusted. He will meet you on the ship. I will introduce him as Nicholas."

The thought of not being cooped up in a room for eight days was tantalizing. He also knew that Victor had the upper hand. If he didn't pay up, this Nicholas person would be a liability rather than an asset. He needed to buy as many "friends" as he could. Reluctantly, he agreed to Victors demands.

The moment of truth had come. Romilov got in line with the maintenance workers boarding the ship and pinned the ID badge to his lapel. As the line moved forward, he hardly noticed the cold light drizzle of rain starting to soak the outer layer of his long workman's coat. Thoughts of leaving Marlena behind, of opportunities lost, his life in Russia and life on the farm, his parents, and the war streamed through his mind. Through the sadness and clouded joy of these memories, there emerged a sense of excitement and anticipation of a new and hopeful final chapter in his life. Feelings of hope, freedom, and fulfillment overshadowed the task at hand.

Yuri had stuffed the inner lining of the coat with eighteen thousand dollars in one hundred dollar bills accumulated over the years and the rubles from the car sale. His research, personal records, and proof of identity had been into scanned onto memory flash drives that were sewn into his leather belt. In his pocket was a small nickel-plated revolver handed down from his grandfather's service in the Crimean War. He would keep it ready at all times. He would rather die than spend the rest of his life in a prison that no one knew existed. He clutched a small bag stuffed with personal belongings and moved along the line.

As he reached the end of the line he could feel his pulse quicken. The badge inspector was barking out assignments and group designations. His badge read Ivan Growski.

"Growski...level two…section 12…follow group C!"

He had made it on board. The first phase of his odyssey was completed.

He was soon met by Victor who introduced him to Nicholas as planned. Yuri handed Nicholas an envelope with the eight hundred dollars. Nicholas produced a sheepish smile but said nothing. They led him to the storage room deep in the bowels of the ship. On the door a sign read DO NOT ENTER HAZARDOUS MATERIALS, accented with the universal skull and crossbones symbol.

As promised, the room was well stocked with food and water. Nicholas left and told Romilov he would be back the next day. Romilov was given a key to use if an emergency exit became necessary.

"Well Comrade," said Victor extending a handshake. "I wish you a good trip and good luck. Sometimes I wish it were me going. The truth is, my wife would find me and kill me!" Laughingly, he paused, "Oh, and lastly, two more things. Even though it was not in our contract I took the liberty of providing you with two bottles of my favorite vodka. Nicholas also likes a drink now and then. There is also this."

Reaching into his jacket pocket he produced an envelope.

"This was given to me by a pretty lady with a promise to be sure to give it to you, only after you are on board the ship."

He handed Romilov an envelope and left.

As Romilov watched Victor walk away he remembered something Spikes had told him….an old cliché.

"There is always some good in everyone. All are born good and pure...then get beat up by life."

Knowing intuitively who the envelope was from, he opened it, and yes, it was from Marlena.

Dear Yuri,

I am very sad that you are leaving without me. The time was not right. It was too sudden. I made the long trip to deliver this letter to Victor hoping I would not see you and suffer the pain of another goodbye. Surely you know that I love you and always have. I didn't want you to leave thinking anything thing else.

You were right about the government looking for you and asking me questions. I showed them the plot and told them we raised fresh vegetables and nothing more. They don't scare me.

When you reach your final destination and are settled, please find a way to get word to me. It should not be too difficult. Unless I hear to the contrary I have decided to try and join you. I have the blessing of my boys. Until then, be well and safe journey, Love, Marlena.

Romilov was moved by Marlena's expression of love and desire to see him again. A joy had entered his heart. He told himself to believe the feeling in his heart that anything is possible and that you're never too old to live happily ever after. He carefully folded the letter and placed it in a zippered compartment of his bag. The ships loud foghorn could be heard signaling that the departure was eminent. He felt the first sensation of movement. The voyage had begun.

Chapter 15

Jeff's work at GenOnc was going well. The team was preparing data to be presented for publication. He was working in the animal lab and thinking about the contribution animals have made to the advancement of science benefitting mankind. "Where would we be without animals that have helped mankind on so many different levels? Farming, transportation, food supply, and now partners in life saving research. Surely they occupy a special place in God's plan and are all deserving of respect, kindness and protection."

Just then Jeff could feel his cell phone vibrating and looked down to see who it was. It was Amanda calling.

"Hi sweetie. What's up?"

"Quick, turn on channel 5. Jessica Blumenthal is about to give another special report on unrest in Iran. Remember at the meeting when she said she didn't know how long she could keep the lid on things? Gotta go…we'll talk about tonight."

Jeff got to a television just as the report was starting.

"It has been confirmed that the Ayatollah Muhammad Almasiri , leader of Iran's ruling party has died under mysterious circumstances. This follows reports of other untimely deaths among the ruling class. Sources report that many of Iran's ruling class have been absent from the public eye raising questions about a possible shake up at the highest levels of government. Iran's president Basara Metangari announced the official cause of death as complications following a routine gallbladder operation. There have been reports of wide spread unrest and student demonstrations. CNX believes that more moderate political factions are vying to fill the void left by these untimely deaths. Spokesperson for the state department expressed the hope that a more moderate régime friendlier to the West might emerge. We will continue to monitor these developments. I'm Jessica Blumenthal for CNX."

That night Amanda was running late. She had a meeting with her Faculty advisors to discuss the progress and direction of her research project which had already been approved by the panel. Rushing into the small conference room she realized that the advisory panel of three professors was already seated.

A quick glance of her watch confirmed the fact that she had made it on time by one minute. Gathering her progress notes she thanked everyone for being there and proceeded to present her calculations, thus far, as they related to her work in understanding the relationship of time and travel.

The panel listened quietly and intently as she began to outline Einstein's theory that time is relative to distance and that time is not linear but instead warped with peaks and troughs creating a fabric like structure that can be folded into pleats. This makes it possible for 2000BC to be very near to 2000AD providing that the speed of light could be reached and exceeded theoretically making it possible for a traveler jump from peak to peak.

She covered the chalkboard with mathematical theorems and formulas which demonstrated to the panel that she had a firm understanding of Einstein's theory of relativity and possibly a new direction to explore it further. After a lively discussion and questions from all, it was decided that she would be allowed to proceed independently. Another meeting was scheduled. She couldn't wait to tell Blake how well the meeting had gone.

When she got home Jeff was already busy at cooking supper. He had acquired an interest in cooking while on tour of duty in Iraq and developed a special liking for food cooked with the savory flavors of Middle Eastern spices. On menu tonight was chicken breasts smothered in a thick and chunky vegetable medley flavored with curry and cardamom over balsamic rice. Heavenly aromas filled the small apartments air.

"Oh my God, its smells so good in here. What a guy! Good looking, smart, sexy... and he cooks! I'm not letting you out of my sight!"

When she gave him his "I'm home kiss" she added, "You smell like curry!" To which Jeff replied jokingly, "The mark of a good cook is attracting the aromas of the food he or she is preparing."

Amanda proceeded to tell Jeff all about the faculty meeting, how well it went, and how excited she was to get the green light on her project. They opened a special bottle of wine to celebrate and talked about the news reports, wondering if it had anything to do with Spikes and all his drama.

"By the way, Jeff said...Where has Spikes been? We haven't heard from him in a while."

"I would rather not talk about him tonight if you don't mind. I kind of like our lives without having to think about those issues."

Jeff had put a little too much hot stuff in the pot but otherwise the meal was quite a treat for both of them. To complete the Middle Eastern theme of dinner, Jeff was making a savory cup of sweet Turkish coffee when the doorbell rang.

Jeff looked at the front door security camera that he had installed several months earlier. It was their old friend agent Rossi looking rather disheveled and agitated. For a moment, remembering the night on Dwight Street, he hesitated opening the door but then gave in to the urge to find out what Rossi wanted.

Rossi was sweating and slightly out of breath. His coat and shoes were wet from the cold drizzle of the day. He was shaking a little from the cold and blowing warm breath into his hands as he rubbed them together. He seemed anxious about something and not completely in control. Something was obviously wrong and Jeff's first instinct told him he was not going to like whatever Rossi had come to tell them.

Rossi had grown up a poor kid in Quincy and spent the better part of his youth helping his Mom raise his younger sister. After a stint with the Marines and service in the Gulf War he attended and graduated from City College on the GI Bill. He wanted to join NSA but didn't get in. His background training in counter intelligence during the Gulf War made him a top recruit for the FBI. Under his rough around the edges manner lived a bright and dedicated patriot not to be underestimated.

"Do you remember me? Agent Rossi from the FBI. Sorry to bother you guys like this but I really need to talk to you both. It's important. Is your pretty lady home tonight?"

Jeff knew this wasn't going to be good.

"Come in and get that wet coat off. Have a seat. I'll get you something hot to drink."

Rossi settled into Jeff's comfortable recliner and motioned that coffee would be great. Amanda, sitting just across from Rossi, sensed that he hadn't eaten all day and brought him a warm dish of leftovers with the coffee. She acted like they were expecting him, with a welcoming greeting and small talk. She didn't let on that she too was concerned about his impromptu visit.

"I'm really sorry for barging in on you guys like this but I'm a little worried that you both might be in danger. I'm not supposed to be here and if my bosses found out about this it would be curtains for me at the agency. There's a lot of crazy shit, oh excuse my French, going on at the agency about you guys and this guy Spikes."

Amanda focused her gaze on Rossi getting his full attention.

"What's going on? I thought you said the case was closed."

"Not anymore. They're talking about picking you both up and sequestering you for interrogation and possibly detaining you for a long time."

"Can they do that?"

"They can do whatever they want."

"Look, I think I'm being followed but I'm pretty sure I managed to lose them. They can't know that I tried to warn you. I'm working off the clock now. This thing with your friend Romilov and this guy Spikes has really blown up into a big deal. When the Russians tipped us off about Spikes, the FBI got involved, figuring something important was going down.Turns out your friend Romilov was not killed in a car accident after all."

Both Amanda and Jeff were visibly relieved letting out a sigh and hugging each other.

"The press release of the crash was bogus. The license plate numbers in the picture of the wrecked vehicle didn't match the numbers on file at the Moscow DMV of Romilov's car. A guy fitting Romilov's description turned himself in at the Canadian border claiming to be him, and asking for political asylum. They believe it's him. He gave your names as references. They have him in custody and are putting him through the wringer. There's a lot more that I could tell you but not now. "

Jeff was obviously elated to learn that Romilov was still alive but there was one thing he had to know.

"Agent Rossi, why did you come here? Why are you trying to help us?"

"It's the dreams Doc. They're driving me nuts. I get these crazy dreams telling me to do stuff... and if I don't, really bad things will happen. The dreams tell me to protect you and your girlfriend at all costs. I know it sounds crazy... and maybe I am... but I believe the dreams are real. I don't do drugs. I don't even do pot. I got so worried about my head, I asked a MRI hospital tech who owes me a favor to do an MRI of my head, after hours, off the books, and guess what? No brain tumor. I don't hear voices or anything like that. I'm not schizoid. You guys are doctors. Do you think I'm crazy?"

Amanda took Rossi's hand. She could see that this guy, who is used to being in charge and in control, felt like he was losing his grip on reality

"You're not crazy. We've had the dreams. A lot of people have had the dreams. It's how he talks to us."

"Who? Who talks to us?"

She explained to Rossi that the dreams are a form of communication initiated by Spikes.

"Who the fuck is this guy Spikes?"

136

They told Rossi everything they knew about the mysterious Mr. Spikes and what he had told them that something very important was about to happen. They filled him in on the meetings with Father Dolan and the fact that no one seemed to really understand who Spikes was, but only that he might have come to give a warning.

Jeff had been pacing around the room. He got down in front of the chair where Rossi was sitting and got in Rossi's face.

"I want to see the professor."

Rossi looked up.

"I'll try to make that happen but can't guarantee anything.

"What's our next move Agent Rossi?"

Doc, I've been thinking about all this and I have come up with a strategy that just might help you both."

Rossi was adamant that he should set up a meeting with the FBI higher ups and make it look like Jeff and Amanda had contacted Rossi asking for the meeting to take place. It would preempt the FBI's move to sequester them and make them look like good citizens coming forward on their own with information to help the government. This would help to remove any suspicion directed toward them. It might just help to place them in the position of being of part of the solution rather than part of the problem. Jeff and Amanda agreed and gave Rossi the green light.

"Before I leave I've gotta tell you guys to start watching your backs. Start thinking about your own personal security. Be aware off your surroundings. Call me if you see anything out of the ordinary. Your names seem to pop up somewhere

137

on every investigative lead. Foreign agents looking into these matters know your names. Be careful."

Amanda and Jeff began to worry that what started out as an odd curiosity was turning into real life problem. Their lives would now change. They needed to get answers. It would be a beautiful weekend coming up and they had to get away. Vermont was on the list of favorite places.

Chapter 16

Jeff mounted the bike rack and two bikes onto the back of his six-year-old BMW SUV while Amanda packed some healthy snacks for the ride to Stow Vermont. It was a beautiful sunny day with a snap of coolness in the early spring morning air.

City traffic was light as they worked their way North. Soon the landscape began to change, morphing from the flat area of coastal southern New Hampshire to the more rural and beautiful rolling mountains and valleys of Vermont. They decided to pull off the highway at Quechee Vermont for some lunch.

Quechee was famous for its breathtaking gorge. There was always a crowd of tourists peering over the short bridge at the incredibly deep and winding stream weaving its way through the jagged shoreline so far below. It made you wonder how the earlier settlers were able to overcome these formidable geographic obstacles in their push northward, the hardships they must have endured, and how tough they must have been.

Within walking distance of the gorge was the quaint Vermont Country Store full of local crafts, art and farm fresh goodies. There was even a miniature train ride for the kids that wound its way through an array of wooden carved animals. No stop was complete without exploring the store and picking up some maple sugar treats or knickknack's.

Jeff and Amanda were shopping around the store picking up a few fun things when Jeff noticed two men wearing dark suits who seemed out of place.

"Who wears a dark suit in the Vermont Country Store?" He thought to himself.

They were lingering by a display of artesian soap bars sampling the different fragrances. It was one of those unexplainable moments when the antenna goes up like something's not right.

He motioned to Amanda to get going and pay for their stuff. They wanted to get a quick lunch and make it to Stowe before it got dark.

The Quechee Diner was right next to the country store. It was an historic landmark edifice, original in every way. Built in 1948, it offered diner food in a truly retro old time setting. The place was decorated with an incredible collection of old tabletop radios from the fifties harkening memories of classic doo-wop music. The place had original Formica counter tops, trimmed with chrome edges, wooden booths, and middle-aged waitresses wearing white aprons who didn't want to be called servers. Jeff was hoping that the fresh homemade blueberry pie he remembered from last year's trip was still on the menu. They sat in a booth that looked out over the parking lot. The homemade meatloaf with mashed potatoes, covered with gravy, topped off with the blueberry pie and coffee for desert, satisfied their need for old-fashioned comfort food.

Pointing out the window, Jeff turned toward Amanda.

"See those two guys over there lingering in the parking lot? Something tells me that there not here for the maple syrup."

Amanda took Jeff's hand and looked out the window.

"Are we being followed? Agent Rossi told us to be careful. They look like two foreign tourists lost in America. Maybe we're being paranoid. Let's get going and see what they do."

Jeff paid the check and together with Amanda, walked across the parking lot. They passed by the two strangers without making eye contact. As they got into their car and started the engine they noticed the two men getting into their black Ford Escape. It was starting to become clear that they were being followed…but by whom?

The speed limit on 89N was 65. Jeff cranked the Beemer up to 85. Sure enough the black Ford Escape kept pace. There was no doubt now, they were being followed.

Jeff took exit 34 off Interstate 89 North marked Windsor, and pulled in to a small country eatery called Charlie's. Jeff had been there before and knew that there was a small dirt service road in the back not visible from the front. They went inside and sat at table facing the door.

Jeff noticed that the black Ford did not pull into the parking lot but instead stopped and parked just outside the entrance to the dirt parking lot behind a row of bushes.

"Amanda, we've gotta shake these guys but first I need to know who they are. Order something to eat . When the food arrives pay the check. Tell the waitress you're in a hurry and ask her to bag it up for takeout. Then go to the ladies room and lock the door. Wait for me there.

"What are you going to do?" Amanda said.

"Never mind, don't worry, I know what I'm doing."

Jeff walked through the swinging doors leading to the kitchen. The din of clanging pots and pans abruptly stopped. He could see the surprised reaction looks on the faces of the young workers. A total stranger had just walked into their workplace.

"Sorry guys, is there back way outta here? My ex in coming in and well… I owe her a few bucks. You guys understand? Things could get pretty awkward."

"No problem," one of them said, as the others chuckled. The worker motioning toward a back door and pointed the way.

Once outside, Jeff made his way around to the the black Ford Escort parked along the country road at the entrance to the dirt parking area. Getting up close, he could hear the two men inside speaking in unmistakable Farsi. It had been a long time since he heard that language spoken and felt the bad memories that it came with. Sneaking up on the passenger side

142

door, he quickly opened the door and in an instant grabbed the passenger out slamming him to the ground. As the man hit the dirt, a 9mm handgun fell out of his suit jacket. Jeff grabbed the gun, chambered a round, and in what seemed a split second, had the drop on both of them.

Yelling, he ordered the men to get on the ground face down and not move or say a word. He then removed another 9mm from the driver and frisked them both men, making sure there were no other weapons. He ordered them off the road and into the woods, leading them to a small isolated clearing.

"Take off your pants, shirts, and jackets and throw them over here," he said in a menacing voice. "Get down and keep your hands behind your heads."

Jeff could see that they were acting like men who feared they were about to be executed. Rifling through their wallets he found Iranian diplomatic IDs. His former military badass persona had emerged and was serving him well.

"Which one of you is Yasim?" One of the men produced a timid answer.

"Well Yasim, I'm going to ask you a question, and if you don't answer my question I'm going to put a bullet into your buddy, Kadim, over here. Then I'm going to ask you again. If you still don't tell me what I need to know, I will bury you both, right here, in an unmarked grave. This way, you both get to spend eternity in my favorite state of Vermont. Do I make myself clear?

They both sheepishly nodded.

Just then Amanda appeared through the thick brush. "What's going on here?"

Still holding the gun on the two men Jeff glanced at Amanda.

What are you doing here? I told you to stay at the restaurant. Get back. Don't get close to these guys."

"Don't tell me what to do! You think Id actually let you go it alone?"

Jeff knew she was right. He turned his attention back on the two men.

"Why are you following us? Who are you working for?"

"Yasim began in a low voice.

"We were sent by our government and told only to follow you both and document everyone you come in contact with. Surely, you have heard of the strange deaths occurring in our country involving prominent citizens? They think you and your government have developed a new mind control type of weapon capable of producing mental instability"

"What makes your government think that?"

Jeff cocked the hammer of the 9mm.

"They all report having horrible dreams foretelling a nuclear holocaust. They see the deaths and hear cry's of their loved ones, incinerated in the flames, right in front of their eyes. The dreams recur over and over again, almost every night, driving them mad, and in some cases causing them to take their own lives."

Jeff got down on the ground behind Youseff and stuck the gun in the back of his head.

"Maybe it's your God warning them to abandon their lust for world domination. Why are you armed? You were planning to harm us!"

"No no no! ...We were told that you are a very dangerous person and that we may need the arms to defend ourselves. We are not killers, only diplomatic functionaries."

With a menacing look on his face, Jeff got down on one knee closer to the two men.

"Here's what I'm going to do. I'm going to let you go home to your families and live out your lives. Tell your government we have no such weapon but that there is an outside force that has made itself known and whose mission it is to save us from ourselves. This outside force has powers that no one on this earth can comprehend. He has the power to produce dreams that compel humans to certain actions. We are going to leave now and you two will not follow us. I spared you once, but you won't be so lucky next time."

Jeff clicked the safety on and ejected the chambered round from one of the 9mm, and then handed it to Amanda. He picked up the Iranians' clothes and threw them deeper into the woods. The two embassy types had no stomach to follow and were glad to have escaped with their lives.

Jeff and Amanda got back in the car and took off heading north determined to get lost for a couple of days.

"I've never seen that side of you before" Amanda said.

Jeff remained quiet concentrating on the road.

Inside her heart she was proud of Jeff and the handling of the situation. She had witnessed the brave warrior and protector. She finally understood the medals he kept tucked away in a box in the upstairs dresser.

"Don't ever leave me alone locked in a bathroom again."

He smiled and kept on driving.

Chapter 17

Isfahan, located 110km northeast of Iran's Karakas mountain range, was founded in the 10th century as a small fortified village. It's known for a delicious fig that flourishes in the desert soil. It is a village unchanged by time. Old and weathered architecture, winding narrow streets and a small classic Middle Eastern central bizarre preserves the perfect backdrop for ancient traditions surviving to this day.

What is not known about this remote and forgotten place is that Isfahan harbors a dark secret. Under one of its ancient buildings resides a complex. A secret network of tunnels and open chambers packed with miles of fiber optic cables, computer servers, and sophisticated communication equipment. It is the control and command center for one of the world most dangerous and dedicated terrorist organizations, Islamic Sons of the Mahdi.

Despite the West bringing to bear its most sophisticated spy technologies, this place has escaped detection. The Mahdi's were an extreme wing of the Islamic State feared even by the Iranian government. They are ruthless murderers of Muslims, Christians, and anyone who gets in their way. They are hell bent on fulfilling the prophecies of Islamic world and imposing Sharia Law worldwide. Well financed, they gained support from Arab governments through intimidation and assassinations.

The old rooftops and domed buildings glowed in the color of burnt umber as the sun began to set in the west. The soulful call to Maghrib or evening prayers echoed through the hot village air. The ritual of washing began as supplicants prepared for evening prayer. It was the fourth of the five daily prayer rituals.

Mustafa al Homsi was 29 years old and a student of Islamic studies preparing for life as a religious community leader when the slaughter at the World Trade Center took place. He remembers feelings of pride that the Great Satan had been finally dealt such a heavy blow.

Four weeks later he suffered the reality of the vengeful might of the American people in the foothills of Bora Bora when bombs rained down on him and his family with no mercy. That night he became an orphan. Hatred and vengeance burned deep in his soul. As with many Jihadists, a once kind human being had succumbed to extreme religious beliefs emptying his soul of good and filling it with pure evil. Logic no longer existed, only the belief that non-believers had to be eliminated. What Mustafa never learned was the time-honored truth of Western Civilization that throughout time and memorial, in the end, Good always triumphs over Evil.

The fortified hideaway was dimly lit. On this night the ambient air had a gritty feel. The ventilation was constantly breaking down, and many had taken the precaution of wearing face masks adding to the already sinister feel of the place. Armed guards stood just inside the entrance and at all three exits, just out of site of any passerby. Tonight was to be a special night. A meeting and briefing to the inner circle on a project most anticipated.

Mustafa gathered four trusted comrades in his small dimly lit office and closed the door.

"You are my technical team. Professor Benani, the geologist, is coming tonight. He will present the engineered plans and precise coordinates necessary for my plan to succeed. I know you have all been waiting and working very hard on your piece of the puzzle. You have not been told the completed plan for obvious security reasons. After tonight we will be the only ones to know the entire plan. Be warned that any breach of security or betrayal could only come from inside this room. Remember that we operate independently from any government and answer only to Allah. The parts of my plan will be put together tonight for you to see and everything will become clear."

"When that greedy bastard Benanie gets here I need you all to pay close attention to every word he says. Every detail must be clear to you all. You are all experts in your fields and have swore allegiance to our cause. I expect you to ask questions. For the plan to succeed there can be no mistakes. Let me provide you with how I came across the plan."

"I have made a habit of watching American television in an attempt to learn more about our enemy. I can tell you that I learned much about their decadent culture, lifestyle, and beliefs. Several years ago I watched a program on an American channel called Nat Geo. It stands for National Geographic. There was even a program on our famous ancient Syrian ruins of Palmyra. I was impressed by the degree of accuracy in describing the history and geography of Palmyra , a place so close to our hearts."

"In America, there are many places called national parks where the infidels bring their families on holiday. They are places of great natural beauty and untouched by civilization. I became fascinated with one of these places called Yellowstone, named after the river that flows through it, with its yellow stone walls. The park is almost five thousand and six hundred kilometers square of wilderness boarding three of the United States."

"But the most important fact my friends are that this beautiful tourist attraction sits atop an active volcano!"

"And comrades, this is no ordinary volcano, but what is called a super volcano! The belly of the volcano which holds the superheated molten rock lava is called the caldaria or giant

150

pot! It is 72 kilometers wide and 54 kilometers long, and has a destructive force larger than anything man could ever create."

"So, my friends, Allah seems to have placed the world's largest bomb in the belly of the beast! They all bowed their heads and in a chorus and chanted, "Praise Allah."

"The Infidels are expecting attacks in major cities or places where large numbers of their citizens gather. Instead, we will give them the surprise of their lives and with the help of Allah deliver a death blow."

"I traveled to Mexico and crossed into the United States. I learned how easy it was to enter their country. I simply walked across the Mexican border into Arizona. When I was apprehended, the idiots welcomed me and gave me food and water. After answering a few stupid questions and giving a false Spanish name, they asked me where I wanted to go. I couldn't believe it. They were not going to send me back. I told them I always wanted to see Yellowstone, and they complimented me on my choice. They gave me instructions to report to an immigration office in a place called Cooke City in the state of Montana. They provided me with fifty dollars and a bus ticket. I told them that I spoke English to avoid speaking to a Spanish interpreter. They never noticed that my accent was not Spanish but instead Middle Eastern. What Cretins!"

"When I arrived I was met by friends sympathetic to our cause who provided me with sufficient funds necessary for a prolonged stay. I made it my business to explore and learn as much as I could about this place. There are many old abandoned mine shafts that can be found everywhere. Some are as deep as five kilometers. I found and copied detailed geologic maps and surveys readily available on the internet. The idiots give away everything!"

"The most amazing and at the same time delightful thing about this place called Yellowstone is the fact that the ground is literally on fire. Boiling water and steam were coming up through the surface of the ground. The land in many places looks like it is about to explode. I became convinced that Allah had given us a gift and directed me to this place."

"Their own scientists have concluded that there have been three eruptions over the past 2 million years, the last having occurred 625 thousand years ago. The eruptions were cataclysmic in scope and produced destruction and mass extinction over two thirds of what is now the United States."

The whole area is unstable with hundreds of small earthquakes recorded annually. The scientists agree that a major eruption would destroy and render uninhabitable a good part of the entire United States. It would be the final battle as foretold in the prophecies."

"Brothers, our plan will be to create an explosion deep in a strategic area initiating a chain of geologic events leading to the eruption of the Yellowstone volcano of a magnitude which the world has never seen. The great Satan will be destroyed once and for all and the fulfillment of our sacred scriptures as prophesized will be realized."

The conspirators again bowed their heads again chanting, "Allah be praised."

Chapter 18

"Take this goddammed hood off my head." No one told me I would be subjected to such indignities! I have not been paid enough to put up with shit like this."

"Don't worry Professor Benani. Please accept our apologies.It is for your own protection. The whereabouts of our meeting must remain a secret. We are almost there."

Professor Benani was a geologist with global credentials. A graduate Cambridge Institute of Earth Studies his publications were respected by many in the geology community. Before Khomeini he worked for the régime of the Shah side by side with the American and British oil companies developing

Iran's then nascent oil discovery and extraction industry. As a Sunni he preferred a more secular life. He was disillusioned and became a cynical opportunistic in a new world of religious tyrants and limited possibilities. He had lost his way.

The driver and bodyguard led Benani from the Range Rover into the compound. Clutching his attaché case containing the details of his work they removed his hood. Sweaty and grimy from the trip he was offered warm wet towels, cold water, hot sweet tea, food and again their apologies for the inconvenience.

"When you are ready you will meet and report on your work."

"I'm ready now. Let's get this meeting over with so I can get out of this shithole. Who will I be meeting with? Be sure the next payment is ready. Nothing starts before I see the money."

He was led to the room where Mustafa and his comrades had gathered. His maps and slide presentation were readied.

"Welcome, Professor Bernani. We have been looking forward to your long awaited arrival. I apologize for the harsh circumstances of your journey and any inconveniences. I trust that you have been made more comfortable since your arrival."

Realizing he was in the prescence of the feared Mustfa himself the professor quickly put on his more dignified and personable persona. He was well aware of Mustafa s monsterous reputation and realized this would not be the place or time to be talking about money.

"Im fine, just not used to all this secrecy and security measures. Thank you for your generous hospitality."

Mustafa,by his sheer presence, knew that he had put the professor in his place .The professor made his way to the table where a screen and writing board had been set up for his presentation.

"Let me begin by congratulating you all for conceiving such an ingenious and bold plan. When I was first approached, my initial reaction was skepictal to say the least. However, after a long study of the geological maps and surveys, you provided, I began to believe that the objectives you desire were, at least, in theory, possible. I can offer you no guarantee that your plan will succeed but will present my best recommendations on how to accomplish it."

He began his proffessorial presentation.

"Think of the volcano as a pressure cooker. The only thing preventing an eruption is the pressure weight of the rock on the lid.The lid is the Earth crust. The pressure is released as a result of tectonic plate movement, earthquake or the crust wearing down over time. Anything that disturbs the crust could trigger the release of the contents from the volcano. The crust at Yellowstone is extremely thin as evidenced by the volcanic activity at the surface. This works in your favor."

He then proceeded to show detailed drawings of the old mine shafts and their angle of entry into the volcano with calculations of the roof pressures derived from measurements of the thickness and density of the stone.

"I have concluded that the placement and detonation of sufficient explosives in these critical locations, could result in the triggering of a significant break in the thin crust found in Yellowstone" I have also provided the specifications of the munitions required."

The conspirators asked numerous technical questions concerning depth of penetration and blast force direction vectors. Benani provided detailed answers to all their questions.

At the end, Mustafa shook Benanii hand and thanked him for his cooperation in this endevor. He reassured him that the last payment would be transferred to his account when the banks opened in the morning.

Turning to his comrads with his arms outstreached in a grande gesture Mustafa said, "The professor has decided to forgo our invitation of lodging in favor of leaving tonight.We will grant him his wish and bid him a good trip. Call the driver and bring the car here now. Ready the plane."

The drive to the isolated desert air strip passed through dark and dusty roads lit only by the full moon that night and the headlights snaking around the curves. Before long, the sharp mountain walls lining the road gave way to the flat desert land. Finally they reached the dark and deserted air strip where Benani had first arrived. He quickly noted that there was no plane waiting.

"Where is the plane?"

Two shots rang out from the front seat. The first bullet pierced Bernani in the forehead sending blood and tissue spalattering onto the back window. The second traveled

156

through his chest embedding itself in the fabric of the back seat. Bernani had met his fate. His body was buried in an unmarked grave. His family would never see him again.

Chapter 19

"So, professor Romilov, tell me again the reason you left Russia under such circumstances and why you chose to defect to the United States? This business of losing your travel privileges and fearing forced retirement just doesn't seem to be enough to reach such an important decision, especially given your age. We have reason to believe that you are involved with this Mr Spikes and must hold you until such time that we are certain that you have no other agenda."

The interrogator, Agent Robert Hall, looked like he had just walked out of the wasp daily register. Crisp white buttoned down shirt, muted tie, spit shined wing tips, pinned stripe suit and an air of superiority, fit the mold of the career security operative. Romilov, for his part was tired, disheveled and getting angrier by the minute. His patience with the system was running out. His pride was bruised. He wanted so much to finally breathe a sigh of relief. His journey had been so long and his decision to defect so stressful. He had had enough.

"I have told you over and over why I left my home and came to this country. I will answer your questions only one more time then you must make a decision concerning my disposition. Either allow me entry or deport me back to face my punishment. I don't care what you do. I'm sick of your questioning. You gave me a lie detector which I passed. What more do you want? Romilov began again.

"I felt marked for extinction before my time was over. I always dreamed of coming America where my work could flourish. I wanted to enjoy a breath of freedom and pursue the projects I knew were important and not the direction of study I was given by the authorities. I wanted to be respected for my contributions and not to be treated like an old man whose usefulness has been served. I have no relatives and very few friends back there."

"As for your Mr. Spikes, I only knew him as Orlov. He spoke perfect Russian. He told me he was born in Kiev and studied in Poland. We struck up a professional friendship and he offered useful critiques of my work. That is all. Now, I demand to see my friends and be given asylum in this country. I have nothing more to say."

Hall turned to his assistant trying not to show disdain and anger toward someone dictating terms to him. He motioned to the security detail to escort Romilov back to the detention area.

"We have nothing more to get out of this arrogant bastard. Notify this guy, Dr Blake and his girlfriend, what's her name, Amanda, that they can come for him. Prepare the necessary papers for provisional entry and alert Homeland Security to put him on the watch list for at least ninety days. Keep an eye on him, his whereabouts, associations, the usual."

The detention area was actually a small but comfortable apartment consisting of two rooms and single bath well appointed clean with flat screen TV, radio and a fridge well stocked with non-alcoholic drinks, fresh fruit, and snacks. Meals were taken in a separate area in the quiet presence of various sundry guests all wondering what each had done to be given such unique hospitality.

Three days had passed since the end of interrogation with no resolution. Romilov entered the dining area for supper and noticed that he was the only guest. The attendant brought him a tray with a hot meal consisting of roast beef, creamed potatoes and salad, and left him alone in the room. He was becoming used to this American fare but would but do almost anything for a glass of red wine.

Out of the corner of his eye he noticed a man sitting in the corner table facing the wall. How could he have not seen him just a moment earlier? Without turning, the stranger spoke in perfect Russian.

"Are you not going to say hello to your old friend Olav?"

Romilov was stunned to see his friend and research collaborator Olav, a man he thought he knew, but now after all the questioning during the interrogation, doubted that he knew him at all.

"What are you doing here? How did you get in here?"

Olav got up and moved to Yuri's table sporting his famous grin."

"Did you think I would let you go to America without me? I want that rematch."

Romolov had all he could do to compose himself. He had so many questions. Olav looked straight into Yuri's eyes producing a calming, quieting and almost hypnosis like tranquility.

"Yuri, I want you to look at my face and remember back to that horrible day when as a child the Germans came and destroyed your village .Tell me what you remember."

Yuri strained to remember the details of that painful memory concentrating with every fiber in his body. Suddenly he reached a shocking revelation.

"I see clearly now. It was you, the German soldier who led Marlena and I to safety. I remembered thinking how you spoke Russian without a German accent. How amid all that chaos noise and smoke you had a calm about you that made me feel safe. I remember how everything seemed to move in slow motion. You look exactly the same now as you looked then except for the albino features. You haven't aged at all. How do you do this? Who are you?"

"Yes Yuri, it was I who showed you and your friend to safety that day. You see, I needed you to survive. I needed you to become the man you are today. You have a higher purpose. You are destined to make the world a safer place and I will help and guide you in this endeavor.

"But who are you Olav?

"Look into my eyes and I will show you."

Yuri stared into Olav's eyes and was gripped by a force that seemed to transport him through time.

There were vivid scenes, of an emersion quality, in the reality of his boyhood. He saw his parents in long forgotten scenarios of daily life on their farm. He could feel their kindness and love again, stirring feelings lost to time. School friends and teachers long forgotten played out in his memories. The war, love found and lost...all fleeting at a rapid pace. The joys of discovery, disappointments, and failures, all running like the wind and morphing into a darker more somber light, signaling the future of mans folly. Where would it all end? He felt cravings for hope dashed by uncertainty. What did it all mean?

A loud noise seemed to slap the professor back to reality. It was the sound of the attendant yelling, "wake up! You have visitors. I think they're going to let you go. Hurry up and wipe your face. You look like you just ran a marathon. Drink some water. Get yourself together before they change their minds."

Looking around Olav was gone.

He ran into the bathroom and began splashing water on his face and hair and wondering how Olav had simply vanished. Looking up at the vanity mirror he was startled by his own

162

reflection, a pale old man looking afraid and bewildered. He had to pull himself together. He decided to give himself a brief time out, blocking out the sound of the attendant summoning him to get going.

Sitting on the toilet seat in the small dark quiet bathroom gave him a sense of isolation he desperately needed at this moment. The revelation that he had met Olav as a young man so many years ago frightened him. To think that such a thing was even possible gave him an unsettling feeling that he had entered a world both unfamiliar and fearful. Olav's message simply added to the mystery. With his head in his hands, he repeated quietly affirmations that had gotten him through difficult moments in the past. Affirmations of hope, thanks and blessings.

"What are you doing in there?" The attendant yelled. "Reliving your youth?"

Romilov had no idea who the visitors might be and was not looking forward to meeting another one of Americas finest. The thought of going through another round of repetitive questioning was more than he could bear.

The cool water felt good on his face, refreshing and offering a respite from the wave of anxiety that previously engulfed him. Managing enough to freshen up, he accompanied the attendant down the stairs and prepared himself for whatever lay ahead. He had given little credence to the attendant's words of possible freedom.

"Go right through that door over there marked Visitors Room and good luck."

163

He opened the door and to his utter delight, there stood Jeff accompanied by Amanda with smiles and open arms. Overcome with emotion at the site of his old friends, a wave of joy and comfort swept over him as if to say, you're safe now, the odyssey is over, it's going to be all right. There were tears of joy, embraces, and words of genuine affection.

Jeff and Amanda where pleased to see that although the professor looked tired and gaunt from his ordeal he had not aged much from when they had seen him last. Jeff motioned with a hand full of release documents to get going knowing that the entire scene was being monitored by surveillance cameras and audio. Just then Agent Hall entered the room.

"Doctor Romilov, you are being released in the care of Dr.Blake and his fiancée Amanda Fiore. The conditions of your release are provisional. You will reside for a minimum period of sixty days at 271 Dwight Street in Boston Massachusetts and must inform this office of any changes in your domicile. This will be followed by an additional period of ninety days provisional status. Furthermore, you will be required to report for a monthly meeting at this office until such time as provisional status is terminated and you have been adjudicated to remain. You have been provided with a social security number to aid you in securing employment. Any breach in these terms will result in you being classified as fugitive subject to arrest and deportation."

"Do you have any questions? No, came the response.

"Welcome to the United States of America."

Traffic was light on Storrow Drive as the trio headed toward the apartment.

"This is just how I imagined Boston to look like. Is that the Charles River? I want to do the, how do you say, Duck boat?

"Yes Yuri," Amanda said, "It's all part of the Duck Tour of Boston."

Jeff and Amanda couldn't contain the laughter.

"What is so funny that you laugh? "You are, Yuri. You're like a kid in a candy store."

When they reached the apartment Amanda showed Yuri to his own bedroom that had its own bathroom and shower welcoming him into their home with genuine hospitality and affection.

That night, the professor got to indulge in his craving for red wine recounting the details of his escape adventure and plans for a new life in America. The stories filled the evening with love and camaraderie.

Chapter 20

The six-hour time difference between Boston and Rome is something every traveler to the Eternal City struggles with to adjust on the first day of arrival. The effects of the all night flight linger until the following morning. Not having had the luxury of a first class ticket, Father Ryan was feeling its effects. The appointment with Vatican officials was for eleven in the morning. It was a rush from the airport from the moment he got off the plane. It wasn't every day that a priest gets summoned by the Pope himself. He intuitively knew that this must have something to do with the Leonard Spikes affair. After all, the Pontiff knew of the mysterious goings on attracting world attention amongst the world's elites and the flurry of emails Ryan had received from Vatican officials.

The ride from the airport was as frightening as ever. Italian cabbies stay true to form. Speeding up only to come to screeching stops, creating their own lanes and for the most part ignoring stop signs. Traffic laws in Italy are interpreted by Italian drivers as recommendations rather than the law. The police exercise lax enforcement resulting in the cacophony of horns and the famous chaos of traffic in Italy.

After the harrowing ride, the cab skidded over the cobblestone street to a halt just at the entrance to Vatican City.

The cabbies name was clearly displayed on his dashboard license. It read Armando Busilli.

"Armando, I have blessed this cab for you but also for your passengers, that they arrive at their destinations in one piece." said Father Ryan.

Pointing to the Rosary Beads hanging from the rear view mirror and laughing the cabby shot back.

"Thank you Padre. I have been delivering souls to their destinations for over twenty five years and with the exception of a few minor fender benders, all in one piece. I have faith that God has his hand firmly over the roof of my cab." They both shared a good laugh and wished each other well.

At the first sight of Saint Peters Basilica Father Ryan was overcome with awe at the majesty of this place. It was the same feeling he recalls when he first saw it over forty years ago as a young seminarian. To think that this was Peters Rock upon which God commanded him to build his church was still as inspirational now as it was so long ago.

He made his way up along the far side of the square reaching the medieval gate and archway manned by a member of the Swiss Guard wearing the traditional orange blue and red uniform recognized the world over. "The Guardia," as it is known, have been guarding the Pope and the Vatican since the time of Columbus and have done so with unwavering honor and distinction.

"State your name and the nature of your business"

"Father Timothy Ryan. I have an appointment with Monsignor Brunetti at eleven this morning."

After checking the appointment schedule and Father Ryan's passport identification the guard returned. "Proceed to the second "camera" and take a seat. The Monsignor will meet you there."

The long corridor adorned with ancient frescos and sculptured archways gave way to a large open room or "camera" decorated with splendid paintings of biblical scenes. Ryan noted that the musty scent of old stone, worn smooth by eons of time, the dim lighting, and the smoky hint of wax candles, was still a part of the charm reminding visitors of the antiquity of their surroundings.

It wasn't long before the Monsignor arrived. He was diminutive man with graying hair, refined facial character and a warm smile. Although he had an unmistakable Italian accent his English diction was impeccable.

He wasted no time in greeting his guest and welcoming him with banter and pleasantries about his trip and his appreciation for the effort put forth. Brunetti was a career

Vatican functionary who had become both a friend and confidant to the Pope. It was rumored that his skills at Chess made him an indispensible asset to the Pope, rumored himself to be quite the Chess player.

He motioned the priest into a private elevator and remained uncomfortably quiet as the elevator moved the fifth floor. The door opened to a quiet, small but well appointed office that looked more like a library with walls lined by books bound in leather. Brunetti took his place behind the leather-covered desk and motioned Ryan to take a seat.

"Thank you for coming all this way at the behest of His Holiness. You have distinguished yourself as an academic theologian and your writings have gained you His Holiness attention and admiration.I don't need to tell you that we are all very concerned about the revelations and rumors circulating amongst us which may in my opinion undermine the very tenets of our faith. The fallen angel has always fought to destroy what the Lord has built and I for one feel that we are facing our greatest challenge in preserving our beliefs and the devotion of the faithful."

Ryan sensed that maybe the Monsignor was seeking validation of his position. He wasn't about to give it. He wondered whether or not the Monsignor held positions were shared by the Pope. Something told him that maybe they were not and that Brunetti was looking for a willing ally.

"I share your concerns but believe that these revelations may, in the end, actually bring about a more detailed understanding of the origins of our existence and the role of

Our Savior. I will offer you more of my impressions when we get into the specifics of our discussion."

Ryan could see by the Monsignor's facial expressions and body language that he had become disappointed in this response and perspective. He wondered again if the Holy Father shared the same point of view.

Just then, the creaky door just to the right of the room opened. A cleric dressed in a long black robe entered and announced in a commanding voice, "Papa Alexandro il Secondo!"

In walked the pope himself in white robes smiling and waving his right hand in the traditional welcoming manner. Ryan and the Monsignor quickly jumped up from their chairs and knelt before the Pope with their heads bowed. He put forth his right hand presenting the papal ring of Peter while making the sign of the cross with his left hand and blessed them both in the Latin verse," Vi benedica nel Nome del Padre, Figlio et Spiritus Sancto". They both kissed the ring and remained kneeling until the Pope motioned them to stand and take a seat.

Servants brought in an assortment of Italian cookies and a pot of Café Americano on an ornate silver tray. Napkins with the embroided Papal seal completed the elegant presentation.

Pope Alexander the Second was the first American Pope ever elected to the Holy See. He grew up the grandson of Irish immigrants in the borough of Staten Island, New York. He rose through the ranks and distinguished himself as Bishop when he defied Rome during the church sex scandal and became a victim's advocate. His no nonsense approach to defrocking priests gained him worldwide recognition and admiration for his principled stance.

He had been leading the Church as the Vicar of Christ for seven years. Alexander was considered by most to be more moderate in his views on matters of marriage, family life, homosexuality, and other issues of modern life. He enjoyed popularity even amongst the more secular faction of American Catholics. The American Pope was known for his openness and desire to make the church as inclusive as possible. By all accounts he was succeeding with church attendance trending upwards even in the most secular nations.

"Welcome to my humble abode Timothy. Oh, may I call you Timothy?"

"Yes, of course, Your Holiness."

Small talk broke the ice and put Ryan at ease, but it became clear that the Pope wanted to get down to business. Smiling, he moved closer to his guests.

"I called you to Rome to discuss and hear your opinion as to what is going on in regards to this mysterious Mr. Spikes and his admonitions. I have learned that you have considerable knowledge and contacts with people who have had contact with the mysterious Mr. Spikes."

"Like you and many others I have had the dreams and have been moved by certain revelations. The dreams have shown me things that would rival the book of revelation. I have seen the past and the future."

Alexander's facial expression grew more serious.

"The central themes of these revelations seem to be wrapped in the spirit of a warning, a warning of an impending cataclysmic event."

The Pope moved around the room with his arms folded and his hands tucked into the voluminous sleeve folds of his robes, looking up at the volumes of old texts that lined the room. While the Pope was speaking Ryan and Brunetti were following the timed honored and respected protocol requiring that others remain silent until the pope indicates that they may respond or add to the conversation.

"My first thought was that this power or entity that had entered my mind was a challenge from the Prince of Evil. It would not be the first time that the Demon had tried to influence or tempt the Vicar of Christ. The Gospels tell us he tempted Christ himself in the Judean Desert after the baptism by John the Baptist. I tried to cast out this spirit repeatedly using the words of Our Savior himself, "Be Gone Satan," but to no avail."

Alexander walked to the large window overlooking the majestic Saint Peters Square. The sun was beginning to set casting an orange glow to his white robes adding to his already strong yet pious persona.

"I would like to relate to you both an event not revealed before."

That caught their attention.

"Several weeks ago I was alone in the papal gardens asking the Lord to grant me wisdom. I noticed a man sitting alone on one of the benches. Wondering how he got in

172

undetected by security guards I approached him. I am not supposed to do that, but then, there lots of things I'm not supposed to do. When he saw me he quickly got up then dropped to his knees and apologized for disturbing me. I asked him his name and he responded, Leonard Spikes."

"I immediately knew who he was and became defensive not knowing his motives for this visit. At the same time, I was immensely excited to finally meet this person of whom I had heard so much and possibly get answers to my questions and concerns. My suspicions that he could be the Evil One were quickly dispelled. There are items I carry in my pocket at all times."

Reaching in the folds of his robes he produced two small gold cylindrical containers and placed them on the table in front of Ryan and Brunetti. Pointing to the containers he said,

"This one contains Holy Water from the springs of Fatima, and in this one, the Holy Eucharist that I personally consecrated."

"I approached Mr. Spikes and anointed his forehead with the Holy Water and offered him the Eucharist which he took." He displayed no resistance. He knew this was a test and that it would clear him of any suspicion as to his origins. If he were the Evil One, he would have repelled, and never accepted. In fact, he would have cowered and fled at the very presence of these most Holy objects of our Lord and Savior.

"When nothing happened he made the sign of the cross, looked up at me smiling and said, "Now can we talk?"

Brunetti jumped up and began to ask one question after another while Ryan sat silent. Pope Alexander motioned the Monsignor to remain quiet and take his seat.

Walking toward the bookcase containing old hand written manuscripts, Alexander removed an old hand carved wooden boxes from the shelf. Opening the box, he removed one of the hermetically sealed in plastic manuscripts. It was a fifteenth century monk's transcription of a work by Saint Thomas Aquinas. He read from the old Latin text.

"Before the End, there shall be a warning to man, to heed and accept the help of one who will come to save the world from darkness. He will be ridiculed and branded a liar, a charlatan, and a false prophet. The powerful will be loath to share or relinquish their power. Their eyes will be blinded by the sin of pride."

He then carefully placed the manuscript back in the box and turned back toward his guests.

"The mysterious Mr. Spikes told me that the time had come to reveal the reason for his appearance. He prefaced his statements by stating that there would be many reveals made public that would be difficult, if not terrifying, for the common man to comprehend. He further stated that many will not believe and reject his message."

"He made it clear to me that he makes no claims to be a deity or the creator, but is of extraterrestrial origin. He will reveal himself in a way that will leave no doubt as to his origins.

"You can imagine my shock and disbelief at this revelation. He could feel my skepticism and began showing

174

me things that were clearly not of this world. He asked me to look into the pool of the fountain by the garden, dedicated to Saint Francis.

In the pool, I saw images of mans very beginnings. There were primitive two legged creatures foraging in the wilderness and communicating with signs and guttural sounds. There was a grittiness quality of these images different than anything Hollywood could ever produce, a realism of actually being there replete with sounds and smells and even the wind against my face. I knew that I had somehow been transported back in time to the actual place, like an invisible observer.

"Then, he showed me something that shook me to my very core."

"I was standing on a dusty hot and dry hillside, surrounded by what appeared to be Roman soldiers. They were not shiny and disciplined as portrayed in the movies but instead disheveled wearing tattered tunics and worn leather harness like belts. Their weapons were crude and also worn. Rough bladed long knives and spears with wooden handles were strewn about. They seemed undisciplined and bored. The sky was overcast and dreary. There were men and woman mulling about in dirty and squalid like conditions. I remembered thinking how short statured everyone was. It wasn't until I looked up the hillside that I saw the three crosses."

"I was at the crucifixion of our Lord and Savior."

The two men bowed their heads and blessed themselves making the sign of the cross.

"I identified our Lord and Savior by the wooden sign above the cross written in Latin, Hebrew, and Greek. " Jesus of Nazareth, King of the Jews." His cross was not in the center but instead to the far right. He did not look anything like the depictions we see today but was instead smaller with dark hair and a full dark beard. He was in the throes of dying but managed to open his eyes ever so slightly revealing their green color. For an instance our eyes locked and a barely perceptible smile swept over his face. It was then that I heard a faint voice saying, "You have come from the future. Go forth and fulfill your mission."

"The pain and sorrow I felt that moment was like nothing I had ever experienced."

Ryan and Brunetti were speechless. Tears formed in Alexander's eyes.

"There is more." The Pontiff said.

"Spikes revealed to me that his world is located in the solar system closest to ours. We know it as Proxima Centuri. It is part of the triple star system known as Alpha Centuri and is 4.2 light years away. Our modern space telescopes would have detected their planet if not for the fact that its position in relation to the Earth is directly behind our sun at all times."

"He explained that after centuries of technological advancement his species realized that their physical bodies were the single most limiting factor in space exploration."

"Centuries later they achieved the technology of teleportation, making all the machines for space travel that they had developed, for the most part, obsolete. With that

176

development came the accidental side effect of near immortality, exponentially increasing life span and decreasing the quantity of resources necessary to sustain their civilization."

"He claims that they discovered the earth in its formative phase before mankind existed and assisted in its biological development depositing genetic material from their extensive depository of diverse life form templates. Over time, they would return and observe our development and at times intervene with help as man evolved from savage animal to an organism capable of reasoning and changing its own environment."

"Many of our ancient civilizations bear the marks of their influence. They established a permanent colony on the dark side of our moon and have been observing our development for centuries."

Alexander moved closer to the Monsignor and Father Ryan and looked directly into their eyes, as if to say with his body language, that he was about to give his final word on these strange developments.

"Well gentleman, I have accepted these reveals and find them to be consistent with our beliefs."

"God, the creator of the universe and all things, sent his only Son, Jesus Christ, to save us from original sin. He has nourished us as we grow into the beings we are destined to become to fulfill his plan for us."

"Now we know that we are not alone in the universe, but that He has provided for us a family. Knowing that we have been blessed with brothers and sisters, in my mind, only enhances the Glory of our God and Father."

"If and when the existence of our extended family becomes known, I believe that with the right message, our beliefs will be more inclusive and stronger than ever before."

Alexander had a smile on his face as if to say, much ado about nothing.

"When that day comes when we finally know that we are not alone, we will go forth and spread the good news."

Father Ryan and the Monsignor nodded in agreement and again made the sign of the cross. There were lots of questions still unanswered but this did not seem to be the time to persist in questioning the Pontiff. He seemed to have reported all that he knew of the most revealing encounter with Spikes yet.

"Oh, and one other thing," said Alexander turning to Father Ryan, "When you get home be sure to contact a Dr Jeffery Blake and make him aware of these revelations. Spikes was very clear about that."

"Do you know Dr Blake your Holiness?" Said Ryan.

"I know of him. I've never met or spoken with him, but know from my friend in the garden, that he is a good man who has been chosen to take up the sword against those who would do us harm."

Alexander opened a desk drawer, produced an envelope, and gave it to Ryan. The back of the envelope was sealed with red wax bearing the papal seal.

"Give this to Dr Blake with my prayers."

Chapter 21

Jeff was running through his morning routine knowing that this day would be busy. There was a morning meeting with the student advisory panel and before lunch the staff meeting at the lab to discuss whether or not the preset research benchmarks that measure progress were being met. He knew that the work were going slow and having a demoralizing effect on the staff.

Amanda was already up fixing the professors favorite American discovery, hash browns. The professor was excited for his first appointment with Dr Gilardi. Gilardi was chairman of Harvard's molecular genetics department. Everyone was hoping that the Professor would find a position in the department. Jeff had plans to bring Romilov on to the staff at GenOnc as a consultant but knew that Romilov would need to first establish a relationship with the university and academic credentials. The professor was reading the daily news online as part of his morning routine when Amanda placed the first batch of hash browns in front of him. He looked down at the hash browns and paused before diving in.

"I understand that these delightful hash browns were invented by someone named Mc Donald. He must have been a true genius."

"No Professor, they are an old American potato recipe. Some of the finest hotels in New York City began to serve them somewhere around the 1890s. A company called McDonalds helped to popularize them." Amanda said.

Jeff couldn't believe the trivia that Amanda could come up with. "Wow, how do you know all that stuff?"

"Simple, I Googled it once."

Just then, a text came through on Jeff's cell phone. It was David Misner from the lab. "Get down to the lab sooner rather than later today. I need to talk to you. It's urgent."

Jeff put the phone in the side pocket of his jacket he tried not to look alarmed by the abrupt wording of the text. It indicated to him that something had happened that couldn't be discussed over a cell line.

"Amanda, do you mind calling a cab for the professor to get him to his appointment? Something came up at the lab that needs my attention right away, and I won't have time to drive him down there today."

"I've got time. I'll drive him." She replied, thinking that whatever was in that text must be pretty important for Jeff to cancel out. He so wanted to be with his friend on the day of this important interview.

Jeff grabbed his coat and sped out the door. The drive seemed exceptionally slow with traffic crawling along Storrow Drive. His anticipation of the nature of the "summons like" text message continued to grow the closer he got to the lab. He kept reminding himself to keep cool no matter what the situation was.

The doors swung open to the entrance hallway where David Misner was already waiting, motioning Jeff to a small conference room to the immediate right. Jeff could see the worried look on his face telling him that Mark had something upsetting to tell him.

"Jeff, someone hacked into our computer system."

"How bad is it?" Did they get the backups?" Please tell me they didn't get the backups."

"That's the funny thing Jeff, all the data is still there. Seems like they got in and actually added stuff. There's more data files in the system than there were before."

Misner moved to a nearby workstation and plugged in his user ID and password. A black screen opened with the message, "The Truths are in the Strands."

"What does that mean? Have you told the others about this?"

"Only that our system had been compromised and that the data was still there. I didn't tell them that the data might possibly have been altered. The backups have been compromised in the same way. We won't know the full extent of what's in there until we get into it. I haven't called IT to report the breach. I wanted to speak to you first."

Jeff's brain was going a mile a minute looking ahead at all the possible consequences of the hack.

"Do we know anyone in computer forensics we can trust to look into this and keep it quiet for now?"

"I'm thinking Alan Brodski, said David. He's a genius and cool with stuff like that."

"Ok, get him. Tell the troops to carry on as usual but not to upload anything to hard drive until we give the all clear."

"Jeff, you know that our data system is not connected to the internet?"

"I know, I know. That's the most disturbing thing about this whole situation. It had to be someone from the inside. Until Brodsky tells us differently we need to go on that assumption"

Jeff walked down the hallway past the "restricted area" signs posted where the main lab was located. Everyone was waiting for a briefing as to what actually happened. Putting on his optimistic face, he addressed the group telling them that some files had been corrupted. He was careful not to mention the word "hacked." He gave the impression that the problem might be a hardware issue and that IT would straighten it all out. Luckily for him, no one asked any questions. No questions from a group like that signaled that they knew there

182

was more to the story. The awkward meeting ended with everyone's facial expression unmistakably wary.

Jeff started to make his way toward the door. David then caught up and asked Jeff to wait up, as there was one more issue to discuss. His eyes gazed downward avoiding direct eye contact.

"Jeff, we've all noticed that you're spending a lot less time here at work. The troops are starting to think you've lost interest in our work. Its having a demoralizing effect and rumors are swirling around."

"What kind of rumors?"

"Rumors that things aren't good between you and Amanda or that you're looking at another position."

"I know. You're right. I was waiting for you to say something and can't believe you've all been so patient with me."

Jeff motioned for David to sit with him taking his position at the conference table and asked him to close the door as if to say this is going to take some time.

"Remember when I came up with the new theory about ligands that changed the direction of our research? Well, the truth is, it was not my idea. It was an idea given to me by a strange acquaintance I've met. I kept it from you so as not to have to get into the whole explanation of who this strange acquaintance is because, as crazy as it sounds, I myself don't know his whole story.

Jeff got up and made them two coffees from the Keruig machine, then placed a cup in front of David.

"David, I'm going to tell you stuff that is totally crazy, but true. You're going to think I've been smoking something really nasty, but I swear to you, that what I'm about to tell you is true."

For the next hour Jeff revealed to David the whole encounter with Spikes and his impressions of all that had taken place. Needless to say, David expressed skepticism throughout the whole story. However, at the same time, coming from Jeff Blake, a man he respected and trusted, he let himself believe the possibility that it could all be true. The story and possibilities it opens captivated David's imagination.

"Had I come to you with this you would have thought I was nuts and probably tossed the idea out. I never intended to take credit for it. But, I can't even prove to you that Spikes actually exists.

" Amanda and I have been drawn into a web of future events to come that are too bizarre for me to get into right now. I need you to believe in me and hold on to the the fort. I need you to help me. You have to trust me now and know that I'm committed to the work. But right now, I need a little slack."

"Jeff, I want to believe everything you just told me but I've got to be honest, it's not easy."

After a long pause, David replied. "Ok, you've got the slack you need but I'll expect you to keep me in the loop."

"That's a for sure." Jeff replied.

Chapter 22

Amanda waited in the car with anticipation. The professor would be coming out from his interview and she hoped the news would be good. The car was doubled parked and the pouring rain was making a racket on the roof.

Finally, there he was, at the exit, fumbling with his umbrella and getting soaking wet. When he spotted Amanda, he gave up on the umbrella. Rushing toward the car door, she could see a smile breaking out over his face telling her that things had gone well. Dripping from the rain, he jumped in and slammed the door shut. He turned to her still sporting a smile.

"Well my dear, it seems that I am now adjuvant professor of molecular genetics. I am charged with creating a lesson syllabus for under graduates and presenting speaking topics for my new role as guest lecturer."

He was smiling and trying to suppress tears of joy.

"And, can you believe it, they are going to pay me a handsome sum, indeed!"

Amanda , almost reflexively, leaned over and gave him a big kiss on the cheek. Having become used to the lack of human contact and affection, he summoned up all the strength he had inside to keep from become emotional.

"This is cause for a celebration." She said. "Tonight you will be introduced to Italian food, North End style."

That night, they all met at Vincenzo's, the best red sauce Italian restaurant in the North End. Baked lasagna and red table wine were in abundance as the trio celebrated Romilov's big success in transitioning to a new life in America. Things seemed to be coming together for him, a successful escape, a path to citizenship, and now, a job.

The rain wouldn't let up. The only sounds on the ride home where those of water splashing over pavement riding along the uneven Boston city streets. Gazing out the wet car window, he starred at the rain droplets running down the fogged glass and began to reflect out loud.

"You both have been so good to me. Just when I thought my life was coming to an end, a whole new chapter has opened up. I left someone behind. Someone I cared for very much. Maybe the universe will be good to me one last time and grant me the wish to see her again."

Jeff was driving and decided to remain silent. Amanda turned and looked toward the professor sitting in the back seat.

"Remember what they say, It's never too late to live happily ever after. And, wishes do come true."

They pulled into their parking space at home and the professor said,

"It's only eight o'clock. Why don't we all have some coffee? There are things I would like to tell you both. Things we need to talk about. There's been no time since I arrived."

Amanda prepared some decaf and Jeff started a cozy fire in their antique marbled fireplace that dated back from the construction of the old brownstone, almost one hundred years ago. They all sat down. It had become the norm to let the professor have Jeff's favorite chair, a comfortable high back with armrests.

"Jeffery, I sent you a letter some time ago that was mailed from Paris by a friend telling you about a discovery I had made. I have discovered something that may someday have an enormous impact on global food production. I must confess that this discovery was not of my making alone. I had help from an unusual individual who befriended me. His name is Olav."

"To my amazement he appeared to me as if out of nowhere, again, at the embassy while I was waiting for a decision on my status. He reminded me of something that I had almost forgotten."

"He reminded me, that he had visited me when I was a boy, and saved me from the Germans when my village came under attack. He is a truly remarkable person who possesses special powers, skills, and knowledge. He is able to transcend time and space and, to be honest, he scares me. I don't know where he is from. Now, please don't judge me insane, but I believe he is not of this world. He knows about you and Amanda. Again, don't ask me how, because I don't know that either."

Jeff and Amanda looked at each other and instinctively knew it was Spikes. The professor excused himself, disappeared into his room and quickly returned with his laptop computer and a large notebook which he neatly laid out on the coffee table.

"Olav provided me with an insight into unraveling genetic information which led to my discovery. Surly you must be aware of the new technology known as CRISPR."

Jeff nodded affirmative.

Amanda turned to Jeff. "What the heck is CRISPR?"

Jeff raised his eyes.

"Believe me ,you don't want to know what it stands for."

"Yes I do!" She retorted in her firm don't patronage me voice.

"Ok, you asked for it. Clustered Regularity Interspaced Short Palindromic Repeats."

"Your right, I didn't need to know that. What does it do?"

188

Jeff turned to the professor as if to ask permission to provide the explanation. The professor lowered his gaze and nodded ok.

"Amanda, it's a technology that makes it possible to delete or insert a specific gene from a strand of DNA. We use this technology at GenOnc under license from the FDA. David Misner is a whiz at it. In this country it is purely investigational. It has the potential of curing cancer or creating new organisms. It's very exciting and very scary at the same time. Imagine a cure for cancer and at the same time the creation of a bug that could wipe out the entire human race."

"Jeff is right." The professor lowered his voice to almost a whisper and leaned closer to Jeff and Amanda.

"Olav gave me a new and closer insight into CRISPR .What I am about to tell you both cannot leave this room. When I am finished you will both, without doubt, think that I am crazy, but I assure you that I am not."

They both went quiet, in anticipation of what the professor was about to say.

"Olav showed me that DNA, in its infinite complexity, can actually communicate to us in an intelligent format."

Jeff and Amanda looked at each other in silence knowing they were both thinking the same thing. "How is this possible?"

"Olav told me to think of DNA as a living organism constantly evolving and adapting. DNA is what gives us life and is present in every cell in our body. It is everywhere on this planet.

"You both know that the greatest minds in statistics and probability have reluctantly concluded that the enormous complexity of DNA could not have happened by sheer chance or probability, but is instead, part of a GRAND DESIGN."

"Olav taught me to understand that WE and our DNA are one and the same. Our DNA is what every living thing actually is. It works every moment of every day to sustain our existence. It is our very essence."

"I struggled with this concept as I am sure the two of you do now. When you look down at your hand you see the functioning tissue made up of complex proteins created by DNA which are being constantly maintained and replaced by DNA itself. This is our living body. It's as alive as the thoughts are in your head."

It was easy to see that the professor was becoming visibly excited the more he got into his explanation. His passion for science and newfound discovery were shedding years off his persona replacing it with youthful exuberance.

"This explains why the two most fundamental urges of all living things, self preservation and desire to reproduce or procreate are present in every living thing, whether it is plant or animal. Our life cycle is such that once we have procreated or reproduced, our bodies wither and die. It is because we have fulfilled the mission for which we were created, which is the preservation and passing to the next generation of our DNA. It is the DNA that contains the knowledge, and life force, that is eternal."

He began to wave his arms about like an orchestra conductor bringing life and emphasis to his newfound knowledge.

" Everything there is to know, every secret of the universe, every wisdom, every question that needs to be answered is contained in the genetic coding system, of which we are all one and part of."

Jeff motioned that he had questions but was restrained by the professors quick facial expressions telling him to wait until he was finished making his point.

"The vast diversity of living organisms are fundamentally nothing more than a universal matrix with a singular purpose. Its purpose is to expand, grow, evolve, and pass on its DNA to following generations, perpetuating life for all eternity."

"Furthermore, Olav stressed to me that these reveals were not to be shared with the masses at this time in the evolution of our species. Revealing them would be disruptive in this phase of our society's evolution."

"Olav explained to me that mankind passed through the first or primitive stage of evolution somewhere around 5000 BC and then began the second or enlightened stage after 400AD. This was followed by the third stage, at or around 1890. According to him, we are approaching the fourth and most dangerous stage. He likened it to a coming of age, or adolescent stage .We have acquired the ability to destroy ourselves but not the maturity to realize the stupidity of such actions. The fifth stage or transcendent stage will require over one thousand years of peace to initiate. During that time the notions of war and self destruction will have become obsolete."

The professor paused then took another sip of coffee.

"When I asked him what phase his society was in, he replied that they were three million years into the transcendent stage where time, space, and physical barriers have been overcome. The transcendent phase is the last stage before reaching the final or ONENESS stage with the CREATOR."

Jeff and Amanda were mesmerized by the concepts revealed to them by the professor and by extension by the mysterious Olav, alias Spikes. The more they thought about them the more it all made sense.

These reveals, although wondrous, were a sobering blow to man egocentric view of the world promulgated by philosophers and theologians throughout the ages. The notion that we may only be tiny specks in a molten sea of life and not the masters of our own universe would be a hard pill to swallow.

Jeff got up from his chair." Whew, I need another glass of something stronger than coffee."

He ran both hands through his hair in a motion to clear his head.

"So let me get this straight. DNA creates all living things then uses living things as a conduit to insure that it will survive in perpetuity."

"No," Romilov jumped in.

"It does not create but is one and the same with all living things. Creation is in the mystery of the Grand Design!"

Jeff continued while pacing around the room focusing his gaze on Amanda who was waiting her turn to jump into the conversation. Jeff continued.

"It has the capacity to communicate with higher organisms with whom it is one or singular. That would explain the message on the black screen that appeared in the lab after the hack. "The Truths are in the Strands" It's starting to make sense. But, what's the key? How is the communication opened?"

Amanda got up and smiled at the professor.

"All this is giving me a monumental headache! There's only one way the communication could take place with no margin of error in interpretation. The answer is obvious to me. It has to be mathematics."

"Yes, said the professor, mathematics!"

"Olav sat in front of my computer and asked me what I was looking for. Then, he asked me to produce for him a decoded segment of the gene sequence from the plant I was working with. He proceeded to enter into the computer what looked like a long mathematical command. Within a minute or two, there appeared a gene sequence slightly different from the one I submitted. He told me to use CRISPR and create the newly sequenced gene."

"I worked secretly in the lab during nights and weekends when no one was around. I then introduced the gene sequence modification into the plant genome by way of CRISPR and wala, my discovery was born."

"A week later I saw Olav again. I thanked him and inquired about the mathematical command he used. You can imagine how astounded I was at this revelation. I wanted to know how it worked, how he came to know such things, everything I could"

"He reached into his pocket and handed me a flash drive and said, "Here is your ROSETTA STONE. Guard it with your life. Keep it safe from those who would use it to do harm. Do not release it in its entirety. Mankind is not ready to know its power. It is too early at this time in evolution, to comprehend what I have revealed and gifted to you. Its secrets must only be revealed very slowly and passed along over the next several generations. Entrust it only to those that profess to honor this sacred covenant I make with you this day. Breaking the covenant will have grave consequences.""

The professor produced the flash drive from his watch pocket and in a surprised gesture handed it over to Amanda.

"Take this and study it. Using your knowledge and gift for mathematics, unlock its secrets and use it for the good of all. I am old now and my time is coming to an end. As I have been instructed, I am passing it on to you both. I know in my heart that you both will be worthy keepers of its power and might. You, Amanda, are the mother of this new knowledge and you Jeff will be its protector.

Amanda took the flash drive and looked down at it. She clutched hands with both Jeff and the professor creating a circle as if to signify the creation of an inner circle.

194

"We are not worthy of such a responsibility. I only hope that we can fulfill the covenant."

Chapter 23

Sally Reynolds , lab chief administrative assistant knocked then poked her head through the door.

"Sorry to disturb you Dr Blake, but there's a man at the door who says he's a friend of yours who wants to see you."

"What's his name Sally?"

"He wouldn't give his name. When I told him he would have to make an appointment and state the nature of his business he seemed to get a little agitated. He's out there now and won't go away."

"Not now Sally. I'm in the middle of something. Tell him he needs to make an appointment. If he won't give his name or gives you a hard time call security."

Just at that instant the door opened. Agent Rossi burst into the room with a hurried look on his face.

Jeff turned to Sally.

"Sally, it's ok. He's an old friend. Just close the door behind you."

"Rossi, what are you doing? You can't just come barging in like this. How the hell did you get passed the locked door?

"Doc, I'm sorry. Locked doors are no problem for me. I've come to tell you they're on their way to pick you up right now for questioning and maybe detain you. Now listen up. I might be in the room when they question you so remember you only saw me once outside your house on that first night. They have that guy Spikes in custody. They say he insists on talking to you."

"Nobody can hold Spikes unless he lets it happen," said Jeff.

Jeff tried to call Amanda but there was no answer. Sirens could be heard just outside getting louder. Rossi bolted for the back door and Jeff went to the entrance so as to avoid an ugly confrontation in front of the staff.

Two men in dark suits and long top coats accompanied by two uniformed Boston Police officers were standing outside the glass doors with badges held up and looking annoyed. They kept pressing the entrance buzzer over and over signaling with urgency that they were too important to be waiting outside. Jeff opened the door.

"Dr Blake?"

"Yes?"

Still holding their badges up.

"You need to come with us."

"Not until I know how my girlfriend Amanda Fiore is."

"She's fine and waiting in the car for you. Now let's get going."

"What's this all about?"

"Certain people need to talk to you right now. Come on."

Jeff was escorted into the back seat of the black Chevy Tahoe, and just as the agent said, Amanda was there in the back seat wearing cut offs, and flip flops with her hair in a bun. Obvious signs she got picked up with no time to get ready. She clutched Jeff's hand and cuddled herself against him. He leaned into her and whispered in her ear.

"Don't worry. This day was going to come sooner or later. We're going to be fine. Remember we only saw Rossi once that first night. If they split us up, clam up, and remember, I love you sweetie. Oh, and by the way, you look wicked hot." She poked him in the ribs while mustering up a smile.

"Where are we going?" Jeff asked. No answer came.

Not a word was spoken for the next thirty minutes until the car stopped. One of the agents opened the door. Jeff could see a sign off in the distance reading Hanscom Field, a former small Air Force base just outside of Boston, now converted mainly to light civilian traffic.

The unmistakable noise of helicopter blades and smell of diesel fuel gave away the next move. They were going on a trip.

As they entered the helicopter they were both relieved to see Agent Rossi sitting there with a barely perceptible smile on his face as if to say don't worry I've got your back.

"Welcome aboard Doc, you too Miss Amanda."

He handed them both a pair of earphone mike units.

The helicopter made its way through some dense bad weather clouds bouncing along in a stomach-churning ride. Jeff and Amanda wondered with some apprehension where they were being taken. After about sixty-five minutes of rock and roll flying things began to settle down. Darkness had just settled in and they could see the lights of a large city growing brighter the lower they got. The final approach to landing was smooth with a gentle touch down.

"Welcome to Langley," Rossi announced. I'm told there's food and drinks waiting for you before the briefing. Take advantage of this time to relax and get freshened up. The briefing is scheduled for fourteen hundred hours."

Langley Virginia, just outside of Washington DC is the home of the CIA. Twenty one thousand employees and a fifteen billion dollar budget make it the largest intelligence gathering body in the world. Jeff knew they were about to meet the heavy hitters of the intelligence community. He knew that they would try to intimidate them with a lot of cloak and dagger bullshit. He had made up his mind that he would have none of it.

They entered a small building sparsely furnished with cinder block windowless walls painted in army drab green. Obvious video cameras marked the room's four ceiling corners. As promised, they were greeted by a quality buffet dinner, complete with wine, which helped to take a little of the edge off. Two military personnel armed with side arms stood in silence by the only two doors in the room. Just as things couldn't get crazier the door opened and none other than professor Romilov was ushered in.

"Well looks like they got us all, "said Romilov. "Reminds me of home."

The last remark sparked a moment of levity and cut the tension in the room. After that, everyone had something to eat. It wasn't long before the trio was led into another black SUV for a short ride to the location where the briefing would take place. Jeff motioned to them not to talk as the SUV was probably bugged.

They were led down a long corridor flanked by a military escort to an elevator. Everyone noticed that there were only two buttons on the elevators control panel, up and down, indicating a single destination only. The ride down was a long one. Wherever they were going, was a long way down, probably a nuclear hardened site.

When the door finally opened the trio realized that they had been transported in one of the most secure command and control centers of the US government.

The enormous room was bathed in the eerie light of giant computer screens perched high along the walls creating an intimidating environment for the uninitiated. At least a hundred workers in military uniforms could be seen in the darkened background. They were manning the yards of computer terminals crunching mega terabytes of incoming intelligence data. The room had a star wars quality about it.

Jeff, Amanda, and the professor were seated in the middle of the large oblong conference table spotlighted by an array of overhead LED lights. They looked like a small group of mice awaiting the slaughter.

Just then, the entourage of military brass came walking in almost in lock step.

"My name is Brigadier General Bernard Morgan, chairman of the Joint Chief of Staff. You have all been brought here at the President's request to discuss your involvement with a certain Leonard Spikes. We are currently holding Mr. Spikes, who has implicated you three, in what we believe to be a plot against the United States of America."

The General seemed somewhat diminutive for a man of his rank, self-assured and clearly trying to give the impression that he was posturing from a position of strength. He spoke with a slight southern drawl giving away his Virginia roots. From what Jeff could see, he was accompanied by two bird colonels, three lower officers, and two suit and tie types, probably CIA station chiefs. There were no welcoming smiles or pleasantries, only a play for intimidation, and domination of the circumstances.

Jeff glanced up from the table, nodded to the professor and Amanda, and addressed the General.

"Well general, first of all, the story that you're holding Spikes is bullshit .Nobody holds Leonard Spikes unless he wants to be held, which I doubt he does. Spikes can walk through your walls, disappear into thin air or with one look put every guard you have to sleep. Nothing you have can hold him. You probably know that already."

The General, visibly agitated, by this show of bravado turned to his subordinates then back to Jeff. He didn't want to lose control of the moment.

"I can tell you this Doctor. I can hold you and your friends for a very long time until I find out what I need to know."

Jeff wasn't about to give up an inch.

"Intimidation is not going to work. You need us. I know it and so do you, otherwise we wouldn't be here. The sooner we get some civility in this room the better we can begin to get to work."

Jeff got up from the table and started to slowly move around to the head of the table while addressing the group of government officials.

"Gentlemen, were all on the same side. I'm not even sure if there are any sides in the conventional sense. We're not the enemy, or your problem. We're part of the solution, so I suggest we start all over again and think about working together. You will treat us as partners and not as prisoners. Are we clear on that?"

The General nodded affirmative and barked, "Let's get some coffee in here."

"Ok Blake, I like your style. A badass with degrees. Kind of reminds me of myself. You're record shows that you demonstrated   courage under fire during your service to your country. I think we're going to get along just fine. I need you to tell me what you know about this character, Spikes, who seems to be going around spooking a lot of higher ups and stirring up a lot of crazy notions about some sort of cataclysmic event in our future. The President has asked us to investigate this matter and it's our job to get to the bottom of this."

Romilov stood up from the table and stared into the group assembled on the opposite side.

"Before we begin I have a question for you gentlemen. Do all of you posses an opened mind? Because if not, we are all wasting our time and it will be a very long day indeed. You must have the capacity to accept certain truths which, shall we say, defy conventional wisdom."

Just then, one of the suits and ties chimed in.

"My name in Gordon Pointdexter, director of the CIA. If you're asking us if we believe in extraterrestrials, we've been winking back and forth at them for over forty years. So let's move on from there right now. Do you think you can keep that a secret, at least, for now?"

Wow! Just like that. The first ever admission by a government official confirming the existence of extraterrestrials.

Fixing his gaze on the trio, Pointdexter continued.

"We know that almost every head of state, religious leader, influential media outlet, so on and so forth, has been visited in one way or another by this guy Spikes who goes by various names and assumes different identities. We know that he claims to represent some higher power and that he has come to warn us about some sort of danger. We know that he is able to communicate through dreams and represents himself as a friend. He wants us to believe that he does not pose a threat to us."

"Finally, we also know that he's the real McCoy. His powers real. Some of our best people who know, and investigate stuff like that, say it's real. His advanced knowledge, through what he calls his reveals in science, engineering, and just about everything else, are nothing short of astonishing. We're treating these reveals as classified and top secret."

Pointdexter looked at the others with a long and directed look. He then paused for a moment, as if to indicate his frustration with the whole issue. He had made a decision to stop beating around the bush and come clean with he wanted.

"What we don't know, is what he or they really want? What, where and when is this supposedly catastrophic event suppose to happen? Why doesn't he just wave his all powerful magic wand and do what he says he wants to do, just help us? Finally, why has he chosen you three to be major players? You're all accomplished in your own fields but with all due respect, just ordinary people."

As if almost on cue, Amanda got up and put her two hands on the table leaned in to the group and responded.

"Director Pointdexter, please allow this ordinary person to give you a woman's perspective. Try to consider for a moment the phrase "it is what it is." Mr. Spikes has always maintained that he came to help us. He has done nothing that would lead us to not believe him. Not a single thing. You have already acknowledged the existence of extraterrestrials. Then,

204

if so, why not the notion that they would want to help us? As to using his magic wand, he has always explained and emphasized over and over that he or they cannot interfere with our free will but can only point the way."

Her eyes gazed down and after a moment of contemplation looked up straight into the eyes of her audience.

"I have accepted what I consider to be the simple truth that we are not alone in the universe, that our neighbors had a significant hand in our development, and that they have developed, despite our considerable shortcomings, a protective role much like a mother over her children."

Looking over her shoulder at Jeff and the professor she added,

"When the time is right they will show us the way. It'll be up to us to choose to follow."

She folded her hands in front of her and sat back down.

"There you have it! You wanted my perspective, now you have it!"

"It is what it is."

There was a relative silence in the room as heads nodded in general agreement. Everyone got up and began to engage each other in conversation. The entire tone of the encounter seemed to change.

The meeting continued for another hour in a more informal atmosphere. Information and insights were exchanged and speculations discussed in earnest. Everyone agreed that the meeting had been productive. They agreed to keep close touch and communicate any new developments. The General apologized for all the cloak and dagger stuff and any anxiety it may have caused. Before leaving he quipped "Maybe we should have just called you guys instead."

Back on the helicopter it was just the trio and Rossi who couldn't wait to be alone by themselves. When the door closed Rossi released his seat belt buckle and moved closer.

"You guys were amazing!"

"Standing up to those stuffed shirts! I'm glad everything's out and in the open now. We're going to be a kick ass team."

Chapter 24

"WE are beginning our descent into Boston's Logan International airport and estimate our gate arrival time at 11.42 am."

Father Ryan looked out the window of the MD80 airliner and could see the wing flaps being lowered. He could feel the sensation of wind drag slowing the plane into a descent. The water of Boston Harbor was coming into view revealing tiny ships and fingerlike jetties projecting out into the sea. He carried the letter Pope Alexander had charged him with delivering to Jeffrey Blake. He fought to suppress the desire to know what the letter contained, but at the same time felt his strong obligation to keep faith with the task he had been given. He began to wonder why and how Jeff Blake played such an important role in the events unfolding. At the same time, he had confidence that, at some point, he would know what message the letter held.

Ryan's phone buzzed with the arrival of a text message from his assistant, Sister Ignatius, who he affectionately referred to as Aggie.

"Members of the group are calling for another meeting. Should I set one up?"

He sensed an urgency about the request and texted her back.

"Email the members and set it up as soon as possible."

Just then, he felt the jolt of the touchdown and the scream of reverse engines breaking the plane to a taxi. His Rome odyssey had ended.

It wasn't long before the meeting convened. Jeff and Amanda had decided to bring the professor and had given Ryan the heads up before the meeting. He gave them the green light and welcomed the professor to the meeting. On the way over, Jeff glanced at the rear view mirror and could see the professor sitting in the back seat deep in contemplation. Jeff turned briefly to Amanda who was sitting shotgun and said,

"Ok guys we need a plan. I say we keep quiet about the Langley thing. Before we go in there we need to decide what were willing to share. Any thoughts? Amanda?

"I say we share nothing. A lot has happened since the last meeting which we both thought was going to be the last. I'm not at all comfortable sharing what we now know with a bunch of strangers we hardly know at all. I say we keep quiet and listen. Maybe learn something we don't already know. There has to be something new for this meeting to have been called."

Jeff nodded in agreement. "Ok, we go in for fact finding only."

The professor, sitting in the back seat had a grin on his face.

"Don't worry. I promise to keep quiet and not give any lectures. But in case I forget, I give you both permission to kick me under the table!"

As usual Ryan was waiting outside at the door and greeting the members as they arrived. It was the same crew except for the senator John Mitchell was absent. Ryan welcomed Romilov and made sure the door was closed behind him.

"I want to start by introducing Professor Yuri Romilov, distinguished Russian molecular geneticist who recently sought political asylum here in America."

There was a light welcoming applause from the group.

"As some of you may know, I returned from Rome yesterday after visiting with the Holy Father. It was a fruitful meeting. However, I am not at liberty to report the details. Suffice it to say that His Holiness remains very engaged. Who would like to begin?"

Jessica Blumenthal of CNX got up. She posed quite a commanding figure dressed in her ON AIR designer suit and matching shoes.

"Lots of dark clouds are gathering in the Middle East. The mysterious illnesses of top Iranian officials continue with no improvement of those afflicted. More troubling are reports that the disease is beginning to spread to the population in general, especially affecting grade school children. Schools and parents are reported to be in a panic. There's a tight lid on the story by their state controlled media. Sources tell us that the Iranian government is beginning to think and suspect that this may be a biologic attack by the US. Rumors are spreading in our own intelligence that possibly a third party may have perpetuated an attack. Our people are thinking that the culprit might be ISIS engaging in a strategy to provoke a war between the Iranians and the West. I'm reporting on this story tonight. I didn't call for this meeting but thought I would come anyway thinking that someone in this group may have something to add."

Jeff raised his hand and stood up.

"Are there any numbers as to the death count thus far?"

"That's another interesting thing. No one seems to die from this condition but become seriously disabled by it. It becomes chronic with no improvement. Those affected seem to languish requiring long term care. Our sources again tell us that researches from China and Russia are working on it. They have isolated a peculiar virus which defies classification and hold out little hope of finding a vaccine. Other Arab nations are announcing travel restrictions. Our CDC has advised the white house of these developments and their holding a meeting with advisors as we speak."

The Rabbi got up next.

"Is that why this meeting was called? To hear about tonight's news a few hours ahead of time? Surely there has to be more.?

Looking around the room, Father Ryan asked, "Who was it that called for a meeting?"

Everyone looked at each other but no one took responsibility. Maybe whoever called the meeting had a reason to not come forth or maybe the meeting was called from someone outside the group who had knowledge of the group's existence.

Romilov spoke next and went off topic.

"Can you get me the names of the Russian scientist working on this problem? I know many of them. Maybe I can help."

"I'll do what I can." Blumenthal responded.

They exchanged cell phone numbers. It seemed that there was nothing else to talk about. All the members filed out in silence. Father Ryan motioned to Jeff to wait behind. Jeff told Amanda and the professor to go ahead and he would catch up.

"Dr Blake, I have a message from his Holiness that he asked me to give to you."

Father Ryan opened his black briefcase and handed Jeff the letter the Pope had given him to deliver. Blake was astounded that the Pope even had knowledge of him, let alone the fact that the Pope had sent him a message. Ryan fixed his gaze on Jeff.

"I want you to know that I have no idea what is contained in that letter. I was simply instructed to give it to you personally."

Jeff nodded his head as if to say thanks but resisted the temptation to get into a discussion with Ryan surrounding the circumstances of the letter. He placed the letter in his coat vest pocket and walked out the door in silence. He wondered whether or not he should open the letter in private or share it with the others when they get home. He opted for the former.

The ride home was quicker than normal. Traffic was whizzed along well on Storrow Drive, a sign that the Red Sox were playing an away game that night.

Amanda turned around to the professor.

"What did you think of the meeting? Did you think it productive or a waste of time?"

"A waste of time? I think not. On the contrary. I think that we three, were directed to be there. I think the meeting was called by our friend Spikes for our benefit. Maybe Jeffery will share with us what Father Ryan said to him when he asked him to stay behind. We learned about the spreading viral infection and the difficulties in finding a cure."

Romilov leaned in closer from the back seat.

"I, for one, took that as a personal call to action. A call to get involved. Remember, we have been given the Rosetta stone. It's the tool which could crack the genetic code of this strange virus and possibly lead to a breakthrough vaccine for this new and devastating malady. Think of the implications beyond the obviously humanitarian ones if we were able to affect a cure. Maybe we were given more than we think. Our Mr. Spikes works in mysterious ways."

Amanda turned and starred at Jeff.

"Well, what have you got to say?"

Jeff fidgeted for a moment and decided it was time to come clean now rather than wait until later.

"Yuri, I've gotta say that you're quite the perceptive fellow. I was going to wait but you are right. We were given a lot more. Ryan gave me a letter from the Pope which I have not opened yet. He told me he has no idea what it contains and I believe him. Ill open it when we get home.

Looking astonished Amanda turned to Jeff then to the professor.

"From the Pope! How does he know you?"

"He doesn't and I'm as amazed and as curious as you both are. I've never communicated in any way, shape or form with the Pope ever!"

"It's our friend Spikes. He's the connection. He's orchestrating this whole thing," said the professor leaning over the front seat.

The anticipation of opening the Papal letter was visible on the faces of the trio as they rushed into the apartment, removed their coats and sat down. Amanda grabbed a bottle of wine and poured three glasses. Jeff produced the letter and placed it on the coffee table. The rich and textured vellum of the envelope and red wax Papal seal on the back gave an heirloom quality to the object in front of them.

"Let me handle this." Amanda said, as she gently picked up the envelope. "I'll do the honors."

She carefully broke the seal so as not to tear the envelope, removed the letter, and handed it to Jeff. As Jeff unfolded the letter, three scapulas of the Blessed Virgin Mary fell out onto the coffee table. Amanda picked them up and held them in her hand. Jeff began to read.

"Dear Dr Blake,

"Although we have not yet met I feel as though I know you through our mutual friend, Mr. Spikes. He has told me that you posses a good heart and love for your fellow man. In addition,he has led me to believe that you have been blessed with strong moral values and a fine medical education, and also that you have dedicated yourself to finding a cure for the scourges that plague all of mankind. You have demonstrated both a courageous and compassionate heart during your life."

"It is my belief that our friend Mr. Spikes has come as an emissary of the Creator to save us from our own folly."

"The first time the Creator saved us, it was from original sin, and the power of the Evil One. He wanted our souls to be clean and contrite, so that we may join Him, for all eternity in the Kingdom of Heaven. The first time He sent his only son. This time, He sends our brothers and sisters."

"The Lord knows that I had my doubts. I'm sure you had your doubts also. Let me assure you that I have accepted what the Creator has directed us to do. I am asking you to do the same. You, and by extension your closest confidants, have been chosen to take up this most noble cause. It is a mission that cannot fail. You must prevail."

"Enclosed are three scapulas that I have personally blessed for you and your two closest allies. They will help and guide you. They will keep you safe. Wear them at all times. When all seems lost, hold and evoke their power."

"There will be a plague of biblical proportions that if left unchecked will engulf the whole world. You must find the cure and make it available to all who suffer. You must then reveal to all that the knowledge to accomplish such a feat came from a higher power. Mankind needs to understand that someone is looking after them and cares about their wellbeing and survival. They need to have hope, but there is more."

"It was revealed to me that there is a plot to cause an explosion in a critical area of the Yellowstone National Park. The aim is to trigger a major eruption of the super volcano which lies beneath the park. A similar event took place over 600,000 years ago and devastated two thirds of North America."

"When the terrorists who brought down the World Trade Center on 9/11 crashed the planes into the buildings, they had no idea, nor did they expect, the two giant towers to actually collapse. When they did collapse, it was a unexpected bonus for them and their evil cause. This time, they again, know not what they do."

"It seems that the plotters do not know that, deep beneath the Volcano, there is a fissure that reaches all the way to the Earth's core. The explosion and eruption could force shocks to the center, resulting in the entire Earth fracturing into fragments and hurling all of humanity into the oblivion of space."

"It would mean the end of our planet and millions of years of evolution by the hand of the Creator. This cannot be allowed to happen. I believe this plan of destruction and extinction is inspired by The Prince of Darkness himself. I have been assured that the evil plan is in the very beginning of the planning phase. There is still time to thwart the evil deed. You must prevail. You three cannot fail. The Graces to succeed have been bestowed upon you."

Jeff folded the letter and carefully placed it back into the envelope. He turned toward Amanda and handed her the letter.

"Tomorrow, bring this to the bank. Get a safety deposit box with three keys and three signature cards. Then call Rossi and tell him it's time to talk."

Chapter 25

David Misner had just settled in to his morning routine at GenOnc when Alan Brodsky called to report his preliminary findings on the computer hacking of lab data.

"So David, as far as I can see, it seems that you were right about there being more data than before the hack. Nothing has been removed or transferred. Instead, there's evidence that some pretty complex mathematical formulations have been added in different locations of the DNA sectional input points, almost as if to point the way, or suggest applying them precisely at a certain point. Whoever did this had a sophisticated knowledge of both math and how you guys study DNA. You need to find someone who's really good at math to figure out these formulations. Its way above my pay grade. If you want, I can take the math formulas out and list them in a separate file for you guys to play with."

"No, don't do that! They need to stay exactly where they are. I'll find math whiz to do as you suggested."

"Oh, there's one more thing." Brodsky said. There's an embedded program running in the background that seems to know exactly where to stick in the formulations. I have no idea what that's all about."

A subtle smile spread across Misners face as he realized the implications of what Brodsky's work had found. He remembered the story that Jeff had told him, about the encounters with Spikes and at that moment felt the chill you get when you realize that something really creepy may have just happened. He tried not to believe that maybe the hack was not an inside job but instead the work of Spikes inserting a little help into the project. After everything Jeff had told him it seemed the most plausible explanation.

"I love you man! I really owe you one!" David told Brodsky.

"No probelema, just remember to tell the boss what a gifted IT geek I am."

"Will do, you can count on it!"

"Come on, answer!" Misner whispered under his breath as he desperately tried to reach Jeff on his cell. "I need you to answer now."

Finally, the call went through and Jeff picked up.

"Get down here as soon as you can. Brodsky came back with his analysis of what happened in the hack and I'm beginning to believe the crazy stuff you told me about your buddy, that Spikes fella."

"I'm actually on my way there now. Amanda and the professor are with me. We've got a lot of work to do. See you in a few minutes."

The trio arrived and was quickly whisked into conference room two. Misner was pleased to finally meet the professor, a man he had heard so much about. The exchange of information went quickly between the four people who understood the same language. Jeff needed to brief David.

"David, we've been given a new task. Surely you've heard about what's going on in the Middle East. I have it on good intelligence that this illness is going to spread rapidly beyond the region. It's going to be our job to find the cure. There'll be no time to screw around with time consuming protocols and all that crap. We're going to have to break some rules. We need answers fast. I need you to call your connections at the CDC a get samples of the virus already isolated from the victims."

"I've already done that." David answered with a subtle smile on his face.

"How the hell did you know to do that?"

Looking down at the table and then up at Jeff's eyes he answered,

"I had a dream."

Smiles broke out in silence over everybody's face. Amanda took David's hand.

"You're one of us now."

David moved his glasses up over his forehead and looked directly at Amanda.

"I don't want to be one of you. I'm perfectly happy being one of me."

"Show me the math formulations that Brodsky found, "said Amanda as they all huddled around the computer monitor. Let me see if I can make some sense of them."

As David brought the first formula up on the screen Amanda began to furiously write notations in math speak , that funny language math people write on blackboards, that makes everyone else feel stupid, but at the same time, so grateful that you never had to learn it.

Her face lit up. "Oh my God, this is so cool. So genius in its simplicity!"

"Are you going to tell us what you're thinking or do we have to wring it out of you?" said the professor as he gently rubbed her back in a circular motion.

"Ok, it has to do with that CRSPER technology you explained to me before. It's an instructional command. First it contains a mathematical map of the entire genome with numbers for each position of a gene connection found in sequence. They number in the trillions. Then, it tells you the exact location where the same substitution must be performed in order for the whole thing to function. I guess if a gene(s) is removed and substituted, let's say, in position X, then the same substitution needs to be made in other locations for the genetic message to stay in sync."

David rolled his chair back and stretched out. Putting both hands behind his head he seemed to be looking up at the ceiling in disbelief.

"This is the Holy Grail of genetic engineering! It moves us ahead at least fifty years!"

The professor had tears in his eyes. Jeff began to clap his hands in a manic display of joy.

"Between this and the Rosetta Stone key there will be virtually nothing we can't do!" He said. "We're gonna cure cancer!"

David shot a quick glance over at Jeff.

"What Rosetta Stone?"

Jeff caught himself. Oh nothing, something crazy, something I'll tell you about later. Did I just say something that sounded like a freaking mad scientist? Please forgive me."

The others smiled in agreement and a little in disbelief of Jeff's display of emotion. It seemed a bit out of character but again the whole scenario was like something out of a movie and not real.

At the same moment they realized that this knowledge can be used for evil as much as it can be used for good. How is a technology like this kept secure from those who use it to create a biological weapon capable of destroying crops or deadly disease that could bring about man s extinction? Unscrupulous use of this knowledge could produce an abomination of life forms completely upending the balance of nature.

The mood in the room changed from elation to somber. They knew that they had been given a gift that they were not ready to handle, a responsibility too heavy to bear.

"Where is Spikes now when we need him?" said Amanda. "We need direction. We need him to show us how to protect this knowledge. Sooner or later it will get out. When it does, the consequences could be catastrophic."

They all set out at the task at hand. Samples if the virus arrived from the CDC and they wasted no time in putting all there procedures in motion. The revelations could not be shared with the staff and access to the computer output data was controlled. Only input data was allowed. Brodsky was called in to create dual programs with sensitive formulations removed. One designed for general consumption and the other containing the formulas included for certain eyes only. Amanda and the professor took up a full time presence at GenOnc and requested leave of absence from their other obligations. The employees were told that the new additions to the staff were brought in to work on a new top-secret government project with security clearance for only a few. It was a full court press to find the vaccine.

There was only one loose end, David Misner. He was at the wrong place at the wrong time.

Supper time at the Blake household was becoming kind of a ritual where everyone had a job to do. Amanda was the executive chef with the final word on all matters culinary, Jeff, the souse chef, doing the chopping and mixing, and the professor put in charge of the wine. Clearing the table was a collaborative chore. A new little family had formed on Dwight Street. They all got along. They accepted each other's idiosyncrasies and had become harmonious in their now common mission.

"You did it again, Amanda."

"And what would that be Dr Romilov?

"Created a simple, yet delicious, and might I add, healthy dinner."

Jeff brought over the coffee tray, placed it on the table in front of the professor and moved toward Amanda standing at the sink

"Even though that's true, you're going to give her a big head with all the compliments you give her all the time." came Jeff's comment, as he placed his arms around Amanda's waist and smooched the back of her neck causing the professor to look the other way.

"It's time I found my own place to live. You love birds don't need this old man hanging around getting in the way of your private moments."

"Private moments? I love that," Amanda said while looking directly at Jeff. "Professor, please tell this wonderful man that we need more private moments!"

Then, turning her attention back to professor,

"Don't be silly. There's plenty of time for that. You just got here, and beside, Dr Blake needs to hear those words and profound insights from a distinguished gentleman such as yourself."

Jeff with his hands still on Amanda's waist Jeff looked up smiling.

"Ok, Ok. I get it. I yield to the consensus. I'm the lucky one and I know it."

The banter of the evening settled down and the professor was getting ready to go to his room as was his custom. Spring was well on its way and the days were getting longer. The lingering light delayed the sense of day's end. Jeff made the decision to bring up the subject that was on everyone's mind that evening rather than wait for the next day to discuss it. He motioned to the professor to wait up a minute.

"There's an issue we need to resolve and I know we've all been thinking about it. I think it better that we discuss it now rather than tomorrow."

"And what issue might that be. Said the professor.

"What to do about David Misner?" Amanda said.

Jeff walked over to the window and started thinking out loud.

"He's a good man, a brilliant and dedicated scientist , he's someone I could trust with just about anything."

Looking over at Amanda he continued.

"But I don't think he was supposed to be there when you started to explain the meanings of the formulations." Amanda looked up at Jeff.

224

"I know you're right. I was so excited when I saw the breakthrough I blurted everything out without thinking. I realized what I had done almost the instant I did it."

The professor took the last sip of his favorite after dinner drink, the hazelnut liqueur, Frangelico, placed the glass on the table, and made a sigh.

"I agree. I like and respect David very much, both as a brilliant scientist and as a human being. But remember, that we three, and we three only, entered into a covenant, to protect and pass down these secrets and powerful reveals in a slow and step like fashion to future generations, and only when they are deemed ready to accept them. We are the temporary keepers for now, a great responsibility. Rest assured that our benefactors will appoint generations of keepers after we are gone. We pledged to use them only to advance and alleviate suffering, to never take credit for their wisdom, but instead make sure that credit be given to our benefactors so that people know that they are not alone in their struggles and never lose hope. I say that for now we do nothing. Not to worry. I am confident that this situation with Dr Misner will be resolved with the help of our friend."

The work to identify the genomic pattern of the Middle Eastern virus, under the direction of David Misner, was progressing well. Professor Romilov, with his experience using the gene insertion technology of CRSPER, was given the job of getting everything ready for gene insertion and substitution. Amanda and Jeff had the task of decoding the formulations and locating the exact location of gene insertion and substitution. Dividing the project into compartments insured that their work, using the secret math formulations, could be kept from the others.

Reports of the virus spreading through the Middle East were becoming more frequent and demonstrations against the West more violent. The Mullahs seemed convinced that they were under a biologic attack from the West despite pleas from western leaders to the contrary. Offers of international help from the West were summarily rejected and sabers were rattling.

Misner called a meeting with the labs inner circle to discuss the projects progress.

"Well, I have to tell you guys that I have never seen a project move ahead so quickly. Yesterday, we tested the first batch of vaccine on live virus and we're still waiting to see one particle replicate."

He then focused his remarks directly to Amanda and the professor.

"I thought I knew something about CRSPER, but the gene substitutions and locations you guys submitted were spot on, in the first batch. That should of taken months of trial and error, and in the end, resulted in a one or two percent success rate at best. I don't know how you're doing it, but however it is, don't change a thing. Truly remarkable work, congratulations."

Amanda, Jeff and the Professor looked at each other with disbelief that David would make such a statement. He knew about the secret formulations and had himself declared that they had pushed up the research by fifty years. What was going on?

226

"Maybe you'll let me in on your methods when this is all over." David said.

The Professor took the lead, and put on his fatherly persona. He walked up behind David and put his hand on David's shoulder.

"Back at the Institute we developed some tricks to speed things along. Don't worry David, I'll let you all in on it when this project is over."

It was clear that Spikes had worked his magic again!

Chapter 26

The full moon cast its glow over the ocean white caps producing a shimmering light show. The moons eerie glow dimly lit the small stretch of sand just north of Cannon Beach. Oregon's coastline is famous for its majestic rocky beauty and this night was living up to its reputation.

The chosen location had a small but sturdy wooden walking bridge leading from the dirt access road to the sandy beach. A black van was backed up to the beginning of the walkway with its back doors wide open, waiting in silence.

Mustafa al Homsi waited on the beach sitting on a small blue cooler. Dressed in his LLBean dark green field jacket, jeans and hiking boots, he blended in with the mostly upscale gentrified types common to the area. Underneath the jacket was his Oregon State University tee shirt. The binoculars slung around his neck gave him the look of any other college senior majoring in photography wanting to make an artistic nighttime moonlit ocean shot. In his wallet, next to his driver's license was an Oregon State University student ID card with his picture. The name printed on the card was Miguel Hormosa. Miguel, a former student at Oregon, had died two years earlier in an auto crash but his information was still available on Facebook for anyone to steal.

The cooler was your standard WalMart variety containing two, of all things, ham sandwiches, and a cardboard four pack of supermarket Gallo red wine. Next to Mustafa, a tripod with a professional grade camera was set up. Fifteen feet to his right, sitting on a rock, and out of sight in darkness was his Glock 45 loaded with a fifteen round clip. Next to that, a small handheld Geiger counter and tablet computer.

Before settling in for what could be a long wait, he walked one more time along the small perimeter of this sandy spot with his tactical flashlight lighting the way. He was making sure there was no one around or approaching. He felt secure that his cover as an amateur student photographer taking panorama night shots was believable. He visited this spot at the same hour seven nights in a row. This gave him confidence that no one was likely to be strolling by. If he was wrong there was always plan B.

The repetitive sound of the waves and flickering moonlight had a hypnotic effect. Mustafa began to dose off. It had been a long and tiring ride from Big Springs, Idaho followed by seven sleepless nights surveying the landing site. He found a place to stay in Big Springs. It was a trailer park. The kind of place where no one talks to each other and everyone minds their own business. It was a one-hour drive to one of Yellowstone's most popular attractions and near the site that Bernadi, the geologist, recommended for placement of the bomb.

Just then, bright intermittent flashes of light came across the water from about fifty yards off shore grabbing his attention. He sprung to attention, glancing around quickly and making sure he was alone. He picked up his flashlight and began responding to the signals with multiple signaling flashes of his own. Next, he grabbed the Glock, stuck it the back part of his belt under his jacket and headed toward the water's edge.

The long awaited delivery was about to become a reality. Even this evil bastard himself, couldn't believe that a former aspiring religious teacher and community activist was so far away from home in a foreign land. He was convinced that his way of life and religion were under attack and that his role as defender of the faith had been preordained. It was a battle in his mind that had grown to consume him. What he didn't know, was the cruel and simple fact, that no one in America actually gave a shit about him or his religion.

A shiny moonlit object bobbing on the water was getting closer and closer. As it approached, it became clear, it was a large stainless steel box sitting atop a black inflatable raft. Four heavily armed men in black frog men scuba suits were guiding the cargo into shore. They were definitely military.

230

The two in the back of the raft were walking back sideways with their weapons pointed to the side and behind making sure those areas were clear of any threats. The ones in front concentrated the barrels of their automatic rifles toward the shoreline.

Mustafa approached them and put his right hand flat against his chest. He bowed his head in the traditional gesture common of a Muslim greeting.

Before he could utter a word, one of the two men in the front grabbed him by the neck with a powerful grip, forceful enough to cut off his air supply. At the same time the man gripped Mustafa's right wrist with a quick downward motion, violently pinning him to the ground. Mustafa found himself weak and defenseless, desperately fighting for air. It was quite the role reversal for a vicious monster who relished his power over the life and death of others.

While the first frogman held him down, the second conducted a body search for weapons. They found the Glock and tossed it aside. They pulled off their goggles revealing menacing Asian faces.

Finally, after what seemed like an eternity, Mustafa began to feel the grip around his neck loosening. His face was a dusky blue from lack of oxygen.

"Are you alone?" The Korean said, in clear and commanding, heavily accented English, as his comrades stood guard.

Coughing and sputtering after a near strangulation, Mustafa forced out a response.

"We are alone. My name is..."

His attempt to give his name was immediately cut short.

"I don't give a shit who you are. You were given a code. Give it to me now or I'll kill you right here."

Mustafa struggled to reach inside the side pocket of his jacket. His captor grabbed his hand pulling it out still clutching a folded piece of paper. The paper read CGxT4Z7cY.

The leader let go of Mustafa's neck and stepped back.

Mustfa was clearly shaken. He got up from the ground covered in sand. He brushed himself off while trying to regain his composure. He was not accustomed to being ruffed up and humiliated. He struggled to keep his cool. He wanted to grab his gun and kill them all but resisted the urge, in favor of not risking the mission.

"Complete the transaction!" Yelled the leader.

"Show me the goods!" Mustafa yelled back showing his indignation and then mumbling in Arabic. "You infidel pieces of shit."

The men hauled the box onto the sand and removed the shrink-wrap it had been sealed in. Using a Phillips head screwdriver the top panel was removed revealing a black heavy lead cast container with a digital coded lock on the top lid. Mustafa kept one hand high in a "don't shoot" gesture as he slowly retrieved the Geiger counter and brought it over the container.

Turning it on, it registered only a small amount of normal environmental background radioactivity. He then entered the code from the paper he had placed back in his coat pocket.

The front panel popped open and the sound of a hard drive whirling started up. Complex wiring leading to an array of colored LED lights came alive as if to say, "I'm waking up. What do you want me to do now?"

The inside top panel of the unit had detailed schematics with Korean characters. He waved the Geiger counter again over the guts of the device and watched as the needle jumped off the dial. A red warning light lit up, and the Geiger sounded a high pitched shrill warning sound, indicating a large degree of radiation detected.

The Korean bent over, reached into the box and pressed a button on the left hand side of the unit that shut the whole thing down. He held a flashlight in Mustafa's face.

"Opening the lid automatically starts whatever sequence you programmed it for. Once the sequence begins the device cannot be stopped even with the pass code. It has not been programmed yet, so I was able to shut it down."

The Korean handed Mustafa a military style computer tablet.

"The bomb is armed by contacting it via a cellular connection using this tablet. Once the contact has been established, the line remains open, waiting for whatever detonation code you set up. Then, it can then be remotely detonated from anywhere in the world using a cell phone. This tablet connects to a Chinese communication satellite that leaves no IP address. It is important that there be a strong cellular connection on both ends for the device to receive the instructions you send it. There are coding instructions inside written in English. There is a CD in the sleeve behind the tablet that will enable you the make arming dry runs to be sure you get it right. Try not to blow us all up until we are at a safe distance in about twelve hours."

"How crazy was that?" Mustfa thought to himself. "An instruction manual for a nuclear bomb!"

Mustafa looked up at the Korean and smiled knowing that this was the real deal, a small self-contained nuclear device. Maybe the first of its kind. It was purported to be powerful enough to take out a medium size city, but of course he had bigger plans.

The Korean nodded at Mustafa.

"Ok, are you satisfied?"

Mustafa nodded back "yes."

The Korean produced a hand held tablet outfitted with a satellite antenna and handed it to Mustafa.

"Transfer the money."

Mustafa had made a deal with the North Korean regime to purchase the device for 25 million US dollars. He entered the codes to a Swiss bank account authorizing the transfer of payment to a secret account held by the North Korean regime. Hundreds of coded numbers scrolled down the screen in a rapid pace suddenly stopping with the words TRANSFER COMPLETED flashing.

The Korean shouldered his weapon. "Now we wait."

They all waited in awkward silence, the only sound being the eternal rhythmic sound of the ocean water lapping the shore. After what seemed like an eternity, the Korean's satellite phone rang. A long exchange occurred between the

Korean his presumed superior, with the Korean repeatedly nodding his head in the affirmative. Then holding the phone to one side he looked at Mustafa.

"His Excellency, the Supreme Leader, sends you his personal congratulations for a successful mission and wishes you success in the struggle against our common enemy."

Without another word spoken the leader turned, put his face gear back on, and together with his men disappeared into the dark ocean waters.

Mustafa struggled to get the heavy device into the van. He gave thanks to Allah for the wooden bridge over the sand which made moving the heavy delivery much easier. He performed a perimeter inspection of the van making sure that everything was in order, nothing had been left behind, and that all exterior lights were functioning well.

 The last thing he needed was a routine traffic stop for a burned out light. Next, he ran the Geiger counter around the van checking for any radiation exposure that might be detected. There was none. He had heard that homeland security had vehicles outfitted with radiation detectors and he was taking no chances.

The drive back to Big Springs was over eight hundred miles. Mustafa knew that he would have to get some sleep after the long night on the road. Getting the van containing the nuke back to his base of operation undetected was the next challenge. He rationalized that there would be less highway patrol on duty during the night shift. He knew what he would have to do if stopped and was ready with a deadly plan of action. No one could be allowed to search the van. His plan for the trip back was to spend only one day in a motel. The least conspicuous the motel, the better.

The sun began to rise over middle Oregon casting a beautiful burst of color over the sharp ridge peaks that lined the highway. It had been over five hours since Mustafa had left the Oregon coast. He had been careful to set the cruise control to five miles per hour below the speed limit. He had set the odometer to zero before setting off. It now read 392 miles. He was almost half way home and to relative safety when he spotted a sign reading, "Mesa Motel, Ten miles, free internet." It was time to find a place to crash and get something to eat but most of all, a few hours of precious sleep.

The Mesa was your typical middle of nowhere run down and forgotten highway motel. It was a throwback to the late fifties before the interstate highway system was built. These now iconic "motor hotels "dotted the landscape. Next door, within walking distance, was a small freestanding store with a sign that read "Steaks and Good Eats." Two old fashioned pumps with crank up flow starters dispensed a no name brand gasoline.

There was only one other car parked in front of the motel tagged with New Jersey plates. The parking lot extended to the back. Mustafa made sure to take a slow ride around the back. He noticed that there was only one small blue Toyota pickup truck with Idaho plates, probably belonging to the one only motel employee on duty at the time. More importantly, there were no cameras anywhere. He noticed that the back parking lot abutting the building was shaded at that time of day. He parked the van in the back so it wouldn't be visible from the

236

road. He grabbed his shoulder bag and walked around to the front office.

The check in desk area was small and dingy with papers scattered about.

Old sun bleached yellow wallpaper lined the walls with a portrait of President Trump hanging in a prominent place. Even at the presence of a new visitor, the old black Lab retriever lying on the floor, soundly sleeping, never stirred. A No Vacancy sign was propped up against the wall behind the desk. There were no surveillance cameras anywhere. No computer screens, only an old-fashioned register book.

"Welcome to the Mesa Motel. The names Jack. I'll be your motel clerk today if you need anything. Looking to stay with us a spell?"

Mustafa was taken aback a bit. Jack was wearing camouflage pants, sand colored military boots, and your standard issue US army tee shirt. He had seen his fair share of young US soldiers back in his homeland. He needed a split second to gain his composure and respond in a nonchalant way to this simple inquire.

"Yes, I've been driving all night. I am tired and need a place to get some rest for the day. Looks like you've got plenty of empty rooms available."

"Yup, right now you've got pretty much the whole place for yourself. It picks up on the weekend but I will admit, it's quiet around these parts. Mister, I guarantee you can get all the rest you need."

"We get sixty nine dollars a night plus tax and that includes cable TV with premium channels. Check out time is ten thirty in the morning. Oh, and included, is this here coupon for a free breakfast in the morning right next door. I'll need an ID to register. Will that be cash or credit?"

Mustafa reached into his pocket and produced a crinkled fist full of twenties and tens. He handed the clerk the Oregon State University ID card with his name and picture on it.

Handing him back his ID, the clerk glanced up with a grin on his face.

"Ok, Mr. Miguel Hormosa, you're all set. Hope you have a good rest now."

Mustafa kept his gaze on the clerk,

"I parked my van in the back out of the sun. Is that ok?"

Handing Mustafa the key to room 16 he said,

"No problem. It'll be safe back there. Do you need a hand with any of your stuff?"

"No, I'm good."

He wondered why the clerk would be offering him help. The Mesa wasn't the type of place that helped you with your bags. Their clientele weren't the types who needed or expected it. He sensed that something wasn't right with the cheerful and helpful clerk.

Maybe he wasn't as dim witted as he sounded or looked. Maybe he wanted to get a look inside the van?

Questions began to swirl in his mind. Had the clerk served in the Middle East? Had his Middle Eastern accent betrayed his fake identity?

238

Paranoia began to sink in.

Mustfa began to obsess and think, " of all the shitty dirt bag motels along this route I had to pick the one with the ex military suspicious son of a bitch." The need to sleep was becoming stronger but also the worry that his mission had possibly been compromised.

On his way to room 16 he noticed that the owner of the last remaining car in the front lot with the New Jersey plates was packing his bags in the trunk and leaving.

He opened the door to room 16 and tried not to look at the bed that looked so inviting. The room was neat and clean. The air was heavy with a slight musty smell. He found the window air conditioner and turned it on to high. With the door wide open it helped to push the heavy room air out. The combination of sleep deprivation and that bed became too much to resist. After closing the door, he plopped down on the bed fully clothed and succumbed to sleep.

The loud roar of an unmistakable Harley engine racing down the highway just outside the motel woke him. A quick glance at his watch revealed that he has slept for a little over four hours. He got up and made his way into the bathroom. The bathroom was clean with a nice shower, tub and fresh towels.

Standing in front of the toilet he started to take a piss and in that moment of solitude tried to clear his mind. He looked up at the small window directly in front of him that looked out and on to the back parking lot. There was Jack, the clerk, standing behind his van with a pad in his hand copying down the plate number.

239

Mustafa's eyes went dark. He rushed back into the bedroom and retrieved his bag. He opened the bag, removed his 45cal Glock, and methodically screwed on a black silencer. He moved the slide back chambering a round and then stuck the gun in the back of his belt under his jacket.

Jack was still behind the van when he was confronted by Mustafa.

"What are you doing?"

Jack looked up and smiled.

"Oh, I'm sorry. I forgot to ask you for your tag number. The law requires that were supposed to do it for every guest then record it in the motel register. I really just started here. I'll catch hell from the owner if I mess up."

Mustafa began nervously looking around making sure there was no one around.

"No problem. It's important you do your job well. You know, I've decided to take you up on your offer to help with my stuff."

Mustafa opened the tailgate doors.

"I've got this heavy box in the back. I wonder if you'd help me move it toward the edge here. Need to get some stuff out. I'm nursing a bad back and well, as long as you're offering, I'll take you up on it."

"My pleasure Sir. My Dads got a bad back and I help him all the time with stuff like that. Better be safe than sorry."

He motioned for Jack to go in first and take the front end of the box.

When Jack reached the deep rear of the van the killer drew his gun and without a moment's hesitation fired two rounds into the young man's back. Jack slumped forward.

The killer quickly jumped into the van and dragged the dead clerk's body out and on to the parking lot surface as fast as he could. He wanted to minimize the amount of blood in the van. Taking a breath, he took one last look in the van before closing the doors. Good job he thought. Very little blood to clean up.

Looking down at his victim, he retrieved the note pad with his tag number on it and stuffed it in his jacket pocket. For insurance, he fired one last round through the back of young Jacks head and made sure to pick up the three shell casings. He left Jacks body on the back parking lot and rushed around to the front of the building.

He looked around again to double check for cameras. No cameras anywhere. He was alone. He put on surgical gloves that he always carried in his travel bag. He dashed into the office and hung the no vacancy sign in the window. He ransacked the office to make it look like a robbery had taken place. He grabbed the cash, the motel register, and a .38cal sub nose revolver he found in the desk drawer. He placed the key to room 16 back on the room key rack, went outside, got back into the van, and drove off.

At Jacks burial the minister gave an inspiring eulogy telling all who had gathered how Jack had just enlisted in the Army to fulfill his lifelong dream of serving in the US military. That was never to be. Jack had the misfortune of meeting the enemy right here at home.

Chapter 27

Jeff had been summoned back to Langley under escort to report on progress being made on the vaccine. Amanda and the professor would stay behind this time to focus on the work which was a top priority.

They would be sending a car for the ride to Hanscome Field in Bedford Massachusetts to pick up the helicopter. From there he would fly to CIA headquarters in Langley Virginia, just outside of Washington. Agent Rossi would be present at the meeting.

After the landing, the car ride to Langley seemed longer than the last one Jeff remembered. Maybe because there was no banter from the escorts, only an official cold military silence the whole way.

As they approached one of the multiple entryways to the post, Jeff noticed that this particular checkpoint was much more secure than the previous one he, Amanda, and the professor had entered.

It consisted of a three-stage process. The first was examination of the usual credentials and inspection of the occupants in the car. The second was a thorough inspection of the vehicle including the under carriage. In the third step the occupants were put through an airport scanner then waited outside in a glassed off secured area guarded by armed personal standing in a three tiered formation.

Jeff turned to one of the uniformed escorts.

"What are they doing now with that gizmo?"

"That is the vehicle authenticator. We're driving a secured vehicle with a coded processor that is encrypted with identifying codes linked to our ID badges and the vehicle itself. Before the vehicle leaves the garage it is given mission number and ID codes that only the computer knows. Prevents anyone from duplicating the vehicle and tampering with it. It also automatically scans for bugs or munitions.

"Why all the extreme security?"

"You'll see when we get there."

They got back in the car and drove into a garage almost as big as an aircraft hangar. Everyone got out. Jeff noticed more than one black limo bearing diplomatic plates. The limos were surrounded by armed guards wearing dark suits. These guys were clearly not our guys.

Jeff was led down a long dark corridor to elevator doors that could be opened only by finger print identification scan.

When they got in, there were to more print scanners marked M and D. Directing the elevator once inside required a different authorized print be scanned than the one used to open the door. They were going to M floor.

The ride down was a lot longer than a few floors. When the door opened Jeff understood why the security was so tight.

There were four obvious Arab heads of state accompanied by their male secretaries. Jeff recognized General Pointdexter and agent Rossi who quickly came over to greet him and took him by the arm.

"Hey Doc, so nice to see you. Don't let all this spook you. We heard you're close to finding a cure for that Blue Dot thing and these big wigs are here to negotiate."

"Negotiate what?"

"You'll see. Have a seat over here." Rossi said as he pulled up a seat for Jeff.

Just then, President Steven Cabot, the nation's 53r^d President entered the room. In unison the entire American contingent jumped up and stood at attention out of respect for the office and the man. Cabot had come up through the military as a distinguished Air Force fighter pilot before becoming a U S senator from Oklahoma.

The President quickly took charge and motioned everyone to take a seat.

"Before we begin, let me introduce to you all Dr Jeffery Blake who is directing the research into this mysterious illness."

He paused then slowly lifted his eyes staring directly at the heads of state assembled before him.

244

"Many of you have fallen victim to the rumors that this calamity has been engineered by the CIA as a weapon to destabilize your government. I am here to tell you, that nothing could be further from the truth."

The President was interrupted by a loud bang on the table as an angry Atwan Imani, envoy from Iran, jumped up from the table.

"What about the dreams driving some of our leaders to go mad? I supposed you had nothing to do with that either! Our patience is running out. I am telling you Mr. President, either you control your people, or we will act in a most forceful manner!"

Jeff stood up and faced Imani directly, pointing his finger and red faced with frustration.

"When are you people, yes I said , you people, going to understand that this is not about you, but about all of us, all of humanity."

The President raised his voice, "Everyone settle down, or we won't accomplish anything."

The lights in the room began to flicker as if to signal that something was about to happen. Everyone was looking around the room in silence. The smell of ozone began to permeate the air The lights went very dim. Only the table was illuminated in a pale yellow glow against a dark background.

The room was becoming gripped in an eerie panic. The participants could feel their bodies becoming heavy...so heavy that they were unable to move. They were stuck in their chairs with their hands glued to the table palms down.

A small ORB of blue light got brighter and larger as it approached the table finally morphing into a figure of a man dressed in traditional long flowing gandorra, a garment worn by men in the Arabic world. Everyone's eyes were fixed on this strange specter. As he came closer Jeff could see that it was Leonard Spikes sporting his characteristic grin albeit it more subtle.

"Well, well, well, it seems that I finally have all of your attention. Many of you know who I am. For those of you who don't , let me introduce myself. I am your friend. I am the same friend that brought you the dreams, the same friend that brought you the condition affecting your most precious possession, your children. Forgive me, but I had to get your attention."

A long pause followed. One by one he made glancing eye contact with each of them and then continued.

"I am the same friend who has advanced your technology to bring you all a better life.

"I am the friend who offers you all a second chance, to not suffer the consequences of your own selfish folly. I am, in short, the best friend you will ever have...that is, of course if you permit me."

As he spoke he continued to slowly move around the table with a fluid like motion, looking at each one in the eye with a deep and penetrating gaze, that seemed to reach into their very soul.

"Let me tell you who I am not."

"I am not your God. You know him by different names. I am not the Creator. The same Creator who created you, created me. The time has come for you to step back from the evil that tricks you into believing that you are more than just a tiny grain of sand in the cosmos. Rejoice instead, that you have been given the precious gift of life. If you fail to step back from the evil that makes you love yourself more than your children, and your fellow man, a great sorrow will befall you all."

"You see, it is the evils plan to lead you into self destructive folly using the fatal flaw you all share...a flaw called Pride. The choice will always be yours but Pride is a powerful flaw embedded in each and every one of you. It drives you to believe that somehow you are better, stronger, smarter or more entitled than others around you."

"In reality, consider for a moment that you were all created equally and that only through a series of random circumstances of birth, life experiences and privilege, were you led you to your current station in life. Hard to believe or accept, isn't it? Try to imagine who you would be today had you been born to a different mother, or in a different place, or of a different race. Life is not a straight line but a series or twists and turns around events that can cause profound changes in direction. An illness or accident, a missed opportunity, a chance encounter. The most mundane occurrence has the power to change everything. Only when you strip away the flaw of pride can you begin to understand how ordinary you all are, and be grateful for the privilege you have all been given. Don't misunderstand my remarks.

Rejoice in your personal accomplishments. They are worthy of recognition and personal pride."

"Let me give you a glimpse of your future if you choose not to heed my warnings and continue on the same path."

He positioned himself behind each one sitting at the table. They were all still silent and unable to move. He placed his hands on their shoulders producing a glow around each one.

They shook with fear at the site of personal scenes and sounds of horrific death and destruction of their families and their world. They shut their eyes tight trying to black out the images but to no avail. When it was over Spikes commanded them to open their eyes and focus on what would be his final words of the encounter.

"I am sorry to disappoint you all, who have gathered for a report and a negotiation. You have had your report but there will be no negotiation today."

Pointing to Jeff Blake he said, "Under my direction the doctor and his cohorts are making good progress in developing a vaccine that will bring your children back to health. This is my gift to you."

He slowly moved his extended arm over the entire group.

"None of you can take credit for this discovery which eludes your most gifted scientists. Your citizens must know and believe that this gift has come from a higher power. Use your creative abilities to come up with a suitable but truthful explanation. I promise you that failing to carry out my wishes will make the vaccine ineffective. The blame for all the sorrow that will follow will be on your shoulders for all to see."

Slowly, the specter of Spikes began to transform into an amorphous ORB of light that vanished into the darkened background. The captive grip loosened eventually freeing everyone. Mobility was restored. All were visibly shaken, looking at each other in a way that confirmed that they had all shared the same experience.

President Cabot regained his composure and somberly addressed the group.

"Well, I guess there is not much left to say. We have all seen and heard from our mysterious visitor. I recommend we take this opportunity to put our differences aside and heed the warning."

The members quietly nodded mumbling to each other. They were led out of the room and into the elevators. Rossi motioned to Jeff to wait up.

"Dr Blake, I'll meet you by the holding area. We need to get out of here and grab a beer. There's some stuff I need to talk out with you. I'll get you back home by tonight. Enough crazy shit for one day!"

Governors Grill, located just nine miles from Langley, looked like your usual upscale pub except for the fact that on any given day probably half the well-dressed patrons were packing heat. It was a favorite hangout for NSA and CIA middle level operatives. It was a busy lunchtime crowd and Rossi looked around checking for anyone he might know. Rossi chose a corner table away from the bar and away from most of the action. The waitress came over.

"What can I get you guys?"

"A double shot of Dewar's. Then bring a 16oz Guinness with the biggest, juiciest medium rare burger and fries platter you have."

"Make that two." Blake chimed in.

"You guys must be celebrating something." said the waitress as she placed napkins and silverware on the table.

"Yeah, we're celebrating the cure for stress!" Said Rossi

The drinks arrived and Rossi lifted his drink for a toast. As the glasses clinked, he leaned over and starred at Jeff,

"To the craziest, creepiest, fucking, far out day I ever had." Jeff nodded in agreement.

"So Doc, do you ever wake up and think to yourself that none of this is real? That maybe it's possible to have nightmares while you're awake or those maybe you'll wake up in a hospital bed and find out you've been in a coma and all of this is just a bad dream?"

Jeff smiled and nodded in agreement then took another sip of the Dewar.

" My whole life has been turned inside out. I feel like I've lost control of my destiny… like I'm caught up in a giant wave. I can't fight it. You know what you have to do. You know you don't have a choice. Do you know what I'm talking about?"

"Yeah, you bet your ass I do. They give me assignments and all I want to do is chase after the weird shit that's going on with us. It's like I'm disconnected with the company. Some days I get the feeling that I'm going rogue. Then some days I get the feeling that I'm using my skills and connections for a

250

higher purpose... for something that's more important than anything else. Then I think, what if all this crap with Spikes all is just bullshit? Then what?"

" Doc, Amanda sent me a text not long ago telling me there was something you needed to talk to me about. Is this a good time?"

Jeff looked up to respond and just then the food and the 16oz Guinness arrived and broke the moment.

"Look Rossi, this food looks great. Let's enjoy it first and talk later."

Both men smiled in agreement, picked up their scotch, motioned for another toast, and downed the drinks in one gulp.

The comfort food was as comforting as they hoped it would be. The buzz from the drinks was settling in, reducing the stress of the day's events. Rossi pushed back from the chair, finished the last bite, downed the last swig of beer, and let out a sign of relief.

"You know Doc, sometimes you nee, melt in your mouth burger, just to remind yourself of how good being alive can feel."

"Well Rossi," Jeff jokingly said, " I figured you for a pretty good defender of the nation but had no idea you were also a philosopher with a profound insight into the human condition."

Both men clicked their glasses again and had a good laugh.

"So Rossi, I need to tell you about some more weird stuff and get your input as to what direction to take if any at all. I'm talking to you first and not to Pointdexter and the rest because

I trust your instincts. You're smart and have been in this business awhile and besides you're my friend and I know you wouldn't let me down.

"Ok, shoot, what is it?" Rossi said.

"I have it on good authority that a terrorist group is planning to set off a nuclear device in, of all places, Yellowstone National Park."

Rossi was understandably skeptic.

"Would you mind telling me who this "good authority "was who told you about this?"

"The Pope." Jeff said, as he watched with anticipation the look on Rossi's face.

Rossi looked up at the ceiling, made the sign of the cross, and clasped his hands.

"Oh, the Pope huh?" Rossi said, as he rolled his eyes and looked toward heaven again.

"Doc, I thought we agreed that there was already enough crazy shit happening for one day. What am I supposed to do with that? Run off and begin an investigation just because the Pope told you something? What was the Pope doing talking to you? Maybe you ran into him at Starbucks. Maybe his holiness drank too much altar wine. God forgive me. I don't know, just saying."

Jeff was smiling and enjoying Rossi's colorful reaction to the news and at the same time thinking, "you can take the boy out of Southey but not Southey out of the boy."

"Are you done now?" Jeff asked.

Rossi put his head down and nodded. Jeff began again.

"He sent me a letter. In the letter he told me he got the information from Spikes."

"Oh, from Spikes? Holy shit, no pun intended. Why didn't you just tell me that in the first place?"

"Because you wouldn't let me!

"Of all the places to do damage, why Yellowstone? More critters than people around there."

"The plan is to set off a volcanic eruption. It turns out there's a giant volcano under the park. It's no ordinary volcano, but one the experts call a SUPER volcano. The last time it erupted was 600 thousand years ago. It took out almost two thirds of what is now the United States"

"Holy shit, sorry again, is that really true?"

"Not only is it true, but that's not the worst part."

Rossi covered his face in disbelief then looked up at Jeff.

"Ok, there's a worst part?"

"Spikes told the Pope that the terrorists have no idea that there is a deep fault line in the volcano that reaches to the core of the Earth. In a big enough explosion, it could potentially rupture, and destroy the entire planet. Nobody knows about the fault line. It hasn't even been discovered yet!"

Rossi starred down at the table while rummaging through his pockets producing a pack of cigarettes. He motioned to the waitress to bring the check.

"Your right, it does get much worst. When is all is suppose to happen? Doc, I need a cigarette. Let's go outside."

The check arrived. Before leaving Rossi left enough cash on the table to pay the bill and leave a generous tip. Outside, Rossi was quick to light up. With his head down he began pacing in a small circle and mumbling something about options. Jeff looked on giving him a moment to figure things out in his head.

"Ok Doc, so if I go to my boss and tell them about this it can go only two ways. One, they'll believe it, and call out the cavalry, and turn the park into a war zone. It would take more than every resource we have to cover an area the size of Yellowstone. Without location details, it's a logistical nightmare. It would alarm the public and maybe hastily move the bad guys to change plans or worse, pack up and go somewhere else. Then we'd be starting all over again."

"Or two, they'll launch an investigation reaching all the way to Rome. You, your girlfriend, and maybe even the Pope would spend a shit load of time answering questions and facing possible sequestration. Why doesn't this guy Spikes just tell us the who, the when, and where of it all?"

Jeff could see the frustration on Rossi's face. Jeff knew it was time to remind Rossi of something.

"Because he can't." He got this thing about free will, about us making all the decisions. He made it very clear from the beginning that he cannot directly intervene, but that it's up to us to do the right thing. Every time I see Spikes, I become a true believer. But during the long intervals of his absence, the notion that maybe all of this could be some kind of a hoax starts to creep in. I start to doubt everything. I start to question my commitment. The whole thing is so unreal. I long for the

254

days when I took care of real people with real quantifiable medical problems. It's not easy chasing this stuff around."

"Yeah, we're both in the same place." Rossi exclaimed.

"I miss chasing real flesh and blood bad guys and locking them up. Now, it's like I'm chasing a phantom. But, I gotta tell ya doc, at the last meeting, with all them Middle Eastern yahoos there, when Spikes appeared to us, and I saw the looks on their faces, I became a true believer all over again."

Jeff, made eye contact with Rossi, nodded his head in agreement and added,

"I'm starting to understand how he works. He knows when we need him. When the time is right, he'll give us a plan. We just need to have faith."

Chapter 28

The little mice wiggling their noses between the wire mesh looked healthy enough even though they had infected with what was now known as the Blue Dot Virus. They had little white tags on their tails with coded information as to the time and date of inoculation.

The virus was named for the small concentric mark of blue dots that appear on all of its victims. The dots appear on different parts of the body. Parents are instructed to look for them on their kids if they develop a fever or begin to sleep excessively. The illness was still mainly confined to children. Adult caretakers in close proximity to stricken children seemed to have immunity. No deaths were reported, but fear was growing, that at some point, supportive care with IV fluids and tube feedings would not be enough. The CDC sent out a warning to the government to consider imposing a travel ban from the infected area surrounding Tehran.

The first step was to determine the incubation period...the length of time between the infection and the emergence of symptoms. An incubation period of eight to ten days was established but not certain. The mode of infection seemed to be from child to child. Schools were closed.

Test mice were divided into groups. The group of little critters with red tags on their tails were the ones who were sick and showing signs of the illness, drooping around, or already in a coma like state. The white tagged group were those critters who were healthy and not inoculated with virus. After them, came the group that were loosing the battle, and facing death, not from the virus but from lack of nutrition and dehydration. They were wearing blue tags.

Professor Romilov, in his long white lab coat, was clearly energized, as he moved around the lab with a newfound purpose. He had found his mojo and gained the respect and affection of the entire staff.

Amanda was holed up in an adjacent room with her computer models and secret algorithms given to them by Spikes, churning out the instruction template commands for gene modifications.

David Misner and the crew referred to them, out of earshot, and with a little envy, as the Dynamic Duo, a reference to Batman and Robin.

Romilov bent over and peered through the clean room glass into the cage containing the white tagged group of critters.

"You, my friends, are going to tell us if our vaccine can prevent the illness. Your, not so fortunate friends over there, pointing to the red and blue tagged groups, are going to tell us if our vaccine will save them. Thank you all for what you are doing."

"The first batch of our vaccine has arrived from the CDC, Misner said, as he rolled a cart into the room. The small vials of 5ml each neatly lined up in the eggshell travel tray were still cool from the dry ice packaging. Each vial was protected from contamination in a clear sterile plastic wrapping marked in red, Hazardous Material. Romilov and Misner watched as technicians dressed in hazmat suits, stationed behind the glass, of the clean room, accepted the vials though the sliding pre chamber drawer. Next, they began the task of inoculating each one of the little critters with 0.1ml of the vaccine, marking the time and batch numbers.

It would be several days before the preliminary results would be in.

David Misner carried himself with authority and purpose. His head was up and looking straight ahead as he walked down the long corridor toward conference room 202. He carried a black leather bag that looked like something from the old days when doctors made house calls and all the medical technology they had was in that black leather bag.

Upon entering the room, the loud chatter of the group that had assembled quieted down almost immediately. There was no need for him to call the meeting to order. He already seemed to have everyone attention. He stepped up to the podium and using the panel controls dimmed the overhead lights and turned on the spotlight illuminating the podium. The large screen monitor behind him came to life with a white blank glow.

Looking out over the staff who had gathered, he could see the looks of anticipation on their faces. He felt their eagerness to finally learn some of the details of the project they had been working on at such a feverish pace.

"Thank you all for being here today."

"As I'm sure you all know, our latest project was conducted with great secrecy. I've heard all the rumors circulating about and must congratulate all of you for your collective imaginations! You've come up with some amazing theories I would never thought about."

"Because of the sensitivity of this project you all have been kept in the dark. Please accept my apologies, but it was necessary. I can assure you all that this is about to end."

Just then the large screen monitor came to life. There appeared a radiant blue complex genetic structure slowly rotating revealing its three dimensional architecture and capturing everyone's attention. Misner motioned toward the image, then turned to the group.

"Ladies and Gentlemen, let me introduce to you the Blue Dot Virus."

Excitement spread throughout the room as rumors were being confirmed that they had indeed been working on this worldwide threat. He waited for the excitement to die down and then continued. Using a laser pointer he pointed to a specific area on the image.

"Please focus your attention on this segment."

The programs powerful image enhancer focused on a tiny segment of the complex genetic structure and magnified the segment to over ten thousand times bringing into focus the actual sequence of genetic code contained in that segment.

The group erupted with awe over what they saw.

"Ok everyone, settle down. Settle down."

"As you have all already noticed, the sequence of purine and pyridium bases repeats its self from position 2989 all the way to position 4375. It's as if the code got stuck, and cannot express itself to conclusion. We have concluded that this explains precisely why the clinical effect of the disease process, characteristic of Blue Dot, stops and does not progress beyond a certain point. As you know from the reports, the Blue Dot renders its victims incapacitated but no deaths have been reported. Imagine how we could use this knowledge in the future. For starters, knowledge of this nature could enable us to change a swift and deadly killer into a more manageable more chronic condition. It could buy us time to further crack the entire code and produce a cure."

"I'm here to tell you all, that we would have never made this finding, if not for your incredible work of producing research samples of a purity far exceeding anything you have ever produced. You guys completely blew away industry standards!"

"I want you all to congratulate each other for an outstanding job well done."

Everyone did just as Misner had asked. Amanda, Jeff and Romilov sitting in the front row got up and went through the staff shaking hands and expressing gratitude for their good work.

As the meeting regained order Amanda, Jeff and Romilov joined David Misner at the podium.

Amanda stepped up to the podium. David Misner handed her the black leather bag. She reached inside and held up for all to see a clear glass tube containing a green iridescent liquid that cast an eerie green glow against the warm light of the overhead spotlight. She then held it up to the group with her other hand pointing to the screen.

Another image appeared on the screen. This time the image was iridescent green, not blue as before. Moving in three dimensions it also revealed its complex architecture captivating the attention of all. Amanda turned toward the group and with great fanfare announced.

"Ladies and Gentlemen, let me introduce to you the Green Monster." A reference to Boston's iconic Fenway Park.

"The Green Monster is going to kill the Blue Dot! It's our baby, and it has only one aim in life!"

The group went wild with cheers and laughter. The sense of pride in having been a part of such an accomplishment was palpable. The nickname given the new creation using the Boston Fenway Park baseball moniker was the frosting on the cake.

Jeff stepped up to the mike.

261

"Our baby is killing Mr. Blue in the lab and we will be starting human trials by the end of this week. We'll be going directly to the Middle East for testing on real volunteer subjects, and on this one, completely bypassing the FDA, for now. The situation is urgent."

Romilov stepped up to the mike next.

"Your attention please! One more thing you all need to know before we adjourn."

The group quieted down showing their respect to the elder professor.

"First of all, let me thank each and every one of you for accepting me into your lab with friendship and camaraderie. You are all so young, so smart, and so capable. You remind me of the children I always hoped for but never had. You are the future and I can see that it will be a bright future indeed."

"Although we all worked hard and can be proud of our accomplishment, we cannot take full credit. We were given a key by an outside source without which none of this would have been possible. I am not at liberty to discuss the source at this point in time, but can assure you all, that it will be revealed, and it will be a wonderful thing for all to know. The press will be contacting you when they hear about our wonderful creation. Be sure to include this fact in your statements. Resist the urge to take full credit. The success of the vaccine may depend on it."

As the meeting broke up Jeff noticed Director Pointdexter and agent Rossi in the back of the room. Jeff made his way through the crowd to the General and Rossi.

"Director, Agent Rossi, what are you guys doing here? Have you been here long?"

The Director took charge.

"Let's just say just we're taking care of business. We're ready, on our end, to begin human testing. We've been here long enough to see this impressive group of great Americans. Tell your people to be ready at o eight hundred hours tomorrow morning. Get some rest. It'll be a long trip."

"I won't be going," Said Jeff.

"Amanda and the professor will be conducting the trials. I have work to do here."

Pointdexter was somewhat taken aback by Jeff's statement. After a long moment of hesitation he nodded his head to signal OK and proceeded toward the exit. Rossi glanced at Jeff as if to say, "well done." Jeff held up his hand to Rossi in the universal "call me signal" They had plans of their own. Plans to take a trip.

Jeff went back to congratulate David Misner again and wish him luck and a safe trip to the clinical trials. Amanda, Jeff and the professor gathered up their things and headed home but not before stopping at Vincenzos for a good luck dinner before the trip. The professor never turned down the opportunity to visit Vincenzos always lamenting the fact that he had missed out on what now had become his favorite cuisine, Italian food.

The waiter had just finished clearing the dishes and gathering up the crumbs with that ingenious device that seems to magically sweep them up from the cloth covered table.

Patrons were beginning to leave. There was still a half carafe of red burgundy sitting on the table calling out to be consumed. There had been no talk of the trip Jeff and Rossi were about to embark upon but there were things that needed to be said. Amanda took Jeff's hand while pouring the remaining wine into all three glasses in equal amounts.

"Jeff, I know this trip you and Rossi are going on is something you two have to do, but I'd be lying, if I didn't tell you how worried I am that something could happen to you. You have no plan. You don't even know where to begin looking, let alone, what, exactly you're looking for. Maybe you should rethink the whole thing and let Rossi take the lead on this one."

Just as Jeff was about to respond Romilov interrupted. Pushing his chair in tighter he moved his glass more toward the center of the table and leaned in toward Amanda.

"It's ok to be worried about the safety of the man you love. But, you know that he must do this thing. You understand that only he can do this thing. It has been made abundantly clear. He, you, and even I... all of us, have been chosen. We entered into a covenant."

"When we bought in to this incredible journey and accepted the covenant we knew there would be dangers and doubts. Remember, Jeff will be guided and protected by the ones sent here to help us all. Try to derive comfort from that knowledge."

"What if you encounter the terrorists? Your life could be in danger," Amanda said, looking straight at Jeff and seeming to completely ignore the Professors words.

Jeff got up and walked behind Amanda, put both arms around her bent over and kissed her cheek.

"We are going to be fine. We are just going to snoop around and see if we can find out something, anything. I promise. I'll keep in touch by secure satellite phone. Before we leave, Rossi and I are meeting with Marty Rosenberg, department head of geology, at the university. He's written papers on the study of volcanoes and was advisor to the geological team from the University of Naples, Italy. He was instrumental in helping them set up a kind of early warning monitoring system for Mount Vesuvius, the volcano that took out Pompeii in 76AD."

"We have some ideas of where to begin looking around. We asked Rosenberg to come up with areas where, in his opinion, there would be the greatest likelihood of an eruption, if one were to occur. That's the area where we'll begin looking for any reports of suspicious activity."

"If we come up with anything we call in the cavalry, I promise."

She got up, took Jeff by the shoulders, and starred directly into his face. Her voice came down a notch. She seemed calmer. Romilov smiled, happy that her fears had been addressed.

"Ok, don't forget to call every day, and again, be careful." She said.

Rossi and Jeff's appointment with Marty Rosenberg was for ten AM .The men had never met before. They made their way up to the third floor of one of the oldest buildings on campus where Rosenberg's was located. Looking down the long and dimly lit corridor they could see a short overweight man fiddling with keys trying to get into room 353. As they approached he turned to them still struggling with the keys and looked up.

"You guys must be Dr Blake and Mr. Rossi. Marty Rosenberg here. Sorry, I'm having some difficulty getting in to my own office. I need a minute to figure out these keys. My wife tells me I carry too many keys, and of course she's right. It's an old habit I got from my father, who was a jeweler, and had lots of stuff under lock and key. He insisted on keeping all his keys, on his person, at all times."

Rosenberg finally got the door open and welcomed his guests inside. Jeff and Rossi looked at each other not expecting to see a little old man with Albert Einstein hair. They had researched his bio. He was a guy that climbed mountains and descended into the craters of volcanoes. They had seen pictures of him wearing a fire retardant suit hanging from a rope, in order to get up close and personal with his lifelong fascination.

The office was small, cramped, and cluttered with books and reams of scientific manuscripts strewn about. From what they could tell, it looked like he was a one-man show with no secretary or assistant. Only one desk, one chair and a small leather sofa just big enough for two, fit into his tiny office. Obviously, from looking at his digs, it was clear that the department of Geology was on the lower end of the university's funding budget.

"So which one of you did I speak with on the phone to set this meeting up?"

Jeff nodded.

"Well, it's not every day I get to meet the university rock stars. You guys over at GenOnc are grabbing all the headlines with this Blue Dot virus thing. Nobody gives a shit about this rock we live on except the oil people. Anyways, what can I do for you?"

Rossi stepped forward.

"Doc, first of all, thanks for agreeing to see us on such a short notice."

Rossi concocted a bullshit cover story that Jeff had to endure. He watched Rossi take the stage.

"I've always been fascinated with volcanoes and the like. It's sort of like a hobby of mine. I've got some ideas for a book I've been thinking about. By day, I'm a special agent with the FBI. I'm doing an , under the radar investigation, on the possibility that someone, with the right knowledge, might be able to take advantage of any vulnerabilities a volcano might have, and provoke an eruption, if that's at all possible. You being an expert on volcanoes and all, I was hoping you could tell us something about this big caldera thing over at Yellowstone. We know this thing is boiling under the ground and could blow at any time. In your opinion, is there a place or specific area where an eruption is more likely to happen, sort of like a weak spot? My friend here, Dr Blake, told me that if there was anybody around who could give an opinion on something like this it would be you."

"Well special agent Rossi, you've come to the right place."

Rosenberg went into a file cabinet and started rummaging through reams of written reports.

"One of these days I'm going to digitize all this stuff. Everyone's after me to do it before I croak. Ah, here it is."

"I spent many a day over at Yellowstone. This is my report containing the information you are looking for. It shows the coordinates of what I believe to be the area where the mantle is under the most pressure or what I like to refer to as the lid on the teapot."

"I'm, however, intrigued by your question on eruption provocation. I've been working on designing a system to vent pressure build up in an attempt to prevent an eruption. We are still a long ways away from this goal. The engineering involved is the stumbling block and proving to be quite challenging. The plan is to someday have in place an installation at each volcanic site found to be at risk, or better yet, a mobile apparatus supported by a consortium of nations ready to bring it in, as a rapid response plan."

"As to your question, I guess the reverse of venting, and preventing pressure buildup, is certainly possible. An intervention that rapidly increases pressure would create the opposite effect and blow the lid off. But why would anybody want that to happen?"

Rossi and Jeff turned and looked at each other with eyebrows lifted. Rosenberg sat down and pushed his chair back.

"Especially at Yellowstone. It's one of the largest calderas on the planet. We know that baby has blown three times, at intervals of about every six hundred thousand years. Rock strata studies confirm the approximate dates. Destroyed about sixty percent of North America."

Chuckling in a macabre display of humor, Rosenberg continued.

"No doubt, a tough day for the dinosaurs. Certainly must have brought true meaning the phrase Crispy Critters."

Nobody laughed except Rosenberg.

He then handed the report to Rossi opened to page 126, and pointed to the map on the page. He placed his index finger over the area marked exo mantle.

"If it ever blows, this will be the spot. It's actually bulging here."

His finger covered a place called Pocatello, Idaho.

.

Chapter 29

The C17 carrying the entire American research team and a portable hospital lab descended below the clouds revealing for the first time the parched desert landscape stretching for as far as the eye could see. Most travelers have seen images of this ancient and foreboding land, but to the uninitiated, the first real sight of this vista leaves quite the lasting impression. Two Iranian fighter jets quickly appeared flanking the C17. They would serve as escorts during the landing at Tehran International Airport.

The C17 taxied toward the central large terminal. There was a large convoy of buses and military vehicles awaiting the new arrivals. Amanda, Romilov, Misner, and the five technicians who accompanied them were met and greeted by a government functionary who escorted them to waiting limousines, assuring them that their equipment and supplies, would be secured and safe.

The plan was to set up a clinic at the Tehran Hospital to treat and monitor the first fifty patients before releasing the vaccine to all who needed it. They had brought one thousand doses of vaccine with them. The first fifty test subjects were to be chosen by Mohamed Kaspani, a noted Iranian virologist.

"Welcome to Iran. My name is Habib. I will be your facilitator and escort during your stay here. I have been instructed to make you comfortable and grant you any reasonable request. I will take you directly to the hospital where we have provided comfortable living quarters for you and all your staff. You will have ample time to recover from your long journey."

Habib was a small man both in appearance and outward confidence. Constantly chattering, smiling, bowing his head and apologizing for everything from the heat to the distance to the hospital. He was wearing his best suit showing signs of wear, an ill-fitting white shirt, and a food stained tie. Everyone just hoped as Jeff said, he would just "shut the fuck up."

With Habib by their side and chatting incessantly, they all began the trip to the hospital, approximately thirty minutes away. After a short while outside the airport gates, the outline of the city could be seen on the distant horizon across the vast flat and arid desert landscape. The group expressed to each other concern with the heavily armed military escort. Why was as this necessary?

The answer soon became apparent.

At the city gates, the Americans began to see crowds forming on the side of the roads. At first looked they like curiosity seekers trying to get a glimpse of the American scientists, but as the new arrivals got closer to the hospital, the crowds got larger and were behaving more like protesters.

Loud voices could be heard yelling and holding signs in English and Arabic with words like, "Murderers, Infidel, and Satan Go Home." Police in riot control gear were everywhere, pushing the crowds back. Habib could see the worry on everyone's faces. No one had expected this. Habib got up and went to the front of the bus with his arms raised in the air.

"Please, please everyone. There is nothing to worry about. Many of our people believe that this illness affecting their children is the work of your CIA."

Romilov got up and pointing at Habib and yelled out.

"That is because your government has deceived them and fed them lies!"

Habib was clearly rattled, but able to muster up a reply.

"Be that what it may, I can assure you that you are all safe. The hospital is just a short distance ahead."

Amanda turned to Romilov.

Yuri, that's how you buy yourself a lot of trouble over here. You of all people should know that."

The hospital came into view and the buses where being directed toward the back where an extended canopy, much like a jet way had been improvised. The front entrance of the hospital was crowded with parents and children in wheelchairs and stretchers clamoring for admission and help. It was nothing short of chaos.

The Americans were hastily ushered into the hospital and led down a long corridor to a large gathering room. They encountered no one in the corridor. The gathering room was furnished with cots, desks, and plenty of electric strip outlets , separated by folding room dividers. So much for privacy. This was going to be barrack living at its best. The ceiling was high and the room well lit. There was air conditioning but no windows. Male and female rest rooms with shower facilities were provided. A long table at one end was well stocked with fruit, pastries, coffee and tea. A desk with telephone had been set up just outside the entrance door in the hallway. It would come to be referred to as the "The guard's station."

Habib placed himself in the center of the room looking anxiously from side to side with his hands clasped in front of him.

"I trust you will find everything satisfactory. I recommend you get some rest before dinner at seven tonight. You will meet and be dining with Doctor Kaspani. I will be just outside the door if you need anything at all.

Everyone took advantage of the respite to get some sleep and clean up.

Promptly at seven thirty Habib entered the gathering room and declared,

"Your attention everyone. I see that you are all ready. I thank you for your punctuality and I will ask you all to follow me."

He led them down another corridor to what appeared to be a larger function room with plenty of floor to ceiling windows. The Sun was setting casting a glow through the sheer full-length curtains, illuminating the colorful array of Persian rugs covering the center floor.

Standing at attention against gold colored floral adorned walls were a row of male servants impeccably dressed in white, replete with white gloves. A sumptuous display of Middle Eastern food contained in silver bowls and dishes lined the woodened hand carved serving table. To the delight and relief of everyone, utensils and serving spoons were provided. The prospect of eating while sitting on the floor was daunting enough. Worse, was eating with bare hands and not knowing the proper etiquette.

Kaspani entered the room with two associates dressed in a long white Arabic Robe. There was also a cadre of five others dressed in western attire thought to be government functionaries. Kaspani had studied and spent three years at NYU School of Health Sciences. His English was excellent. Waving his hands like a politician, he proceeded to the front of the group of visitors who had assembled.

"A welcome to my distinguished colleagues from America. I am looking forward to our collaboration. I have been authorized to thank you in the name of the Iranian people. We have had our differences, but this is not a time for differences. This is a time for coming together in a common

274

cause to fight this Blue Dot scourge. I have brought with me members of my trusted team to aid us and learn of your methods."

Amanda addressed Dr Kaspani and his associates. She wore a headscarf in respect for her host's customs.

"My name is Amanda Fiore, and together with all my colleagues, whose names have already been provided, I would like to thank you for the hospitality that you have shown us. We have brought with us a vaccine which we feel confident will help to reverse the effects of the Blue Dot virus, affecting so many children in this part of the world."

"I must be honest with you. In the spirit of full disclosure, I will tell you that this discovery could only have been made with the help of an outside party who gave us the key to being able to make the right genetic substitutions necessary to create this vaccine. This outside party will soon make his presence known and then you will all understand his significance."

"We have prepared a short video to show you how the vaccine was made."

Everyone took their seats and turned their attention to the large screen monitor.

They were shown the same video presentation that had been shown the staff containing detailed graphics of the gene substitutions used. There followed many questions as expected and lively discussion around the social atmosphere of a sumptuous welcoming dinner.

While sipping on sweet tea and exchanging pleasantries, Amanda and Romilov quietly walked out onto an adjacent small courtyard, away from the others with Kaspani. Kaspani turned to Amanda as she struggled a bit to adjust her headscarf.

"You can take that off if you wish. I will not be offended."

The truth was, she felt more uncomfortable wearing it while in the presence of Iranian men. She was also dressed and covered from head to toe. She wore loose fitting dark slacks. She understood the disdain Muslim men had for western women. They consider them to be whores for the way they dress and express their independence. In the Muslim culture, a woman's body should only be revealed to her husband. Amanda was uncomfortable being placed in that position. Men were starring at her and she could sense what they were thinking.

"Thank you, but I prefer to leave it on."

"As you wish."

"Dr Kaspani, Dr Romilov and I want you to know that we have a great respect for your scientific achievements and feel honored to be able to bring you this discovery. We appreciate that this situation may be somewhat awkward for you. It is by no means a reflection on your abilities or those of your team. I must warn you that our methods at this time are to remain nebulous. Our benefactor has assured us that this knowledge can only be used for good. Once he becomes confident of this requisite, it will be revealed as a gift to all. Again I repeat, only at a time when he is satisfied that only good will come of it.

276

Kaspani chuckled. His face produced a demure smile. He started strutting around like an arrogant asshole.

"You don't need to explain anything to me. I too have had the dreams. I know all about your Mr. Spikes. I also know that he is the culprit who has brought this scourge upon our people. He has done this to make a point and get the attention of our leaders."

"We shall see if he prevails. No one is more powerful than Allah. In time, we will learn his true identity and expose his powers for what they are, parlor tricks."

Amanda and Romilov looked at each other realizing that Kaspani had closed his mind to change.

"Why did he choose you, representatives of the US to reveal these scientific secrets? If he is truly a friend of all mankind, as he purports to be, why does he not share these revelations with all of us? Why does he punish our people?"

Amanda moved closer to Kaspani and mustered up her American, I'm your equal and you're not going to condescend me, persona. She whipped off her headscarf letting it fall to the floor and shook her head, releasing her dark and lustrous hair that fell over her shoulders framing her beautiful face. She wore it like a badge of courage- defiant and strong.

Kaspani was visibly startled by this display of a take-charge American woman who had suddenly created a scene and revealed that she submits to no one. Romilov was thinking, "Ok, now you pissed her off. Here it comes."

"Dr Kaspani. You asked an important question which I will now answer."

"We were chosen because our hearts and minds are not closed. We have accepted the changes that are about to happen and are trying to prevent a cataclysmic event revealed to us by Mr. Spikes. We do not yet have the details of this event, but have enough confidence is his warning to not dismiss it as a parlor trick."

"He is not a citizen of any country on this earth. He represents no government. He is not The Creator in whom we all believe. He did not come to undermine or change your beliefs. He came to save us from ourselves. We were hoping that your ideology would not get in the way of your good scientific judgment. I am disappointed that you cannot rise above it. In any event, we have come here with a job to do, and we intend to do it."

Without saying a word, Kaspani led the group back into the function room, thanked everyone again, and told them to all meet in the clinic at eight AM the next morning. Amanda and Romilov joined with their colleagues who were having a good time at the reception dinner. They quietly got the attention of each one and let them know that there would be a short meeting back at the "hotel "as it was called.

Back at the "hotel," Amanda gathered the group without making a sound putting her finger vertically over her lips in the universal be quiet no talking sign, and waving her arms in the gathering motion. They all huddled in a corner of the room and she began to whisper.

"Ok Guys, we couldn't find any cameras but as you know and learned in our security prep back home, we have to assume that they probably have ears on us."

She turned to David Misner and motioned to him to come in closer to the group.

"This guy Kaspani has turned out to be a major asshole. His ego and skepticism is preventing him from accepting the truth. He can't be trusted. There's a risk that he could sabotage the whole trial."

"No one is to handle the vaccine except us. No exceptions. I'll make that clear to everybody tomorrow and say that we are following a safety protocol. If they object Ill threaten to pack up and go home. We need to stick to our guns."

"David, you checked the vaccine containers. Anything to report?"

"No, not so far. Most of you know that the vaccine vials are sealed in groups of twenty four, with a cellophane wrapper. What none of you know, is that the wrapper contains a line of nano particles that when broken emit a signal. I have an app on my phone that picks up the signal. It's something new, not in production. We agreed to test it for the Geek Squad at MIT. When we open the containers tomorrow, I should get a signal. If the signal comes through, it'll mean that the nano strip worked and the vials have not been tampered with. If no signal comes through, we can only assume there's been no tampering, but won't know with absolute certainty."

Morning came with no fanfare. David Misner was up early preparing the fifty vials of vaccine and securing the remainder.

Lot numbers were recorded against a list of the fifty difficult to pronounce names of patients who were to be the first recipients. When he broke the cellophane seal, his cell sounded an alert. The nano particle security strip worked. The vaccine was secure. The Geek Squad back at MIT also got the alert and went berserk with joy knowing their latest cool project was a success. A decision had been made that Misner would stay behind during the administering phase of the medication to guard the remaining inventory of vaccine against any possible tampering.

Habib could be heard just outside the room reciting his morning prayers. Minutes later there was a knock on the door and Habib entered. He was accompanied by two white clad waiters rolling a cart with coffee and morning pastries.

"I hope everyone slept well. Please enjoy these refreshments. The test subjects have arrived and are being prepared in the treatment area. I will return in thirty minutes to collect and escort you."

The treatment area had a sterile feel. The white tile floor and walls had a retro look and made the acoustics bright to say the least. There were no shades on the large windows. The morning sun was bright, casting long shadows from the beds and fixtures onto the floor. Five rows of ten beds each were set up with a chair on each side of the bed. Each bed was separated with cloth room dividers and room enough to walk between the beds. A clipboard hung at the foot of each bed to record the subjects name, sex, date of birth, beginning time of infusion, any known allergies, current medications, and lot number of vaccine vial used.

A distant sound of demonstrators demanding treatment outside could be heard. Iranian nurses dressed in white burka were comforting the grateful parents and placing the IV lines into each child. Some or the nurses wore sandals and were sporting manicured polished toenails with bright colors, probably in a desperate subconscious attempt, to have some expression of their femininity. Others wore clogs. Two soldiers were posted inside wearing side arms. Three translators were provided to facilitate communication.

When Amanda, Romilov and the team entered, the room fell silent. An uncomfortable awkwardness took over. Amanda, after a moment of hesitation, seized the situation and quickly moved to the center of the room. She summoned one of the translators to her side.

"Thank you all for your gracious hospitality. I am looking at your children and see how beautiful they truly are. I can also see the love and devotion in your eyes, the special and profound love, that all parents, of all faiths, in every part of our world, have for their children. We have come here to offer you a possible cure for the terrible illness that has robbed your families of the joy of healthy children. I admire all of you for your courage in being the first to try this new but unproven treatment. I pray with you, that it restores your children to the happy and healthy children they deserve to be."

"It is important that you know that we were given the key to this cure by a higher power. We cannot take credit for it. We are simply the conduit through which these revelations or gifts are brought to you. We have been told, that soon we will all better understand the nature and purpose of these gifts. Thank you."

After a short moment the room erupted with applause and shouts of "God is Great."

Romilov took Amanda's hand, bent over and whispered in her ear, "well done."

The American team took charge, and drew up into the syringes, a premeasured dose of vaccine for each child, to be administered by IV bolus injection. One by one, the vaccine was administered.

Amanda and Romilov walked through the grid of beds greeting the parents and examining the children to verifying the presence and the exact location of the blue dot .They were struck by how serene and healthy each child looked. Their eyes were open and heads slowly moving as if they were looking at something only they could see. They remained unresponsive to sound, light or touch but continued staring with an occasional subtle smile at something in the distance. The Iranian nurses commented how, even the stick of the IV needle, produced no reaction at all.

As for the parents, they were extremely polite and affectionate, profusely expressing their gratitude to the Americans with bows and, as is the custom, to kiss the hand of the visitors.

"Yuri, we've been here for over two hours and Kaspani hasn't showed up yet. I can't believe it. Where do you think he is? I thought for sure he would be here strutting his arrogant ass around. Maybe he's somewhere hatching a plan to throw a monkey wrench into this whole thing. I don't trust that bastard."

" I agree, Amanda. Wait here. I'm going over to talk to our friend Habib."

Habib was standing around playing word games on his Android phone when Romilov approached him.

"Mr. Habib, I was wondering if Dr Kaspani will be joining us this morning. I am frankly surprised that he is not here. I hope there is nothing wrong. I especially hope that he was not offended in some way by something we may have said. Please communicate my sentiments to the doctor and tell him that if we offended him it was purely unintentional. We have great respect for him."

Habib began to fidget uncomfortably and began to mumble that the doctor had taken ill and was resting at the moment. His eyes and body language betrayed him. Habib was a bad liar. He turned away from Romilov and walked a few steps away for privacy. He made a quick call on his cell and a minute later he was back.

"The doctor is feeling better and hopes to join you later on today."

Romilov walked back over to Amanda, reported his conversation with Habib, and joined her in their bed-by-bed evaluations. Almost three hours had passed since the first vaccine infusion.

As they approached bed #36 they could see that the parents, seated at the head of the bed were smiling and looked hopeful. Amanda and Romilov were standing on both sides of the bed. A burka-clad nurse was standing at the foot of the bed with her head in a bowed position.

The nurse lifted her head and in perfect English asked Amanda and Romilov how they were holding up. Before they had time to react to her question she reached over to both sides of the bed and took their hands as if to say a prayer.

In a split second, a wave of strange energy flowed through their arms producing an almost paralyzing sense of calmness. The room went quiet and darker. There was no motion. The three were instantly isolated and separated from the reality of their surroundings. A luminosity they had experienced once before began to well up under the burka and shine through the face opening. Spikes had come to pay a visit.

"Hello, my friends. I have come to thank you and offer you a bit of assistance. You have been doing a wonderful job helping me and, by extension, all of you, in advancing our agenda."

"I had the pleasure of meeting Dr Kaspani today. A very bright but unfortunate man. Unfortunate, in the sense that he suffers from the affliction of PRIDE, a debilitating condition that renders its victim incapable of seeing past their own ego. Let's just say he has been enlightened. You will find him to be more personable and accommodating and, shall we say, endowed with a new found capacity to help his own people.

Still holding both their hands he concentrated on Amanda.

"Amanda, I am here to tell you that Jeff and Rossi are safe but are about to begin a dangerous phase of their work. I cannot guarantee their safety but will keep a watchful eye over them."

His grip began to loosen. The energy flow diminished and the isolated reality dissipated. It was as though a forward button had been pressed and time started up again without skipping a beat.

It was obvious that no one had noticed a thing. Every action and circumstance just took up where it left off. Spikes seemed to have the ability to stop time and create a no time zone where you could work or communicate in a suspended reality but still not disturb the fabric of time. Quite an amazing tool. It was clear to Amanda and Romilov that, whatever civilization Spikes came from, had learned to conquer the time-space compendium, one of the Holy Grails of modern physics.

The next morning Habib was again escorting the team towards the treatment room. By now everyone understood that they weren't going anywhere alone. Wide eyed with excitement, Habib walked quickly and kept looking back at everyone nervously wringing his hands. Half way down the hall they began to hear a sound they had not heard since their arrival. It was the sound of children's voices.

Kaspani was at the entrance with a joyous smile on his face holding his hands together in a prayer like manner. The children were awake, happy, and laughing. Mothers holding their children with tears of joy and fathers holding them both.

A cheer went up as the team entered and then a spontaneous rush to engulf them all with embraces of gratitude. Kaspani hugged Amanda and shook everyone's hand.

"I have been shown goodness this day and it is a beautiful thing, indeed." Kaspani said.

Misner grabbed the satellite phone and called the lab workers waiting at home for any news.

"It worked! Tell everyone! Call the media! Get productions going! We need a hundred thousand doses as soon as you can churn them out!"

Next, Misner handed the phone to Amanda who quickly called Jeff to report the good news.

Amanda was sobbing as she described to Jeff the joyous sight in front of her. To Jeff there was no distance between them. He could feel her joy and responded in kind,

"I knew it would work. I never doubted it for a moment! Honey, this is the beginning of something big...really big!"

"You be careful" She said. "Spikes told me you and Rossi are in danger. I want you home safe and sound. Remember, safe and sound!"

"I love you honey. I'll see you in a couple of weeks, max...safe and sound."

The team was feverishly taking cell phone video and posting it on social media to show and tell the world of the great success. Without running it by the boss they were adding the hashtag, "Thank you Mr. Spikes." The team knew more than they let on and in their moment of exuberance let the cat out of the bag.

The Iranian guards began an attempt to subdue the parent's outburst of joy but finally gave up with Kaspani waving them off. News of the success quickly went viral. It wasn't long before the news media started asking the question, who is Mr. Spikes? Talk shows bristled with debate on the mysterious Mr. Spikes. Who is he? Where is he from? What does he want? Does he even exist?

Reporters descended on GenOnc labs. News stories covering the backgrounds of the principals of the company were everywhere. Jeff was a war hero. Amanda wasn't even a doctor, only a physics student. How could she have been instrumental in the development of the vaccine? Was Romilov defection to the United States legit or was he some kind of spy or Russian operative? Conspiracy theories were everywhere. The press was having a field day. Even Maggie was on CNX and FOX being hijacked with a mike stuck in her face trying to escape being interviewed about Jeff.

"He is a wonderful doctor, and I have nothing further to say!"

The trio had become famous overnight and the pressure was building. There were reporters camped outside their Dwight Street apartment waiting for their return. Anyone who had any connection with the trio was asked the same question. Is there a Mr. Spikes and has anyone seen him?

Famous and notable people around the world started coming forward with bizarre stories about Spikes and the dreams. Some were true and others pure fabrications. Government officials were coy and evasive referring all questions to higher authorities. Those in the know were stonewalling hoping it would be a fifteen minute of fame type thing and die down as it usually does.

A federal judge from Middlesex County ordered a gag order on all employees of GenOnc under the guise that the company's proprietary intellectual rights needed protection and the work was top secret. The military, not the company, petitioned the courts citing national security concerns.

Jessica Blumenthal's news reporters gut told her the lid on this story was about to be blown off. She and her producers decided to do a special in prime time on the mysterious Mr. Spikes entitled "Friend or Faux." The special was not going to happen...at least not now. The Feds pounced on the network with every injunction known to mankind ordering the network executives to put a temporary hold on the report. The network had no choice, but to temporarily relent.

Chapter 30

The black van looked innocent enough. Professionally applied graphics in gold lettering gave the impression of a first rate legitimate business, "Evergreen Engineering" It was complete with a web site and an eight hundred-contact number.

The web site offered services ranging from surveying and soil sampling analysis to environmental compliance planning. A call to the eight hundred number was answered by a call center with a quick sales pitch and request to leave a brief message as to the nature of the inquire.

Mustafa had thought of everything...even a powerful portable compressor and pneumatic drill with rock bits and long extension hoses. He also had a spool of hundred and fifty pound nylon line, 3000 feet long to be used to lower the device into the mineshaft. The device weighed 65 pounds.

His inner circle had joined him coming in through Mexico and had taken up residence in a trailer park just outside Big Springs. They all had the mindset of a suicide mission knowing full well that if the plan succeeded they would be willing to be part be part of the carnage. However, the cowardly bastards also had an escape plan. The device timer would be set for a forty-eight hour countdown after it is activated remotely from anywhere in the world using a cell phone with a dedicated non-listed number. In an emergency, a secondary, five minute alternate timer, was programmed.

They assembled in the van all wearing blue jump suits bearing the company logo. There would be a brief meeting before setting out in search of a suitable location to plant the device.

"These are the maps Bernani gave us. The locations of many old mine shafts are supposed to be located along this route twenty. The largest caldera will be located a few hundred meters just west of route twenty and will be right under our feet."

"I visited the local historical society and learned that there are old service roads all along this route. They are used by hunters and hikers. Some of them lead to old abandoned mines from the late eighteen hundreds. The mines had no names, but instead were given numbers. Only one mine was given a name. It was mine number 166 which later became known as Bartlett mine, named after three brothers who perished when they were overcome by methane gas. The land is still owned by the descendants of the original mine owners, a family that resides in Colorado. The Bartlett mine was said to be two kilometers deep. We need to get as deep down as we can. This mine would be ideal if we can find it. There are no signs or directions, only a general area. Any questions?"

No one responded. Mustafa got behind the wheel. The others sat in the back on cushions.

Abdulla, an expert bomb maker, had grown up in the same village as Mustafa and became a trusted jihadist from the beginning. His mother and sister had also been killed in the bombings after 9/11.

"Mustafa, the news is full about of the cure of the Blue Dot by the Americans."

"Yes, my brother. They bring the disease upon our people then provide the cure. How convenient! They are true heroes. They think we are stupid but together with the help of Allah we will show them who is stupid. We will be rid of the devils once and for all. Now, all of you keep a watchful eye. I need you to help me look for something that resembles a path or road along here while we still have daylight."

After almost one hour driving they did not see anything that looked like a service road. The men were beginning to complain, that without a specific location and directions, they could be driving around in the wilderness forever.

"Brothers, do not lose faith. We will find what we came here to find. The Prophet will guide us."

The tattered wooden sign ahead read Bobcat Saloon one mile. After a slow approach they pulled into the gravel parking lot. Mustafa lingered inside the van giving the place a through once over look. He glanced at the others with a look of disdain. They looked like a demoralized bunch of losers slouching on the floor of the van.

"I am going into the bar and see what I can find out. I will go in alone. Stay in the van and out of sight.

"We have to piss. What are we supposed to do? Piss our pants?"

"Go piss in the woods but stay out of sight. I don't want to raise any suspicion."

There were three dirty beat-up pickup trucks parked in the front and another to the far left side. The inside of the bar was your typical Billy Bob shithole dive. Knotty pine covered the whole place. A light cloud of cigarette smoke lingered by the dimly lit light fixtures hanging over four pool tables. The air was saturated with the smell of stale cigarettes and beer.

There were six patrons who could have passed for brothers. Big, burly, and stupid looking. Unkempt hair sticking out from under sweat soiled baseball caps, gnarly beards and shit kicker boots stained with oily garage grime seem to be the dress code. Two at the bar, two at a table, and two more milling around one of the pool tables. Behind the bar stood a morbidly obese barmaid sporting a massive cleavage and a nasty grin.

Mustafa walked in and looking like a fish out of water. His spiffy blue jumpsuit with company logo drew stares from all. He immediately realized that going in this bar was a mistake, but overcame the urge to turn around and walk out. The barmaid's eyes lit up looking at Mustafa.

"Well looky here. What have we got here? Looks like Captain Kurt come to pay us a visit. What can I get you, Captain Sir?"

The others stood in silence with menacing frowns fixed on Mustafa.

"Actually, I was hoping to get some information. You see I was hired to do a survey of an old mine around here once called Bartlett or number 166. Do any of you know where I might find it?"

"Information?" One of the men shouted.

"Information's not cheap. Information like that got to be worth at least a hundred dollars. That would be a bargain for a big shot surveyor man like you."

The men moved in closer and one of them stepped forward in Mustafa's space.

"Hey! I think we got ourselves a fuckin towel head. I killed some of you motherfuckers over in Afghanistan. I know a fuckin towel head when I see one."

He glanced around at the other Neanderthals looking for approval. He found it, noting the shit eating grins on their faces.

"The information just went up to two hundred." Said another one of the group.

Mustafa knew he was in trouble and had to think fast. He had left his 9mm in the van and regretted telling his men not to come in. He blurted out.

"Hey man, I was on your side. I rode with the 101 out of Bradley as a translator and spotter. Saw a lot on action with guys just like you."

The Neanderthal paused for a moment and looked around. First a smile, and then a laugh, bellowed out through his dirty beard as he turned to the barmaid.

"Get this man a drink, on me."

"No, no thank you. Thank you. I am driving. Thank you for your time." Mustafa managed to sputter out as he headed toward the door.

"Wait friend. Don't you want to know where Bartlett's mine is?

Mustafa looked at him with an incredulous face not believing what he had just heard.

"When you get to the Snake River pull over and hike up about half a mile north, till you see a big arrowhead shape rock. The mineshaft is just about ten yards to your left. It's covered in all kinds of shit from the earthquake of 1879. And sorry for the towel head shit. You guys saved our asses more than once over there."

Mustafa nodded, turned, and quietly walked out of the bar happy that the mission had not been compromised and that he was still alive. No sooner had Mustafa left, that the Neanderthals looked at each other and had a good laugh.

"Wait till that fella runs into the shiners holed up in them parts. They won't take too kindly to folks like him. He'll be lucky to ever see his towel head kin again."

"Look alive! Wake up!" Mustafa yelled, at his comrades some of who had fallen asleep in the back of the van.

"I have secured the directions to the mine. It is not far from here. We still have time to find the site and learn what preparations will be needed. Please be sure to remind me when our mission is accomplished stop here again."

Abdulla looked at him with a roll of his eyes.

"What for? Did the menu look that good?

"No my brother. I want to kill everyone who may be inside and then burn the building to the ground."

"But why? They will perish in the explosion anyways."

"Why? Because my soul requires it to find peace."

It wasn't long before the river came into view. It wasn't much of a river, only about fifty feet wide, shallow, and rocky. They parked the van in a narrow dirt road just off the main road. The road only went into the woods for a distance of about ten yards. A narrow single file path continued on deeper in the woods. Mustafa grabbed a briefcase containing phony engineering paperwork and surveys in case anyone questioned what they were doing.

"Bring the nylon line. We need it to measure and test the shaft if we find it."

Hot and buggy was an understatement as the four men trudged their way through the path. One of the men remarked not to forget bug spray when they return for the real thing. The path started to gently turn to the right and begin a moderate upward stretch toward a ridge. The men were whining and complaining about the uphill hike when Mustafa abruptly stopped and turned to his men. He held his arm high motioning for them to stop.

"Silence!" Can you smell wood burning?"

They nodded yes. "Somebody is up there burning wood or brush. We do not want any encounters with locals if it can be avoided. If we encounter anyone we stick to the story. Let me do the talking. I have the best English."

As they approached the ridge, the woods gave way to a small clearing. That's where they saw the arrowhead rock formation. The smoke was coming from behind the ridge past the rock formation and down the other side of the hill. They kept their heads down and looked to the left of the formation as they had been instructed.

The opening of the mine was not hard to find. The smell of methane led them to a pile of rocks. Abdulla placed his hand near the rocks and could feel a draft of cool methane scented air flowing out between the cracks. One by one they began removing the rocks trying at the same time not to attract attention. Soon they had cleared an opening with access to a pit of about five feet in width.

"Bring the line over here and find two good size stones." Mustafa commanded.

Mustafa took off his watch and got ready to use the stopwatch feature.

"Ok, drop the first stone in and listen carefully."

296

They all agreed to having heard a faint splash at 8 seconds. He plugged 8 seconds into the formula of height=1/2 x (gravity (9.8)x seconds)squared. The answer? 1029ft deep to the water popped up.

Next, they securely tied the second rock and lowered it together with a thermometer to 1100 feet. They pulled up the rock still wet and the thermometer read 196 degrees.

"Brothers, Allah has brought us the right spot, over the belly of the beast, but not hot enough to destroy the device. Pull up the line and let's get out of here."

On the way back down the hill they were all boasting that they had accomplished their mission without attracting any attention. When they reached the van the mood quickly changed. Flashing lights of a park ranger police truck spelled trouble.

As they moved toward the truck they saw only one officer standing by the vehicle.

"Everybody smile and be relaxed. If he tries to take us into custody we must overcome him at any cost. Be calm."

"Hello officer. Very hot today. How can we help you?"

"Saw your van and stopped by to see what you were up to but mostly to give you a little warning."

In anticipation of producing some documentation of their purpose, Mustafa reached into the briefcase and removed some of the papers he had brought. All he could think of was to be calm and stick to the script.

"We are under the impression the land was privately owned. I hope we are not trespassing. The owners hired our company to take soil samples from the old mine and check methane levels. We don't know what their plans are but this is what they are paying us to do."

"You're right about the ownership. We go in from time to time. There are moonshiners working their stills around there. They can be very nasty to folks who have the misfortune to stumble across their criminal activities. There have been a number of disappearances over the years. So, you'd best be careful up there. I recommend you get your work done and don't be a lingering in them parts too long."

"Thank you for the advice, officer. We have actually concluded our work in there for today. We will be coming back one more time before we are finished. Thanks for the warning. We will keep everything you said in mind when we return."

The officer got in his truck and waved once before leaving. The quartet hugged each other and praised Allah for having dodged another bullet.

Chapter 31

Rossi's eyes were getting tired after hours on mountainous roads that require the driver's full attention. He and Jeff had gone on a quick unofficial road trip to try and find out if there was any evidence that terrorists were working the area designated by Marty Rosenberg. Rossi used his credentials to get information from local law enforcement. He was tired and frustrated at their lack of leads.

"We've been driving for hours without a single lead. This is turning out to be a bad idea. The local cops haven't noticed anything unusual. The park ranger's office told me the same thing. Hardware and heavy equipment dealers I contacted report no unusual sales. Maybe were in the wrong place.

Yellowstone is a big place. Too many miles to cover without a specific spot to focus on. They could be anywhere."

Jeff gave out a sigh and put the map he was holding down.

"I trust Marty Rosenberg. If he says this area is the best spot to plant a bomb then this is the best spot. Maybe the bad guys are not as smart and picked a spot hundreds of miles from here, but doubt it."

"Anyways, all hell is breaking loose back home with the press all over Amanda demanding to know who Spikes is after the name was leaked. Amanda called me to check up. She told me that Romilov came up with an ingenious bullshit explanation to feed the inquiring minds of the press. He told them that Spikes is not a person but simply a made up avatar we thank when were stuck on something and finally come up with a solution. She thinks some of them may have bought it. I should be there with her instead of this wild goose chase. Anyways, were leaving tomorrow."

Rossi shared Jeff's frustration.

"Yeah, my station chief is all over my ass asking me where the hell I am. I told him I'm following a lead and will have a report in forty-eight hours. I can't stall much longer. I think the lid on this whole thing is about to pop off. Let's get some lunch. I'm starving. I'm pulling over. I can't drive another mile."

Rossi pulled the blue rented Nissan Rogue over so Jeff could take the wheel. Luckly, for the two weary travelers, the Snake River Diner was just up the road. Rossi got out first and ran inside before Jeff.

"Gotta take a leak before I piss my pants! I'll meet you inside."

The dinner menu was full of comfort food favorites. Jeff found two stools at the red formica counter that wrapped around center of the establishment. There were booths against the back wall, and tables along the front windows, overlooking the parking area. Jeff knew that Rossi, unconsciously, always chose a spot in a public place that offered the greatest overall view and the quickest exit strategy. For better or for worse Rossi's, FBI training had become embedded in his everyday life and Jeff was catching on. When Rossi came back, the first words out of his mouth to Jeff were," Hey, good spot."

The menu had all the good comfort food that Jeff secretly enjoyed in the age of health food police. Jeff would sometimes think that, if Amanda knew of his occasional dietary indiscretions, there would be hell to pay.

The service was fast. It wasn't long before the hamburgers, and fries arrived. Both men ate in silence both knowing that they'd be heading back the motel for a nights rest before getting back to reality and the real world. They were feeling like failures, and their exuberance, in their impromptu mission was fading fast.

From their position at the counter, it was hard not to notice the old dusty blue Ford pickup truck that pulled up to the front of the diner close to the windows. A small dark skinned boy got out from the passenger side by himself and walk to the front door. He looked to be around six or seven years old. Too young to be entering the restaurant unaccompanied. The boy struggled with the heavy glass door finally getting it open and letting himself in.

The boy stood in front of the cashier's station carefully looking at all the tables and patrons until his eyes fell upon Jeff and Rossi. Walking with confidence directly to them, he got behind Jeff and poked him with one finger getting his attention.

Jeff turned around and looked down at the little boys shiny jet black hair and inquisitive wide-eyed expression.

"And what can I do for you young man?"

"Are you the doctor from Boston?"

"I might be the doctor from Boston, but who are you?"

Still with a wide-eyed expressionless look on his face he responded.

"I'm Charlie Evans."

"And what can I do for you, Charlie Evans?"

"My great, great, great, grandfather, Joseph Shortsleeves wants to tell you something."

"That's a lot of "greats" to describe your grandfather. Don't you think?"

"Joseph Shortsleeves is very old. Some people say he is the oldest person alive on the Earth. His two daughters take care of him and they are ninety-one and ninety-two."

Rossi got up off his stool and knelt down on one knee next to the little boy.

"How did your grandfather know that the doctor was here in this restaurant?"

302

"Joseph Shortsleeves knows many things. He sees and hears things that no one else can see or hear. He is a Holy Man. The white men call him Shaman. The Earth talks to him and tells him secrets. Many people of the Black Foot Nation and even the whites go to him for advice."

"He told me to tell you that he knows what you are looking for. You must come with us now, while it is still light. Joseph Shortsleeves does not see anyone after sunset. You and your friend will follow my older brother Daniel and me. Daniel is shy and does not speak."

Jeff and Rossi looked at each other and knew intuitively that this was the break they had been hoping for. Jeff leaned over and got closer to the little boy.

"Take us to Joseph Shortsleeves."

Little Charlie left the restaurant and got into the pickup next to his brother. They pulled the truck out to the road and waited for Jeff and Rossi to pay the check and get behind them. Jeff took out his phone and looked at his weather app. It read sunset at 7.33PM. It was now 1.15PM. He figured it gave them plenty of time to make the meeting.

By this time the two men had become used to all kinds of weird shit going on and stopped asking questions. They had learned to go with the flow, knowing that there was a higher power guiding them.

Jeff was driving and following the two boys blue pickup truck as it turned left off the main road. They followed them onto a dirt road. The two men were both getting exited and a little anxious as to what was in store for them. Jeff noticed that Rossi was unusually quiet. Jeff nudged Rossi on the shoulder.

303

"Hey, this guy Shortsleeves may be the real McCoy. Before leaving I did a little research on the areas indigenous people. This area is home to the Black Foot Indian Tribe. They were here way before the white man arrived and survive today .Unlike the Comanche tribe, who nearly exterminated the Apache, the Black Foot were peaceful. They had a great respect for Nature and the bounty it provided. They worshiped the mountains and rivers and killed only what they could eat. Only what they needed to survive. They just wanted to live in peace and be left alone. In fact, when the white man came they tried to coexist but learned some hard lessons. They were looked down upon and feared by the early settlers, leading to a lot of unnecessary confrontation."

The road continued higher and higher until a clearing was reached. There were magnificent views of the mountain ranges and majestic valleys. One could imagine God looking over His dominion at the beauty of what He had created.

An old farmhouse stood perched on the very top of the clearing. The farmhouse was wooden, parched, and bleached from the sun. The covered porch offered protection from the suns direct rays and shade for the front windows. Charlie and Daniel pulled up to the side of the house, got out, and signaled Jeff and Rossi to follow.

As they approached the house on foot they could see two old women sitting on the porch. They were dressed in black with snowy white hair worn in a bun. Each wore one black feather piercing the hair bun like a hairpin, reminding anyone who saw them of their proud heritage.

They sat in silence, each with a basket of clothes, needles, and thread, wearing thimbles on their index fingers. The old women brought back memories of the past long forgotten by Jeff. He remembered his mother darning socks and tighten buttons on Dads work clothes after dinner. He remembered her sewing basket of tangled threads and mismatched buttons, and how difficult it was for him to thread sewing needles as a child, and how his mother would thread them effortlessly.

Jeff and Rossi stepped on to the porch and paused for a moment to smile at the old women and acknowledge their presence. They quickly realized that the gesture would not be reciprocated as the two women only briefly raised their eyes then lowered them again to concentrate on the task at hand.

Charlie and Daniel opened the screen door and paused in the threshold turning to Jeff and Rossi. Charlie got up on his tiptoes and the two men bent down to hear what he was about to whisper.

"Don't talk to him unless he asks you a question. Never touch him. No hand shaking."

The boys led Jeff and Rossi into a dark room. In front of a window facing the back of the house was the silhouetted figure backlit by the light coming through the window.

"Grandfather, I have brought the doctor and his friend as you wished."

An old and raspy voice answered.

"Good boy. Now leave us to discuss our business. Make sure you offer them something to drink or eat before they leave."

The old man swiveled his wheel chair around revealing a weathered face whose deep creases looked like they could tell a thousand stories. He nodded to the two men. He wore sunglasses and seemed to stare out the windows into space, like a blind man. A neck dress of colored feathers and animal teeth adorned his chest. His snowy white hair was tied in two side pigtails held together by rawhide bands. It reminded Jeff of the Shawmut Indian logo made famous by the Shawmut Bank of Boston.

Jeff and Rossi could smell the unmistakable scent of ozone in the air.

"Did they tell you not to talk to me?"

With hesitation, Jeff replied.

"Yes"

"You may speak to me freely. I will answer any questions that you both may have before I tell you why I brought you here. You will call me Mr. Shortsleeves.

Jeff and Rossi looked at each other as if to ask who would go first. Rossi won.

"Well Mr. Shortsleeves, small Charlie tells us that you are the oldest living human on this Earth. Is that true?"

"I do not know. I know that I have memory from before the white man arrived. The Gods will not grant me the gift of eternal peace that I so desire, even though I implore them. Instead of the gift of peace, they have given me the gift of sight. The ability to see things that no one can see. I hope someday to earn their mercy, and that they will grant me respite from the burden I bear. In the meantime I continue in their service."

Jeff began to move closer. The old Indians voice was beginning to fade in and out.

"Do not come closer! Do not touch me! I would not want to transfer to you an energy force that could ruin your progeny"

"Progeny?"

"Yes, doctor, progeny. Amanda will bear you two children. The first will be a male child who will possess all your qualities of intellect, sprit, character, and goodness. He will be like you in every way. He will be destined to make great contributions to the Earth. Your daughter will inherit Amanda's strength, intellect, and beauty. Together, your children will continue the legacy you will both leave behind."

Jeff was blown away by the Shamans prediction.

Meanwhile Rossi was standing around feeling totally neglected and not part of the conversation. He was thinking, maybe I should go outside and wait. Better yet, maybe I should get back in the truck and go home. Then, without warning, the old sage raised his feeble voice.

"And as for you Agent Rossi, banish those thoughts from your mind! Your efforts in this cause will not go unrewarded. They will not go unrecognized."

Holy shit, Rossi was thinking. The old man can read minds! Jeff and Rossi nodded to each other signaling that Joseph had captured their undivided attention.

"I have brought you here for an important reason. The land has been very anxious, more so than usual over the past several months. There have been numerous small tremors that I alone can feel. They warn me of something terrible that is on the way. The birds are flying in unpredictable patterns and the winds have become erratic in direction. Nature is entering a period of chaos. The land senses something worst than an earthquake is coming. Something that will change the balance of nature."

"I had a dream that commanded me to find you and tell you what you are looking for.The place you seek can be found next to the big arrowhead rock located on private land high on the hill in the region of route twenty. There are dark shadows in that place. Go there prepared to meet danger. There is still time to prevent destruction of the land. You must act soon."

Jeff and Rossi looked at each other and smiled, knowing that Spikes had come through again. Jeff approached Joseph Shortsleeves.

"How did you know where to find us?"

Mr. Shortsleeves took of his sunglasses revealing severe cataracts of both eyes.

"I see things that many cannot see."

Jeff thought he had just seen the worst case of cataracts he had ever encountered and reflexively offered help.

"Mr. Shortsleeves, I can get those cataracts removed and artificial lenses placed. It could give you back your sight. Let me help you."

"Oh no, Doctor Blake. I thank you, but I see much more clearly this way than before. This is part of my gift."

"I understand Mr. Shortsleeves. I have no more questions except to ask you, why are there tears in your eyes?"

"The land is crying. I cry with the land."

Jeff and Rossi were lost for words. They moved closer to the Shaman and bowed their heads in respect. Jeff needed to say something to the old Shaman before leaving.

"You have done the world a great service Mr.Shortsleeves. Agent Rossi and I will do everything in our power to prevent the terrible event. We ask you to please use all your powers to help us succeed. We need all the help we can get. I hope we meet again someday."

Joseph Shortsleeves nodded and put his sunglasses back on, turning again toward the view of the mountain.

Jeff and Rossi walked back to the car and said their goodbyes to Charlie and Daniel. Jeff guided the Nissan down the mountain road going faster than he should skidding on the gravel turns. He handed Rossi the map.

"We need to find that place."

Rossi started Googling "Arrowhead Rock,"and came up with a reference to Arrowhead Hill off of route twenty along the Snake River.

"Jeff, it's less than an hour from here. We should get there by three. That gives around four hours to look around and get back to the car before sunset."

The traffic was light along route twenty. When they reached the small bridge over the Snake River they knew they had gone too far. Jeff made a u turn and put on the hazard flashers as they crept down the road in the breakdown lane looking for a clearing or somewhere to pull over.

Rossi spotted the clearing first.

"Over there. Pull in over there. Look there's a walking path over there."

Rossi opened the glove compartment and produced a loaded Smith and Wesson 9mm and two loaded 8 shot clips he kept as a backup to the weapon always strapped to his side. He handed it over to Jeff who wasted no time ejecting the loaded magazine, pulling the slide back, checking the chamber, and then replacing the magazine. He chambered the first round, and clicked the safety on.

"Jeff, remember your training. If someone is up there, chances are they've posted a guard to sound a warning and take us out. No noise, stay low. If we come to a clearing or see the arrowhead marker we split up and secure the perimeter before we look around. Hand signals only." Jeff nodded.

Both men made their way through the narrow path and endured the heat and the bug bites in silence. Then, there it was, the arrowhead rock. They were surprised at how small the rock was. They expected something much larger. Rossi signaled Jeff to go right. Rossi went in the opposite direction.

After making the circle Rossi signaled Jeff with the all clear sign and Jeff did the same. They began looking around the arrowhead rock. Jeff was the first to smell the methane gas which led them to the mineshaft opening. They could see by the disturbed ground that there had been recent activity. Peering over the edge they saw nothing but the dark abyss.

Rossi proceeded to get readings from a miniature Geiger counter attached to his belt. It detected nothing but low-level background activity, normal for a rocky landscape. Rossi flashed Jeff the all clear signal.

"Well looky here!" The voice came from behind.

Rossi spun around, drew his gun instinctively, and yelled "FBI! DON'T MOVE!"

There were three of them. Bearded, dirty and mean looking with their shotguns trained on Rossi and Jeff.

"Well, looks like we got ourselves what they call a Mexican Standoff." Said the one in the middle.

Dangling from his lips was what looked like a cheroot cigar, thin and crooked after drying from the liquor dip.

By this time, Jeff had drawn his gun and taken position behind Rossi.

"We been up here near two years cooking moonshine and aint never seen anybody snooping around these parts. Now, seems like folks have taken a shine to that old mine. Maybe there's something hidden in that there mine that everybody wants."

Rossi kept his gun trained on the moonshiners and knew he could take out at least two of them before being blown to pieces by a close range shotgun blast. He couldn't show that he was scared shitless. He needed to show that he was in command of the situation.

His training taught him to instantly figure out who the leader was. It was usually the one doing all the talking. The others will take their cues from him. Once the leader is identified, he was trained to never take his eyes off the eyes and trigger finger of the leader.

"We don't give a shit about your moon shining operation! Put your guns down now, and we all go home to our families tonight!"

Rossi noticed the leader's finger back off the trigger and his eyes unfocused from them, instead, glancing from side to side at his two buddies, as if to signal them to follow his lead. Body language that told Rossi he was getting through to them.

"So, let me get this straight, Mr. FBI man. We put our guns down and nothing's going to happen to us. We free and clear?"

"That's right .You have my word. Now put your guns down slowly and step back!"

The leader went first. One by one they did as they were told.

"Now turn around and put your hands high over your heads. I'm not going to arrest you. I just need to be sure you don't have any other weapons."

As Rossi held them at gunpoint, Jeff collected the guns, removed the ammo, and made sure they had no other weapons.

"Ok, you can all turn around and relax now. All we want is information. We need your help in an investigation and promise nothing's going to happen to any of you. Tell me who's been snooping around these parts?"

The leader slowly took another puff of the crooked cheroot dangling from his mouth as if to savor the brandy it had been dipped in. Then took the cheroot out his mouth and spat on the ground.

"Well, a few days ago ,some fellers dressed in blue jumpsuits came up here and spent the better part on the afternoon checking out the old mine shaft. They had some fancy equipment that they lugged up the hill and ran some sort of tests or something. They were talkin some kind of gibberish. We kept out of sight but I'm sure they could see the smoke from the still over yonder."

Jeff stayed behind Rossi continually watching the perimeter as Rossi asked questions.

"Did they leave anything up here or put anything down into the shaft?"

"Not that we could find, and believe me, after they left we took a good look around. What's down there that everybody wants?"

"Nothing we hope. We have reason to believe that those guys you saw may be planning to put something down in there that could damage the land or water"

Rossi reached into his pocket, pulled out a card with his contact information, and handed it to the leader.

"If you see those guys up here again, do not approach them. They're dangerous. Call me directly, immediately, day or night. Do what I say and who knows, you guys could wind up heroes if we catch those bastards."

"Oh, and a couple more things. Finish up whatever you're cooking and move the still somewhere away from this place. Won't be long before this hill will be crawling with federal agents. And another thing, don't be sticking your head over that shaft with that lit cheroot in your mouth or the last thing you'll be hearing will be the sound of a loud boom!"

Jeff and Rossi knew that there mission had been a success. They were confident that they had found the precise place where the terrorist had chosen to place a bomb. They had gone out on a hunch and a wild goose chase. It wasn't as stupid as is sounded. They had faith that a higher authority would guide them. They were right. The search for the perpetrators could now be narrowed.

Rossi called Pointdexter and reported their success. The area had to be secured and surveillance set up. It all had to happen quietly. The bomb had to be found and secured if it had not been already planted. That was the number one priority. They still had no leads on the bombs whereabouts.

Rossi sent the exact coordinates of the location to the FBI on a secure cell channel. The FBI had to contact the CIA to get satellite surveillance on the location before a stealth team of spotters could be put in place. At least they could watch the area during daylight. A trap had to be set. A large security presence would scare off the bad guys ruining any chance of an apprehension and the bomb secured. The assets had to be put in place without detection. Backup had to be nearby and completely out of sight. No one could know about the operation. Even the local and state police would be kept out of the loop.

Jeff would have to wait until he got home to tell Amanda and Romilov about their adventure. By now there were no secrets among the trio. Jeff and Rossi had no idea that while

314

driving back to their hotel to gather up their stuff and get back home they had passed a black van coming in the opposite direction.

Mustafa and his gang were on their way to plant the device under the cover of darkness. The sun was setting behind the mountains. They would be in and out before any team could be put in place.

Chapter 32

The black van pulled onto the now familiar clearing just off the highway where the path to arrowhead began. This time it was parked nose facing out to reduce its profile. A black tarp was placed over the nose of the van to prevent any reflection off the glass headlight covers which might potentially be seen from the road.

The sky was overcast that night. There was no moonlight. It wasn't long before the forest turned black with darkness. This time the crew was heavily armed. Each member carried an AR15 assault rifle and sidearms outfitted with silencers. This night would be the culmination of years of planning. Mustafa and his men were determined that nothing would get in their way.

They gathered outside the van and put on night vision goggles. The eerie green glow seen through the goggles not only illuminated the forest but revealed the spooky lit up eyes of critters roaming around the woods looking for food. They seemed to be everywhere. The men began to express trepidation of their newfound friends. Mustafa motioned to them to come together behind the van.

"Don't worry about the animals. They were here the other day just as close only they are now. They are experts at staying out of sight. They fear us as much as we fear them. Only the mountain lion and grizzly bear found in this area pose any threat. If we have the misfortune of encountering one of them, we have enough firepower to eliminate them. Now pay attention to the task at hand."

The explanation seemed to satisfy everyone

The device which had been amply wrapped in heat resistant wrap was carefully unloaded and placed on a gurney type stretcher that could be carried by four men. Mustafa checked it again for any radiation leakage that could possibly be detected and there was none. They reached the clearing at the arrowhead rock and placed the device down near the opening of the mine. They removed the camouflage stones that had been placed hiding the opening.

A portable wench was erected and the device lifted to a position over the mineshaft ready for descent. One last check with the remote cell phone detonator showed a four bar cell signal strength. They were good to go.

Just then, a crackling snapping sound of twigs breaking warned them that someone was approaching. Through the green haze of the night vision goggles they could see three figures stumbling through the dark then turning on flashlights. There was no time to take cover. The visitors were upon them.

"What would you boys be doing up here in the dark? What's in the box?"

Before a word could be said, multiple thud like sounds rang out from silenced shots. The three intruders were shot multiple times and down in an instant. They never knew what hit them. Abdulla walked over and shot each one again through the forehead, execution style, as Mustafa and the others looked on.

"Abdulla, go down to where we saw the smoke the last time. Find the camp. Make sure there is no one remaining in their camp. There can be no witnesses. We will dispose of these bodies."

The bodies of the three men were dragged and thrown down into the mineshaft. A distant splash was heard as each one hit the water below.

Abdulla had no problem finding the camp. Light from the embers burning in a fire pit were still visible glowing in the night vision goggles. He found a young woman and small child cowering under a blanket.

"Get out from under there!"

"Where is my husband and my brothers?"

"Never mind that. Get up and come with me!"

He led them back to the mine bringing them to Mustafa.

"I found these two. What should we do?"

Mustafa walked over to the little girl, bent down to her eye level, and removed his goggles.

Her mother screamed pleading to leave her daughter alone. He took the girl by the hand.

"Let's go see your daddy."

With a kind smile on his face he brought her to the edge of the mineshaft, gently kissed the top of her head, and pushed her over the edge to her death while her mother screamed in horror. He quickly turned to Abdulla and yelled.

"Shut that woman up!"

One shot to the woman's temple and the night turned quiet again.

Without skipping a beat the men cranked the device down the shaft to a depth of 1000 ft. The wench was folded down inside the shaft and bolted into the rock using stone anchor bolts. Just in case something went wrong, the wench was down far enough and out of site, readied to be reused if needed. Twenty five million dollars in the bottom of a pit couldn't just be left there without a retrieval plan. What if something went wrong?

The men covered the opening, gathered up all their gear, and made it back to the van.

Their plan was to drive to Miami and wait to dial the fatal number triggering to bomb to explode with a lead time of forty eight hours. Mustafa made sure to put the number on speed dial. That would be enough time to charter a boat to Cuba where they could get a private jet to North Africa and back to Iran making a clean getaway. A second number that bypassed the delay was also programmed into the phone giving the option to detonate quickly.

The bomb would be detonated on Mawlid al-Nabi,the birthday of the Prophet Mohammad, six weeks away.

Chapter 33

Jeff's plane was about to touch down at Logan Airport just as the rush hour traffic was building in downtown Boston. As the plane descended below the cloud cover, he could see and pick out familiar places from a much different perspective. How small everything looked from only around fifteen hundred feet up. To think that everything in his world could be so small when seen from a larger scale perspective was humbling. He recalled the words of Spikes talking about grains of sand in the cosmos.

The overcast skies of Boston were in sharp contrast to the blue skies of Idaho. He was so happy to be seeing Amanda that he never gave it a thought. Rossi nudged Jeff's arm and said,

"Home sweet home."

Jeff began thinking how that the gritty feel of a northern city, overcast with clouds, was strangely comforting to someone who had spent his whole life there. Memories, connections to people, places and things, had all taken place under those clouds. It was home, with that feeling of comfort that only home could give.

"Jeff, first I'm going to pick up the guns at the firearms check in desk. Then I'm going to grab a cab. Then, I'm going to grab a thick steak and a beer. Say hello to Amanda and don't forget, heads up. They'll be a lot of curious types who will want to know how you and your brainy team came up with that vaccine. You don't have to tell them shit."

Jeff stood on the pickup arrival sidewalk waiting for Amanda to come by. He had texted her while she waited in the cell phone parking lot awaiting his arrival. He spotted her driving their trusty old Beemer in the long line inching up to where she could pull over. He could see the trunk popping open readied for him to throw in his bag. A signal telling him that she had seen him too.

At that moment of anticipation of seeing Amanda again, he felt the strong comforting feeling of having a partner in life. That comfort of knowing that someone has your back. That, no matter what happens, there is someone that will help you get through whatever life throws your way. He was reminded of how much he really loved her.

He jumped in the front seat next to her and before a word could be spoken, almost on cue, they both embraced and kissed with total disregard for the cars and taxies behind them honking to get out of the way. Her familiar scent and soft cheek against his face were reminders of their bond and what they meant to each other. Romilov was in the back seat with his head sticking out from the back window swearing in Russian at the cabbies telling them to go around.

Not letting go, she pulled her head back and looked straight into Jeff's eyes.

"Don't you ever leave me alone like that again."

"I won't. It was a mistake and stupid not to bring you. I won't do it again. I missed you so much."

On the way home Jeff recounted details of the adventure with special emphasis on the story of the Shaman and his help in locating the location of interest. Amanda and Romilov, for their part, recounted the public commotion caused the discovery of the vaccine and the press coverage just now starting to ease up. She warned Jeff that there were still some reporters outside the condo and camped out at the lab and to be ready for all the attention that brings. The drive home seemed to pass quickly.

Amanda pulled the car into their parking space behind the condo, turned the ignition off, but did not open the door. Everyone had noticed that there were only two reporters lingering outside a news van parked across the street from their condo. She turned toward Jeff.

"They're going to be asking a lot of questions about where you went and what you were doing."

Jeff reached out and held Amanda's hands.

"We say nothing. We just do a lot of smiling and nodding. We need to fade out of the limelight. The more meat you give them the hungrier they get. They'll get tired and move to more fertile ground."

Romilov leaned in over the front seat.

"So good to have you home again young man. I was worried about your safety."

He put his hand on Amanda's shoulder.

"We were both worried."

Rather than exit the car immediately, they paused for a moment. Everyone sort of took a deep breath. The professor leaned back in the seat, peered out the window, and began to muse.

"Well, looks like our adventure with the infamous Mr. Spikes is coming to a close. When the authorities apprehend the criminals, all should be right in Oz."

"On the contrary, Yuri. This odyssey is just beginning. I don't think we've seen the last of Mr. Spikes. He's here on a mission much bigger than I think we know. It's not over yet."

They made their way inside the house waving off the reporters who spotted them. Once inside they were just getting comfortable when Jeff noticed a text on his phone. It was Rossi.

"Sorry Bud, I'm on my way over."

Jeff wondered what could have happen that Rossi, who he had just left, was coming over. He let the others know that they would be having a visitor. Romilov threw his hands in the air.

"For the love of God, can we have no peace? At least for one day."

Amanda shrugged and started adding more coffee to the coffee maker and setting another place at the table. Romilov noticed that the Boston Police had pulled up by the news van out front and gotten them to move along. It wasn't long after that Rossi arrived and went inside. Being the gentleman that he was, he went right over to Amanda first.

"Sorry to barge in on you like this. I know you all need a little down time but something's come up that I need to tell you all about, before you see it on the TV. I had my friends on the Boston PD move those idiots outside so I wouldn't be spotted coming in."

They all sat down around the table as Amanda poured the coffee. Rossi had everyone's attention.

"We have assets all around the bomb site and there has been no activity noted. Satellite eyes haven't picked up a damn thing. There's a biker bar down the street from the site. Somebody went in there and shot up the place then burned it to the ground. Three dead. There was one survivor who reported that there was more than one gunman and that they were driving a black van with some kind of business logo on the side. They didn't take anything. By all accounts the attack was unprovoked. One thing though. The survivor thinks the shooter was Middle Eastern. That got my attention. I know, I'm not PC, but I don't give a shit. There might be a connection between our bad guys and this event. Just sayin. Everyone's looking for the van."

Rossi paused for a minute. Jeff commented that the surveillance team was jumping the gun and needed to give more time. Amanda began to fret that maybe the Intel regarding the bombs location was incorrect and everyone's wasting their time. Rossi echoed that it was a possibility.

Romilov took his glasses off and began rubbing his eyes before looking up toward Rossi.

"Dear Agent Rossi. You fail to remember that the circumstances that led, both you, and the good Dr Blake, to that place was engineered by the one and only Mr. Spikes. His fingerprints are all over it. You're forgetting that he is never wrong about anything. Don't lose faith. You were in the right place. Of that, I have no doubt."

Rossi had his head down holding his face like someone frustrated and grappling with difficult problem.

"Thanks professor. Of course it's the right place."

Rossi's speech began to hesitate before beginning to speak again like somebody searching for the right words to say, careful that it comes out right.

"Prepare yourselves for what I am about to tell you. The real reason I came over today. It's something I was briefed on before I even had time to unpack my bags. It's something that will change the world forever."

An expression of alarm spread over everyone's face.

Chapter 34

Jet Propulsion Laboratory
Pasadena, California
One week earlier

Elizabeth Enright was only 23 years old when she learned that she was the recipient of the J. Harvey scholarship for excellence in aerospace science. A recent graduate from Caltech with a degree in aerospace engineering, the award had earned her the opportunity to intern at the Jet Propulsion Lab for one month before starting her Master's Degree program.

She had always been a little on the geeky side. While her friends were winning awards for sports that impressed everyone, she was quietly acing the most difficult science courses that no one gave a shit about. On the other hand, she was going to the JPL and they were not. To say she was excited was an understatement. After all, this was the place that developed America's first orbiting satellite, and manages NASAs deep space probe programs. There's probably more brainpower per square foot in the JPL than in any other place in the country. She was determined to make a good impression and had prepared for her first day.

She entered the visitors lobby and couldn't help but notice the impressive large marble and bronze plaque on the wall depicting the Earth with satellites whizzing around it. She checked in at the security desk giving her name and student clearance number and scanned her fingerprints which matched with her application prints. The desk verified that she would be coming in that day. They gave her security badge with instructions to report to the third floor section G. The picture on the badge was a good likeness, but as any woman would, she grimaced when she glanced at it.

Before swiping her badge through the security lock to section G she paused to take a deep breath and compose herself. This was the moment she had dreamed about during her entire undergraduate life while taking courses with names that most students would run from.

Her straight blond hair was perfectly cut to shoulder length, resting on her white blouse. A tasteful gold chain given to her by her parents held a gold charm replica of the wall plaque logo of the JPL, the same one she had just seen in the lobby. It depicted the Earth , flanked by a tiny rocket and satellite. It had been custom made by the family jeweler just for her. Her face glowed with just a touch of blush. A tasteful black knee length skirt and short-heeled matching shoes finished her professional look. She swiped the card, listened to the loud buzz, and waited a few moments as the door clicked open.

"Hey, I'm Dr Bryant. You must be Elizabeth. Welcome to JPL. Follow me."

As she followed Dr Bryant she quickly, and duly noted, that the Doctor had her hair in a bun, and was wearing no makeup. Worst than that, she was wearing jeans, a polo shirt, and black rubber clogs.

The walk through passed by all kinds people, presumably engineers and scientists, working on computers or drawing out complicated formulas on clear glass boards with colored magic markers...all wearing jeans, polo shirts, and clogs for the women or Lands End leather deck shoes for the men. Not a single white lab coat in sight.

Mortified that she stuck out like a sore thumb, she took comfort in the fact that she hadn't put on the lab coat she had folded in her bag. She was directed to a small area open the the workroom, where there were lockers. Dr Bryant gave her a key.

"This is where you'll put your stuff."

Then turning to the group of workers in the work room, Bryant raised her hand to get their attention.

"Attention everyone! This is our new intern. Her name is Elizabeth. Please try not to be too rough on her. Remember people, she might be your boss some day! Stranger things have happened around here."

Everyone gave smiles and welcoming nods.

"Sorry Elizabeth, but you arrived at kind of a awkward moment. I wanted to give you the grand tour, kind of show you the lay of the land and explain your assignment. But, it just so happens, that we have a staff meeting literally starting right now. Everyone will be tied up for about an hour. I'll have to leave you alone until we are out"

"So, in the meantime have a look around on your own. Don't touch anything. Read your security rules folder. That's the first thing we will be going over."

Dr. Bryant looked down at her watch then back to Elizabeth.

"I wish I could invite you in, but you're not cleared for a class 3 meeting yet. If anything blows up, just come in and get someone."

Dr Bryant looked as Liz's eyes went wide after hearing the words, "blow up."

"Just kidding." She assured her.

"Please Doctor Bryant, just call me Liz."

"Ok Liz, I'll see you in about an hour."

The conference room door closed behind her with a sign dangling from the back reading, MEETING IN PROGRESS. RING BUZZER TO INTERUPT ONLY AT YOUR OWN RISK, with a smiley face emoji. Liz looked down and saw the buzzer button with a small speaker confident she would never ring it.

With everyone in the meeting, the work area took on an eerie quiet solitude, with only the sound of machines humming and an occasional beeping sound, reminding any listeners that the technology is at work twenty-four seven. As Liz moved slowly around the area, she noticed a wide open door leading to another room. There were colored lights flickering from the inside reflecting against the walls. Remembering that she was given permission to look around as long as she didn't touch anything, she poked her head inside to take a look.

"OMG" , she whispered to herself. There it was, on giant HD screens, the live feed of the Mars Rovers space vehicles Curiosity and Opportunity. Both of these rovers had exceeded their planned missions and life expectancies, dutifully sending back a goldmine of data and images. They move at a snail's pace sending video and sound, collecting Martian soil samples, and reporting everything from air quality to soil composition. In fact, it took five years for Curosity to travel only eleven miles. Liz knew that it takes, depending on the solar winds, fourteen to twenty minutes for the communication signal to travel the three hundred and fifty million miles back to Earth.

She began to stare at the image sent back by Curiosity. Orange sand and rocks for as far as the eye could see in spectacular detailed high def. A never changing jagged horizon in the distance and a strange luminescent dusky sky gave the feeling of a desolate, sad, and lonely place. A place devoid of life.

She wondered if the thousands of people around the world monitoring the live feed on the NASA live internet channel were experiencing the same feeling these images gave to her, to fully appreciate a world blessed by life and all its beautiful diversity, rather than the empty void, of a world without life. NASA keeps the live feed up to spark interest by the public and help keep the funding coming.

The periphery of the screen was packed with numbers giving data on atmospheric pressure and composition, temperature, wind velocity, and a lot more. Hardly any oxygen, lots of carbon dioxide. No barometric pressure, just a vacuum, that could suck the oxygen out of your lungs, cause your sweat to boil, and kill you, in about fifteen seconds if you weren't in a spacesuit.

She looked down at her watch. Still another forty-five minutes before the meeting would end. Now would be a good time to go over the security manual for what would be at least the fourth time. She reached into her bag behind the lab coat she was so glad she hadn't put on knowing, that the manual was under it. Just then the Curiosity monitor started to beep.

Glancing back at the screen, she saw a small flashing message in red on the lower left side of the screen.

"MOTION DETECTED"

Scanning the screen she saw nothing moving. Just the same lifeless image of a barren wasteland. Then, a red circle, like a target bull's-eye, appeared on the screen and zoomed in to a spot, far off in the distance. In the circle was what appeared to be a black dot.

She began to feel a sense of panic sinking in. What should I do? Should I disturb the meeting and report this? Will I look stupid or piss somebody off? On the other hand, maybe, they would be like, "why did you wait to let us know about this you jerk? She knew she had to do something.

The motion detection warning kept flashing and beeping and wouldn't stop. The black dot was getting larger.

Liz made a beeline for the meeting room door, looked down at the black buzzer button. She pressed it. A male voice came through the speaker box.

"What is it?"

"This is Liz, the new intern. I'm really sorry to bother you, but the screen on the Curiosity feed is flashing a motion warning signal and I thought you'd want to know."

"Thanks Liz, replied the voice.

"Come on in."

The buzzer lock release sounded and the door opened. Liz stood by the doorway looking worried. One of the men at the table raised his hand looking toward Liz.

"Hi Liz. I'm Jack Butler, Curiosity project manager. That dam warning comes on all the time for the slightest disturbance. Usually wind just stirring up some dust."

He turned his focus on the team member sitting directly across the table.

"Neal, weren't you supposed to decrease the motion sensitivity this week? I thought we already talked about that.

How long is that going to take? These false alarms cut in to productive work time."

"Right boss. My team is working a software command to decrease motion detection sensitivity without affecting Curiosities 'sound module. Motion and sound functions are connected more than we realized. Should be ready to test soon. I'll break for a sec and turn the thing off."

Neal got up moved toward the door. Jack nodded toward Liz.

"Oh Liz, welcome to JPL."

"Thank you Sir."

Liz followed Neil toward the Curiosity monitoring station feeling the obligation to apologize for the intrusion.

"Sir, I'm sorry for disturbing your meeting. I hope I didn't get you in any kind of trouble but..."

"My name is Neal. Just call me Neal. You did the right thing anyone in your circumstance would have done. No apologies necessary. Jack is a great boss. Sometimes his old astronaut commander stuff comes out. We all humor him."

Neal looked at the screen for a very long time. With a look of astonishment on his face he blurted out, "Holy Shit!"

He turned around, and without saying another word ran to the meeting room door which was still open. Grasping both sides of the doorframe, and out of breath, he leaned forward inside toward the group.

"Ok people. You'd better get your asses in there right now. You all need to see this!"

The room emptied like someone had yelled "Fire!"

334

Everyone huddled around the screen while Liz stood by the side wondering what the hell was happening. Jack took the lead.

"What the hell is that? Said Jack, pointing to the black dot that seemed to be getting larger.

"Did somebody put something up there we don't know about? Is the CIA or NSA fucking with us? Somebody turn the feed off now! The public can't see this!"

Neal reached over and threw a switch that produced the message, TECHNICAL DIFFICULTIES, PLEASE STAND BY on the third screen, the image that the public sees.

From the moment the feed switch was switched off, no one but the team could see this incredible sight unfolding before their eyes. The public, now shut out, had seen a lot more than they should have.

"Call the director. Get security to shut down the grounds and secure this building. Nobody goes in or out until we figure out what's happening."

The black dot continued to become larger. The team began to see the outline of a humanoid figure approaching Curiosity. They watched, mesmerized by the figure which appeared to be walking like a human slowly toward Curiosity.

Details of the figure began to emerge. It was definitely humanoid. Tall and slender, with what looked like a black stocking like covering or maybe skin. No bulky space suit.

An almost panic like state began to take hold with everyone shouting out comments and questions at once. It was pandemonium. Jack stood up from the console turned to his troops with as distressed expression on his face and yelled in a loud voice.

"OK, everybody, shut the fuck up! Quiet! One at a time! Were getting nowhere like this."

" Make sure the recorder and the sound is on."

"It's always on." Came a voice from the group.

"I know that! Just make sure it's on NOW!"

"It's on now chief. No worries."

The mysterious and astonishing figure walked up to within two feet of Curiosity's camera lens. It leaned forward and looked directly into the lens with a close-up of its eye that looked like the eye of anyone in the room.

It then moved back enough that its head filled the whole screen. Facial features were not discernible. The black surfacing of its body seemed to be some kind of black smooth coating containing tiny raised yellow dots.

Then still looking directly at the cameras lens, it declared in perfect English...

"HELLO. WE'VE BEEN WINKING AT EACH OTHER FOR THE LAST FIFTY YEARS. I THOUGHT IT TIME WE MADE EACH OTHERS ACQUAINTANCE."

Everyone in the room gasped. There was no way to respond. No two-way communications on Curiosity. Besides, the signal averaged fourteen to sometimes twenty minutes to travel one way depending on the atmospheric conditions on

336

Mars. All they could do was stare and listen in awe. The message continued.

"You can call me Leonard...Leonard Spikes. It's a name I've chosen for myself that seems to suit me well. I've been moving around your lovely world for quite some time now and have had the pleasure of getting to know some of you. Please excuse the dramatic venue I have chosen for my introduction. I wanted to get your undivided attention, and dispel any doubts concerning my authenticity."

"One more thing. You have nothing to fear from me. I assure you that my presence here is a good thing. However, I must warn you. You have a lot to fear from each other."

"We will discuss more about that in the near future. I will make my presence known to the whole world soon via an exclusive broadcast during a meeting from Switzerland at the site of your new linear accelerator. Again, I repeat. You have nothing to fear except each other. Until then, I would advise world leaders to make preparations for this historic event."

Spikes then turned and slowly walked away from Curiosity leaving footprints, clearly visible, in the sand.

Jack Butler quickly took command.

"Everybody back in the conference room. You too Liz. You're part of this now whether you like it or not."

The group filed back into the conference room in silence. Neal closed the door. Then Jack took up position at the head of the table pausing to gather his words.

"I think what we all saw in there was real. We need to assume that for now. You can bet we're going to check the feed line code on the stream segment to be sure it's our code. That'll make sure that no one hacked the feed."

Jack turned somber as he continued to address the group. He felt humbled by what he had just experienced. He knew that everyone in that room had chosen the field of aerospace science and committed their working lives to this endeavor for the same reason. To answer the question. Are we alone?

"People, if this is real and I think that it is, then, to the best of our knowledge, we will have been the first to make official contact with intelligent extraterrestrial life. I want you all to think long and hard about the implications of this event both in general and to each of you personally."

"We've all been given an amazing privilege. With that privilege we've also been given a great responsibility. We have the responsibility to handle this like the true professionals that we are. Our responsibility extends to our employer, to our government, our nation, and the entire global community."

Jack walked slowly around the conference table where everyone was seated as he spoke. Even though they were beside themselves with excitement and wonderment, no one was making a sound.

"I'm going to contact and report this event to the CIA, NSA, and the White House through the usual secure channels. Your job is to sick to the security rules you all signed and pledged before taking this job. You will speak to no one about this matter. No one especially includes your families. It won't be easy, but that is what YOU all will do."

"In the meantime we will continue to monitor and support the mission as usual. I don't think they'll be able to keep the lid on this one for long. My guess is that a new era is about to begin. Don't worry, when the time is right, you'll all be able to write your books, memoirs or whatever. You'll get your fifteen minutes of fame. But for now, this event is classified top secret. Are we all clear on that? Are there any questions?"

Everyone stirred uncomfortably looking around at each other. Then, out of the group, came a reply.

"What about the lockdown?"

"I going to lift it right now and tell the security chief it was a false alarm. I'll tell him it was my mistake. Bryant, get a team together and go over the video clip with a fine toothcomb. Make sure there is nothing we missed."

Jack went over to where Liz was standing bewildered.

"Liz, you're one lucky girl. Someday you'll be telling your grand children about this day."

Nervously moving her eyes from side to side she answered.

"Yes sir, can I go home now?"

Chapter 35

"Sorry everyone but this can't wait. Ok everybody; now hold on to your hats. You're not going to friggin believe this!"

Romilov, losing patience, jumped in "For God's sake, what the hell is it!"

Rossi took a deep breath and began.

"Spikes made contact with a group of scientists at the JPL... from Mars! Walked right up to the Rover Curiosity like someone on a Sunday stroll, looked right into Curiosity's lens and basically said, we're here! The cats out of the bag now. Top military brass, white house, and everyone else are running around like crazy trying to figure out what to do."

"They're putting together a statement. Consensus is building that the answers to the question of "are we alone" can't be kept a secret anymore. The global UFO community is going ape-shit. They got enough of a glimpse on NASA live feed to know something big just happened. They're demanding answers."

"The President has decided to make an announcement soon. The news outlets have not been prepped. He's put the military on alert. The speech writers are hard at work. All hell is about to break lose."

Everyone stood silently looking at each other as if to say, now what?"

Romilov again was the first to open up.

"It's about time! This is a good thing! As long as the visitors are peaceful, only good things can happen. Already, good things have happened! Spikes has already moved science ahead by fifty years."

Everyone nodded in agreement with the professor's remarks. Rossi wasn't finished.

"One more thing. They found the van we think belongs to the terrorists. An employee in an auto storage facility in Miami called the authorities to report five Middle Eastern looking guys who rented a storage space for a black van with Idaho tags and the words Evergreen Engineering on the side. There were blue jumpsuits in the back together with all kinds of geological stuff and a bag containing survey site maps of the area where the mine we checked out is located. Looks like they rented a Ford SUV from the storage place and gave them a credit card and driver's license issued to a Miguel Hormosa."

"We ran a background check. Turns out that this Hormosa guy was s student at Oregon State who died in a MVA two years ago. There's a full court press out to find these guys and an APB out for the SUV."

"Here's the scary part. They wouldn't have left the area unless the bomb was already planted and ready to go. Our guys on the ground report no movement at the site at all. There's equipment and guys ready to go down the hole and look for it. We have to pray that it's there or were up shits creek. A two hundred mile radius will need to be evacuated if we don't find and neutralize it. I'm leaving in one hour to Miami to help find those bastards. They've either set a timer already or have a remote. My moneys on the remote."

Jeff looked over his shoulder at Amanda and then back to Rossi.

"Is it possible that they put some kind of a lead shield or something to block any radiation detection? Remember, you had a Geiger counter that didn't show jack shit."

"Anything's possible."

Jeff gazed downward while he unloosened his tie then looked up toward Rossi.

"What can we do? Did the President say when the announcement was coming? Do we know when Spikes will speak again?"

"Right now, we don't know the time table but word has it that it's going to be real soon."

342

Rossi paused for a moment then motioned for everyone to sit down with a look of resolve on his face.

"So here's the deal. You three have had the most contact with Spikes. Everyone knows that. Word has it that you three will be called upon to make a public statement following the President's announcement."

"They want you to make a statement about Spikes. They want you to put a positive spin of the situation. Tell people not to be afraid. All the big wigs are scared shitless that the public may go berserk thinking that doomsday has arrived. Civil unrest, violence, suicides. That sort of stuff. They need credible people who are not in the government to calm the public's fears."

Amanda jumped in.

"I'll take care of that. Tell them not to worry. I'm not going to bullshit anyone. We'll tell the truth about Spikes, everything we know, our honest impressions. That's what we'll do. This is no time for spinning any stories. Facts and the truth. That's what everyone needs to know. I'll start working on it right away."

Rossi started to head toward the door, almost forgetting to let the others know his next assignment.

"I'm leaving for Miami this afternoon. See you all when I get back. Wish me luck."

"Wait. Jeff said. I'm coming with you."

"No, I need you to stay here. Director Pointdexter has ordered us on this mission and made it clear that there will be no civilians. Agents from the Miami office will meet me there and help. The President will be counting on all three of you to calm the public."

Amanda grabbed Jeff's arm clearly signaling him that he wasn't going anywhere. She went over to the door and put her arms around Rossi.

"I want you back here in one piece...be careful and remember... you're like a brother...you're one of us."

Rossi smiled and looked over toward Jeff and the professor. The smile quickly changed to a look of determination.

As Rossi had predicted, the trio were summoned to the White House for a meeting with the President. They were becoming frequent flyers at the Hanscom Field military airport. What a thrill, as they landed on the White House lawn!

Each of them was thinking how crazy it was that they were actually having a private meeting with the President of the United States. Romilov was thinking. "If only my friends back home, and those KGB assholes, could see me know. I'd love to see the look on their faces. If only Marlena was here to share this excitement."

Jeff remembered his mother and father and hoped they could look down from heaven and see their boy, now, on this day.

Amanda's memories of her parents and of her humble beginnings welled up in her mind. She gave thanks to God for all her blessings.

They were greeted by Pointdexter and White House security personnel. Pointdexter put out his hand.

"So nice to see you all again. Thank you for coming. The President will see you as soon as we get inside.

A light drizzle was falling. The lawn was a lush green from all the moisture. In the middle of all this, Amanda began to worry that her hair would frizz up just before she got to meet the President.

They were led inside and brought directly to the oval office. Nothing could have prepared them for the simple elegance of the room. From the long windows flanked by textured drapes to the presidential portraits and Native American wooded sculptures, they found themselves immersed in a tradition of history, pride, and strength. The President's desk was larger than it seemed in pictures but very ordered.

The sitting area consisted of two sofas face to face divided by a coffee table and two fabric chairs at each end. One blue and one matching the sofa fabric design. Everyone noticed the large monitor set up in front of the sitting area.

They were offered coffee or tea and directed to take seats in the sitting area leaving the blue chair for the president. Pointdexter sat on the far right sofa representing the CIA. He introduced everyone to Daniel Strattford, secretary of defense sitting to his left. Stratford looked different than he did on the television news shows. He was older and shorter, both in height and personality. He kept rifling through a folder of notes looking like a nervous college student preparing for an exam.

No more than a minute later President Cabot entered through a side door with a quick step and forced smile on his face. Everyone rose to their feet. He motioned everyone to sit down and wasted no time in getting down to business.

"I take it you've all been introduced?

Looking specifically at the trio he continued.

"I want to thank you all for coming on such a short notice. In the matter we are about to discuss, time is of the essence. There is something I want you to see."

The lights dimmed and the monitor lit up with the video of Spikes introducing himself to the staff at the JPL. When it was over he addressed the group.

"Ladies and gentlemen, this is not a hoax! The signal carried the imbedded security code only the Curiosity cameras can transmit. We've known about these "things" for years. They've always stayed on their side of the fence and we on ours.

"Roswell was bullshit but running in to them on the moon was not. Why do you think forty years after the moon landing we never went back?"

"We can't keep this a secret any longer. I've personally contacted over twenty world leaders and the UN president informing them of the event and our upcoming announcement. As you can imagine, we are worried about worldwide panic, demonstrations, breakdown of law and order, and of rogue nations taking advantage of the situation to start something. Moreover, there's still the problem of knowing the true intentions of our new visitors. If you recall, it didn't turn out well for Native Americans when Columbus arrived."

Next the President turned directly toward the trio.

"You three have had the closest contact with the entity who calls himself Mr.Spikes. I need your thoughts and impressions on him, his motives, his abilities, how many there are, where they hide, that sort of thing."

Everyone glanced at each other for a moment not knowing if there was a protocol. If there was Amanda broke it first.

"Mr. President, thank you for the honor of being invited here. May I speak openly?
The President nodded in the affirmative.

"With all due respect I would refrain from referring to our new friends as "things."

Jeff and the professor had to suppress a slight grimace at Amanda's statement. Even the President lowered his eyes and mumbled something like "Of course, of course."

"Secondly, I know I speak for my colleagues when I tell you that we are convinced Mr. Spikes has come in peace. He has told us over and over that he is here to save us from ourselves. His powers are extraordinary. He could have caused chaos. Instead, he chose to warn us of an impending terrorist plot which, with his help, is being thwarted as we speak. He revealed to us genetic breakthroughs that are astounding and have the potential to cure cancer. He sent a warning to those who would risk the existence of mankind in the form of the Blue Dot virus then provided a cure to assert his power but show that he is not a threat. He is a benevolent being, and that is the message we must tell everyone who will listen."

Daniel Strattford leaned in from his position on the sofa directly toward the President.

"What if this is all a ruse to let down our guard?"

"What guard?" Said Jeff, looking at Strattford. "You have no guard. You're powerless against Spikes! Why don't you get that? He's trying to show us how to get out of the mess we've created for ourselves. Why don't we just let him do that and listen to him?"

Romilov added.

"Mr. President, he has moved science ahead by fifty years and has asked for nothing in return."

The President got up and stood in front of everyone with a commanding presence.

"We have to believe that everything you three are saying is true. What choice do we have? Spikes said he is going to make his presence known to the whole world in a broadcast from Switzerland. My people tell me it's coming up three days from now. There is nothing we can do to stop it without looking like desperate bullies. Nor do I think should we try."

"I'm going to prepare a thoughtful message directly after he speaks from Switzerland. It will be tweaked as needed depending on what he has to say. I will introduce you three afterword to say something and take questions from reporters. Unless something changes I will welcome Mr. Spikes and thank him for the advancements in science he has given us. Frankly, I don't know what else to do. By the way, before you, Pope Alexander will address the world from Saint Peters Square. He has assured me his message will be one of peace, reconciliation, and joy, rejoicing in the fact that we are not alone."

"Also, in the meantime, Agent Rossi, who has done remarkable work tracking those sons of bitches plotting to blow up Yellowstone is being assisted by Homeland Security personal and our best people from the CIA. We need to stop them and bring that threat to a safe conclusion."

The President directed his next comment to Amanda.

"Amanda, may I call you Amanda?"

"Of course, Sir."

"Please have a copy of your statement to the public on my desk as soon as possible. I need to review your comments prior to broadcast."

It was clear that no one would be leaving Washington until the announcement was over.

Chapter 36

It wasn't every day that an Air Force Galaxy cargo plane landed at the Billings Montana International Airport. Airport personnel, civilian travelers, and visitors watched in awe as the giant plane taxied to a remote corner of the airport. There were four busses and two eighteen wheelers positioned to meet the plane.

It didn't take long for word of the landing to get out. News vehicles began to descend on the airport. Reuters news feed began to buzz with announcements of the landing to news outlets throughout the country. What's the military doing in this remote area?

Around a hundred combat equipped troops exited the plane and got on to the buses. They were followed by large military camouflage containers loaded onto the tractor-trailers. Three

Humvees, and an army helicopter equipped with search and rescue lights, and what looked like an armored personal vehicle rolled out of the Galaxy and on to the tarmac. Lastly, out trotted a dozen German Shepherds, led and leashed by their military handlers. They all lined up forming a convoy and were escorted out by airport police with lights flashing . There was nothing secret about their arrival. The cavalry had landed. Their destination? The Bartlett mine.

"Sergeant Castillo! Get me the chief of police of Pocatello on the line!"

"Yes Sir, Colonel Peters, right away."

Charlie Peters founded the Army's first formal ordinance training school at Fort Devens in Massachusetts over twenty years ago. He was a tough combat veteran respected not only as a warrior but also as an academic. Peters pioneered methods of underwater bomb diffusing and recovery. His team was responsible for the recovery and disposal of two nuclear bombs lost in the Pacific Ocean in 1997. His mission? Search, recover, disarm, and dispose of a suspected nuclear device somewhere in the vicinity of Bartlett Mine.

Sergeant Castillo handed the phone to Colonel Peters.

"Chief Morrissey? This Is Colonel Charlie Peters, US Army."

"By order of the President of the United States, I'm commanding a convoy of one hundred and thirty personnel to be deployed in and around the old Bartlett mine. I am not at liberty to discuss the nature of our mission at this time. We should be out of your hair in about eighteen hours. I'm asking you to cooperate by keeping your people out of our perimeter

351

and keeping any curious civilians away. Traffic will need to be diverted. Can I count on your cooperation?"

"Well, it would help us, Colonel, to know what's going on, but I understand if you can't give us the details. Colonel, you can count on us, but let me know about anything that could put my people or the citizens of Pocatello in harm's way."

"Will do, and thank you."

The convoy arrived at the site at around two PM. By sundown the one hundred or so armed troops set up a one-quarter mile perimeter around the Bartlett mine site. There were bright LED white light lamps to illuminate the forest giving the whole area a surrealistic and eerie glow. The helicopter hovering ran a strafing pattern of searchlights overhead.

The Colonel came chomping through the brush with his crack team towing an equipment slide carrier. He stopped by the large arrowhead rock and yelled over the noise of the chopper.

"Who's in command here!"

"I am Sir. I'm Captain Roger Travis!"

"Ok Travis, where's this god dam mine shaft?"

Travis led the team over to the opening of the mineshaft where they quickly began setting up equipment to descend and explore to mine.

"Colonel, we were going to drop a rope down there and have a look, but Central Command ordered us to stand down and wait for your arrival. Sir, my guys were happy for that order. It's nasty down there. At first, smelled like methane but now smells like something died down there. Probably some poor critter. Hope you brought your gas masks along."

"Don't you worry, we got everything we need."

Sergeant Matthew Powers was team leader of the Colonels bomb disposal team, so it fell on him to put on the harness that would lower him down the mineshaft. He performed a radio check and made sure his gas mask was well secured before the order to lower him was given. He had just begun his descent when he yelled through the radio.

"Hold up Colonel. There's what looks like a wench attached to the rock about ten feet down. There's a heavy-duty line attached going down the shaft. Looks like those bastards left a retrieval system to bring whatever's down there, back up, if need be. What do you want me to do?"

"What a break! Let's use it and see what happens .We can always go back to plan A. Bring it up here."

Captain Travis went in and removed the wench from the rock using bolt cutters and brought it to the surface. They connected it to their own power supply at the egde of the shaft and bolted it to the ground. A six foot arm was extended over the edge and the process of slowly lifting whatever was at the end of the line began.

Travis remained suspended over the line holding a powerful light down in the hole.

"I see something coming up! Hold it right there! Oh fuck! Keep going!

The winch resumed pulling upward bringing a large rectangular box dripping with muddy water and hot to the touch. Everyone looked on with disgust at the partially decomposed body draped over the top.

The arm of the winch swung over away from the shaft causing the body to slide off on to the ground in a muddy pile of jelly-like goop.

The Colonel began barking out orders.

"Bag this body! Set up the basket! Powers, get down there and see what else you can find. Get your fire suit on. It's going to be hot down there. Like going into hell. Bring up anything else you find but take no chances. We got what we came for. We'll pull you out at 160 degrees or if you stop talking for more than ten seconds. Watch out for booby-traps."

"Call forensics and tell them to get ready for body identification processing. Whoever this is deserves a decent burial and some justice."

"Clean up the package. Looks like it's got some kind of thermal wrapping around it. Get it on the leveler and set up the exam protocol. Check for radiation. If it really is a nuke, we've got to get it out of here ASAP."

The wrapping was carefully removed revealing the smooth shinny surface of the device. Captain Travis was kneeling in front of the box with the Geiger counter in his hand looking up at the Colonel.

"Sir, the Geiger's going crazy! Needles buried in the red and she's screaming like a banshee!

"Ok, bag it in the lead box, and get it ready for transport. Can't risk having a look here. Tell them to get the plane ready with minimal crew. Nothing gets loaded on the plane except the disarm kit and x-ray machine."

"Call the White house. Tell them were headed as far south as we can get from the Bikini Atoll and still make it back. That should get us at least a thousand miles away from any population center. Tell them to stand by for air refuel. If we can't disarm it, we drop it in the ocean and hope for the best. Tell them I'll need Intel, in real time, on our efforts to find the detonator."

The colonel gathered the fifteen disarm experts he had brought with him. They were the best of the best. He needed to brief them. He had to yell over the noise of the chopper overhead.

"Looks like we got the real thing here boys. We'll know for sure after we x-ray it on the plane. We're going to go by the book and follow the West Coast disposal protocol. We're going down to Oceana. That's gonna be our plan. We've got a problem. The bad guys still have the detonator and are still at large. They could set it off in five minutes or five days. There's no sense in all of us getting blown up. I need three volunteers."

Every man in the line immediately stepped forward.

"I appreciate that, really! Draw straws or something and meet me inside the APC."

The device was placed in the armored vehicle with the Colonel riding shotgun. By now the operation had become media frenzy. The public came out in droves to watch the spectacle of the convoy headed back the airport.

The jet turbines of the behemoth plane were already fired up when the armored personal vehicle containing the device drove up the tail ramp with the Colonel and three of his men on board. The Colonel jumped off and ran forward to address the crew. They handed him four pairs of earphones with mikes for communication purposes. The noise was deafening.

"Have you guys been briefed?"

"Don't worry Colonel. We've got our heading and are ready to take off on your command. Our runway has been cleared. You do what you have to do back there and we'll take care of everything up here."

The Colonel ran back to his men who had already loaded the bomb in the x-ray machine and initiated the sequential program that takes multiple shots of the device at different angles. A composite image appeared on the monitor. Using the control toggle switch, the team carefully examined the device.

"It's the real thing; all right. Looks like it has a modified PIFA and a folded loop dipole antenna. There's no way we'll be able to jam that. Whoever made this thing knew what they were doing."

The Colonel clicked on his mike button and gave the command to take off. The giant Galaxy rolled down the runway like a heavy bowling ball. Just when it felt too heavy to ever get off the ground the nose tilted upwards and it was airborne.

Chapter 37

"Mustafa, when are we going to get out of this shit hole? We have completed our mission. My wife and children probably think I'm dead.

"We have not completed our mission until the bomb explodes and the world sees the glory of Allah. Yusuf, you have done the work of Allah and he thanks you. We have all received his His blessings. We remain alive and free, and ready to leave the land of Satan to be reunited with our loved ones, yet you continue to whine and complain like a spoiled child."

Yusef plopped down in a chair eyes down with a subservient gaze starring at the rug. Then he mustered up the courage to speak up.

"What about the American President? He will be speaking to the American people tonight in one hour about an important matter. The motel manager told me that everyone will be watching. Maybe they have discovered our plot!"

"If they had discovered our plot we would already be dead. We will watch the President's speech but afterward, I have a surprise for all of you.

That caught their attention.

"Our brothers, who became martyred after 9/11, also spent the night in Miami before going to Boston. They spit in the eye of Satan by frequenting a gentleman's club here called TENs, pleasuring themselves while defying Satan's control and influence. We will follow in our brother's footsteps by going to that same club tonight. Allah offers his warriors a sinful indulgence when they are about to achieve greatness in his name."

"Tomorrow, we will rendezvous with the chartered boat which will take us to Cuba. From the Havana airport, we will fly to Sudan, and from Sudan to home where we will rejoice with our comrades and loved ones. The Cuban government has guaranteed us safe passage. I will detonate the device from the plane before takeoff."

Holding up the cell phone to his men he explaned the dialing instructions.

"The bomb has two detonation sequences. The 01 suffix sequence has a 48-hour delay while the 02 will explode the bomb in five minutes. In the event that I have become incapacitated one of you must take command and perform the

358

detonation. I have programmed the speed dial for 1 or 2. Any questions?

It was seven PM when a commotion could be heard outside the motel room. It was the sound of people running up and down the hallway. Cars were beeping their horns from the street and adjacent parking lot. Something was happening.

"Yusuf, go out and see what's going on."

Yusuf went down the halls and out to the reception area. He noticed the motel manager fiddling with the channel changer of the small television at the desk. The front glass entrance door had been locked and there were people clamoring at the door outside wanting to get in. Those who had managed to get in before the door was locked were standing in the reception lobby starring up at the television that hung from the wall. The screen was all snow and static. Yusuf went back to the desk and poked his head in getting the attention for a brief moment of the manager who was still fussing with the TV.

"What's going on?"

"Get back in your room and turn the TV on."

Yusuf ran back to the room, swung open the door, and yelled, "Turn on the television! Something is happening!"

The TV picture was cutting in and out with intermittent snow and static sound. In between the poor transmissions were messages from CNX New York anchor desk stating that their signal was being compromised by an outside source and they were fighting to regain control. They were not the only network dealing with this problem.

Soon the intervals of clear and snowy transmission improved. Jessica Blumenthal appeared at the news desk obviously not prepared to be on camera, wearing jeans, a tee shirt, and no makeup.

"We are experiencing a very unusual phenomenon. Our global affiliates are reporting the same problem, as are other television outlets, all over the world. The FCC has alerted us that there is no emergency and urges the public to remain calm. They state that they were recently made aware by the White House that this event would take place, but were not sure of the exact time or date. The President has assured us that there is no danger and that he will speak to the American public live after the event."

The screen went black. Within moments a message appeared on the screen.

AN IMPORTANT MESSAGE OF GOOD NEWS WILL BE BROADCAST WORLD WIDE IN TWO DAYS AT 7PM US EST

The message remained on the screen for a full hour then disappeared. There followed speculation about the message with heated discussions across the political spectrum.

Yusuf turned to Mustafa.

"Something crazy is happening."

"Never mind that. It is a distraction. We will watch no television. We will go to the club tonight and fulfill a tradition that will bring us luck. Nothing must stop us from completing our mission. Whatever this foolishness is, we will learn about it in two days. By then, we will be well on our way home and the infidels will know what it is to suffer the wrath of Allah."

360

Mustafa was beginning to feel that things were coming unglued. He was determined that nothing would derail his mission. He contemplated detonating the device before the next day, ahead of plan, but was fearful that all ports and airports would be closed after an event of this magnitude. His pride of being able to enjoy the honor, in his world, as the man who defeated the Great Satan, was getting in the way of his cold and pragmatic self.

Chapter 38

Rossi and his team arrived in Miami with not much Intel to go on other than the location of the parking storage facility where the gang left the truck and rented a vehicle.

When they arrived, a team of forensic agents had already finished taking fingerprints, fiber samples, photos, DNA swabs and more. They were preparing to tow the vehicle out of the garage and transport it to the crime lab facility. Rossi got a briefing form the agents assigned to the case.

"Where's the manager in question? Rossi said, looking around the fume smelling haze of auto emissions wondering why there wasn't better ventilation and how long working there would result in death."

"That guy over there." They replied pointing over to the small lit booth.

"He's the manager who rented the car to the suspects but hes not the one who called it in. We still dont know who that was."

Ironically, he was of Middle Eastern descent himself having come to America on a political asylum visa. He claimed he was escaping the Syrian revolution. His name was Assad Abdu Al Bari. He was married with three children and had been living in Miami for three years. His wife was a house cleaner. All her clients had been checked out and fell into the category of upscale white families with no ties to anything.

Rossi flashed his badge and began interrogating Assad with a long list of the usual questions. Assad knew he was under suspicion and was being very cooperative. Rossi was using his "I'm not fucking around" official FBI persona. It was working. Assad was visibly scared shitless. His forehead was wet with sweat. His eyes were moving everywhere trying to avoid eye contact, and he kept shuffling papers in front of him until Rossi reached over and rudely snatched them off the desk.

"Did they indicate where they were going?

"No. The one who was the leader was all business, very serious. The other four were talking, laughing, and acting like stupid children. I overheard one of them say, "Maybe if we are good boys, he will let us go to an American strip club. The serious one became angry and told them to shut up. I, become very upset when hearing this type of talk by my Muslim brothers. They think that when they leave their country and are in a secular country, they are free to commit sins that are an affront to Allah. Misfortune will befall them."

Assad lowered his head and became emotional

"Please, Mr. Sir, don't send my family and me back to the war from which we came. We only want a chance to live in peace."

Rossi leaned over and put both hands on Assad's forearms.

"If you're clean, you'll have nothing to worry about. Call me immediately if these men come back or if you remember anything else."

Rossi grabbed the rental documents .The car they would be looking for was a new Chevy Tahoe, silver with Florida plates KJH 23542.

Rossi went back to his car and asked his team to stay outside and leave him alone for a moment. He slammed the door shut and moved the front seat back all way. He stretched out his legs and lit a cigarette. He desperately needed a lead, and a quiet moment. He needed to really think hard.

There was something Assad had said sticking in his mind. Then he remembered reading reports that the 911 terrorists had been in Miami before going to Boston to board the planes and that they had visited a strip club the night before.

Bingo, it was a long shot but he thought to himself, "what the fuck, it's better than nothing."

He opened the car door letting out a plume of cigarette smoke as he got out. He called FBI headquarters in Washington requesting a databank search for the name of the club. A few minutes later it came back, TENs. He Googled the club wondering if they were still in business sixteen years later. Yes, they were, at 3756 NW Avenue, Miami.

"Hey, guys, who wants to go to a strip club tonight on official business?"

Agent Eddie Barnes, Rossi's old partner, answered first.

"You got to be shitting me! Agent Lori Matthews, the only female on the team, looked at the guys and started rubbing her hands together.

"Oh, this is going to be fun!"

Rossi briefed them on his hunch and the reasoning for going there. They rolled their eyes knowing that Rossi was desperate.

"Let's get back to the hotel. Get some rest. Change into something casual. We meet in the lobby at twenty-one hundred hours. Wear your vests and mic up."

Rossi and his agents arrived a little before 9 pm. The music was loud with a thumping beat that seemed to resonate all the way to the gut. Colored lights twirled around the room like a kaleidoscope. The girls were shapely and beautiful living up to the name, Tens.

The patrons ranged from middle-aged corporate types with after work suits and ties to college boys looking to whoop it up. The agents ordered one drink each against FBI rules, but usually waived for undercover work. They took up positions in different parts of the bar. They all knew what to look for and were focused on finding the perpetrators. They performed a sound check on the ear bud lapel mic system.

"Remember, if they show up, nothing goes down in the club. Last thing we want is a civilian body count."

Rossi stationed himself at the inside the entrance door and pretended to be engaged in a cell phone conversation. The bouncer, who looked like a mountain man with a beard and shaved head, told him he couldn't stand around there and had to find a seat. Rossi told him he was waiting to meet a blind date. A menacing look made Rossi move farther back.

One hour passed then two. Lori Mathews walked over the Rossi.

"Look, Boss, I think we're wasting our time. We gave it a good shot, but I think it's a dead end. The guys have had a good time, but if I have to watch one looser stuff a measly one dollar bill in another G-string, I'm going to throw up."

Just at that moment, in walked five men in a group. They looked like they could have been brothers. Dark skinned, mustached, and dressed all the same in western urban chic. They stood there, checking out the scene and looking for a table.

As Rossi watched them, he was thinking, they looked like they just got off a fuckin camel and put on a pair of expensive skinny jeans, cool shirts, and the latest fashion sports jacket cut short just below the waist."

Rossi turned to Lori, bent down, and whispered in her ear, "Bingo, tell the others. Go out and look for the Tahoe. These are our guys. I can feel it. We wait till they leave then approach them outside."

A waitress, smiling, topless, and wearing revealing fishnet pantyhose came over and led the group of cool looking guests to a table.

Lori came back in the club and ran over to Rossi.

"The Tahoe is out back. The plate number matches. These are our guys alright."

Rossi quickly made a call to Pointdexter.

"I think we have them sir. We're in a club called Tens. It's about to go down now. We'll take them into custody the minute they leave the club. Any news on the bomb?"

"We've already got eyes on the club knowing you and your guys were going there. Colonel Peters and his guys found the bomb just where you said it would be. They're in a C4 Galaxy somewhere over the South Pacific seeing if they can disarm it. I've sent in more agents dressed as street workers setting up a one-block perimeter around the club. Anything else?"

"Yes, set up a conference call line to Colonel Peters. We need to be in real time communication."

"You got it. I'm connecting you now. Oh, and good luck."

"Thank you sir."

In less than ten seconds the screen on Rossi's phone began to blink, " Conference connected."

"Colonel Peters, Agent Rossi with the FBI here. What's your status?"

"Hey, Peters here. Heard you guys are closing in on those bastards. Good work. We're up here trying to disarm this son of a bitch. It's North Korean for sure. We can tell by the radiation signature. Very sophisticated. Those smart bastards have made a lot of progress since our last Intel."

" Right now we got it hooked up to our code scanner crunching a thousand possible codes every minute. We're hoping for a break in finding an arm command code we can block. So far, no luck. We know for sure it hasn't been armed yet. It's definitely a remote trigger. Look for a cell phone. The old flip type ones, not a smart phone, is your best bet. Don't press any buttons if you find one. We found a detonation delay code. Could be a minute or days. Those cowards want the glory more than just the virgins. We're headed to the Mariana Trench. Its 27000 feet deep. If we can't disarm it, we either blow up with it, or ditch it so deep that when it blows, no one will notice."

The gang was having a good time and breaking every rule in the Koran when after about an hour, Yusuf got up and went to the men's room. Rossi followed.

Rossi lingered by the sinks washing his hands while Yusuf took a piss in the urinal. When he finished, Yusuf came over to the sinks and began washing his hands. Three sinks separated the two men. Yusuf kept looking over at Rossi and into the mirror with menacing eyes. They both noticed their eyes connecting to each other in the mirror. Both men knew that something was up. Yusuf, still staring at his reflection in the mirror said in his Middle Eastern accent,

"Do I know you?"

368

Rossi instinctively stood up, stepped back two steps, and in one motion pulled out both his gun and FBI badge, holding them with both arms extended, straight out at Yusuf.

"Agent Rossi, FBI! Keep your hands where I can see them! Get down on the floor! I need to ask you a few questions!"

In a split second, Yusuf lunged at Rossi knocking the gun out of his hand and pinning him to the floor. The gun slid across the floor under the sink out of arms reach. Yusuf pulled a knife and began furiously stabbing at Rossi whose training kicked in, twisting and turning his upper torso under the weight of the son the son of a bitch , somehow avoiding a direct stab. The stabs hit the ceramic floor with such force that the knife blade snapped off. Rossi landed a punch to the throat. Yusuf clutched his throat and struggled to breathe, giving Rossi enough time to roll him off and get him in a chokehold. Rossi kept him in the chokehold while Yusuf struggled to get loose again. Yusuf went limp and lost consciousness. The men's room door opened. The bouncer walked in and looked down at Yusuf and Rossi on the floor.

"What, the fuck, is going on here?"

Rossi, out of breath and bleeding from small cuts about the hands and neck managed to respond.

"Oh, my friend here, had too much to drink, and passed out. It took a little bit of persuasion to get him to behave. I'm taking him out for some fresh air. He's fine. He does this all the time."

"Get him outta here. We don't need this kind of shit in this establishment."

Rossi slung his arm under Yusuf and dragged him out while the bouncer looked on. The bouncer knew full well that Yusuf was seriously hurt but didn't want any part of it happening under his watch.

Rossi knew that Yusuf was dead and that he wasn't given a choice. He looked up the street and saw the Tahoe parked about a fifty feet from the entrance. Reaching into Yusuf's pocket he found the car keys and a cell phone. He clicked the fob and watched as the Tahoe's lights flashed twice confirming its owners. He carried Yusuf's body into an adjacent ally and propped him up against the wall in the dark where no one would see him.

"No fucking way you're getting back in Bud."

The big, badass, bouncer stood firm at the entrance blocking Rossi's way.

Rossi got up in the big boys face and flashed his FBI badge and credentials, at the same time exposing the grip of his Glock 45cal.

"Look, you fucking Neanderthal. One more peep out of you and you'll be facing charges of interfering with an official FBI operation. Keep your mouth shut. Do your job! We'll be out of your hair before closing. I already cleaned up one mess for you. Be grateful! No calls to anyone! Do something stupid and I'll make your life a living hell. Got it!

The bouncer backed off with his eyes gazing downward in submission and nodding yes.

It wasn't long before Mustafa noticed that Yusuf had not return from the men's room. He got up from the table rudely pushing aside one of the strippers who had joined them, and began visually scanning the room. He was always paranoid that something would go wrong. He told the others to get the check and get ready to leave, then began making his way through the crowded club. He stopped short of the men's room door before opening it and took one last long look around for Yusuf.

Two patrons were at the sinks. He checked all the stalls but no Yusuf. Panic set in. He ran back causing a commotion, bumping people, and spilling drinks.

"Let's go, right now, quick!"

Rossi and his Agents saw that the gang had caught on that something was wrong and were heading out of the place in a hurry. He gave the signal to his agents to follow them. In their haste to get out, Mustafa tripped and fell with a hard landing. As he struggled to get up, his eyes somehow locked on to Rossi, who had moved in much closer. He saw Rossi talking into his microphone. In an instant he looked around and spotted the other agents who had all moved in very close. He thought to himself, "How could I have missed this? How did they find us? It's all over right here and right now. I must act."

His men were pushing away patrons who were trying to help Mustafa get up. They were confused in the chaos of the moment but knew that something had gone terribly wrong. Mustafa got up with a subtle smile on his face as if to say, I'm ready to die. He didn't try to flee but instead reached into the side pocket of his sports coat and pulled out a flip cell phone.

In a frantic gesture he fumbled around trying to dial the fateful number, but the pounding music, dim lighting, and pulsating strobe lights were making it difficult. Rossi saw the flip phone and without hesitation dove over a small café table tackling Mustafa who had begun yelling Allahu Akbar!"

In the struggle, Mustafa reached into Rossi's jacket, pulled Rossi's gun and fired two shots. The first bullet pierced Rossi's upper chest fracturing the left third rib. It passed through the left upper lobe of his lung and lodged in the café table that had followed him down during the fall. The second bullet shattered the humerus bone in Rossi's left upper arm and went on to rip the ear off of Spencer Davis who was there celebrating his eighteenth birthday with his older brother.

Mustafa was holding the phone up high yelling naaam! naaam! naaam! Arabic for "yes! yes! yes!

Mustafa's comrades pulled their guns and began shooting up the club. The agents killed all four terrorists in a hail of bullets. The whole shootout lasted all of thirty seconds. Agent Barnes was shot through the head and was later pronounced dead at the scene. Lori Matthews suffered a bullet to the neck that missed major blood vessels and her spinal cord by a few millimeters. Everyone else in the club, remarkably, escaped running out into the street including the big bad bouncer.

Rossi was going in and out of consciousness while being attended to by paramedics. He was slowly bleeding to death from the chest wound. By this time, the EMT's had arrived, and were bent over him trying to stop the bleeding by applying compression to the wound. With a labored voice, Rossi insisted, "Get me my phone. Call Colonel Peters. Tell him to ditch the bomb."

Thirty thousand feet over the South Pacific Ocean Colonel Peters and his team were trying to disarm the bomb when suddenly the digital display lit up like a Christmas tree flashing red lights and beeping loudly. A message popped up on the screen.

"Detonation sequence loading" with a bar slowly filling in red next to a digital counter indicating two minutes and thirty seven seconds.

"Son of a bitch, those guys are smart! Somebody hit the remote and she's ready to go. Looks like we've got less than three minutes to ditch this son bitch! Prepare for decompression!"

He switched on his mic to the pilots.

"Open the hatch! We have to ditch the cargo!"

"Not at this altitude, Sir! Hook up, hook up! It's going to be rough!"

The men grabbed their oxygen canisters and quickly hooked up to the wall tethers.

The giant fortress went into a steep dive producing a moment of weightlessness .The noise was deafening as the plane fell nearly ten thousand feet. The men watched as the pilot activated the cargo door to open. The plane pitched upwards and to the right as Peters pushed the bomb down the ramp, over, and into the abyss.

The last thing they saw was the flash of bright yellow light through the crack of the closing hatch door. It was too late.

Chapter 39

Rossi didn't have many relatives. His father was killed in the Vietnam War in the service of his country when Rossi was thirteen years old. His mother remarried at around the same time he went off to college. She later died of breast cancer when he was thirty-four. He never developed a relationship with his stepfather .There was a half sister who lived in California that he barely knew.

When Jeff, Amanda and the professor learned about Rossi's run in with the terrorists and his injuries they quickly boarded a plane for Miami.

The University of Miami Medical Center had a top-notch cardio-thoracic trauma team. They managed to stop the bleeding and repair the damaged lung, but not before the severe blood loss he suffered, dropped his blood pressure to a critical point causing his kidneys to fail. He developed pneumonia. His vital signs were unstable. His blood pressure was being kept up with an epinephrine drip and his blood oxygen saturation level was only moderately low thanks to the ventilator. He was put on continuous peritoneal dialysis for the kidney failure. Rossi was in bad shape and clinging to life. The only good news was that the orthopedic surgeons were able to repair and save his shattered arm, and that he was still alive.

There was a 24-hour FBI security outside his room. No one, including a select group of medical staff went in or out of the room without a special security badge and fingerprint scan. When the trio arrived, they were processed downstairs in the hospitals security and given clearance per order of the President.

A nurse was just finishing up checking Rossi's vital signs and replacing his IV fluids when Amanda, Jeff and the Professor came in. Looking up at the visitors the nurse had a look on her face that said, I'm sorry. Amanda went right over to Rossi, held his hand, and kissed him on the forehead. Rossi never stirred. She leaned over to him and spoke softly in his ear, having faith that even in a coma, he could hear her, and derive some comfort.

"Jeff, Yuri, and I are here now. We want you to know that you are not alone. You have a family and we care about you. You're going to get through this and we're here to make sure that you do. You did a very brave thing yesterday and helped

376

prevent a lot of lives from being lost. God is not going to forget what you did. He will bring you the help you need. Your job is to fight hard to get well. I know you're a fighter. I know you can do this."

Jeff knew that Rossi's chances of making it through this were 50/50 at best. They decided to spend the night taking shifts next to Rossi holding his hand , believing that mere human physical contact would comfort him.

It was just after midnight when they decided to start the shifts. The lights had been dimmed leaving only the glow of the monitors and dim night lighting from the outside corridor coming in through the rooms view window. There were two FBI agents posted just outside the door sitting on brown leather recliners trying not to fall asleep. Amanda and the professor were just about to leave to get some sleep when the door quietly opened . A man wearing blue scrubs and a long white lab coat walked in and whispered,

"Hello, my friends. How is our brave patient doing?"

It was Leonard Spikes who simply walked past the guards into the room. The trio recognized him. They were visibly startled and lost for words. He went over to Rossi, put his hand on Rossi's forehead, and looked down on him like a loving father on his child.

"Hello my good friend. You have done a great service and shown not only courage but also the conviction of a good heart. I am in your debt for believing in me. I am grateful to you. You helped me to complete my mission and fulfill my purpose here on your beautiful planet. Surely, you didn't think I would abandon you in your time of need."

Spikes looked up toward the ceiling and closed his eyes. Slowly a glow of white light began to flow from his hand to Rossi's forehead. Amanda got down on her knees and made the sign of the cross. Yuri mumbled a Hebrew saying and Jeff seemed to be frozen in place, mesmerized by the whole scene.

The white light grew more intense covering Rossi's entire body. Soon the light became so intense that there was nothing but the light. It blocked out everything and everyone in the room. It took on the feel of a dense solid like brightness that permeated everything. Suddenly, it extinguished itself, leaving everyone feeling like they had just awoken from a long and restful sleep. Spikes, still looking down at Rossi and was the first to speak.

"Our friend should be feeling much better by the morning."

Amanda ran over to Spikes and hugged him but repelled quickly upon touching him. He was ice cold. She quickly regained her composure.

"How can we ever thank you for what you have done here tonight?"

"You already have. Sorry for the cold shock. My metabolism is a little different than yours."

"Tomorrow night I will make my debut . It should be quite a show. I must confess that I'm a little nervous. I've been waiting for this day for longer than you can imagine. You all must go to Washington tomorrow. Your President needs you to be there .Our friend here will be fine.

Spikes walked away and literally vanished through the door. One of the guards opened the door and poked his head in.

"Is everything all right in there?"

"Everything's just fine. Actually it could not be better," Yuri said.

The guard made a perplexed face as if to say, I wonder what he meant by that?

Morning came fast enough. Rossi had been disconnected from the ventilator and was awake complaining that he was hungry. He noticed Amanda by his side and Jeff and Yuri waking up in their recliners.

"Hey, what are you guys doing here?"

"We are the only family you've got, silly man. Where else would we be?" Amanda said.

"How are my guys? Did the bomb go off? Are the bad guys in custody?

"The bomb went off over the Pacific. The crew of the C4 Galaxy and Colonel Peters were lost. The bad guys are all dead. Lori Matthews was shot in the neck but will be ok. We're sorry, but Barnes didn't make it."

Rossi's eyes welled up and he began to cry. He squeezed Amanda's hand.

"He was good man. He was my partner and friend. He's got a wife and three kids."

"The Bureau will take good care of them, "said Jeff, trying to add some measure of comfort.

That day, Rossi underwent a battery of tests and x-rays. The doctors were amazed that his wounds were not just better but were almost completely healed. A chest x-ray confirmed that the pneumonia had cleared up. His urine output had picked up indicating improved kidney function. His serum creatinine level, a blood test that measures how well the kidneys are working, went from 9.2 all the way to a normal range of to 0.8 over night.

Rossi was disconnected from the peritoneal dialysis apparatus and was scheduled to be discharged and flown to rehab at the Boston VA Hospital.

That day an envoy from the Miami District FBI office came to see Rossi. He informed Rossi that the FBI Director had recommended him for two of the FBIs highest honors; the FBI STAR for serious injuries sustained in the line of duty and the Medal of Valor, given to those in recognition of exceptional heroism and voluntary risk of life in the line of duty.

Jeff, Amamda,and Yuri said their goodbyes and headed back to Washington per request of the President to be on standby for when Spikes makes his global announcement. It was expected to come in two days when the conference in Switzerland was expected to convene.

Chapter 40

The Gateway Hotel was only three blocks from the White House. It was mostly frequented by power brokers who come into Washington peddling influence or trying or get the attention of some congressmen or senator. Elegant and refined accommodations would be the best way to describe this old Washington hotel. Very few families or tourist types ever stayed there.

Jeff, Amanda, and the professor were biding their time on the government's dime waiting the big event that was supposed to happen. It was already 7 PM eastern time and all was quiet. Most of the news outlets had been given the heads up about a possible special event with no details given.

"I'm going to my room and rest for a while." Said Yuri, as he pushed his chair back from the table. "Dinner was outstanding, especially knowing that it was free." Call me if anything happens."

Amanda and Jeff signed the dinner check and went back to their room. Jeff laid down on the bed and let out a sigh. It felt so good to lie down and stretch out. He watched Amanda as she freshened up after the long day. Meticulously unpacking and folding the clothes she would wear if called to the White House tonight. She was so beautiful.

Jeff began patting the bed next to him beckoning her to come join him. No words were necessary. She came over and laid down next to Jeff. He pulled her in close. They both sighed and cuddled together, melding as one, in a welcomed moment of peace and solitude. Her hair smelled heavenly. Her soft warm body was as comforting to him as were his strong arms to her.

"Sweetheart, we need to be doing more of this." He said.

"We used to do this all the time." She answered.

"Yeah, I know. Do you remember that romantic little hotel we stayed at in Venice? We made love every day. It was like being in heaven."
She squeezed him tighter.

"Let's go back and visit Heaven again."

"Yes, lets promise each other right here and right now, that we are going back as soon as all this settles down."

"Yes."

They both succumbed to the desire they had for each other and fell asleep in each other's arms.

"What the hell is that?"

"Someone's banging on the door like there's a fire or something."

Jeff jumped out from his side of the bed and quickly put on the hotel bathrobe before running to the door. Amanda did the same, running into the bathroom.

It was Romilov at the door.

"Quick turn on the TV."

It was Jessica Blumenthal again on TV about to make an announcement.

"Ladies and Gentlemen, we have just been notified by credible sources, and I still can't believe this, that we are about to hear an address by an extraterrestrial. That's right; you heard it, by an extraterrestrial!

"The broadcast is coming from the site of the new linear accelerator in Switzerland. This not a hoax! I repeat, this is not a hoax! We cannot control the feed. The FCC is telling us that that they have no control over the transmission. The global network of telecommunication satellites have been taken over. Your cell phones and GPS devices may be temporally disabled during this transmission. It looks like this event will be seen in every corner of the globe. The President, and later, the Pope will speak after this historic event. The FCC has been informed that our government has known about this for several weeks and that there is no danger. I repeat, we are told that there is no danger!" "

Jessica Blumenthal paused, gazed downward, and pressed her earpiece tightly against her head like she was straining to hear something.

"We are now hearing from the Pentagon that a large explosion has occurred over the South Pacific Ocean near the area of the MarianaTrench. No damage or injury reported. There will be more details to follow."

All non-essential employees at the Linear Accelerator complex were given the day off .The parking lot next to the underground facility was filled mostly with the cars of invited dignitaries from all over the world. They were a mix of world politicians, scientists, newsmakers, and media types.

The mood in the hall was electric, especially now, that everyone was aware of the world –wide broadcast that had just taken place. The attendees were mulling about sipping champaign, renewing old acquaintances, and chatting away with theories and speculation. The lights flashed and a loud voice came over the public address system.

"Ladies and Gentleman, please take your seats. Your cell phones and all other communication devices will not function during this brief address, so we ask you to put them away."

The guests were unaware that outside, the local police and an army of news outlets were descending on the grounds overwhelming the scant security detail scheduled for this event. They had no idea that their desire to get into the event was futile. Spikes had seen to that. The underground facility was completely locked down. In fact it was impenetrable.

As the lights dimmed down a figure appeared in the stage in silhouette. A giant lit screen loomed behind the silhouetted figure. Light from the front then slowly illuminated the figure making him come to life.

It revealed a young man whose face was smooth and had perfect symmetry. His eyes were a slightly luminescent green. His skin was olive brown in color. His hair was stubble like, short and dark. His perfectly proportioned body stood about six foot tall and was draped in same, adhering skin like lining covering, he wore on the JPL video.

"Good evening Ladies and Gentlemen. My name is Leonard Spikes. It is a name I have chosen for myself. Perhaps you have heard of me."

"All of you here tonight were chosen and invited because you all share something in common."

"You are influential in your position or field of expertise. You are global leaders whose opinions, actions, or power over others impacts the common man."

"Please forgive me for entering your personal space, but I am the one who sent you dreams designed to prepare you for my arrival and what I am about to reveal to you tonight. I am the one who brought the Blue Dot virus to some of your children, and then the cure. It was meant to remind you what your most precious possessions are, and the importance of not risking their happy future for the goals of the evil one."

385

"I needed to get you all thinking in the right direction. You see, before I could make myself known, I had to find a way to win your favor and acceptance .Others that have come before me, have suffered your rejection and even worse. I needed to establish myself as a credible persona before my formal introduction."

"In the spirit of overcoming skepticism, I revealed to some of you, in varying degrees, many wondrous secrets of the universe. Least you considered me a charlatan or magician, I gave to you, a ray of insight into the many problems you have been struggling with, in the fields of science, medicine, physics, engineering, and philosophy."

"I have done this to solidify my credentials and authenticity and to lessen the shock of what I am about to reveal to you and all the people of this wondrous planet you call home."

"I am not the creator. You know the creator by different names. You have ascribed to your Creator the characteristic of exclusivity. You are more comfortable believing that your Creator is exclusive to you and your group. Nothing could be farther from reality. There is but one Creator who created all things seen and unseen. The Creators you have chosen for yourselves are one and the same. The Creator that created you created me. So, I repeat. I am not the Creator. Instead,

"I AM THE SEED SOWER."

The audience gave out an audible gasp and a few grumbles here and there. Most were mesmerized by the melodious and unwavering tone of his speech. A sense of calm and goodness permeated the venue and everyone remained silent.

"Our evolution precedes yours by millions of years. When we discovered your solar system and particularly, the third planet from your sun, we were given hope that our species would be able to survive and prosper beyond the age of our planet. Many, like me, were sent here to seed your developing atmosphere with what you call today DNA."

"DNA is the source of all life and contains, in its code complexities, the knowledge of the entire universe. It is ONE with the Creator. The DNA in my body is the same as yours except for a few modifications allowing me certain advantages."

"As you can see, I look like you."

"I'm sorry to disappoint those of you who were hoping for something a little more reptilian."

"I have been asked the question, where is your spaceship? It is in a museum of technologies that failed the challenges of deep space travel. We moved beyond those machines many ions ago."

The audiences laughed gently at the reptilian reference and were amazed at the notion that space travel using machines was antiquated.

"We returned every few thousand years or so to see what our garden was growing, and were very pleased indeed. About one hundred thousand years ago we established observation posts on your moon. The structures still stand today. Your governments have known about us for over seventy years. Why do you think they never went back to your moon in over forty

years? They were correct not to reveal their knowledge. It would have been catastrophic to your society's development."

"I was compelled to make my presence known in order to save you from yourselves. You were about to go extinct! Humanities ignorant folly was about to erase millions of years of evolution."

"By now you have all heard news of the explosion over the South Pacific Ocean. That explosion was a nuclear device of mass destruction that had been placed near the belly of a super volcano located in the beautiful Yellowstone National Park. The evildoers were attempting to exterminate millions of lives from North America. They did not know that a geological fissure located deep in the volcano's core would have ruptured and caused the entire planet to disintegrate into space."

A loud sigh rose from the audience. All over the world, people watching the broadcast cried with both tears of joy and sadness over this revelation.

"Make no mistake. There is an evil in this world that divides us into different groups and pits one against the other. This evil is the cause of all your wars, poverty, suffering, and strife. It is a strong adversary to peace and prosperity and the grand design of the Creator."

"The only weapon you have against this evil is knowledge and free will. Know that evil subverts the feeling of PRIDE

388

into a notion that you have dominion over others. Only the Creator has dominion over his creations. "

"Remember the essence of what we all are. A creation made of the same DNA .The same DNA that makes up our genome holds the "code of life. " It is the most complex code in the entire universe. It contains all of the answers to mans most profound questions. You need to look no further than in your own substance. The answers are literally under your noses. "

"Look closely at your hands and the hands of your neighbor. Are they that different? I think not. We are not different but instead fundamentally the same. You were given free choice. I suggest you use it wisely. "

"One more word. For those of you in positions of power over others and for those of you who exploit your minions, enslave them, or subjugate them to your will, know that your time will be coming to an end. Your people will rise up and see you for what you are, agents of the evil one. It is not too late to find and regain your humanity. "

"I will be leaving you now. Remember, you have been given another chance to realize your destiny and embrace the precious gift of life that you were given. "

"For those of you who still doubt me; look at your moon tomorrow night. I will give you a farewell sign. "

He seemed to simple dissolve away, in front of everyone, in a spectacular exit.

Televisions all over the world flickered back to their normal programming. CNX came back on with Jessica Blumenthal still at the desk. There was a change in the schedule. The Pope would speak first.

"There you have it, ladies, and gentleman. Probably, the most important and historic announcement in the history of mankind. We are not alone! I don't know what else to say. A truly remarkable revelation. My producer is telling me that message from the Pope coming from the Vatican is about to air. Here it is."

Pope Alexander, standing from the window balcony, overlooking Saint Peters square began to speak to the thousands who had gathered below.

"Rejoice! Rejoice! For the Lord and Almighty Father has revealed to us that we are not alone in this vast universe. We have brothers and sisters!

"To our brothers and sisters I say."

"We welcome you! We welcome you!"

"And to the people of this world, let this be the end of our differences."

The crowd below erupted with applause and shouts of support.

The news cycle was almost completely consumed with stories and discussion on the world's first public alien contact. Next, there followed the address from the President and other world leaders echoing the same comments as the Pope.

There was a deafening silence from many Middle Eastern nations with the exception of Israel's President calling for a permanent peace agreement based on commonalities rather than differences.

Amanda, Jeff, and Yuri, fielded numerous questions from the press on a special report. As they had agreed, they stuck to the truth about everything that happened and expressed the hope that mankind could come together for the common good.

President Cabot's UN ambassador introduced a resolution to ban and dismantle all nuclear weapons. The billions of dollars saved would be earmark into a newly created fund to help third world nations revamp their economies raising the standard of living for their people. There would be harsh penalties for those who steal the monies with no tolerance for corruption. All this in the first twenty-four hours.

The next night the whole world watched as the sky darkened and the moon became visible. Just as Spikes had promised a bright light visible with the naked eye could be seen pulsating from the surface on the moon. It had the quality of a very bright LED white light. NASA reported that the light was being emitted from an alien installation that they had known about for years. The pulsations were a coded message looping over and over.

"Live well, all of you, in peace. I will return some day. Farewell "

Amanda, Jeff, and Yuri had become celebrities again and wanted nothing more than to be left alone to get on with the work. They expected great things now that they were given new insights into their science. They wondered if they would ever see Leonard Spikes again.

Chapter 41

Three weeks had passed from the tumultuous day and a lot had happened.

There were uprisings in the Middle East with entire armies laying down their weapons and heading back home to renew their studies, find a job, or start a business.

University students and faculty in these formerly repressive regions no longer feared the powers of oppression and were free to express themselves with a renewed vigor and purpose. Many questioned why all the great scientific achievements of the previous one hundred years came from the West. They began to ask why there were no innovative giants in Pharmaceuticals, Engineering, Cancer Research, or Aerospace Science in their countries. A restructuring of a medieval society into a modern one was underway. It was the beginning of a new Renaissance and intellectual rebirth.

Rossi was recovering from his wounds and released from the VA rehab hospital. Jeff had gone back to the lab which had more funding than ever. Amanda reentered the physic PhD program and was respected by all. Yuri was working on the release of his agricultural breakthrough and fielding offers to speak at scientific conferences around the world.

They decided to have a reunion dinner, to catch up, and renew their friendships. Of course reservations were made at Vincenzos. They arrived all about the same time. Alphonso Chiari, the owner was there to meet them. Greeting them with a European waiters bow as they entered, he led them to their table.

"Signorina, Dottore, Professore, Signore Rossi. It's not every night that famous people come to dine in my restaurant. It is an honor."

"Amanda laughed, but the professor seemed to enjoy the attention. Jeff answered.

"Alphonso, you know us for a long time. Please, we haven't changed all that much. We drink and enjoy the table wine. Remember?

Alphonso nodded yes, then took the standard table wine off the table and replaced it with two bottles of six year old Montepulciano Riserva and adding," un vino speciale per voi coplimentare." (a special wine for you, complimentary of course.)

Rossi looked good. He seemed to have recovered well from his injuries. They all laughed, ate, drank and reminisced about the adventure they had all shared. When things settled down, Rossi looked around the table and said,

"I don't know about you guys, but I'm going to miss that weird Spikes character. There was something about him that sticks with you. He kind of just took off and left without even saying goodbye. Maybe those alien types don't develop relationships. Anyways, I think he was a great guy in his own way."

"Yeah, I'm going to miss him too." Amanda said." He was so interesting and good-hearted. I could talk to him for hours. One afternoon, early on, he came over to the house and we talked about everything. He was amazing. That was the day Jeffery got all bent out of shape."

"Hey! Love of my life. I didn't get all bent out of shape. I was concerned for your safety!"

"I hate to interrupt a good fight but was wondering if I could join you."

Out of nowhere, Spikes was standing before them dressed in a Boston Red Sox sweatshirt, jeans and baseball cap that read "The Stars the Limit."

Yuri, hurriedly got up and made room for another chair at the table. The shock of Spikes popping in and out never seemed to fade. Spikes turned to Rossi and spoke directly to him.

"I'm so glad to see that you are doing so well. You have been a true soldier in the fight against evil. I thank you."

"No, Mr. Spikes, I thank you for saving my life."

"To the rest of you I extend my gratitude and take this opportunity to remind you of our covenant. Stay true to it, and life will reward you. Before I go, there is something that I want to share with you four, and only you four."

"I told the world that I am the Seed Sower. In truth there were many of us tasked with sowing the code of life in your developing atmosphere."

"I do not have a mother or a father. I am a biological creation of my civilization. You see, the biology of the human species is incompatible with deep space travel. The miracle of teleportation, which allows me to disassemble and reassemble my atoms in a different location can only occur with a different cellular structure and altered biology. Therefore, although I am not a machine, I am a synthetic life form, fashioned after the human model with modified DNA."

" My cells are impervious to the effects of radiation. My telomeres only shorten a little each time I teleportate, so I hardly age. My cells never mutate so I'm never going to have cancer. My immune system is stronger than any bacteria or virus. My metabolism is so low, that I can survive for very long periods of time with no food or water. Trauma is the only injury that could possibly end my existence. But even with trauma, my cells heal in seconds and minutes, not weeks and months like yours do."

"We were first created to perform difficult and dangerous tasks. As time went on we developed self-awareness and superior intellectual capacity. With those attributes, came independence and acceptance as equals in our society."

"I share these secrets, with only those of you, at this table. I need to repeat, that releasing these revelations prematurely, before your society is ready, would have a disastrous effects. I gave you the tool to unlock the secrets of DNA. It can be used for good or evil. The tool is a secret that you must use sparely."

"Jeff, you, Amanda and the Professor must focus on eradicating the scourge of cancer. The answer is in gene substitution not medications. All of you now have the key you need to unlock the mystery of cancer and find a cure. This must be your life's mission."

Amanda reached over and took Spikes cold hand.

"What will become of you old friend?"

"I'm not entirely sure." He replied.

Spikes fell silent and began looking around as if to buy time needed to make an unplanned decision. With a certain reluctance, but yet resolve, he turned his head back to the group.

"There is one more thing I've decided to share with you, my trusted friends."

He hesitated with a long pause having second thoughts.

"I am the last surviving humanoid of my planet."

The shock on everyone's face was plain to see. Spikes let out a sigh like someone extremely relieved to get something off of his chest.

"I was on a long-term assignment as director of our lunar installations. It was my job to observe, report, and record all activities on Earth. The UFOs you were obsessed with were surveillance drones under my supervision. We were studying the global atmospheric patterns of your planet, accumulating data needed to someday control the planets weather. We were monitoring all your broadcasts and analyzing patterns of behavior. We were learning your different cultures and planning to choose one, which we could begin, to more comfortably integrate and populate as a permanent colony."

"We saw signs that our planet was getting old and coming to the end of its life. We needed to find a place where we could someday live. You were our insurance policy. We knew that we could be your salvation."

"There were never any plans for conquest. Conquest only brings destruction. It represented for us, an antiquated and barbaric notion, counterproductive to developing a successful society. I was forbidden to enter your atmosphere for fear of being discovered and taken prisoner. I always thought, that knowing my powers, that being taken prisoner was impossible, but those were the orders. Getting that close was the job of the drones.

"There came a time when all my comrades had teleported home. I was left alone to shut down the facility until the next major Earth observation mission."

Amanda interjected.

"Are you telling us that we are the only other intelligent life in the universe?

"That we know of, yes! You on Earth were our experiment. We brought DNA from our world and seeded this planet before there was any life. The universe is infinite and we have explored only the tiniest fragment. We were not looking for intelligent life but instead a place where our life could survive."

There was a silence at the table. Spikes could see that he had revealed too much for them to assimilate, producing more questions than answers. He continued.

"I began the process of teleportation home, when the system, for the first time blocked the reassembly. It is a failsafe system that prevents the atomic reassembly in a physically hostile environment. I cannot teleportate in the midst, for example, of a fire. That is when I learned that my home was no longer there.

"What happened to it?" asked Jeff.

"I don't know. To this day, I still don't know. I found myself stranded without a plan or a direction. The constant communication flow link to the base also stopped. I have received no further communication for over two hundred and fifty three Earth years."

"At first, I thought it had to be a malfunction of my T system. Using modulators from the base I developed a program of earth navigation. It enabled me to call up any coordinates and allow me to teleport to any location on Earth.

Then, I broke the rule and tried it. It worked. The year was 1801.I wondered from place to place and learned more about your people and customs. It was a very primitive world, so different from today."

"I began to make many friends who came into my existence and then died from aging. Earth became my new home. I don't do well living in isolation or without a purpose."

Spikes began to smile and almost laugh. It was very uncharacteristic for him to express levity and it didn't go unnoticed. He put on his mischievous face and said,

"I may have had, from time to time, some fun inspiring some of your more forward thinking people in the development of electricity and computers. Nikola Tesla was a very interesting fellow. Enough of that. It was when I learned of the plan of these evil and misguided religious zealots, that I knew I had to act."

"I couldn't stand by and watch evil destroys the only home we have."

We were under orders never to directly intervene in mankind's affairs no matter how destructive they were. The Creator gave us both free will. We had to sit by and watch, with great sadness, as humans murdered and enslaved each other for thousands of years."

"To answer your question Amanda, I have nowhere to go. This is my home now. The professor knows the gratefulness one feels to having found such a hospitable home."

Spike got up from the table and extended his arms over everyone like a coach over his team before they take to the field. The expression on his face was sorrowful. It was a good-bye look.

"Amanda and Jeffery. The Creator has given you a gift that grows inside of Amanda's womb. A son, who will bring you both great happiness and pride. He is destined to carry on the covenant. A daughter will follow. She will be the embodiment of her mother's goodness and like her brother, carry on the legacy.

Amanda began to cry with tears of joy. Jeff held her tightly and cried with her.

"Professor, my friend. The Creator has not forgotten your brave and loyal soul. Your dream of being reunited with your beloved Marlena will come true. She was allowed to leave her homeland with her two sons and will be arriving in Boston tomorrow. You will have a family to comfort you in your later years. In return, she and her boys, will have a good man to love and protect them."

Yuri grasped Spikes hand in gratitude, and with a trembling voice expressed his gratitude in his native language.

"And as for you, young man, "Referring to Rossi.

"I know that you have a first name, so I will address you as Robert"

"My dear Robert. A certain lovely, kind, and compassionate nurse who took such good care of you, who goes by the name of Keri, is hoping that she will see you again. Let's just say it's a match made in Heaven. You'll find her number in your cell phone contacts. Try not to blow this one."

Rossi looked up at Spikes and noticed moisture welling up in Spikes eyes. Sporting a big smile, Rossi exclaimed,

"Look everyone. Even Aliens cry!"

Spikes nodded in agreement, and then vanished.

No one at the table would ever see Spikes, aka, The Seed Sower, again.

Chapter 42

One hundred years later.

It was almost as if someone had ordered perfect weather. A warm and comforting sunshine cast a soothing light over the Washington Mall. Thousands of people crowded into the Mall from all over the country. Everyone wanted to participate in the centennial celebration of what was now considered to be the greatest event in modern history.

Similar celebrations were being held all over the world. Advances in science and medicine allowed many who were alive at the time, and who had witnessed the original event, to attend. In fact, the average life expectancy had gone from 76 to 136.

They came from all corners of the globe to celebrate the hundredth anniversary of the day the Earth was saved. One hundred years since humanity had been given a reprieve from extinction and entered what was now known as "The Age of Freedom"

Tommy Maldonato was nine years old and was happy to be getting a day off from school. His mother had brought him all the way from Port Jefferson, New York to witness the event. April 27th had become a national holiday. Every school kid in America knew the significance of this day.

Tommy's mom made her way through the crowd with a knapsack on her back, a small folding chair in one hand and Tommy in tow in the other hand. She spotted a small patch of grass about hundred feet from the main grandstand and quickly claimed it for herself.

"Tommy, this is a great spot to watch everything. Pay attention to everything .Someday you'll be telling your grandkids about this day."

"I don't have any grand kids, mom." Tommy said, looking up at his mom with tired eyes.

She opened a picnic lunch she had prepared and placed it on a portable folding lap tray and handed Tommy a half a sandwich of "real flavor" synthetic ham protein, no fat cheese, hydroponic lettuce, and NAD infused whole wheat bread.

For the next hour they listened to music by "Soul Search," one of the most famous synthesizer bands in the country. Most of the speeches from show business types, clergy, and politicians had already been given during the two previous days.

Anticipation was building for the keynote speaker. He was one of the most beloved public figures in America. He was loved for his work as a scientist and for his contribution in finding the cure for cancer.

His global initiatives completely erased the term, Third World. They led to the eradication of abject poverty. Every man, woman and child on the planet now had access to the basics of adequate food, clean water, medical care, shelter, and basic civil rights.

Doing the honors for introducing the keynote speaker was the president of the International Federation of Freedom, Jackson Mujavi. The IFF was formed after the dissolution of the United Nations. Its mission was to defend individual freedoms against any political group or national leaders who would try to subvert them.

"Ladies and Gentlemen. It is my great honor to introduce to you a man whose life has exemplified the spirit of the New Age of Freedom. You know him from all his accomplishments that have benefited all of mankind. You also know him for the historical legacy and unique personal connection he brings to this most joyous event."

"I present to you the President of the United States of America, the honorable Andrew J Blake."

The president walked out on to the stage accompanied by his wife of 62 years, Barbara, and their two grown children Jeffery and Amanda named after their now famous grandparents. He was tall and had his dad's athletic build. With only a few wisps' of white hair, he looked much younger than is age of ninety-seven.

The audience erupted with pride for having a leader of this stature.

"Tommy, that's the President. His mom and dad were the ones who were friends with the Seed Sower."

"I know, mommy. I did a report at school. Don't you remember?"

"Ok, ok, now pay attention."

"Well, here we are now, on this wonderful day. One hundred years ago a good friend, who told us he was the Seed Sower, saved us from ourselves. Today we honor him, for making the decision for intervening on our behalf, and our common Creator, who enabled him to do so. However, we also honor ourselves for having upheld his legacy and for not falling back to the old ways."

"He taught us to appreciate the value of life."

"Just when we had come to believe that we were the center of the universe, he put our existence into perspective. He reminded us that we are just a speck of dust in an infinite cosmos, and how everything we cherish can be gone in an instant."

"Growing up as a boy, I recall hearing the stories from my parents about the events of those days. They were always careful to remind me of what our friend, The Seed Sower, kept repeating. That he was not the Creator but instead one of His creations."

"We can take pride in the fact that there has been no war between nations during these last hundred years. Thanks to universal disarmament, there is no longer the threat of nuclear annihilation. All the resources that were spent on defense are now channeled into projects for the betterment of all mankind."

"Scientific advancements have allowed us to live longer and more productive lives. The resurgence of traditional values have reinforced our commitment to be deserving of the second chance we have been given."

"The major religions of the world honoring the Creator and His Grand Design are flourishing in an environment of tolerance and forgiveness for past injustices."

"A lot of work has been done. Be proud of yourselves!"

The standing ovation lasted a full five minutes with bands playing and flags waving. The President motioned the crowd to pipe down but to no avail. Not even the President of the United States could deny the people their moment of jubilance. He waited for the audience to settle down then took to the microphone again.

"Wow, that was amazing! Thank you all so much! I know you were cheering each other!"

"I have one more surprise for you all!"

There were no more listings on the program of events.

Two young men, dressed in elegant black tuxedos, slowly wheeled a very elderly couple in wheelchairs on to the stage. The crowd immediately recognized Jeff and Amanda and stood again for a prolonged ovation.

They were frail and weathered but still had a sparkle in their smiling eyes. They both managed to stand with assistance and wave to the crowd. Yuri Romilov had passed 21 years earlier. Amanda held a portrait of him that was placed on a large easel for all to see. Jeff senior held a portrait of the now famous Agent Robert Rossi who had also passed. A microphone was brought over to Jeff Senior. He looked up to the sky raising his arms and said,

" Thank you Mr. Spikes, wherever you are."

Just then the sky got brighter and flashed three times in long slow intervals.

Tommy squeezed his mother's hand tightly, clinging to her dress and looked up at her.

"Mommy, what was that? What was that?"

"That was, YOUR WELCOME."

THE END